Praise for *New York Times* bestselling author Lindsay McKenna

"McKenna provides heartbreakingly tender romantic development that will move readers to tears. Her military background lends authenticity to this outstanding tale, and readers will fall in love with the upstanding hero and his fierce determination to save the woman he loves."
—*Publishers Weekly* on *Never Surrender*

"Talented Lindsay McKenna delivers excitement and romance in equal measure."
—*RT Book Reviews* on *Protecting His Own*

"Lindsay McKenna will have you flying with the daring and deadly women pilots who risk their lives… Buckle in for the ride of your life."
—*Writers Unlimited* on *Heart of Stone*

Praise for *USA TODAY* bestselling author Merline Lovelace

"Merline Lovelace rocks! Like Nora Roberts, she delivers top-rate suspense with great characters, rich atmosphere and a crackling plot!"
—*New York Times* bestselling author Mary Jo Putney

"Lovelace's many fans have come to expect her signature strong, brave, resourceful heroines and she doesn't disappoint."
—*Booklist*

"Ms. Lovelace wins our hearts with a tender love story featuring a fine hero who will make every woman's heart beat faster."
—*RT Book Reviews* on *Wrong Bride, Right Groom*

NEW YORK TIMES BESTSELLING AUTHOR

LINDSAY McKENNA

USA TODAY BESTSELLING AUTHOR

MERLINE LOVELACE

STALLION TAMER
&
RETURN TO SENDER

ISBN-13: 978-1-335-00693-6

Stallion Tamer & Return to Sender

Copyright © 2019 by Harlequin Books S.A.

The publisher acknowledges the copyright holders
of the individual works as follows:

Stallion Tamer
Copyright © 1998 by Lindsay McKenna

Return to Sender
Copyright © 1998 by Merline Lovelace

Recycling programs
for this product may
not exist in your area.

Printed in U.S.A.

CONTENTS

Lindsay McKenna is proud to have served her country in the US Navy as an aerographer's mate third class—also known as a weather forecaster. She was a pioneer in the military romance subgenre and loves to combine heart-pounding action with soulful and poignant romance. True to her military roots, she is the originator of the long-running and reader-favorite Morgan's Mercenaries series. She does extensive hands-on research, including flying in aircraft such as a P3-B Orion sub-hunter and a B-52 bomber. She was the first romance writer to sign her books in the Pentagon bookstore. Visit her online at lindsaymckenna.com.

STALLION TAMER

Lindsay McKenna

To Dan York,
who's way ahead of his time, and a good friend.

Chapter 1

No! The cry careened through Jessica Donovan's head. She tossed and turned on her old brass bed, one of the few items taken from her life on the Donovan Ranch before she'd fled at age eighteen. Her blond hair swirled across her shoulders as she moved from her back to her side. The dark cloud was pursuing her again. Only this time it was even more malevolent. More threatening. She began to whimper. Her small, thin fingers spasmodically opened and closed in terror.

That black cloud reminded her of one of the torrential thunderstorms that every summer rolled across the Mogollon Rim and then across the expanse of the Donovan Ranch. Those terrifying downpours of her Arizona childhood were every bit as devastating and unrelenting as the monsoons of Southeast Asia and India, or so she'd been told. As lightning and thunder now careened and rolled through the black cloud in her dream, Jessica's breathing became shallow. Faster. Her hands curled into fists as she saw the black cloud begin to take shape.

For whatever reason, the normally lethal, roiling cloud that often chased her was now, for the first time in a year, beginning to take form. Jessica saw herself on the mesa, on the Rim, watching the bubbling cauldron of a storm racing toward her. The wind was tearing at her clothes, punching and pulling at her. Her blond hair streamed out behind her shoulders. As scared as she was, she lifted her chin and directly faced the oncoming, savage storm.

Her mother, Odula, an Eastern Cherokee medicine woman from the Wolf Clan, had not taught her to be meek or mild in the face of fear. No, Odula had always counseled Jessica to face her fears. Not to run away from them, but to work through them and stand her ground no matter what.

Jessica moaned and rolled onto her back. The storm cloud was taking on the appearance of something. An animal? A man? She expected it to be her abusive ex-husband, Carl Roman. Her heartbeat sped up as she saw the lightning stitch and lance through the black-and-green clouds. The winds began to screech like a banshee. An old memory surfaced…old and wonderful. Exhilaration momentarily wiped away the fear she could taste in her mouth. And then it slipped away from her, blotted out by the savagely moving storm.

Jessica felt as if she were going to die. It was a feeling she'd felt often in real life, while married to Carl. Was she remembering the time he'd sent her to the hospital? Tears trickled out of the corners of her eyes as she faced the storm. This time, she knew, it was going to consume her. Kill her. Oh, she'd been near death too many times already! She was tired of being afraid. Her soul was dying. She knew that. Somehow, even while caught in this nightmare, which haunted her several times each week, Jessica knew her soul was withering, dying like a beautiful flower not given enough care, love or nurturance.

The wind picked up, pummeling her bodily. Jessica's turquoise eyes widened as she watched the black clouds take shape.

It was a horse! A black horse. Her breath hitched in her throat as she watched the beautiful, threatening animal form midway up that spiraling, anvil-shaped mass towering forty thousand feet above the Mogollon Rim.

For an instant, her fear turned to awe. She saw the finely dished head of an Arabian stallion—ebony colored, his nostrils red and flaring. His eyes were black and wild. White and red foam trailed from the sides of his mouth. As the front half of his magnificent body formed out of the clouds, Jessica gave a cry of recognition. It was Gan! The Donovan Ranch Arabian stallion! Gan was the horse that her father, Kelly, had repeatedly abused, trying to beat him into submission. During one of his frequent drunken rages, Kelly had even used a whip.

Jessica sobbed. She watched as the figure of Gan developed fully in the writhing, roiling clouds. The stallion was at once beautiful and terrifying as he seemed to gallop, free at last, across the darkening sky. Jessica's hands flew to her mouth as she watched Gan's savage, primal beauty. He was big boned for an Arabian, his raw power evident in the taut muscles that rippled with each long stride he took. His black mane and raised tail flew like

banners, proclaiming his freedom from man's hands—
or more to the point, from Kelly Donovan's cruel hands.

Jessica felt tears streaming down her face. She began
to sob harder as she watched the powerful celestial vision. Gan had wanted nothing more than to roam freely
with his herd of purebred Arabian mares. Her father had
always kept him in a small, eight-foot-high corral where
he couldn't stretch his long limbs or truly exercise. And
a stallion servicing a hundred mares a year needed exercise. Kelly had been so cruel to the stud.

During one of his drunken bouts, Kelly had won Gan
in a high-stakes poker game in Reno, Nevada. Gan was
brought home by Kelly to procreate black Arabian off-
spring. Black was a rare color and in high demand in the
equine world, for there were few true black Arabians.
Gan was able to throw that color eighty percent of the
time. Often Kelly had lost mammoth sums with his gam-
bling ways, but this time he'd walked away with a prize.

But what he'd won, Jessica thought as the stallion and
the thunderstorm began to fade away in her dream, was
trouble with a capital *T*. Kelly had expected a submis-
sive stallion, not the fighter that Gan turned out to be.
In some ways, Gan was like her—badly beaten. And
like the stallion, she was bloody, but unbowed. Thanks
to her mother's spirit, her nurturing, Jessica had managed to hold her head up through her disastrous marriage and successfully carry on.

It was Jessica's own sobbing that awakened her. In the
early morning grayness, she opened her eyes and slowly
pushed herself up into a sitting position. As she leaned
forward and brought her knees up beneath the downy
quilt, she placed her hands against her face and felt the
wetness of spent tears on her cheeks. Her silky hair fell

around her face, covering it like a curtain as she took in a deep, unsteady breath.

That dream, that nightmare…why did it haunt her still? It had since she'd gotten the call that her father had died unexpectedly in an auto accident. Lifting her chin, Jessica sniffed and reached for a tissue on the nightstand. Blowing her nose and wiping away the remnants of her tears, she gazed out the window near her bed. Her mother had been a medicine woman, and she was Odula's daughter. She had the mystery, the magic of her mother's blood running through her veins. She knew dreams were not sent without a reason. Jessica knew she had to try and understand the context of the nightmare.

Shafts of grayish dawn penetrated the Victorian lace curtains at her bedroom window. Jessica lived north of Vancouver, British Columbia. How she loved the area, having been here since age eighteen. The pristine big Douglas fir forest that surrounded her home provided a wall of safety for her. She loved the scent of the pines, and unconsciously breathed in deeply now. Even in the coldest of winters, Jessica kept her window slightly cracked to let in just a little fresh, outside air. Odula had had the same habit.

A soft smile played on Jessica's lips. In so many ways, she was the image of Odula—at least inwardly. As far as outward looks went, she wasn't. Kate and Rachel, her older sisters, had gotten her mother's black hair. Where Jessica's blond hair had come from was beyond her! It certainly wasn't in Odula's Eastern Cherokee lineage. At least her large, expressive blue eyes were her mother's gift to her. The Cherokee people were lighter skinned than other Native American tribes, and some had blue, green or hazel eyes. The Cherokee people also had brown and reddish brown hair in their genetic background, too. Odula had had ebony hair, shiny like a raven's wing in early morning light. And while Kate had Odula's dark hair, Rachel's strands had a decided reddish gold cast to them.

Jessica had to get up. Today was the day. The day she would leave Vancouver to start her long drive home. Fear struck her as she eased her slender legs from beneath the covers. The white, knee-length flannel gown she wore kept her warm against the chill of her room. Even in early May, Canadian weather was cool. In her hometown of Sedona, Arizona, it would already be in the nineties on some days, with lots of brilliant blue skies and un-relenting sunshine—unlike Vancouver, which had days of grayness interspersed with shafts of rare sunlight.

Jessica would miss her little cabin, surrounded by its massive tree guardians. Her lovely fir trees had acted as a barrier against the world. Hurriedly, she got dressed in a pair of well-worn jeans and a pale pink, long-sleeved, jersey shirt. With a colorful scarf she tied up her hair in a ponytail before heading for the warmth of her tiny kitchen to make herself some scrambled eggs and coffee.

On the maple table stood one of her favorite orchids. Spontaneously, Jessica went over and stroked one long, oval leaf, which felt like leather.

"You didn't have any nightmares, did you, Stone Pinto?" She smiled admiringly at the lovely Phalaenopsis orchid's first blossom. Phals were known as moth orchids, their blooms looking like the outstretched wings of a very huge moth—only the orchid's colors were far more spectacular than any moth! Stone Pinto was a white Phal with violet-colored dots all over her large petals. Although it emitted no fragrance, Jessica admired the plant's incredible beauty as it graced her table. How could anyone live without an orchid in each room of the house? It was beyond Jessica, who was sensitive to the energies not only of people, but of animals and plants as well, and knew how much certain plants improved the atmosphere.

Hurrying back to the stove, she added some sprinkles of shredded cheddar cheese to her scrambled eggs and placed the lid over the skillet for a moment. She looked sadly around her small cabin. She'd lived here since her divorce, two years ago, and loved this place. So had her orchids and the other flowers she'd raised for her company, Mother Earth Flower Essences. Yes, the dream her mother had had for her daughters had really taken root in Jessica. Of the three sisters, Jessica walked most directly in her mother's medicine footsteps—but in her own unique way.

At ten o'clock she would be leaving her place of safety and moving home—back to the Donovan Ranch. It would be different this time, Jessica told herself sternly as she dished up the eggs onto a stoneware plate covered with a bright, pretty wildflower design. Very different.

A knock on her door interrupted her thoughts.

"Come in," Jessica called breathlessly. She quickly brought down another plate from the cabinet as the door opened. A young woman about five foot ten, with long black, shining hair and lively forest green eyes, entered.

"You're just in time, Moyra," Jessica said in greeting. She placed half her eggs on the other plate and beckoned her best friend to come and join her for breakfast.

"Oh," Moyra whispered, waving her long, ballerina-like hand, "you go ahead and eat, Jessica! I'll just grab a cup of coffee." She took the percolator off the stove and reached for two cups decorated in a flower design.

Jessica eyed her. "Have you *had* breakfast?"

"Well…" Moyra said in her low, purring voice, "not really, but—"

"Then sit," Jessica demanded with a flourish. "Here you are, helping me pack my orchid girls for the trip, and what kind of hostess would I be if I didn't feed my help first?"

Moyra grinned broadly and placed the steaming cups of coffee on the table. She sat down and graciously accepted a plate with half the scrambled eggs on it. "I'm going to miss you terribly," she said, picking up the fork and knife.

"I know.…" Jessica felt a terrible sadness. Moyra had entered her life unexpectedly two years ago when Jessica had been in the middle of a messy and life-threatening divorce. A young woman in her thirties, Moyra had come from South America. In Jessica's eyes, she was an incredibly gifted person with a wild beauty to match her mysterious lineage. Because Moyra had been raised in the jungle of Peru, she was quite knowledgeable about orchids. She had helped the Mother Earth company grow and become financially solvent, assisting Jessica in expanding the distribution of the healing orchid essences around the world.

"Well," Moyra prompted between bites, "you'll get on well back home. I just feel it, here in my heart."

Jessica tried to smile. "I hope you're right.…" She had tried to talk Moyra into coming south with her to Arizona, but her friend had refused, saying the hot, dry weather wasn't for her. She was used to the warm, humid Amazon jungle and loved the rain, which Vancouver had a lot of. Now Jessica would be without help. She would have to train someone down at the ranch. But who? It was a real problem, because orchids needed unique care and sensitivity on the part of those who worked with them. And most people didn't have the level of sensitivity that Jessica desired.

"Besides," Moyra continued, wrinkling her long, chiseled nose, "leaving Vancouver and getting away from Carl stalking you is the best thing that has happened to you."

Glumly, Jessica nodded as she sipped her coffee. Normally, she loved this time of day, the talking and sharing that went on between her and Moyra. Each morning, Moyra would come and they'd talk over what had to be done during the day: what orders needed to be filled, which essence was to be made or what orchids carefully tended, watered or fertilized. But today Jessica felt her heart breaking.

"I had that nightmare again," she finally confided.

Moyra's eyes narrowed. "Again?"

"Yes." Jessica finished off her eggs and put the plate aside. She wrapped her slender fingers around the warm mug of coffee. "Only this time it was different...." She shared the frightening vision with Moyra.

Tossing her head, her black, long hair thick and curled with the humidity, Moyra nodded thoughtfully. "Where I come from, my people—my grandmother, who was a jaguar priestess—would say that your nightmare is telling you something. The threat of the clouds turned into a stallion. What does that mean to you?"

"Isn't that the sixty-four-thousand-dollar question?" Jessica asked with a chuckle. She sipped her coffee, wanting to prolong her last morning with Moyra as much as she could. She would miss her wisdom. Perhaps they were so close because Moyra's background paralleled her own. Her Peruvian friend came from a mixture of Indian and Castilian Spanish aristocracy. Her mother's side of the family were known to be members of the powerful and mysterious Jaguar Clan. Legend had it that those who carried the blood, the memory of once having been a deadly, powerful jaguar, could, when they wanted, go from a human form into a jaguar form in times of threat or emergency. It was called shape shifting. Jessica had only seen Moyra turn into a jaguar once, but she felt her friend's incredible energy—an energy that was very different from any other person she'd ever met. At times, Moyra's green, almond-shaped eyes, would turn a distinct yellow color when she was angry, and Jessica would almost swear she could see a jaguar overcome Moyra's human shape, could see the face of a jaguar staring back at her.

Nonsense? Maybe. Moyra had been Jessica's right hand since the divorce. And on more than one occasion, Moyra had stood up to Carl, who'd come to stalk Jessica, to harass her and hurt her. In this way, Moyra truly was a jaguar who had guarded and kept her safe. Now, where Jessica was going, there was no safety. Carl had threatened to find her and kill her—that hadn't changed. But perhaps it was time for this chapter of her life to close. A new one was certainly beginning for her. Would Carl try to follow her to Arizona? A shiver of dread wound through Jessica.

"Are you glad to be leaving? Going home?" Moyra asked as she finished off her eggs with relish.

Shrugging, Jessica sighed. "I don't know. Part of me

is. I've missed my family terribly. It's like a hole in my heart that never got fixed."

"Family wounds are the worst," Moyra murmured, buttering her toast and adding orange marmalade. And then, with a husky laugh, she said, "Not that I'm one to talk!"

Jessica nodded. The air of mystery around Moyra was always intact. After two years Jessica still knew very little about why Moyra had moved to Canada. Family meant everything to her. So why didn't she go home?

Home was several places to Moyra, though. She had family in the jungle of Peru as well as in Lima, its capital. Jessica did not pry, however. Like a typical Native American, she figured if Moyra wanted to tell her something, she would share it. Otherwise, it was not on the table as a topic to be discussed.

"The only thing I've got to do this morning is put my orchids in my pickup, and then I'll be ready to go." Once Jessica had made arrangements to bring the plants across the Canadian border, she had rented a large trailer to bring the rest of her supplies—the beautiful one-ounce, cobalt blue bottles, the eyedroppers, labels and other office items that were needed. Her computer, printer and files were already packed. She had fifty orchids of different varieties and types from around the world, and they would need careful temperature and humidity control. To expose them to chilly Canadian temperatures could kill them, as most orchids could not survive below fifty-five degrees Fahrenheit. Only her truck with the cap on it would be able to transport them properly. Moyra had fixed the heater in the truck so that the warm air would flow back into the bed where the orchids would be packed.

The Peruvian woman stood up, tall, lean and graceful. She even moved like a jaguar, Jessica thought, smiling to herself. Moyra was, indeed, more jaguar than human most of the time. Maybe that's why they got along so well, hidden out in the forest, absorbing the peace and quiet of their natural paradise. But then, Jessica knew her own Cherokee blood had given her a need for such surroundings rather than the craziness and the stress of city living. She could never survive in a city! Nor could her orchids, which were quite sensitive to air pollution.

"I'll start up the truck and get the heater going," Moyra said. "We need to warm that bed area for them. I'll make sure there are no leaks so that colder air can't get back there. I've got the temperature gauge set so you can just turn your head, glance at it and know that it's in the right range for your girls." Moyra leaned over and delicately touched the Phal. "How I'm going to miss Stone Pinto. She's so lovely!"

"I know." Jessica rose and put the plates in the sink. "Worse, I'm going to miss you…."

Moyra hugged her. "I'll be around in spirit. You know that. Once a jaguar priestess adopts you into her family, you are one of us, and you come under the protection of the jaguar goddess herself." She frowned, her thin brows knitted. "And I hope Carl has the good sense not to follow you to Arizona."

"He wouldn't dare," Jessica whispered, her throat automatically closing with fear.

Moyra threw back her head and chuckled. "Ha! That poor excuse of a man would do anything! He's capable of anything." The smile disappeared from Moyra's full mouth and she studied Jessica, who was inches shorter than her. "And you, my fine, delicate wisp of a friend, need to embrace the power of your Wolf Clan. You've run from your own power all your life. You're so much your mother, and yet you're afraid of the power of the wolf." She gripped Jessica's shoulders, deadly serious now. "I ran from the Jaguar Clan for years, but don't do as I've done. Our life path is part animal, part human. We are here in this lifetime to learn to integrate both halves into ourselves so that we are whole."

"I know you're speaking the truth. I feel it here, in my heart," Jessica admitted.

"Well," Moyra growled, sounding exactly like a jaguar in that moment, "you are going home to complete the first circle of your life. Claim the Wolf Clan power that is rightfully yours. Don't keep running from it." Allowing her hands to slip from Jessica's shoulders, Moyra added primly, "That dream of Gan, the Arabian stallion, has something to do with this. I know it."

Jessica felt lost suddenly. "What am I going to do without you?"

Moyra smiled enigmatically. "My jaguar sight tells me there is a man in black who will be near you soon. He will be someone you can trust, so run to him."

Jessica eyed her jadedly. "Oh, sure, a man. My track record with men is horrible and you know it. Besides, I don't trust them anymore…."

"Carl was a mistake." Moyra closed her eyes and took a deep breath. "This man who is coming into your life is dangerous—not to you, but to himself." She continued in a low voice "I see him…swathed in black. Covered in darkness. But it's not a dangerous darkness like Carl has around him." Opening her eyes, she smiled down at Jessica. "And don't ask me any more questions because we both know that discovering the truth on your own is the only way to do it. I've said enough! I'm off to the truck. Meet me when you're ready and I'll help you load your orchid girls."

Jessica felt a heaviness in her chest and knew it was sadness at leaving Vancouver, Moyra and the many other friends she'd made here. Canada had been good for her—a home away from home. How she loved this beautiful country and its wonderfully friendly inhabitants!

Jessica's heart ached. And yet, as she finished washing, drying and packing the last of the kitchen supplies into one final box, another part of her was very excited about seeing Kate again. Their sister Rachel could not come home for a while because she had to fulfill her teaching contract at a college in England. But by December, Rachel would be moving back, too, and then what was left of the Donovan family would truly be home for the first time since their chaotic childhood.

As she carried the box outdoors, Jessica saw that the dawn had brightened, revealing a pale blue sky. She smiled. Even Canadian weather was going to bless her travels—blue sky and sunshine in early May was wonderful!

At least she wouldn't have to struggle through snow, sleet or rain on her southward journey back to the States…back to Sedona, Arizona.

Moyra had the pickup backed up to the small, glass greenhouse that housed most of her orchids. Going to the trailer, which would be hitched on afterward, Jessica packed away the final boxes. One of them contained her goose-down quilt, her most precious possession, made by her mother when Jessica was fifteen. Odula's energy, her love, her heart, was in this quilt and no matter how alone or bereft Jessica felt, even in the darkest days with

Carl, she could wrap that quilt around her and feel the love and healing energy of her mother being absorbed into her battered spirit.

Closing up the trailer, her breath white and wispy, Jessica hurried to the greenhouse. Opening the door and quickly shutting it, Jessica saw that Moyra had carefully packed the orchids in plenty of newspaper and then moved them into cardboard boxes so that they wouldn't tip or fall over during the three-day trip down to Arizona. Jessica appreciated Moyra's attention to detail. Many of the orchids were just coming into bloom, their long, thin green spikes about to yield inflorescences or buds.

"Ready?" Moyra asked, looking up from the last box she'd packed with larger orchids already in bloom.

"I think so," Jessica whispered. She looked around the greenhouse. Kate had made her one exactly like this back at the ranch and it stood waiting and ready for her orchids—for her new life.

Moyra smiled gently. "Little Jessica is once again closing one chapter in her life and opening up a new one. You have to be excited."

"And scared," Jessica admitted softly, easing her arms around the first box of orchids.

Laughing, Moyra took another box and followed her out to the pickup. "Be scared, but stand in the storm of fear and walk through it, my friend."

"Spoken like a true jaguar priestess," Jessica teased, smiling over her shoulder at Moyra. The woman positively glowed with life, her green eyes sparkling mischievously. Jessica knew that Moyra was psychic. In the past, she had used her abilities to warn her when Carl was in the vicinity. Jessica had been able to call the police and avert Carl's stalking each time. She shuddered now. She didn't know what Carl would do if he got his hands on her again. For two years, ever since Moyra had magically walked into her life to become a big, cosmic guard dog of sorts, Carl had not been able to fulfill his threat that he would hunt her down and kill her if she divorced him.

They put the first boxes in the pickup, the warmth satisfactory for Jessica's orchid girls. Hurrying back and forth, both women finally got all the boxes in place and the cap closed to protect the orchids from the chill of the Vancouver morning. Then Moyra maneuvered the pickup to the trailer and they quickly hitched it up.

"There," Moyra said, rubbing her hands and grinning. "Don't look so sad, little sister. I'll be with you in spirit, looking over your shoulder. You know that."

Tears filled Jessica's eyes as she looked up at Moyra. "You've been a true sister to me. I don't know what I'd have done without you, Moyra. Really, I don't feel like it's been a fair exchange. You've given me so much and been such a wonderful role model for me—"

"Hush, sister. You are going home to reclaim your power.

"You know, a shaman is always most powerful where she was born. You are a long way from your source of empowerment. Go home. Don't be afraid." Moyra moved closer and placed her hands on Jessica's small, slumped shoulders. "Listen carefully, Jessica. I see much." Her fingers dug more deeply into Jessica's shoulders. "You are in great danger. You will be tested once you reach home. In order to survive this test, you *must* embrace your power. If you don't…" Moyra looked upward, tears in her eyes. "But I know you will. You are a frightened little shadow of your true self. There is a man clothed in black who will help you, guide you, if you allow him to."

"I don't *trust* men!"

"I know that. Carl has hurt you so deeply, he's wounded your spirit, Jessica…but this man, whoever he is, can help you heal at a soul level." She gave Jessica a gentle shake, her voice turning raw with emotion. "Your test is twofold, my sister. You must face your fear head-on and you must learn to trust men again. Neither is an easy task, but you are the daughter of a medicine woman. You must learn to embrace your inherited power from her, and become it. If you do this, your life will be spared. But you will be in danger. Just embrace your wolf senses—your exquisite hearing, your sense of smell—and remain on guard…."

"Sometimes I wish you wouldn't speak symbolically," Jessica said with a little laugh, taking Moyra's hands into hers. "Sometimes I wish you'd just spit it out."

Moyra grinned. Her laugh was a husky purr. "I was raised by my grandmother, an old jaguar priestess. I was taught at an early age to discern and not say too much. Life is a process of discovery, little sister, and it's not my right to take that way from you." She hugged her fiercely and then released her. "Go, Jessica. Drive toward your new life. Trust this man in black. Open your heart to him. See what happens."

Jessica nodded and climbed slowly into the pickup. The sun was just edging the tops of the spruce, making the sky look like a crown of pure, white light surrounding the small meadow where they stood. "And you? What of you? Where will you be?"

Moyra smiled sadly. "I must go home to Peru now, little sister. My people have called me home."

"Which ones? The Jaguar Clan or your family?" She

started the engine, her heart already crying for the loss of her friend. Jessica knew that she'd probably never see Moyra again—except in her dreams, where the jaguar ruled night journeys of all kinds.

With a laugh, Moyra said, "One and the same."

"Stay in touch?"

"I will see you on the Other Side."

Jessica blinked back her tears. "Okay.... I love you, Moyra. You're like a fourth sister to me. You know that."

"Yes, and you've helped heal my heart, you know." Moyra's voice became choked. "You gave me a place to heal, Jessica, whether you knew it or not. You taught me about the goodness, the positiveness of family once again. I needed that. In your own way, you are a great healer." Moyra motioned to the orchids in back of the vehicle. "And look what you do for thousands of people around the world who buy your orchid essences. Look how many you heal in that way. Go, my little sister. Drive toward your destiny. I must go to mine now. I promise, I'll be in touch...."

The driveway blurred in front of Jessica as she put the truck in gear and drove away, leaving behind her cloistered, safe existence. The sunlight glared brightly down on the rutted dirt road. She drove slowly and carefully, not wanting to jar her orchid girls. Sniffing, she wiped her eyes on the sleeve of her shirt. Fumbling for her dark glasses, she put them on. In the rearview mirror, she saw Moyra standing so proud and tall. And then she saw her form change—suddenly a jaguar with a gold coat covered with black spots stood in her place. Blinking the tears away, Jessica almost slammed on the brakes. Blinking once more, she saw Moyra again in human form.

Jessica was grateful that her mother had called Moyra

from South America to be her guardian for these past two years, since her divorce from Carl. Jessica knew her mother could use her power from the Other Side. Odula had embraced her Wolf Clan power, but she herself was afraid of it.

And what about this man in black? Jessica shook her head and paid attention to the winding road. The greenhouse and the log cabin disappeared one final time as she drove around the curve that would take her to the asphalt highway—that would take her home. Her real home.

Fear warred with expectation and joy. Jessica had felt little joy in her life—except when she worked with her orchid girls and made the essences. There she was free—like Gan, the black Arabian stallion—to run wildly without fear. She examined her dream of the night before. A man in black…who was that?

Suddenly, Jessica felt a trickle of hope—something she'd not felt in a decade. Hope had been torn from her the day she'd fled from the Donovan Ranch. Now, miraculously, she felt it coming back—a small tendril of flame, so tiny and weak—yet it was there. Yes! Taking in a deep, shaky breath, Jessica absorbed that wonderful feeling. Just thinking about this mysterious "man in black" lifted her wounded spirits. Maybe, just maybe, as Moyra had said, she was going home to face her old fears, to try to work through them and walk out the other side, healed—finally. With the help of this man in black….

Chapter 2

The darkness gripped Dan Black's belly, twisting his fear into pain. Sweat trickled down from his furrowed brow, running into his eyes and making them sting. The low, husky voice of Ai Gvhdi Waya, Walks with Wolves, trembled through the darkness of the sweat lodge where Dan sat. Ai Gvhdi Waya was an Eastern Cherokee medicine woman who lived up on the Navajo reservation where he'd been born, thirty years ago. She wasn't Navajo, but she was known to be one of the most powerful healers on the res. He focused on her now as she poured ladle after ladle of cooling water on the red-hot lava rocks making them glow eerily through the steam. Why the hell had he come here? Why had he thought this would help?

The pain knotted in his stomach. The heat was building. Her voice was low, powerful and searching. His fear heightened. Squeezing his eyes shut, he tried to control the fear. Wasn't that why he'd come? To walk through his fear, not control it? He'd been taught that fear was not to be ignored or denied. By walking through it, feeling it, allowing it to consume him, he would be healed.

He felt anything but healed. He was scared to death. Death...yes, how many times had he faced that horrible possibility? It hurt to admit he had a fear of dying. Dan hadn't realized the depth of his fear until he'd gone over with his marine reconnaissance unit during the swift-moving Gulf War. Desert Storm had been a living, fiery hell for him—externally as well as internally. *No!* He shook his head, moving his long, roughened fingers along the hard curves and lines of his sweaty face. He tried to wipe away the bubbling fear that was snaking up his gullet.

The medicine woman stopped singing. Dan opened his eyes. He could not see her in the sweat lodge, the darkness was so complete. So terrifying. All he saw was the vague outline and shape of glowing red rocks. He centered all his attention on them. He had to or he was going to scream. And then what would she think of him?

"You are frightened, Dan Black."

Her voice sounded like a bullhorn over his head. Dan instantly jerked upright. It was as if Ai Gvhdi Waya was leaning over him, talking directly into his right ear. Automatically, he moved his right arm outward, but the space was empty. Though he was sitting opposite the door she sat next to, he could not see her at all.

"Tell me of your fear."

His throat closed. He felt the penetrating heat of the steam burning the back of his shoulders and neck. His flesh prickled and he cried out, feeling another type of pain.

"Fear is walking around you. I see you clothed in black. Are you going to become your namesake?"

"No..." Though Black was an honored name on the Navajo reservation and there were many branches of the family, Dan's mother had done the unthinkable— she'd wed an Anglo schoolteacher. Dan was a half-breed, and he'd been mercilessly teased about it as he'd gone through the school system on the res. He'd regained his honor among his family by becoming a tamer of horses. Horses were still a powerful, moving force on this reservation today.

"Sometimes we take on a name to walk through it. How far into your journey are you?"

Dan closed his eyes. "It's so dark I can't see daylight at either end," he rasped, forcing the words between his thinned lips.

She threw more water onto the rocks. The hissing and spitting threw up more billowing, steamy clouds into the closed, confined space. "There are people who have a black heart. You are not one of those. I see your heart in pieces, but it is not dark. It is bleeding. You do not have a black spirit, but I see your spirit clothed in darkness, instead."

Was there any good news? Dan felt his heart pumping wildly in his chest. The heat scored his flesh. The sweat ran in rivulets from his head down across his naked body to the white towel he wore around his waist. He dug his fingers into the earthen floor he sat upon. There was something soothing about the red sand. He'd been born on this red desert, in a hogan in Monument Valley, a hundred miles from the nearest hospital. It was one of the most sacred places on the res. The medicine woman in attendance at his birth had proclaimed him a light among his people.

Some light. His last name was Black. And he was clothed in darkness. His spirit sagged. He felt so damned alone, so afraid and unable to help himself. Maybe part of it was his own fault. He never reached out and asked for help because of his childhood on the res as a half-breed. The Navajo children had tortured him daily at school because of his lighter skin and gray eyes. He had black hair like they did, but that was where similarities ended. They said his eyes looked colorless, like those of a predatory owl. And owls were not looked upon kindly in Navajo cosmology. No, they were the symbol of death.

"I'm dying…." he managed to say, his voice low and terribly off-key.

"Sometimes, in order to move forward, a part of us must die. Cut out the old. Let it go and die. And then you will have space for something new, something better, to take its place."

He wished she wouldn't speak in such riddles. But then, all medicine people did. His head was swimming with terror, with trying to control the pain in his stomach. He was overcome with the same fear he'd felt over in the Gulf War when— Instantly, Dan slammed his mind shut, obliterating that scene.

"Look into the stones. The stone people talk to us in many ways," she directed in a low voice.

Eagerly, Dan focused his smarting eyes on the red-colored rocks in the fire pit. Any attempt to take the focus off his terror and pain was worth doing. The clouds of steam came and went. For a moment, he thought he saw the shape of a face in the glowing rocks. And then it vanished. Was he seeing things? His Anglo side pooh-poohed this stuff. His Navajo side was starved for it. Which to believe? Was he hallucinating or did he truly see a woman's face in those rocks?

"There is a woman coming."

Dan's breath hitched. He snapped a look across the blackness to where Ai Gvhdi Waya was sitting. She saw it too? Then he wasn't delusional? Holding his breath, he waited and prayed that the medicine woman would say more.

"Look again."

Disappointed, he shifted his gaze back to the rocks. She poured more water on them. It was so hot now, so strangling with humidity that Dan thought he was going to die for lack of cool, clean oxygen. Everything was becoming claustrophobic to him—again. A new fear, the fear of being in too tight a place, raced through him.

Concentrate!

He had to concentrate or he would begin sobbing.

His gaze fell to the red rocks, where clouds of mist swirled and moved. He blinked, trying to get the stinging sweat out of his eyes in order to see the rocks better. Would he see the woman's face more clearly this time? It had been so vague before.

There!

He gasped.

Yes! It was her—again. Only this time, the face was far more distinct. Its outline wavered in the clouds and heat rising off the rocks. An oval face. He saw huge blue eyes staring back at him—blue like the turquoise color of the endless sky that blanketed his beloved Southwest. The expression in them tugged directly at his heart. He felt a strange spasm there and the sensation was so real that he automatically rubbed his chest. The feeling continued. There was more pain as he felt something opening inside him like a rusted door that had never been opened before.

Gasping, Dan felt his breath leaving him. He clung to the vision of her face, wavering inches above the heated stones in thick, misty clouds of steam. Pain surged outward, like ripples from a pebble thrown into a quiet pond, each one a wavelet of more intense agony. The sensation continued inside his heart and tripled as it moved outward, expanding rapidly across his chest.

"Release it!"

Ai Gvhdi Waya's order came as a physical blow, her voice low and snarling. His hand fell from his chest and he straightened up and tipped his head back, gulping for air as the knifelike sting continued to ripple outward across his chest. He was having a heart attack. Dan was sure he was going to die.

"Lie down!"

It didn't take much for him to do that. He practically fell over, feeling the warmth of the sand on the side of his face, arm and lower body. Air! There was cooler air near the bottom of the sweat lodge. He gulped it greedily, his breath ragged.

"Let the pain continue."

He couldn't have stopped it if he'd tried. Rolling helplessly onto his back, he dug his fingers deep into the red sand on either side of him. The pain deepened and felt like a red-hot brand now, centered in his heart region. Oh, no, he *was* going to die! The air in his lungs was shallow and he was unable to get enough oxygen because it hurt so much to breathe.

Suddenly, Dan felt a swirling sensation around his

head, and then it moved down, inch by inch, across his body. The more he became enveloped in this cloud, the less of a coherent hold he had on reality. Somewhere in the distance, he heard Ai Gvhdi Waya beginning another song. He tried to hold on to her voice, to where he was, but found it was impossible.

There was a deep, snapping, cracking feeling emanating from within him. He not only felt it, but distinctly heard it. It sounded like good crystal being smashed with a hammer. Almost instantly, he closed his eyes and he felt himself become featherlight. He was drifting in the darkness, but he had no idea where. The need for breath no longer mattered. He wasn't breathing, he realized, but he was still alive. Or was he? Dan was no longer sure. Miraculously, he no longer felt the fear from the Gulf War. No, he felt an incredible sense of peace—and love.

Shaken by the experience, he allowed himself to move. At times, he felt like a leaf that had fallen off a tree and was gently wafting on an invisible breeze. There was a rocking motion to his weightlessness, reminiscent of a cradle. It was nurturing. Supportive. How wonderful it felt not to be pursued by the demons from hell that had lived within him twenty-four hours a day since the war. He breathed in a sigh of absolute relief.

And then he realized that this was what death must feel like—a warm, embracing cocoon that made him feel like an infant swaddled in a blanket, lovingly held. Held by what, he wasn't sure, and his mind wasn't functioning all that well to ask or to care. Little by little, he thought he saw a grayness somewhere above him. It seemed as if he were moving upward, slowly but surely, toward that emanation of light.

Dan watched in awe as the blackness changed to gray,

and then transformed into an incredible gold-and-white light that surrounded him. He should have been blinded by it, but wasn't. Instead, it embraced him, cradled him and held him in a loving security he'd never known before. How he liked being in this place! There was no fear, only an incredible sense of being loved for who he was—faults and all. There were no judgments in this place, only an incredible sense of nurturance. Perhaps this was what white man's heaven was all about.

Out of the light, colors began to congeal. Sometimes they would disappear, but they'd always return, more vibrant than before, eventually taking the shape of a blossom. He had no idea what kind of flower he was looking at. It was white with purple spots all over it.

The apparition danced and moved slowly in front of him, and then it faded. In its place he saw the most beautiful turquoise blue he'd ever seen. In this reality, wherever it was, colors were more vibrant, more dramatic and pure than what he saw with his physical eyes.

The blue color began to take the shape of a set of large, wide eyes. Beautiful eyes, Dan thought as he clung to the gentle love that seemed to emanate from them. And then he began to see the rest of a face fill in around those eyes—the same face he'd seen in the fire. Only this time the vision—of a lovely woman about his own age—was very clear and unmistakable. She had long, straight blond hair that shone like precious gold in sunlight. Her face was oval, her lips full and delicate. Dan didn't know which of her features he liked better. She was smiling, and the fact sent his heart skittering with unaccustomed joy.

He watched as she raised her small, stubborn chin and laughed, her pink lips curving deliciously. The sound of her laughter reminded him of angels singing. It was soft, low, and held such love and nurturing that it brought tears to his eyes. He felt the heat of his tears mingling with the sweat that ran across his face and body in rivulets.

And then her face began to fade. *No!* He tried to call out to her, but he had no voice. His chest region was throbbing with warmth now, not pain. The light began to fade and he felt himself being pulled rapidly back into the cloistered blackness once again. This time he didn't fight it. He surrendered totally to it because he knew he was safe and loved.

The spinning began again, sharp and violent. Within seconds, he felt heaviness. He was in his body once more. He could feel the sand he still gripped beneath his fingers, could hear the ending of the song Ai Gvhdi Waya sang, could feel the prickling heat against his taut flesh and the endless streams of sweat washing off of him.

"You have returned."

He lay there in awe. Dan had no idea how long his journey into the other world had taken. He'd never had such an experience before—ever. But then, he had never sought out the help of a medicine person, either. He'd always gone the anglo route when it came to medicine, rather than rely on his Navajo heritage. Maybe he should have come long ago, he thought wearily. He moved his hand across his chest where an intense, branding warmth still throbbed. There was no pain, just a wonderful feeling of joy. What had happened? What had the medicine woman done? And who was the woman he'd seen in his vision?

"Come out when you want," Ai Gvhdi Waya instructed as she threw open the blanketed door. "Go to the hot springs down the path, wash off and dress. Then come see me at my hogan."

Dan felt incredibly tired, as if his body weighed twice what it should, and he was thirsty, too. It was probably dehydration, the loss of water during the hour-long sweat lodge ceremony. As his mind slowly began to function again, he felt the grit of the sand on his naked back. It felt familiar, comforting. He watched as the medicine woman, who was dressed in a faded cotton shift, crawled out of the sweat lodge and then got to her feet. Outside the door, the sun was shining brightly, the shafts of light piercing the darkness of the lodge.

Closing his eyes, Dan gasped for the cooling air moving into the heated, humid confines. Air! Fresh air. All he could do was lie there and allow his weakened body to recuperate. His mind spun with questions and no answers. Emotionally he felt lighter. The fear was less. Why? What had the medicine woman done to make it so? The questions drove him to sit up and then weakly crawl out on his hands and knees.

The midafternoon May heat moved across the red desert as he stood up on unsteady legs. Rewrapping the white towel low on his hips, Dan picked up his clothing and cowboy boots and headed down a well-worn path toward the hot springs behind Ai Gvhdi Waya's hogan. In the distance, he heard the familiar and soothing sounds of bleating sheep. Right now, he just concentrated on putting one step in front of the other.

At the springs, a natural well of hot water surrounded by smooth red sandstone guardians, Dan lay with his head on a stone that served as a pillow and felt the healing effects of the water on his body. His mother would be proud of him—going to see a medicine person. His father would have told him to see a psychotherapist—which Dan had many times.

Oddly, his fear remained at a distant from him. Before, he'd anesthetized the fear with alcohol. That had gotten him into a lot of trouble, too. When he was drunk, he was violent. He'd spent some time in the Coconino jail in Flagstaff. He'd recently gotten fired from his job on a ranch, where he'd been the head horse wrangler. Alcohol had made his fear lessen, so that he could continue to function in the world. And yet, because of his Navajo blood, he had no enzymes to break down alcohol once it entered his bloodstream, so he went "crazy." His father used the word *berserk*. His mother cried and begged him to seek help of her medicine people.

A tired half smile tugged at Dan's mouth. He lifted his head and knew it was time to climb out, dry off and get dressed. Well, he hadn't been much of a prize to his family, had he? He'd shamed them repeatedly. Now his name was mud. Any honor he'd gained for being one of the best horse wranglers they'd ever seen was now destroyed. It had hurt to see his mother cry when she visited him in that damned jail. It made him angry when his father did nothing but castigate him and tell him to go to a shrink to get cured.

Dan had disappointed them. Shamed them in front of the rest of his large, extended family. Gossip was one of the worst habits Navajos had, and there was plenty about Dan Black, the "black sheep" of the family, and his crazy ways. He was shunned by his own people. Well, why not? Since returning from the Gulf War six years ago, he'd pretty much made a disaster of his life.

Before going into the marines, he'd had a good job on

a ranch near Flag. He'd joined the marines because his father had been one. Dan had wanted his dad to be proud of him. And he was, until Dan was sent to the Gulf, where all hell broke loose. He'd come back broken not only in body, but in spirit. His mother had pleaded with him to walk the Navajo way and get his spirit healed. His father had said that in time his fear would go away and that he didn't need help from some medicine person.

Why the hell didn't he listen more to his mother? Dan thought as he got out of the spring and quickly dried off in the ninety-degree, midday heat. He donned his light blue, short-sleeved shirt, his faded jeans, and settled a dusty, black felt Stetson on his head. Sitting down, he pulled on his socks and badly scuffed cowboy boots. The boots looked like how he'd felt before coming to this incredibly powerful medicine woman.

Standing, he stretched his arms toward Father Sky. The blueness of the sky reminded him of this unknown woman's turquoise eyes filled with such loving warmth. Just remembering the vision of those eyes caused his heart to expand with joy. It took him off guard. What was going on? What was happening to him? Maybe the medicine woman could tell him. Dan hurried up the slope, looking for answers that would explain his vision.

As he rounded her hogan, Dan saw Ai Gvhdi Waya with a white man. Word had gotten around that she was living with an Anglo named Dain Phillips. Gossip had it that he was very, very rich. If he was, Dan didn't see it. The tall, intense-looking man stood near a beat-up old blue pickup that looked a lot like his own—in dire need of a paint job and some bodywork. He saw Ai Gvhdi Waya reach up and kiss him quickly on the mouth. She was once again dressed in familiar Navajo clothes: a long-sleeved red velvet blouse and a dark blue cotton skirt that hung to her ankles. Her hair was in two thick braids, tied at the ends with feathers and red yarn.

Dan stood near the door to the hogan, his eyes averted. But he hadn't missed the love for Ai Gvhdi Waya shining in the Anglo's eyes. Dan wondered if he'd ever find a woman who made him feel that way. So far, his luck with life in general, not to mention women, was pretty bad. He supposed it had something to do with that curse of darkness that surrounded him. When he was growing up on the res, the children had always teased him that his skin was lighter because the copper color had faded away due to the blanket of darkness wrapped around him since birth. And because of this owl darkness, his skin seemed lighter to those who looked at him. Dan hated that explanation. He'd fought repeatedly to defend his honor throughout the twelve years of schooling here. Fighting didn't come naturally to him. No, he'd rather work with horses, to feel in tune with their wild, free spirits, than take on the school bully.

"You feel lighter."

Dan lifted his head, suddenly realizing he was staring down at his dusty, booted feet. Ai Gvhdi Waya stood directly in front of him, no more than six feet away. He looked past her and saw that the Anglo had driven away in the pickup, down the rutted dirt road. Shaking his head, Dan rasped, "I don't know what's happening."

"Come in. You need to drink water."

Her hand felt comforting on his arm. He liked this woman, her quiet power, her ability to soothe him and make him feel decent and not ashamed. "Thanks," he mumbled, and followed her into the cooling comfort of her hogan.

He always felt at home in the hogan, an eight-sided structure made of mud and logs. The door faced east, to welcome Father Sun as he rose each morning. The odor of sage filled his nostrils and he saw that some was burning slowly in an abalone shell on top of the old pine table. She gestured for him to sit down at the table while she went to the kitchen counter and poured two large glasses of water.

"Thanks," he said sincerely as she handed him the glass. Dan drank the contents quickly, his body eager to replace what he'd lost in the sweat. She placed a pitcher of water between them and he poured himself a second and third glass before he was satiated. When he was finished, he sat opposite her at the table, the tendrils of sage smoke drifting upward and spreading out across the hogan. Sage, for the Navajo, was purifying and healing. Whenever he got a cold or flu, Dan would make sage tea and drink quarts of it to flush and cleanse his body. It always worked.

"Tell me what you saw in your journey," Ai Gvhdi Waya urged softly.

He took off his hat and set it on the table. "You'll probably think I'm crazy." He tried to smile, but failed miserably. "Everyone else thinks I am, anyway...."

She smiled gently. "One person's craziness is another's sanity. So who is sane and who is really crazy?"

He laughed a little and tried not to feel so uncomfortable. "Listen, this is my first time with a medicine person. I didn't know what to expect."

"Expect nothing. Receive everything."

He stared at her, more of the tension draining from him.

"You've been called crazy by many, but you are not.

Your spirit is sensitive. Things that wouldn't wound others wound you. The road you walk, Dan Black, is a hard one." She closed her eyes and gestured with her hands. "I see a man walking with one foot on one road, an asphalt one. And then I see him walking with the other foot on the good red road of our people." She opened her eyes and smiled a little. "You carry the blood of two worlds in your body. You are *heyoka,* a contrary. You must learn to blend these two paths you walk into one road and then make it your road."

"Easier said than done," he muttered.

"One path is that of a warrior, the other of a healer. A warrior healer. You have tasted and done both. But neither is comfortable with the other. Your spirit hungers for the touch of our mother, the earth. And for her living things. Today I saw horses surrounding you. I knew of your reputation before you came here—of being one of our best horse wranglers. Horses are important to you. They are part of your healing. Stay with them."

He nodded. "Yeah, I just got a job down at the Donovan Ranch. The ranch foreman gave me a chance. He knew I was a—that I drank too much…."

"Yes." She nodded. "I know him. Sam McGuire is a good man. He will give you the chance you deserve."

Earnestly, Dan met and held her sympathetic gaze. "Look, I came to you to try and stop this fear. That's why I drank. I had to make it go away somehow…it was the only way."

"Not the right way and you know that, Dan."

Grudgingly, he nodded. "My father calls me an alcoholic. My mother cries for me all the time. I had to do something."

Reaching out, the medicine woman closed her work-worn hand over his. "Listen carefully, stallion tamer. You drink to run from the pain you received while being a warrior. There is only one way out of this and that is to walk through it. Alcohol will not cure you. Only your heart's desire to do this for yourself will cure you." She lifted her hand, all the while her gaze holding his.

"I know... I agree," Dan rasped.

"The path you walk is a hard one. There is no disagreement on that. The Great Spirit gives you the strength you need to walk it. All you have to do is surrender to a power higher than yourself and trust what you know instinctively. You use it to tame the mustangs. Why not use it on yourself?"

Dan watched her smile. It reminded him of the coyote, the trickster. He smiled a little, too. "I'm going to try. I've got to save my family's reputation. This is tearing my mother apart. I don't mean to hurt her—I really don't...."

"I understand," Ai Gvhdi Waya soothed. Tilting her head slightly, she asked, "What else did you see in your vision?"

Shaken, he stared at her. "You saw it, too?"

"Yes, but I want to hear in your words what you saw and experienced."

Dan took a deep breath, and, risking everything, told her the details of the vision. She nodded wisely now and then, as if to corroborate his story. Little by little, he didn't feel so foolish. By the time he finished, Dan felt oddly comfortable. He wondered if everyone had such visions in a sweat lodge, but didn't ask.

"What do you make of it?" he asked instead.

She shrugged. "It's more important what you make of it."

Quirking his mouth, he leaned back and tilted the chair onto its rear legs. "I knew you were going to say that."

Ai Gvhdi Waya laughed deeply. "It is your life, your interpretation of events, that counts. What I think about it is unimportant compared to how you feel, how you respond to what you saw."

Nodding, Dan looked up at the earthen ceiling. His voice dropped. "I feel lighter, almost happy…expectant that something good is coming my way—finally. I don't know this woman I saw. I've never seen eyes like hers. She's so beautiful…like a dream I might have. And the flower…it was white and purple. I've never seen anything like it, either." He shifted his gaze to her. "Do you know this flower?"

"No. I've never seen one like that."

Shrugging, Dan eased the chair downward. He placed his hands on the table and folded them. "A woman and a flower. Got me."

"And what did you feel when you saw this woman's face?"

He gave a shy grin. "A lot of things."

The medicine woman smiled back. "Your heart opened. By just seeing her face, some of your injured heart was healed. It is no longer as fragmented. Do you have the feeling that she could heal your heart?"

Dan felt telltale heat creep into his face. That was one of his flaws—blushing. "Yeah… I think she could—"

"No," Ai Gvhdi Waya admonished, "stop saying 'I think' and switch to saying 'I feel'. You must disconnect from that Anglo head of yours and move down to the true center of your being, which is your Navajo heart. There you feel and you *know*. You can know without knowing why you know." She smiled enigmatically. "Your father is Anglo. Anglos think too much. They think only their brain has answers. That is not true. Our heart is our only true voice. You use your heart when you break and train horses. Why not use it *all the time* with regard to yourself? Switch off your thinking. Not all of life is logical. And reality?" She laughed deeply once again. "The Anglo mind sees only what it can weigh, measure or perceive with these two things we call eyes." She pointed to her own eyes. "There are many other realities. When you're with a wild horse, you move into his or her reality, don't you? You are no longer a human, a two-legged. You become like a four-legged, a shape-shifter. You become the horse to feel him, his fears or whatever, don't you?"

Dan had never thought of what he did in those terms, but looking at it her way, he had to nod his head. "Yes," he said slowly, "something does happen, but I couldn't tell you what, or how it happens."

"That," Ai Gvhdi Waya said firmly, "is your skill, your power. That is what you need to embrace twenty-four hours a day. I call it your flow. It is a flow of life. If you can get into it and stay in it, life becomes one unfolding miracle after another. If you will try to stay in your flow, this woman with the flower will come into your life."

He chuckled. "I wish. I'd be happy just to see her now and then in my dreams." Instead of his terrifying nightmares, he thought, but didn't say it.

The medicine woman rose. "Become more aware of what feelings and sensations you have when you work with the wild horses. And then start to feel them in other situations. Watch what happens."

Dan stood and placed the black cowboy hat on his head. He'd brought fifty dollars' worth of groceries to the medicine woman in exchange for her help. He wished he had more, but he was broke—as usual. "I don't know how to thank you...."

"You can thank me by getting into your flow." She led him out of the hogan and walked him to his rusty white pickup. In the back was all his horse-training equipment and other meager belongings. He would head down to the Donovan Ranch and be there by sunset.

Entering the pickup, Dan tipped his hat in her direction. She stood six feet away, with a white wolf now at her side. There was an ethereal presence to this medicine woman; an inner beauty and power resonated from her person. Dan was in awe of her, and he was grateful. As he drove away from the hogan, the woman's face, the one with the incredible turquoise eyes, seemed to hover like a mist in front of him. He shook his head. He had to concentrate on his driving or he'd end up stuck in one of these sandy washes.

Today, he thought, *is the first day of my life. My new life.* In a sense, he felt reborn by the experience in the sweat lodge. He also knew Ai Gvhdi Waya saw a lot more than she was telling him, but then, she was right: his personal discovery of his own process was far more empowering to him than her just telling him. He understood her reasoning.

Dan knew this was his last chance at a good job—a way to salvage his family's name. The foreman at the Donovan Ranch was giving him a break when he deserved none. His first order of business was to tame a black Arabian stallion known as Gan. *Gan* was an Apache word for devil. From what the foreman had said,

Gan hated humans, and had been badly abused by his alcoholic owner. Dan's fingers tightened momentarily on the steering wheel. In front of him rose the red sandstone buttes that were scattered over the red desert of the Navajo res. It was a beautiful sight, one that Dan never got tired of looking at.

Hadn't he been abused daily by his schoolmates when he was growing up? Been called names? Been shunned? He'd always had to defend himself. And how many fights had he lost? How many times had he come home with a black eye or a bloody face? Or worse, a broken hand or nose? Navajo children were not kind to one who did not fit their concepts. Dan wasn't a fighter. All he wanted was peace. So why the hell had he joined the marines and gone into the warrior branch, the Recon Marines? He knew now that he'd been trying to make his father accept him. It hadn't been the right choice.

No, Ai Gvhdi Waya was right—he had to stand in his power as a horse trainer and not always be apologizing for not being a teacher, as his father wanted to be, or the marine Dan had once tried to be for his father's sake. He had to find himself and like himself for what he was. Or else the man clothed in darkness would become a homeless person on some cold street of Flagstaff, looking for handouts, for money to go buy his next bottle of whiskey.

The alternative was no alternative at all to Dan. Somehow, he *had* to save his own life. This was his last chance and he knew it. And the woman with the flower was part of his healing. Did she exist? Would he be blessed by getting to meet her in physical reality? He fervently prayed that it would be so.

Chapter 3

"Welcome home!" Kate cried as Jessica parked her truck in front of the main ranch house and got out. The midday sun beat down as her older sister took the steps two at a time to get to her. Though she was tired and stressed out, Jessica rallied and gave Kate a big smile in return.

"Oh!" she cried, throwing her arms around her tall, lean sister. "It's so good to see you, Katie!" She basked in the love that emanated from Kate, before she finally stepped away.

"I don't mean to be in a hurry here, Katie, but my girls, my orchids…" She pointed to the rear of her pickup. "They've got to have a cooler temperature or they're going to die!"

Sam McGuire, the foreman, came out of the house. He grinned and tipped his hat respectfully to Jessica.

"Did I hear a call for help? Welcome home, Jessica. Kate couldn't sleep at all last night because she was so excited about your coming home today."

"Hi, Sam," Jessica whispered, and hugged the tall, strapping Arizona cowboy. "It's great to be home. Where did you put the greenhouse you and Kate built for my girls? I have to get them into it pronto or they're going to die of heat prostration." Jessica quickly pushed a wisp of blond hair away from her brow. She saw the love in Sam's eyes when he and Kate shared a warm look. If only she could someday find a man like Sam—who loved her, warts and all.

Sam put his arm around Kate's shoulder and pointed to the house that stood to the left of the main ranch house. "That's your new home, Jessica, over there. I'll drive your truck around and back it up to the greenhouse door. Kate put on the humidifier, and the temperature was reading eighty-five just about half an hour ago."

Relieved, Jessica nodded. "That's wonderful. Thanks so much, Sam."

He brushed past her and drove the pickup around to the other side of the cottonwood-enclosed main house.

Jessica gazed up at her sister. "You look so happy, Katie. Love really does work, doesn't it?"

Kate nodded and said softly, "Sam is wonderful. I'm afraid that it's all a dream and that I'll wake up someday and be without him," she confided as she put her arm around Jessica's shoulders and guided her toward her new home.

"Pshaw. Sam isn't some dream. Judging by the way he was looking at you, he's never going to leave under any circumstances," Jessica responded. It felt so good to have Kate's tall, lean body against hers. "Boy, to tell you the truth, Katie, I'd sure like to find a guy like Sam, but my record isn't so good in that department."

Kate touched Jessica's flyaway blond hair. The ninety-degree weather in early May was sending waves of heat across the canyon floor, where the ranch headquarters sat. "Give yourself time. Carl was a real bastard. Not all men are that way."

"I'm worried, Kate. Carl might try to follow me here. He threatened to hunt me down and kill me. I seem to have a curse. All I pick are abusive types."

"Is it any wonder? Kelly was abusive to us. That's all we know." Kate sighed. "And as for Carl following you here, if he has any brains at all, he won't."

Jessica looked up into Kate's face, which was darkly tanned despite the fact that she wore a straw cowboy hat today to protect her skin and shade her eyes. "Then tell me how you ended up with Sam. He's certainly not an 'abuser' type."

Mystified, Kate shrugged her shoulders. "I don't know, Jessica. I really don't." And then she grinned down at her. "You tell me. You're our little spiritual sister out here in the desert wilderness."

Jessica chuckled as they rounded the corner of the ranch house. About three hundred feet away was a beautiful cream-colored, Santa Fe adobe home. It was one of three houses that Odula had insisted be built for her daughters. Kelly had built them, but he'd been angry about doing so. In Odula's world, children not only were raised together, they lived in close proximity to one another even after they were grown. Jessica remembered how Kelly had railed at spending what little money they had on building these homes. Sadly she recalled how their mother had wanted her daughters to stay on after high school, but it had been impossible with Kelly's continual drinking and abusive behavior toward them.

"The house…" Jessica said with a sigh. "You've given it a new coat of paint!" A thrill went through her. Home! She was really home—and it felt so good! A bubbling joy kept moving up through her and expanding her heart until she was breathless from it. Not until this moment had Jessica realized just how much she'd missed her family.

"Actually," Kate murmured, releasing Jessica and opening the gate in the white picket fence, "our new wrangler, Dan Black, just finished painting it."

"Oh, you've got help finally."

Kate grimaced. "We're not in any financial shape to be paying anyone yet, Jessica. Sam knows Dan Black. He's part Navajo and part Anglo. Got a real chip on his shoulder, but Sam said he was good at breaking and training horses. And he's going to be working at taming Gan." Kate moved to the front door and opened it for Jessica with a flourish. "Welcome home, little sis."

Jessica stepped into the much cooler environment of the house. It was empty, but the colorful flower-print curtains on the windows made tears come to her eyes. "Oh, Katie, it's beautiful. I'd forgotten how much I'd come to love this house after Kelly built it." She wiped tears from her eyes as she looked around. Happiness deluged her.

"Grudgingly built," Kate reminded her grimly. "Why don't you go unload your Mother Earth Flower Essence stuff from the back of your pickup into your new greenhouse? I'll get Dan to help unpack your trailer, and he and Sam can move the contents into here."

Jessica sighed, relishing the cool interior of her home.

"Which of the two guys would be more sensitive to my orchids?"

Chuckling, Kate moved to the door. "Sam is all thumbs. If you need help unloading the orchids, I'll call Dan over from Gan's corral to help. Okay?"

"But you said he's got a chip on his shoulder."

"Ah, he's shy and doesn't say much. Like most Navajos, he won't look you in the eye. He looks up, down or to the side, but not straight into your eyes. They think it's rude to stare at a person. Sam says the only time he ever got ugly was when he hit the bottle after coming back from Desert Storm. Dan hasn't touched alcohol since that time, so I think it's in the past. He's been here for a week, and so far, so good. Dan's really wonderful with animals, Jessica. Far more sensitive than Sam. He'll be okay. He takes orders well. I'll go get him and he can help you unload your orchids. Sam and I will move your furniture into the house in the meantime."

Nonplussed, Jessica nodded and hurried out the back door. It was so hard to concentrate on the care the orchids demanded at a time like this. All Jessica really wanted to do was settle into her new home, spend time with Kate and simply reacquaint herself with the place where she'd grown up. With a sigh, she opened the side door to the hothouse. Checking the thermometer and humidity gauge, she noticed the rows and rows of lattice type, wrought-iron shelves that had been set up for the bulk of her orchids to sit on. The environment within the greenhouse felt wonderful compared to the much drier, hotter air outside. The swamp cooler kept the greenhouse at a reasonable seventy-five degrees.

"I hear Dan's going to help unload your orchids with you?" Sam called from the front door.

"Yes," Jessica said, hurrying to where Sam had parked her pickup near the door. "Thanks for helping, Sam."

He nodded. "Dan will be better at this than I am. I'm all thumbs."

She smiled up into Sam's rugged face. "Okay, thanks. I think Katie wants you to help her move my furniture into my house." Sensitive to the need of others, Jessica could feel that he was trying his best to be warm and welcoming to her. She knew Sam was a strong, silent type, and for him to be putting out this much for her meant a lot. She appreciated his trying to make her feel comfortable about coming home.

"Yep, that's where we'll be. When you're done here, come back to your house. Kate's got some nonalcoholic grape bubbly to toast your coming home."

Touched, Jessica nodded. "I will! Thanks for everything, Sam. It means so much...."

Nodding in turn, Sam left.

A few minutes later, Jessica heard a slight, hesitant knock at the side entrance to the greenhouse. It must be the wrangler, the one with a chip on his shoulder, she thought. Jessica chided herself for thinking of the man in that way. It wasn't right. She hurried to the door and swung it open.

For a split second, Jessica froze before the open door. A man, tall and lean, his skin a dark golden brown, and his eyes gray and intelligent, stared back at her. Her heart pounded in her breast. She felt her breath torn from her. It was as if time had halted and frozen around them. She studied the man before her more closely. He wore a dusty, black felt Stetson hat low across his broad forehead. His prominent nose was crooked, as if it had been broken a number of times. A scar along his left cheek scored his hard flesh. His face was narrow, and the lines at the corners of his pale, almost colorless eyes showed he squinted or laughed a lot. On closer inspection, Jessica surmised that he probably squinted more than laughed. This was a man who wore sadness like a huge blanket around himself.

Because of her sensitivity to people, to the feelings surrounding them, she felt an incredible weight settle within her, the weight of his absolute sadness. And yet he stood lean and tall, his shoulders strong and thrown back with an unconscious pride. She saw the Navajo in him, from his shining, short black hair to the leanness of his body to the golden color of his skin. She liked the warmth she saw banked in his gray eyes, eyes that seemed to change color slightly as he stared down at her. He seemed surprised—shocked—at seeing her. Why on earth would he be shocked?

Almost unconsciously, Jessica touched her hair. She was sure it was in disarray and needed a good combing. Why was he looking at her like that? Had she spilled something on her skirt or blouse when she ate that veggie burger on the road? Nervously, Jessica touched her lacy cotton blouse. No, no ketchup there. How about her skirt? She quickly flattened her hands and brushed them over the dark green print decorated with various shades of pink and lavender morning glories. She found no damage to her skirt, either.

Lifting her chin, she frowned as she felt his shock deepen. He was staring at her as if he'd seen a ghost! His gray eyes had widened considerably. Those black pupils had enlarged and she saw an almost predatory intent in his gaze, as if he were an eagle checking out a possible prey. Laughing at herself, Jessica quirked her lips.

"Hi, I'm Jessica Donovan. You must be Dan Black. Come on in." She stepped aside and he slowly entered, still continuing to appraise her sharply. Closing the door, Jessica offered him her small, slender hand. "You can call me Jessica...."

Dan stared at that very white, delicate-looking hand with such slender, artistic fingers. This was the woman he'd seen in his sweat lodge vision! His heart was pounding like a sledgehammer in his chest. An internal trembling began deep within him and he felt outwardly shaky. Unable to tear his gaze from her beautiful turquoise eyes, Dan stood there, looking like a gaping fool, he was sure. How could he tell this beautiful woman of the sky that she'd been in his vision? Automatically, he felt a strange, warm tendril curling around his heart.

"Do you shake hands?" Jessica demanded a little more briskly. "Because if you don't, we have to get to work. My orchids must be cooled down quickly or they'll die."

Rousing himself, Dan jerked his hat off his head and quickly raised his hand, swallowing hers up in his. Her fingers were so soft and firm compared to his dirty, range-worn and callused ones. "Sorry," he mumbled. "I'm Dan Black. Most folks call me Dan unless they don't like me."

Jessica felt the warm strength in Dan's hand. It was a hand that had known hard, even brutal physical labor. Suddenly she felt a new sensation and she didn't want to release his hand. Though she could feel energy and emotions around people, if she touched them she got a far more intimate portrait of them. Dan's strength was there, quiet and deep, like the cold Canadian lake near Van-

couver that she loved to sit beside, watching the wild-
life. The sadness she'd felt melted away, and instead she
discovered the man who was hidden within it. Yes, he
was terribly shy, and unlike the typical Navajo, he *was*
staring at her. As if she were a specimen or something.

Laughing softly, she reluctantly released his hand.
"Am I a ghost to you, Dan Black?"

Shaken, Dan placed the hat back on his head. How
pretty Jessica Donovan was in person. The blouse she
wore had Victorian lace around the throat. The skirt was
full, brightly colored with flowers, and fell to her thin
ankles. She wore some kind of sandals on her small,
perfectly formed feet. As his gaze moved up again, he
noticed how her mussed golden hair fell in a tumble
around her shoulders. She reminded him of the clouds
that moved along the Mogollon Rim above the ranch,
fleeting, ethereal and transparent with beauty. But in
the sunlight, those clouds disappeared. Dan wondered
if she was an apparition. He hoped not.

"No, ma'am…you're not a ghost. You, uh, remind me
of someone I saw one time, that's all. I'm sorry for staring. It's not polite."

Jessica felt heat rise in her cheeks as he averted his
gaze. "Oh, that's okay. I hope I reminded you of someone who was good and not bad." She chuckled, gestur-
ing for him to follow her. A new thrill moved through
her. How handsome he was! Twice in the span of a short
while, Jessica found herself detoured from the care of
her orchids. On a feminine level, she found herself helplessly drawn to Dan Black. There was an air of mystery
around him and it drew her effortlessly.

Even the way she moved reminded Dan of a wispy
cloud. It was as if Jessica's feet weren't really touching

the gravel of the greenhouse floor at all. He shook his head. What was going on? Was he hallucinating? How could this woman be real? Yet his fingers tingled wildly where he'd touched her hand. If she was a ghost, a vision, she certainly felt real. His entire body was resonating with her presence, her impish smile and the kind warmth that danced in her eloquent eyes—eyes that were a window into her sweet, vulnerable soul.

As he followed her to the door where the truck was parked, Dan realized that as closed up and guarded as he was, Jessica was just the opposite: she was open, available, trusting and sweet. So very, very sweet. How did she survive in this harsh world? Early in his life, he'd been a lot like her, but the meanness of the schoolchildren had forced him to close up and protect himself against such attacks.

Looking at Jessica's flyaway, spun-sunshine hair, the almost ethereal way she walked, he realized life hadn't treated her in the same way. Halting, he watched her pull a box out of the pickup, and he opened his arms to receive it. All he saw were a lot of lumps of newspaper in it.

"These are orchids, Dan," she said a little breathlessly. As she slid the cardboard box into his waiting arms, she found herself *wanting* to make physical contact with him again. Jessica felt such hesitancy around him, such excruciating shyness and...what else? As her arms brushed his darkly haired forearms, bared because he'd rolled up the sleeves of his dark red cowboy shirt, she felt something else. It was so hidden and elusive... and yet, as she slid the box into his arms, it was there. What was it?

"Treat them gently. Just start putting the boxes over

there, on the metal table." Jessica found herself wanting to touch him again. How strange! After her experience with Carl, she had learned to distrust men, yet here she was, wanting more contact with Dan. Her emotions were like a roller coaster and she simply couldn't stop the blazing joy that curled through her heart every time she looked at Dan Black.

For the next twenty minutes, Dan helped her bring in box after box. He'd heard of orchids, but he'd never seen one, so he was curious. When Jessica finally shut the door to the greenhouse, her cheeks were flushed a bright red and her gold hair was growing slightly curly in the humidity, framing her oval face beautifully. Dan tried not to gawk at her. He tried not to rudely stare into those beautiful, bottomless eyes that shone with such life.

"Now, watch what I do," she directed softly as she brought the first box over to where he stood.

Dan moved closer. He liked how he felt around her. Remembering Ai Gvhdi Waya's instructions about opening himself up to that mystical flow he always had with horses, he allowed that to consciously happen now. Jessica felt safe to him. In fact, he'd never felt more safe with a person than her. There was nothing dark, manipulative or abusive about her. She was like an incredible rainbow of color to him, and just as otherworldly. He still wasn't sure he wasn't hallucinating. But each time he got to brush her hand or her fingertips, he knew she was very human.

In his world, the Navajo world, he had heard tales of gods and goddesses who turned from animal form into human form. Sometimes, they became human in order to instruct the Navajo people. That was how he saw Jessica—as a goddess from the Other Side, come to instruct him. She couldn't really be human. She was too beautiful. Too loving and open to be like him or the people he knew.

Jessica gently began to unfold the newspaper from one of the orchids she had taken from the cardboard box and set on the metal table in front of her. "Have you ever seen an orchid, Dan?" She thrilled to his nearness. There was such raw, barely controlled power around him. He was a stallion tamer, a man who could handle a thousand-pound horse and not be afraid. Admiration for him spiralled through her and a hundred questions about him sat on the tip of her tongue.

He shook his head. "No, ma'am, I haven't."

She glanced at him out of the corner of her eye. "Please call me Jessica. Ma'am sounds *so* formal. I'm afraid I'm not a very formal person." The warmth in his eyes melted her and she saw one corner of his mouth gently curl. It was a slight response, but she felt the feathery, invisible touch of it upon her.

Out of habit, he tipped the brim of his cowboy hat in her direction. "Yes, ma'am! I mean… Jessica." Her name rolled off his tongue like honey. He liked the sound of it. In his world, names had meanings. Someday he'd like to ask her what her name meant.

Smiling warmly, Jessica met his shy gaze. She saw color rising in his cheeks. Dan was blushing! What a delightful discovery. This hard-bitten man, whose face was carved with sadness, could blush. Jessica felt her pulse speed up as his gray gaze met hers for a fleeting moment. She saw again the hint of thawing in his eyes and felt a shy smile emanating from him. But it never appeared on his hard, thinned mouth. She wondered if Dan's lips would seem fuller if he didn't keep them so tightly compressed, as if to protect himself from what she might say. She sensed that he was like a beaten animal—a beaten, wary animal that didn't quite trust her.

As much as she wanted to be nosy and ask him more, Jessica had grown up with Navajo people and knew they did not like to be asked direct questions about themselves. Perhaps with time and careful watching, Dan Black would be like one of her mysterious orchids. As he blossomed and began to trust her more, she would understand more of these feelings she picked up around him.

"Watch me carefully," she said, and unfolded the newspapers one by one and set them aside. "Orchids are very sensitive plants. They must have a certain range of temperature in order to survive. For instance, many of my orchid girls like the temperature no lower than fifty-five degrees at night and no higher than eighty-five during the day. And—" she pointed to the two temperature gauges hung on a redwood spar "—humidity is an absolute must or they won't bloom or flourish. The humidity has to be set around eighty to ninety percent to create the best environmental conditions for them."

He watched, mesmerized as her hands flew knowingly around the packed orchid. Although Dan wanted to see what one of these plants looked like, her long, beautiful fingers were worth watching. There was nothing but grace to Jessica Donovan. No move she made was jerky or hurried. Everything she did flowed from one gesture directly into another, making it seem as if she were always in motion. He smiled to himself, absorbing the warm, sunny energy that emanated from her. Getting to stand only inches from her, looking over her shoulder as she worked quickly, was pure, unadulterated pleasure for Dan.

"See?" Jessica said excitedly as she pulled the last remaining newspaper away. "This is Stone Pinto!" Her voice softened with excitement as she turned the orchid in the red clay pot around so that Dan could see the spike with twelve blossoms on it. "Isn't she lovely? Oh, I love this orchid so much. She's one of my personal favorites. Here, look at her. Carefully touch her leaves and her flower."

Jessica was delighted to see real interest in Dan's eyes as he moved closer, much closer to her. She unconsciously absorbed Dan's nearness; it was a powerful sensation, but one that did not put her on edge. Ordinarily, if any man got this close to her, she would shy away. But she wasn't afraid of him. Although she was puzzled as to why, Jessica had enough intuitive sense to allow the exchange of energy to take place. In some ways, she was like a starving animal and Dan was giving her what she needed. But when she remembered he was a man, wariness invaded her. Yet her heart whispered that he could be trusted. Could he?

Dan stared at the orchid. "The flower..." he began, choking up. Without thinking, he reached forward and delicately touched the white blossom with the field of purple dots across it. "I've seen this flower before—" He felt his throat close up completely. When he touched the orchid blossom, he felt the strength of it, as well as the velvety softness of the petals.

Jessica saw so many different emotions cross his once hard, unreadable face. She was amazed at his response to Stone Pinto. She'd seen similar responses to other orchids when she'd allowed friends and customers to come in and see the plants from which she'd created the flower essences that cured them.

"You like her?" she whispered, touched by his emotional reaction to the orchid. As he leaned over and carefully examined the orchid, he grazed her arm with his. Being with him, Jessica realized, was wonderful! She'd never felt this way around any man. Ever. Absorbing his profile, she felt confused and exhilarated all at once. "When I did tests with Stone Pinto, I found out her essence was for people who carried too much responsibility on their shoulders or worked too hard. People who saw life as just one big responsibility and had lost their ability to play, to laugh or even smile...."

She reached out and stroked the long, leathery leaf of the orchid. "Stone Pinto is for people who usually have had a very hard, rigid life, Dan. If you took her essence, it would help you unbend, allow you to feel more vulnerable and to be able to laugh or smile again." She shared a soft smile with him as he turned and looked down at her. The predatory look was gone from his eyes now; instead, they appeared to be a soft dove gray, showing his emotions.

"Already," Jessica whispered, "she heals you as you touch her...."

Dan stood there, mystified. He withdrew his hand and stood looking at the orchid on the workbench. "But how... I saw this flower in my vision...." And then he stopped. Most people would never understand. He didn't trust that Jessica would. And when he saw her eyes change, and tears swim in them, he felt his heart opening like that orchid bloom. He was helpless to stop the reaction as their gazes met and locked. There was such an incredible sense of love moving from her to him in that moment that it made his breath hitch in response.

Stepping back, he looked away, unable to understand or digest all that was happening. Embarrassed, Dan moved the hat around on his head. It was a nervous gesture, something he did when he was afraid he'd humiliated himself once more in front of a stranger.

Jessica reached out, wrapping her fingers around his arm and drawing him back to the bench. "Let me show you something. You're part Navajo. You're close to the land, the plants and animals, like we are. My mother was a medicine woman and she passed on much of her skills to all of us." Jessica didn't want to release his hard, muscled arm, but she forced herself to do it. How strong and capable Dan was. Her hands tingled wildly from contact with him. Sliding her fingers around the six-inch clay pot, she drew the Stone Pinto forward.

"You understand that all living things have a spirit, don't you?" Her gaze dug into his widening eyes.

"Yes." He took the clay pot she placed in his hands. The spike on the Stone Pinto arched close to his face, like a bower full of beautiful blossoms.

"All right, then take what you know about plant spirits. They are just like people, aren't they? There're grumpy ones, happy ones, shy ones and everything else in between." Jessica moved her fingers along the leaves in a loving, caressing motion. "They have an aura around them, just as we do. Like people, not all plants are created equal. We know from our belief systems that there are young souls and old souls down here on Mother Earth."

Jessica became very serious as she placed her hands around his. "Dan, when I share this with you, I know you'll understand what I'm saying. I don't normally tell people this because they'd think I was crazy, but orchids are the most evolved plants on the face of Mother Earth.

They are the pinnacle, the most spiritual of all the species of flowers that grow down here. Why? Because—" she slid her hands off his and tapped the bottom of the pot "—orchids do not live in soil like every other plant we know. No, they are air plants. They require absolutely no soil to grow. All they need to not only survive, but flourish, is humid air and the right temperatures. They absorb all the water they need right out of the air."

Jessica sighed and held his awed gaze. "Isn't that something? I'm so amazed by these plants. I feel like a child among very old, learned teachers when I work with my orchids."

He nodded, slowly turning the clay pot in his hand. "So, they are like the stone nation. Stones are millions of years old and hold much knowledge, too."

Jessica clapped her hands delightedly. "Exactly! Yes, you've got it!" She saw the redness in his cheeks and realized she'd embarrassed him. "I'm sorry, I didn't mean to seem to make fun of you, Dan. Just the opposite. Do you know how few people I can talk to about orchids and their spiritual qualities and evolution?" She held up one hand and spread her fingers wide. "Not even five people for the five fingers on my hand!" She laughed.

A hint of a smile tugged at the corners of his mouth as he gently placed the orchid back on the workbench. Jessica's childlike joy was infectious. She made him want to return her sunny smile, her uninhibited joy. "I see. They are flower teachers to us because they are so advanced on their own path of learning?"

With a sigh, Jessica whispered, "Yes. Oh, yes. You've got it, Dan. I'm *so* glad you're working here at the ranch. You really understand. And I need someone to help me. Would you like to do that? I can teach you so much about them, but in the long run, they will teach you ten times more. Just to get to work with orchids is like being in the most wonderful school of life you've ever experienced. I love it! I love working out here most of the day with them. They are so loving, so warm and giving to us." As she gazed at him, she realized the woman part of her wanted him around for other reasons. She savored his maleness because it did not threaten her, rather, it made her wildly aware of herself and her femininity. Each time he looked at her, she felt as if her heart would explode with raw joy.

Stunned, he muttered, "I don't know anything about them, though. I'm afraid I'd hurt them."

"Pshaw!" Jessica handed him another orchid clothed in protective newspaper. "Unwrap this one. Let's see which one she is! I don't believe for a second that you'd hurt a fly, Dan Black." And then she became serious. "Maybe you've been hurt, like Gan out there, but you're not mean and neither is that stallion."

Shaken, Dan stared at her, the silence building. "How— no, never mind...."

"I'm pretty psychic," Jessica said, quickly going about the business of freeing up the orchid in front of her. "It was a gift from my mother, Odula. She had the Sight, as we call it. Kate has good gut feelings and intuition. Rachel has the same thing, but I got gifted with more than them in some ways. I can feel people, and sometimes I'll know something about them without ever having been told beforehand. Don't let it shake you up. If you want to work in here with me and my orchid girls, you'll just have to get used to it."

As he unwrapped the orchid, a beautiful yellow one

with a spicy scent, Dan nodded. "I know a medicine woman who sees like you."

"Will it bother you?" Jessica demanded primly. But from his expression, she knew it wouldn't. As she watched Dan carefully unwrap the orchid, she almost smiled. Despite his long, large-knuckled hands toughened with calluses, he had been ultracautious unwrapping that orchid. Yes, he was the perfect helper for her. Even if he was a man, he had that wonderful gentleness that many Navajo men possessed. She sent a prayer of thanks upward to the Great Spirit for sending such a person to her. Jessica had been very worried about not having help, since Moyra was no longer at her side. And she certainly couldn't ask Kate or Sam to help. They were already working sixteen hours a day to keep the Donovan Ranch afloat. She could not expect help from them.

"You know," Jessica whispered as she set the orchid on an upper shelf, "you are an answer to my prayers, Dan."

His head snapped up and he momentarily froze, the orchid in his hand. "What?"

"I said you're an answer to my prayers. Is that so awful? Judging from the look on your face, it is. Do you not want to help out in the greenhouse? Maybe Sam's given you other duties that I don't know about?"

"Oh...no," he muttered, placing his orchid next to hers on the wrought-iron shelf. "It's not that—"

"What then?" Jessica removed two more pots from the cardboard box. Her heart broke a little at the thought that Dan didn't want to work out here with her and her orchid girls. He seemed so perfect for it. Besides, if she was really honest, she had to admit she liked having him around, shyness and all. He was terribly handsome in a rugged, western kind of way. Maybe he was married, she thought as her gaze went to his left hand. There was no wedding ring on it, but a lot of Navajos never wore much jewelry on their fingers—just on their wrists and around their necks.

"No... I'd like to work out here," he admitted in a low voice. "I'll have to have Sam okay it. He's my boss. My other duty is to try and tame Gan and get him under saddle."

"Big order," Jessica said, relieved that Dan wanted to work in the greenhouse.

For the first time, Dan chuckled. He began unpacking another orchid. The pleasure of having Jessica less than a foot away from him was all he needed. "Gan is wary and he hates men. I've got to get him to trust me even if I am one. That's the first order of business."

"When my father drank," Jessica said in a low voice filled with pain, "he used to beat Gan with a rubber hose." She slid Dan a pained look.

Dan's hands stilled around the orchid. "What did he do to you when you tried to stop him?" He saw her face go pale and those glorious turquoise eyes of hers veil with deep grief and sadness. In that moment, he wanted to reach out and cup her small face protectively.

"I don't want to talk about it," she managed to answer, hurriedly unpacking the next orchid.

Dan felt her anguish and heard it in her strained voice. He'd heard a lot about Kelly Donovan; he knew he had been a mean bastard when he hit the bottle. Frowning, Dan returned his attention to the orchid he was unwrapping. It wasn't the Navajo way to ask personal questions or intrude into someone's life. He'd already overstepped the bounds with Jessica. It was so easy to do, he was discovering, because she was accessible and vulnerable.

Sighing, he realized his vision had been real. And the woman he'd seen in it was Jessica Donovan—a woman completely out of his reach. She was the owner of this ranch. She was rich and had land. He was nothing but a horse wrangler with no money, no savings. Pain racked his chest. Life was cruel, he decided. Cruel and hard and merciless. Here was the woman in his vision— unreachable. Untouchable. In a different class from him. In a different world from him.

His hands trembled slightly as he picked up another orchid. Great Spirit help him, but he wanted Jessica. He wanted her breathless laughter against his mouth, the warm touch of her hands exploring his hard body. He longed to discover every inch of her and love her until he died, knowing he'd given her every ounce of his passion.

Dan was even more unsure about life now than ever before. It had thrown him a curve he could never have imagined. Not ever. What was he going to do? How was he going to handle this hotbed of bubbling emotions in his chest that refused to be stilled or denied? Could Jessica feel it? Feel how he *really* felt toward her? He lived in fear of her finding out because he was afraid she'd misinterpret his feelings. Yet just watching her hurry back and forth, like a fluttering, beautiful butterfly, Dan felt his fortitude dissolve like honey in hot sunlight. He ached to remain in Jessica's presence. And somehow he was going to have to control himself, his emotions and his desires in order to keep his job on this ranch. How was he going to do it?

Chapter 4

Jessica awoke suddenly. She sat up in her old brass bed, the quilt falling away from her. Sleepily, she pushed her blond hair away from her face and looked toward the open window. Outside, she heard wonderful, familiar sounds from her childhood. The soft lowing of the cattle, the call of the rooster and the snort of horses were a welcoming balm to her. Inhaling, she could smell the scent of juniper in the cool, damp dawn air that flowed through the window into the small room.

Looking at her watch, she discovered it was only five a.m. She never got up this early in Vancouver. As Jessica sat there, Dan Black's face seemed to waver in front of her. Her heart tugged, gently stirring her sleep-filled thoughts. A soft smile pulled at her mouth as she eased from bed. Her feet touched the shining cedar floor, which had been waxed to perfection days earlier. Bless

Kate and Sam for their help. Jessica knew that Dan had helped prepare her home, too. That made her feel inexorably good.

Quickly taking a hot shower, she pulled on a short-sleeved white blouse, a pair of jeans and very old but comfortable cowboy boots. She smiled as she stood up. She hadn't worn these since she'd left the ranch. Noticing that the leather was cracked and worn, she ran her fingers across the roughened texture of one of the toes. Despite their condition, the boots were steel toed and would protect her if a horse or steer accidentally sidestepped and came down on her foot. Cowboy boots were an important part of the uniform of the day here at the Donovan Ranch.

Humming softly, Jessica moved to the small kitchen and made some hot, fresh coffee. The odor filled her nostrils as she stood leaning against the beige tile counter decorated with the Cherokee colors of the four directions—red, yellow, black and blue.

As her gaze moved around the silent room, she saw many places for some of her hardier orchids, which would love to live here part-time and bring more color and life into the adobe house. Again Dan crossed her mind. How much fun she'd had yesterday unpacking the orchids with him! He was so gentle. So sensitive. Many times during the day she'd watched him carefully unpack one of her girls, enjoying the sight of a man with work-worn hands using a delicacy she'd rarely seen. She hoped Sam would allow Dan to continue to help her set up her business. She needed to get back on line with her company as soon as possible to take care of her back orders.

Pouring coffee into a dark red mug, Jessica moved out to the roughened log porch that enclosed her home.

As she gently sat down in the swing, her ears picked up music—a Native American flute being played, she realized. The rasping, husky notes seemed to waft on the coming dawn. The sky in front of her was turning from gray to a pale pink color. High above the ranch a few wisps of cirrus, which reminded Jessica of a galloping horse's mane flying outward, turned a darker pink. Sighing because she'd missed the intrinsic beauty of the Southwest, Jessica stood and followed the sound of the flute.

As she rounded the large, freshly painted red barn, which housed thousands of bales of hay for the horses and cattle during leaner times, Jessica saw that both ends of the structure were open to allow maximum flow of fresh air to the broodmare stalls that lined the aisle. A few of the mares near foaling nickered as she walked by, probably thinking she was bringing them their oats for the day. But their meal would come later, when Dan made his rounds.

Behind the barn were several huge, rectangular corrals. All of the barbed wire had been replaced either with heavy wooden poles or, in the case of the Arabian horse corral, with solid and safe pipe fencing. Jessica was glad to see the wicked, scarring barbed wire finally replaced. Kelly had never wanted to spend any money on suitable fencing.

The Arabians in the corral all pricked up their ears as she approached, and a few of them nickered in welcome. Jessica smiled and continued to follow the flute music, which was coming from farther north. Who was playing it? She hadn't had time yesterday to explore the ranch and get a feel for it.

In front of her was a huge, enclosed wooden arena.

As she headed toward it, she realized it was the place where horses were broken and training was begun. The walls were ten feet high so that the horse could not look anywhere but at the trainer and the animal's attention would be focused one hundred percent.

Moving around the training area, Jessica halted. Her breath hitched momentarily. There was Gan, the black Arabian stallion. And Dan Black. Neither saw her, and she remained perfectly still, gazing at the unbelievable sight. Though Gan was now twenty years old and middle-aged, the proud stallion looked larger than life. Gan's size had come from Raffles, a stallion of English lineage and one of the most profoundly influential bloodlines in North America. Gan wasn't more than fourteen hands three, but what he didn't have in height he made up for in muscle and power.

The stud had been a year old when he'd come to Donovan Ranch. Because of Kelly's abuse, the stallion hated all people, and men especially. The only person who'd ever gotten close to Gan was Odula.

Now Jessica's gaze moved from the stallion, which stood frozen, his wide nostrils flaring, his full attention on the opposite side of the corral, to Dan. He was sitting outside the pipe fence, his back to a post, playing his flute. The soft, plaintive notes filled the air, bringing tears to Jessica's eyes.

The music was subduing Gan, she realized. She watched with fascination as the stallion snorted and pawed the ground angrily, the dirt and red sand flying from beneath his sharpened hoof. And then he'd stop, fling his magnificent head upward and listen. At no time did Dan pause to see what the stallion was doing. Luckily, he was in a protected place, where Gan was unable to charge and bite him.

The sky turned a darker pink. Jessica heard the familiar call of quail families, which lived around the ranch. She saw a flock of mallards skimming northward, heading toward the Rim and Oak Creek. Slowly, she lifted the cup of steaming coffee to her lips and took a sip. Enthralled by Gan's attention to the stallion tamer, she smiled. Sam had said Dan was the best horse wrangler in the state of Arizona. Well, his methods were certainly surprising. As the last notes of the mournful flute song ended, she watched Gan.

The stallion shook his head from side to side. He pawed the ground again, a wary look in his eyes as Dan slowly eased away from the post and stood up. It was at that moment that Jessica saw Dan raise his head, take his attention off the stallion and look directly at her. Her pulse skittered. Her heart opened like an unfolding orchid bloom. His gray eyes were dark, the pupils huge and black. For the first time, she saw relaxation in his features—not that hard, guarded look that had been on his face yesterday. Jessica realized Dan was happy. Even more, his mouth, which was usually tightly compressed into a thin line, was now full, the corners tilted upward. She realized she was seeing the real Dan Black now—the man without the mask in place.

Suddenly she felt like an interloper; heat swiftly moved up from her neck, warming her cheeks. She gripped the coffee mug a little more tightly and an apology came to her lips.

As if sensing her embarrassment, Dan pushed his black Stetson off his forehead with his thumb and gave her an uneven smile of welcome.

"May I come closer?" Jessica asked in a low voice. She knew that horse trainers liked to work alone, without interference from other people. They needed one hundred percent of the animal's attention at all times or training didn't occur.

Dan nodded. "Walk very slowly," he told her in a low voice. "No fast movements."

"Right...." Jessica said. She paid attention to the uneven red clay and sand beneath her feet as she walked carefully toward the corral. Gan started, snorted and leaped from the center of the corral to the opposite side, away from her. Her heart sank. She hadn't meant to scare the stallion.

Her pulse skipped erratically as she approached Dan. He stood completely at ease, one foot hitched up on the bottom rail, the flute in his left hand resting across his thigh. How terribly handsome he looked today, Jessica thought, despite the fact that the long-sleeved, white shirt he wore had seen better days. She saw a number of places where the material had been torn and sewn carefully together again. Still, she couldn't help but admire the broad shoulders and powerfully sprung chest beneath that shirt. His blue jeans outlined his lean, hard lower body to perfection and a red bandanna was wrapped loosely around his neck. His cowboy boots were in just as bad a condition as hers, worn and cracked by years of use.

Dan's eyes narrowed as he watched Jessica approach. Had the Great Spirit ever made a woman more beautiful, more untouchable than her? As she closed the distance to him, he thought not. Her gold hair was drawn back into a ponytail that moved with her graceful movements. Her white blouse was feminine and enhanced the blush staining her cheeks. Yesterday she had worn a skirt, but today, he noticed with more than a little interest, she wore snug-fitting jeans and cowboy boots. She was small and delicate. Dan wondered if she had been sick as a child, because she seemed so fragile compared to Kate, who was more solidly built and much taller.

When Jessica lifted those lashes and revealed her turquoise eyes, Dan felt heat gather in his lower body. And when her pink lips drew into a hesitant, almost apologetic smile, his heart opened wide. Again that same warmth he'd experienced during his vision in the sweat lodge avalanched through him. How beautiful she was! How untouchable! Pain moved through him and doused the joy he'd felt. His fingers closed more firmly on the flute as she halted about four feet away from him.

"Your music was beautiful," she whispered with a sigh. "I woke up early for some reason and made coffee. When I came out on the front porch, I heard your song. It was so incredibly beautiful, Dan." Jessica closed her eyes and sighed again. "You should record what you play. It's as good as any other recording I've heard of Native American flute music."

He felt heat tunneling up his neck. With a shy laugh, he pulled his hat back down on his brow, unable to accept the look of admiration in Jessica's eyes. "I'm afraid, ma'am—I mean, Jessica—that my playing is pretty basic. I learned from my uncle, who died when I was a kid and passed on his flute to me."

"So what if you're mostly self-taught?" Jessica said, some indignation in her voice. "You have a natural, raw talent for it. Don't apologize."

With a shrug, he lifted up the flute for her to take a look. "My uncle made it out of cedar. He carved it himself. I remember he used to play it for us kids when we'd get in bed at night. I always liked his music." Sadness moved through him at the memory. "He died of liver cancer. I was real sorry to see him go. He's the one who brought laughter to us."

Jessica set her coffee cup down on the ground and gently took the nearly three-foot-long flute in her hands. The wood was a warm color, a mixture of red and yellow. There was a beaded band of red, blue, green and black around one end of it, and several red-tailed hawk feathers hung beneath the rust color of the feathers matching the reddish hue of the wood.

"This flute feels so warm. So alive...."

Dan studied her widening eyes. "You feel it, too? Why should I be surprised? You're sensitive like your mother."

Shrugging, Jessica moved her fingertips lightly over the wood. "Wood has spirit. So do these hawk feathers. You have a tree and a hawk spirit who work with you when you play this flute."

"Yes." He smiled inwardly, liking her understanding that all things were connected and that all things had spirit. Even though Jessica looked more Anglo than Cherokee, she still had the powerful blood of her mother moving through her, as Kate did. "I guess I have to get used to the fact you've got blond hair, but you're still Indian."

Jessica chuckled as she continued to examine the flute. "I'm the renegade in the family. Mom said she had no idea where my blond hair came from. It sure wasn't from her side of the family."

He enjoyed watching her, studying how she stroked the wooden flute. How would it feel if she touched him the same wonderful way? Dan surprised himself with the thought. Generally, he didn't pay much attention to women, because he'd never had any luck with them. Who wanted a drunken Navajo cowboy for company? Not many, that was for sure. But he couldn't help wondering what Jessica's light touch would do to him. His skin tightened in response. Deep down he knew, but he didn't dare follow that line of thinking. She was part owner of a large ranch. And him—he was just a tumbleweed cowboy without money or property. She would never be interested in him.

"On your father's side, I thought they were all red-haired like he was."

"No, looking back in family photos, I can see that many of our descendants from the Bay of Donovan had black hair or reddish blond hair." She reluctantly handed the flute back to him. Their fingers met briefly and Jessica absorbed Dan's warmth. She withdrew her hand quickly because her heart sped up again, as if to underscore how much she enjoyed his touch.

Dan felt his hand tingle wildly as a result of their contact, and the heat in the lower part of his body flared for an instant. Would she sense how much he liked touching her? He hoped not, or his shame would be complete. Shaken, he unhitched his boot from the rail, leaning down to pick up the carefully folded leather flute case.

"How long have you been working to tame Gan?" Jessica asked.

"Sam and Kate hired me less than two weeks ago. I've been working with Gan about a half hour a day. That's all he'll put up with for now." Dan lovingly slid the cedar flute back into the case and then hitched his boot up on the rail again. Balancing the flute across his thigh, he tied the leather strings at the top so that the instrument would not slide out.

Jessica studied the stallion, which was watching them from across the corral with large, intelligent brown eyes. He was switching his black tail from side to side, as if peeved with their continued presence. His fine, small ears kept moving back and forth.

"I never thought anyone could tame him," she admitted.

"I may not be able to. I'll try. But I'm not going to get killed in the process of trying." Dan placed the flute against the pipe fence and rested both his arms on the rail in front of him.

Jessica moved closer to Dan. She liked his lean, masculine grace. There was never a wasted motion with Dan. She sensed an underlying steadiness in him and knew that he would be someone to rely on in a time of emergency. He was someone she could trust. Moving to the fence, she placed her hands on the rail and watched Gan. The stallion's coat gleamed in the dawn light.

"He's so terrifyingly beautiful," she whispered.

"Well, he wouldn't be so terrifying if people hadn't made him that way," Dan said, absorbing her closeness hungrily. "I sometimes wonder what he would be like if your father had not beaten him into hating two-leggeds. In my mind, when I play my flute for him, I see him coming over to me." He pulled a carrot from his back pocket. "Coming to take this from me."

Jessica shared a brief smile of understanding with him. "Gan, if I remember correctly, loves apples and carrots. That is how my mother got him to trust her. She always brought him an apple or carrot a day. He always waited for her right over there, next to the gate."

"Did Gan ever try to charge her or bite her?"

"No, he was a gentleman with her, like he was to the mares he was bred with." Jessica shook her head. "Gan is a paradox in some ways. He'll bluster and charge you, and I've seen him take a pound of flesh out of Kelly two different times. And he charges with the intent to hurt you bad. But if you turn a mare ready to be bred into his corral, he's such a gentleman. He's never hurt a mare."

"There are some stallions that hurt their mares. But Sam said this stud's gentle with them. He never bites or scares them."

"Then there's hope," Jessica said, "that you can tame him and get his trust. Gan is not completely bad. No animal or human ever is."

Dan grimaced. "I don't know," he muttered, "some of us two-leggeds have pretty bad reputations that we aren't ever going to live down. People's memories are too long."

She looked at him and felt his inner pain and deep sadness. Jessica almost asked him if he was referring to himself, but something cautioned her not to be too nosy about Dan Black. He was a lot like that stallion in the corral—wary of people and not all that trusting. She felt him wanting to reach out, to trust her, and she hoped she could be there for him when he did. She liked his easygoing nature when his mask wasn't in place. Out here on the desert with his untamed stallion, she was privileged to see the real Dan Black.

"I know what you mean," Jessica said. She shrugged painfully. "My track record isn't one I'm proud of, either. Thank goodness it's in Canada, not here. But I know what you mean about gossip and people never forgetting. If you're bad, you're always bad in their eyes.

There's no way to reclaim yourself or try to better yourself. People hold on to what's bad about us, not what's good or decent."

He held her sad, blue-eyed gaze. "Somehow I don't believe that you are bad."

Sighing, Jessica said, "I married a guy, Carl, up in Canada. I'd just arrived there after leaving this ranch. I didn't want to leave, but Kelly was driving us all out. He didn't want women running his ranch. Me and my sisters each left at age eighteen, as soon as we graduated from high school." Her fingers tightened around the coolness of the pipe railing.

"I didn't want to leave Mama. I was the baby of the family, the last to go. She wanted me to stay, but I just couldn't stand what Kelly was doing to her, to the ranch and to himself."

"Or," Dan said gently, "to you?" He knew he shouldn't ask, but something drove him to. He wanted to know more about Jessica, about how life had treated her. In his heart he knew without a doubt that Jessica had the goodness he'd searched for and never found in himself, much less anyone else. It anguished him to think that Kelly might have struck her, for the rancher had been known to be violent and abusive to friends, neighbors, strangers and family alike. Dan could hardly stand to think Jessica might have been hurt by him.

She closed her eyes. "Let's just say that my growing-up years followed me to Canada, Dan." Opening her eyes, she stared sightlessly into the corral, no longer seeing Gan, but her past. "My marriage to Carl Roman was like my life with my father. I spent eight years in a hell with him. *Hell.*" The word came out bitter and hard.

Dan watched her closely. He fought the desire to ask

more personal questions. His Navajo heritage told him not to—that if she wanted to, she would divulge what she felt he should know. He tightened his mouth and stared down at the ground in front of him.

"Hell comes in many forms," he said. "It sounds as if you were not at fault, but you walked into a bad situation with a person with a dark heart."

Jessica took in a deep, shaky breath. "What was it my mother called a person who was a liar? Who chose to use only their bad traits instead of their good ones? A two-heart? Yes, that's what Carl was. He had two hearts, not one good heart. I was too young, too naive and blind to see the real him."

"That is the past now. You're home and you are loved here. Kate has done nothing but talk of you, of your arrival. Sam cares for you as a brother." Dan gestured toward the rising sun in front of them. "Here you are wanted and cared for."

"But I'm not safe here," Jessica muttered, unable to meet his eyes. She felt wave after wave of concern coming from Dan. How protective he was of her! His care was like a warm blanket that could assuage her pain, fear and worry all at the same time.

His black brows knitted and he blurted, "Safe? What do you mean?" Damn! He hadn't meant to probe! Inwardly, Dan chaffed over his rudeness.

Jessica looked up at him, searching his intense features. She was discovering that when Dan was upset, that mask came down across his face. No longer was he relaxed or at ease. Every line in his body had gone rigid with tension. His face was hard now and his eyes nearly colorless. It reminded her of a hawk ready to strike its unsuspecting prey. A shiver ran through her and for a moment Jessica had to remind herself that Dan's demeanor was not aimed *at* her, but rather was a protective response to what she'd just said. Shaken, she managed to whisper, "Carl had always told me that if I divorced him, he'd hunt me down and kill me. He said he couldn't live without me. That if he couldn't have me, no one would."

Dan's nostrils flared and he released a held breath. "The man's crazy, then."

"No kidding. I divorced him two years ago and the most wonderful and strange thing happened. I know if I tell you, you won't think it's bizarre. I was in the middle of divorcing Carl, and I was hiding out in an apartment in Vancouver under an assumed name so he couldn't stalk me. At the time, I ran my flower essence company from my apartment. I was trying to keep my business afloat and stay hidden. I desperately needed help, someone who could assist me with my orchids, fill orders and answer mail.

"One day, I went out in disguise to the grocery store. I was so scared that I dropped a bottle of orange juice in one of the aisles. It broke all over the floor. I was so ashamed, I just stood there looking down at the mess at my feet and burst into tears. I was sobbing almost hysterically when this tall, dark-haired woman came out of—I swear—nowhere. She took me by the shoulders and moved me away from the mess in the aisle, talking soothingly. She just kept patting my shoulder and telling me that it was all right, that I was safe.

"When I looked up through my tears, I saw not this woman's face, but the face of a jaguar! And then the jaguar disappeared and I saw her human face. I was so stunned by it, I stopped crying. I saw her smile and she offered me a handkerchief for my tears. She said her name was Moyra and she was from South America. She told me in a low voice, as an employee from the grocery store cleaned up the mess I'd made, that she had been sent not only to protect me, but to help me for the next two years."

With a nod, Dan said, "She was a shape-shifter."

"Yes," Jessica admitted. "She's a jaguar priestess from South America. She came from an unbroken lineage of the Jaguar Clan."

"The Great Spirit sent her to protect you, then."

"And she did, too. I could never have survived and flourished in these last two years without her help, Dan. Moyra had a jaguar's senses, and she was completely clairvoyant. She knew exactly where Carl was at all times. She helped me find a beautiful cabin out in a meadow north of Vancouver. We moved everything out there and she helped me build a greenhouse for my orchid girls. And if Carl got too close, she always knew it and would tell me."

"You avoided your ex-husband for two years, then?"

"Yes, thank goodness." Jessica shuddered. "I don't know what I'd have done if Carl had found me. I—I'm still afraid. I talked it over with Kate and Sam, and they said for me to come home, that I'd be safe here." She looked beseechingly up at Dan. "I don't know that for sure. I have bad feelings about it. I feel pretty naked and alone without Moyra around. She said she had to go home, that her family was calling her back to Peru, that she was needed there."

"You're feeling vulnerable," Dan said.

"Yes, unprotected. Moyra was a real friend."

Dan saw Jessica's eyes swim with tears and he laid his hand gently on her shoulder. How badly he wanted to say "come here," to open his arms to her and embrace her until she no longer felt so alone and unprotected against her predatory ex-husband.

Dan's hand felt firm and stabilizing to Jessica. She closed her eyes and absorbed his care and concern. "I shouldn't be telling you all of this. You barely know me...."

"What are friends for if you can't unload what worries you?" he asked huskily, and removed his hand reluctantly. "I'm not Moyra. I'm not a medicine man, but if you want, I can be like a big guard dog for you. I'll protect you, Jessica. If you want...." Never had he wanted to do anything more. Dan suddenly realized that he *could* help protect Jessica. He hadn't been trained as a Recon Marine for nothing. No, he was very good at such things. Far better than most men ever would be. Besides, his Navajo side, the man in him, would automatically protect the woman he felt so strongly about. Maybe it was a knee-jerk reaction, but it felt right to offer her his protection.

Reaching out, Jessica briefly touched his arm, feeling the hard, lean muscle beneath her fingertips. There was a dangerous quality to Dan that she'd never encountered until now. She saw it in the wild look in his almost colorless eyes, and she heard it in the grate of his voice. This side of Dan surprised her for a moment, because he'd shown her only his softer, more sensitive side. Now she saw the warrior unveiled. She allowed her hand to drop back to her side.

"No... I couldn't put you or my family at risk if Carl decided to get even with me, Dan. I don't want to put anyone else in danger. He's—he's horrible and he's insane at times...just like Kelly was when he got drunk.

Only," she said, her voice dropping with terror, "Carl was never drunk. He was that way all the time. And I never realized it until it was too late, until after we were married. He hid the real person inside of him until it was too late for me to back out and run from him."

"Listen," Dan said, cupping her shoulders and turning her toward him, "you don't have any say in this matter. There are things you don't know about me, either—good and bad. One thing I can do is help you, protect you, should he ever come here to the ranch." He saw her open her lips to protest. "No," he ordered tightly, "this is not up for more discussion, Jessica. I now know why the Great Spirit sent me here—to help protect you. Because this man is coming here. I don't possess the Sight like you or Moyra do, but I feel it here, in my gut. And I've been in enough situations to trust my gut completely. It's never been wrong."

Trembling, Jessica tried to breathe, but she felt suffocated by the possibility of Carl stalking her once again. Her intuition told her it was only a matter of time. Only Dan's reassuring, strong hands on her shoulders gave her any sense of hope or stability. "Oh, no... I hope you're wrong. Leaving Vancouver, I tried to cover my tracks completely, so he'd never find out...."

Her terror avalanched over him, catching Dan completely off guard. As he felt the depth of her fright, he realized just how much danger she was really in. He wasn't expecting to be that open, that vulnerable to another human's pain or emotions, but it was happening. He felt this exchange of feelings when he worked with horses, but never with humans. Not until now. He remembered Ai Gvhdi Waya's words about allowing himself to shift into that flow, and he did everything in his power to keep his heart and mind open to Jessica.

"You're going to be all right," he said, giving her a small shake. "Look at me, Jessica. Please…." Her eyes opened and he drowned in the blueness of them. "The Great Spirit didn't leave you defenseless by coming here. You traded Moyra for me. I'm just a poor tumbleweed of a horse wrangler, but I have abilities and skills that can protect you. Do you believe me?"

The confidence in his speech cut through her terror. She stared up into his rugged features and absorbed the toughness of his rasping voice. His hands were firm and protective at the same time. "Dan, I can't ask you to do this. Carl is insane and he's manipulative. He was in prison for second-degree murder, but just escaped. The police are after him, but he's smart. They still haven't caught him. He's already killed one human being. I—I couldn't ask you to do this for me, don't you see?"

"Shi shaa, I am not much of a warrior, but I will be like a shield in front of you when Carl comes here, and he will. I know that now. That is my promise to you. Your jaguar priestess may have left, but in her place you find the spirit of the cougar, instead. My spirit guide is just as powerful in some ways as that of my jaguar sister. Trust me. I will be your eyes and ears from now on. You will be able to live here safely…."

Chapter 5

"Hey, how are you doing?" Kate called from the door to the greenhouse.

Jessica jumped at the noise. She whirled around, a plastic sack filled with redwood chips in her hands. "Oh! You scared me, Kate."

Kate grinned and closed the door behind her. Wiping her brow, she took a deep breath. "Whew, it's a lot cooler and nicer in here. Must be close to a hundred degrees outside." Moving over to the workbench, she perused the four orchids in clay pots sitting there. "I dropped by to see how things were going. Sam and I just came off the north range, moving some pregnant cows to a greener pasture." She wrinkled her nose. Untying her dark blue bandanna from around her slender throat, she wiped her perspiring face with the cloth. "Not that there's much green. This drought is a killer. I've never seen anything like it in all the time I've lived here."

Jessica nodded and placed the wood chips back on the bench. "I know. It's awful. So much is dying. And the money you're having to use up to buy bales of hay... yuk."

Kate grinned a little and retied her bandanna. "Little sis, you do not want to look at the accounting books, believe me. Or you'll spend your nights like I do—tossing and turning and wondering when the bank is going to foreclose on us."

Jessica looked up at her oldest sister. Kate had her dark hair in a ponytail, a straw cowboy hat, stained with dust and perspiration from many hours of work, on her head. Tall and angular, she was a living testament to the rugged Southwest and what hard work did to a body. She looked good in her bright red T-shirt, faded blue jeans and dusty cowboy boots. Jessica had always admired Kate in so many ways, even though her sister had spent time in prison for a crime she'd been unjustly accused of. Now Kate's eyes sparkled with happiness, and Jessica knew it was because she was so in love with Sam. Jessica was so happy for Kate. It was about time her sister had something good happen to her.

"Well, if Sam and you will okay it, I could use Dan's help in here to begin processing orders for Mother Earth Flower Essences and start collecting money for that hay you need."

Kate shook her head and put her arm around Jessica's slim shoulders for a moment. "You're so generous, Jessica. I don't know what possessed you to help out so much, but we're all grateful for it."

Jessica put her own arm around Kate's waist and

hugged her in return. "I wouldn't have it any other way. Besides, we're going to get out of this financial nightmare with the ranch someday."

"I hope sooner rather than later," Kate said, her voice strained. She sat on a tall wooden crate next to the workbench and watched Jessica begin to repot the orchids. "Hey, on a happier subject, if you want Dan Black to be your assistant, go for it. Sam would like him to divide his day into working at taming Gan, helping you in the mornings and then helping Sam run the fence and handle the other ranch duties in the afternoon."

Jessica turned the first pot upside down. Old redwood chips fell onto the bench, and she gently drew the orchid's long, white root system to one side. "That's fine." Taking fresh redwood chips, she leaned down, retrieved a new clay pot and put some into it.

"What do you think of him?" Kate asked, watching her sister work quickly and efficiently.

"Who?"

"You know who. Dan Black."

"Oh…" Jessica risked a look at her sister's frowning features. "He's, uh…"

"Aren't you getting along? Did he say something?"

"Now, Katie, don't go jumping off a cliff, okay? No, Dan didn't say anything wrong to me."

"You look…" She searched for the right word. "Uneasy?"

With exasperation, Jessica picked up the orchid, carefully arranged the root system in the larger pot and began to drop small pieces of bark around it. "It's just me and my big mouth, Katie. I barely know the guy, right? What do I do the second day I see him? I blurt out my whole life story."

Grinning, Kate took off her hat and set it on her thighs as she propped her heels up on the box. "What else is new? You always trusted everyone without wondering what their ulterior motives might be. Me? I'm just the opposite of you. I walk in wondering what the son of a bitch wants from me—a pound of flesh?" She chuckled indulgently.

"A little paranoia is good," Jessica admitted, frowning.

"Especially in *your* case," Kate warned heavily. "This thing with Carl isn't over. We both know that."

Jessica shot her a look of anxiety. "I'm worried, Katie."

"The guy is nuts. He's a sick stalker. He killed a guy. He could kill you. He might try it."

"Now you're talking just like Dan."

"Oh," Kate murmured, raising her brows, "you told Dan about Carl, too?"

With a sigh, Jessica placed the newly repotted orchid into a small dish of water so that the clay would absorb some of the moisture for the plant's root system. "That's what I mean—I blurted out everything about my life to Dan this morning."

"And?" Kate asked carefully. "How did Dan react to Carl's potentially showing up here to finish what he started in Vancouver?"

Agitated, Jessica felt fear and consternation roiling within her. She raised her eyes to the ceiling and then back down to Kate. "I was surprised at his reaction, to tell you the truth."

"Tell me about it."

Shrugging, Jessica took another orchid and turned it upside down to loosen the old wood chips around the roots. "He said that he knew now why he was sent here to the ranch." She glanced at Kate. "To protect me...."

"Hmm..."

"That's all you have to say? I mean, I was a little taken back by his passion for wanting to protect me. He doesn't know me! I mean, for all he knows, I could be a murdering thief in disguise."

Kate laughed and shook her head. "No, Jessica, you just don't fit the profile, and Dan knows that." She tapped her fingertip on the workbench. "Dan's a lot like Sam. He's a realist. He's pragmatic, too. He may not value himself as much as he should, but he's good with animals and some people. He's been kicked around enough to know the world isn't a goody-goody place. Unlike you, Miss Idealist."

Jessica grinned a little and set the unrooted orchid aside. "Okay, okay. So I think ill of no one. I don't question people's motives or their reasoning like you do. In most cases, my view of life works."

"That's what got you into trouble with Carl," Kate growled. "You believed the facade he put up for you. You didn't bother to ask what might be behind it."

"Carl's manipulative. It took me a year to know the real man behind the mask. I don't think anyone could have known." Her hands trembled slightly as she put redwood chips into a new pot.

"Listen," Kate whispered gently, "Carl's insane, as far as I'm concerned. And he's dangerous. Sam and I think he'll try and get to you here, at the ranch."

Her heart plunging in terror, Jessica set the pot down and fully faced her sister. "If you honestly believe that, why on earth did you let me come here? Carl could kill *all* of us if he goes off into one of his ballistic rages. He has an arsenal of guns he keeps hidden from the Canadian authorities. He could bring them down here and begin shooting up the ranch."

"Hold on," Kate said, putting up her hands. "Don't get upset, Jessica. First of all, you've got three big, bad guard dogs here at the ranch—Sam, me and Dan. We are being watchful."

Grinning a little, Kate continued, "Besides, Dan Black is a hell of a lot more dangerous than his mannerisms might show. He was a Recon Marine for four years, and according to Sam, he was damned good at what he did. Those men are taught to be invisible until the right moment. Dan got a lot of experience during the Gulf War. He was in the thick of things. And if a worst-case scenario happens and Carl is stupid enough to come down here thinking he can hurt you, well, he'll be in for a few surprises. Dan may not be able to be everywhere with you all the time, but when he is, Sam told him to watch out for you. And if Dan isn't there, Sam will be. Twenty-four-hour protection, Jessica."

"So Dan knew about me already? About Carl?"

"No, Sam told him that you needed to be watched, that was all."

Miffed, Jessica put the repotted orchid aside. Her fingers trembled badly now. "That's why Dan was so intense with me, then. He was all worked up about protecting me."

"He's not getting paid any extra to do this, you know. I don't know where his passion is coming from." And then Kate tilted her head and smiled a little. "Maybe he likes you?"

"Oh, please, Katie! I'm not exactly a great gift, am I? I've got an ex-husband who wants to kill me. Who might be really stupid and drive all the way from Canada to do it. If I were Dan Black, I'd sure stay away from me, with good reason!"

"But you have a lot going for you that any man worth his salt would be interested in. You're pretty, smart and ultrafeminine, just the way a man likes a woman."

"Please...." Jessica begged, truly upset now. She took the third clay pot, forcing her hands to stop shaking so much. "I just wish I had your nerves of steel, Katie. Look at my hands. I'm such a wimp. I think of Carl coming to stalk me, to hurt me, and I feel like I'm falling to pieces all over again. I think about the time he put me in the hospital. The pain. The horrible thought that I had to go back and live with him again. It's as if this nightmare is never going to end." She stopped and forced back the tears that stung her eyes.

"It's not easy," Kate whispered gently, her face soft with sympathy as she got up and walked over to Jessica and hugged her. "It's my fault. I shouldn't have brought this up. You're still tired from your trip. You've got a lot of pressure on you to get your orchid girls taken care of, not to mention a lot of orders that haven't been filled."

Shrugging painfully, Jessica looked up at Kate. "Compared to you, Katie, I've got the spine of a jelly-fish. I wish I didn't let day-to-day pressures and stresses get to me like this...."

"It's not every day you realize your life is in danger," Kate answered wryly, releasing her. She settled her cowboy hat more firmly on her head. "Look, you need help here. Let's rearrange the schedule for the next week. I'll talk to Dan. He can still work with Gan in the early morning, but I think I'm going to ask him to work with you the rest of this week full-time, to help you get on your feet with your business. That way, that's one more stress off your shoulders. Okay?"

Jessica's heart pounded briefly and this time it wasn't out of fear, but rather something else she couldn't identify. Whatever it was, it felt good and steadying. When she realized Kate was watching her like a hawk, she said, "Ask Dan. He may not want to do this. I don't even know if he likes working in a greenhouse with orchids. I mean, he's a wrangler, for heaven's sake. He's used to doing a man's work outdoors, not spending time in some hothouse...."

Chuckling, Kate headed for the front door of the greenhouse. "Oh, Jessica, you are so funny! I swear, sometimes you wouldn't see a Mack truck barreling down on you."

"What's that supposed to mean?"

Kate turned, her grin widening considerably. "You really are naive, little sis. When a man brings 'passion' into conversation with a woman, there's something there, you know? Yep, I'd say that horse wrangler likes you just a little bit."

Heat washed across Jessica's face as she stared at Kate. "You mean, personally likes me?"

"*Arrgh,* I give up!" Kate lifted her hand in farewell and left.

Muttering to herself, Jessica returned to her work. Her fear over Carl's possible appearance and her apprehension over Dan's feelings for her warred within her. Yes, she'd felt something when Dan had gripped her by her shoulders early this morning. She'd felt his care, his powerful protection blanketing her, like something warm and good. Oh, why wasn't she wiser about people? Or, better, wiser about men? She supposed the fact that she'd married Carl at age eighteen, shortly after leaving home and moving to Vancouver, was to blame. She really didn't have any experience with men except for Carl.

No, Kate was right—her naiveté was getting her into a lot of hot water. But how did one become wise in that way? Too bad there wasn't a flower essence she could take to give her that wisdom. She laughed out loud at the thought as she repotted the next orchid. She could make millions if that were possible.

Suddenly Jessica heard the door open and close. She looked over her shoulder and her pulse leaped. It was Dan Black. His mask was in place, that unreadable, hard expression, and his eyes were nearly colorless, measuring her.

"Hi, Dan. Did Kate send you?" The corners of her mouth moved upward in greeting. How handsome he looked!

She absorbed his tall, lean frame and the easy way he walked. She saw his expression soften just as soon as she smiled at him. His eyes changed from colorless to a soft dove gray. The tightness around his mouth eased, revealing the fullness of his lower lip.

"Yes, she did." He gazed hungrily at Jessica's petite form as she stood at the workbench. She had on a dark green canvas apron that fitted her body to midthigh. In her hands was a large orchid in a clay pot. "She said you needed help this next week," he continued, taking off his cowboy hat and wiping the sweat from his brow with the back of his arm. "This place is a lot cooler and nicer than out there, anyway."

She brightened. It was so hard not to stare into his large, intelligent eyes, which seemed banked with so many emotions he fought to hide from her. There was a sparkle in them today, and she felt their penetrating power. Shaken by the sensation, she stammered, "W-well, if it's okay with you, I can use some help getting set up the rest of this week. I know you're probably used to being outside and doing ranch work, and this sure isn't anything like that, but—"

"I want to help."

The words, husky and filled with emotion, silenced Jessica. She saw the honest sincerity burning in his eyes, and the roughened quality of his voice was like a cat's tongue licking her flesh, making it tingle deliciously.

"Oh...." she replied, at a loss for words.

"My people honor the plant nation," he said simply, looking around at the hundred or so orchids sitting at various heights on the wrought-iron steps. "My uncle, the one who died of cancer and gave me his flute, knew a lot about plants. He wasn't a medicine man, but he passed on his love of them to me. I know a lot about the plants that live on the res." He shrugged slightly. "Not in a scientific sense, but I know which ones the Navajo people use for medicine purposes."

"That's wonderful! I've been thinking of expanding my business line to include plants from the Southwest now that I've moved my company down here! Maybe you could help me identify some of them and tell me what you know of them?"

Dan felt her unbridled enthusiasm, her childlike awe and joy. There wasn't anything not to like about Jessica Donovan, he decided. All morning he'd tried to find things to stop himself from liking her so much—from wanting her, man to woman—but he'd found nothing. Now, for better or worse, he was being put to work with her for seven whole days, except for the early morning training sessions with Gan. He frowned. Either this was heaven or his personal hell, he couldn't decide which. It was heaven just to be privileged to be in Jessica's exuberant presence, but it was hell trying to keep his hands off her, to maintain a respectable distance from her and treat her like the owner of the ranch. He had to remember he was only a ranch hand.

"I'd like to learn about your orchids. I know nothing of them."

"And you were so gentle with them," Jessica said. "I would never have thought a man could be like that, but you are."

He held her wide, innocent gaze. "Not all men are like your ex-husband, Jessica. There is a man in Sedona who owns a nursery, Charlie McCoy. He loves his plants like you do. They grow well for him because he cares for them with his heart—like you."

Chastised, Jessica nodded and returned to the workbench. "You're right, of course. I shouldn't be projecting that every man is Carl." And then she laughed sharply. "It's a good thing they aren't!"

Dan followed her over to the workbench. "Show me what you'd like me to do."

For the next hour, Jessica went through everything that Dan would need to know about the care, watering and repotting of orchids. He proved an apt student. Time flew by as she became immersed in her love of the brightly colored orchids that lived in the greenhouse. She enjoyed his nearness, though he seemed somewhat distant compared to earlier this morning, when he'd become impassioned about protecting her.

Finally, she said, "Enough for now. I'm sure your head is spinning with too much information on my girls."

Dan nodded and rested his hands on his narrow hips as he surveyed the many orchids. "There's a lot to them. More than I realized." He noticed a light veil of perspiration across Jessica's furrowed brow. Her blond hair was slightly curly from the high humidity in the greenhouse, and he had an urge to move several strands away from her eyes, but he resisted.

"When you talk about them," he told her, "do you know your eyes light up, your voice becomes excited?"

Laughing, Jessica nodded. "Yes, I've been told that many times before."

"It's your love of them that does it." Dan followed her back to the workbench.

"Don't you think that whenever a person loves, he or she should show it?"

"Maybe," he hedged. "But not many people I know are willing to reveal themselves, their real feelings, like you do all the time."

"Kate's warned me about that. She says I'm too transparent. That I need to put up some barriers until I get to know people better."

"I don't agree," Dan said.

"No?" She looked up and smiled as she washed her hands in bleach and water to keep from spreading potential viruses among the orchids.

"No."

"You hide behind a mask like Kate and Sam do."

"Guilty."

Jessica laughed a little as she dried her hands. She stood aside for him to rinse his hands and dry them off. "But I shouldn't be like the three of you?"

"No." Dan replaced the towel on a hook on the side of the workbench. "I don't pretend to know orchids very well yet, but I think you're a lot like them. You're different. As you said, they don't need soil to survive in, just air and moisture. In my mind, they are plants of Father Sky, not Mother Earth." He turned and held her warm, soft gaze. How badly he wanted to reach out and caress her reddened cheek, touch his mouth to those parted lips that were begging to be kissed. Battling his needs, Dan said, "You are like the sky people. Like the clouds that form and disappear. You respond to sunlight, moonlight and the temperature of things around you, as these orchid people do. You *are* different, Jessica, but that doesn't make you wrong or us right. In some ways you are able to see things better. You don't think badly of anyone."

Maybe he'd said too much. Dan supposed he had. But Jessica's expression changed to one of such sweetness that his hand itched to reach out and stroke her cheek. "Father Sky sees all that goes on down here on his lover, Mother Earth. His eyes are set differently. So are yours. You belong to the cloud people, who see above and beyond what we mere two-leggeds, who are root bound on Mother Earth, can see. So no, do not change. Do not try to become like us." He touched his face momentarily. "Masks are shields. We put them on to protect our soft, inner side. Cloud people do not need masks. They have the safety of Father Sky's embrace to protect them."

Jessica stood there for a long, silent moment, digesting Dan's heartfelt words. His sincerity touched her heart as nothing else ever could. "How you see things is so beautiful," she began in a strained, low tone. "I wish— I wish…well, never mind."

Dan saw her eyes darken. "What is your wish?"

"Oh, it's a stupid one. An idealistic one, as Kate

would say." Jessica could not bear to look at the compassion she saw burning in his eyes. For a moment, she wanted to take those two steps forward and simply embrace Dan, lean against him and feel the solid, hard beat of his heart against hers. This man was surprising her on so many levels all at once that she felt flustered emotionally.

"Would you share it with me?" he asked, moving next to her at the workbench.

His closeness was wonderful. Jessica was only beginning to realize how *hungry* she'd been for a positive male presence in her life. Moyra had often teased her that she didn't know how Jessica had survived two years without male companionship. Moyra had a boyfriend who she saw on weekends in Vancouver, and Jessica had wished for something similar for herself, but it had never materialized. Maybe because she lived in abject fear that Carl would unexpectedly show up to hurt her, she supposed.

Jessica also realized she hadn't been ready to reach out and trust a man, either. Until now. Dan was different, very different from any man she'd ever encountered. He was so in tune with nature, with her flowers and most importantly, with her. It was amazing—and scary. Carl had come on to her like that, too, pretending an interest in her flowers, and in the philosophy of life that she lived every day. Her memories of Carl warred with what she saw in Dan. Was he really like Carl? Her heart said no, but her head was screaming at her to be wary, to watch out and to give things time, instead of rushing willy-nilly into some kind of relationship that might turn out similar to her marriage.

Heaving a sigh, Jessica wrestled with her confusion.

Who to trust? Who not to trust? Frustrated, she finally said, "It's a stupid wish built on fantasy."

Dan heard the finality in her voice, the strength that came up unexpectedly from deep within her. Her tone implied that he was to drop the subject—completely. He would respect that for now. There were many feelings he was picking up around Jessica, he realized, noticing how her fingers trembled slightly as she removed an orchid from an old clay pot. From the stubborn set of her lower lip and the darkness haunting her glorious turquoise eyes, he knew the beautiful cloud person was gone, at least for now. Somehow their conversation had brought up ghosts from her past that now stood between them. He felt badly about that. All he wanted was to see Jessica remain in the clouds, to be that magical, wondrous, happy creature he'd first met.

For the next fifteen minutes, Jessica concentrated on showing Dan how to repot an orchid. He no longer questioned her, but stood respectfully nearby, just far enough away to keep her from feeling threatened.

When Jessica handed him another orchid to repot, he went through each step perfectly. Just the way he touched the plant made her ache for him to touch her in the same way. It was a ludicrous idea, but her body was responding to him even if her mind whispered warnings to her. Unhappy with how she was feeling, she sat on the wooden crate beside the workbench to watch Dan complete the repotting process.

The silence remained between them for a long time, except for the occasional instructions he needed from her. By noon, Jessica felt her stomach growl. Glancing to the left, she watched Dan's angular profile as he worked. His mouth was relaxed now, not thinned.

His black brows were drawn down in concentration as he worked with the fragile orchid, his touch light and careful. A light perspiration made his dark, golden skin gleam beneath the diffused light in the greenhouse. Sweat dampened his white shirt beneath each arm and around his upper chest. She saw the creases and lines at the corners of his mouth and eyes and she wondered how he'd gotten that scar on his left cheek. But, she remembered, there were a lot of things she wanted to know about Dan Black.

"This morning," Jessica began awkwardly, trying to find a diplomatic way of asking what she wanted to know, "you said something to me I didn't understand."

Dan glanced over at her. "Which part of it?"

Knitting her hands nervously, Jessica looked away. In that moment, the brief smile that pulled at the corners of his mouth made him look years younger. Dan had a beguiling face; she knew his rugged features had yet to reveal his every emotion to her. She wondered what it would be like if he really smiled, or laughed fully.

"You said something in Navajo—*sh* something. I didn't know what it meant."

Dan's hands stilled over the orchid. His heart plummeted. "That…" he muttered self-consciously.

"Yes?"

He didn't *dare* let Jessica know what it meant. "It was…nothing. When I get excited, I drop into my own language, that's all."

She watched him closely. His expression had closed up faster than a snapping turtle. It was surprising to her. Her head whispered, *See, he's not to be trusted. He's lying to you. He knows what it means, but he won't tell you.* Jessica tried to ignore her mistrustful thoughts.

"Oh…."

He felt her sadness and looked at her sharply. "It wasn't anything bad, Jessica. I promise you that." And it wasn't. It was a beautiful expression that a man used for the woman he loved. He knew Jessica had grown up with Navajo people, but he was grateful she didn't recognize the wonderful endearment that was only shared between two people who were deeply in love with one another. He had no wish to embarrass her with his slip of the tongue, or the wild way his heart and his passion had galloped away from him in those moments out of time with her. At all costs, he must hold how he felt toward her to himself. She must never know his real feelings, because if she did, he was sure he'd be fired from the job and asked to leave the ranch. And right now, Dan was helpless, unable to walk away. Jessica was like an answer to his lifelong prayers—a woman who could fulfill him on every level. And she could. He knew that as surely as he took each breath of air into his lungs.

Jessica sighed and stood up. "You did a great job of repotting that orchid. Let's go get some lunch. I'm starving to death."

Relieved that she wasn't going to pursue the topic, Dan nodded. He put the orchid on the bench and, grabbing his hat, followed her out of the humid, moist depths of the greenhouse. He wondered how he was going to handle his unraveling feelings for her in the days to come. Yes, he felt like a man with one foot in heaven and the other in hell. Or maybe he was like that man in the Greek myth, who ached to capture the golden fleece that was guarded by a killer giant, but knew he never could. Not ever…

Chapter 6

Where had the first three weeks of her time at the ranch gone? Jessica stood out on the porch of her house, the hot breeze ruffling her hair. In frustration, she caught the tousled strands and put them up in a ponytail. The sunlight was blindingly bright, the sky an incredibly deep, cobalt blue. It was a beautiful day, she thought as she watched Kate and Sam riding off to the north pasture. A lot of new calves had been born, and she knew they wanted to check on them and the mothers today.

In her hand was a list of things to pick up at the Sedona Hay and Feed Store. Sam had asked her to get veterinary items they were running low on, such as antibiotics, hypodermic needles and thrush ointment. At the clip-clop of horse hooves coming around her house, she turned expectedly. Instantly, her heart rate increased. Dan Black sat tall and proud on a dark bay gelding with four white socks. His face was a sheen of perspiration, and she admired once again his powerful chest outlined by the sweat-damp, dark blue shirt he wore. Oh, how she'd missed his company!

Jessica had become spoiled by Dan's presence that first week at the ranch. He'd worked sixteen hours a day helping her get her business set up and running smoothly once again. The only time she saw him now was for an hour—if that—in the morning. Their time with one another was extremely limited. How often she had gone over to the bunkhouse to invite him to her house to eat, only to learn that he was still out on horseback, doing ranch chores somewhere.

She saw Dan's gray eyes narrow heatedly upon her. That mask he always wore softened considerably as he pulled his dusty, sweaty horse to a halt. Putting his fingers to the brim of his hat, he tipped it in her direction.

"Going somewhere?" he asked. Dan knew he should continue to avoid Jessica all he could, but when he'd seen her step out onto the porch, he couldn't help himself—he'd had to ride over to visit with her. It was a selfish decision on his part. He'd just finished herding some broodmares from the south pasture to the west one and was coming back in to grab a late lunch. Now he was hungry on a much different, more galvanizing level.

"Hi, Dan." Jessica held up the paper in her hand. "Sam wants me to go to the feed store and get some antibiotics for him."

He nodded. "Yes, we're going through them lately. A lot of sepsis with the cows and their babies." He squinted at the dry, yellowed pastures. "Might be the drought doing it. Everything's dying."

She sobered and stepped off the front porch. "I can

hardly wait until Rachel gets here. She's got homeo-
pathic remedies that can cure sepsis better than an anti-
biotic, and it will cost us a lot less, too. She left a few
kits here on her last visit, but we've already used them."
She paused, then said, "Hey, why don't you come into
town with me?"

The idea was tempting. "I can't, I got—"

Jessica pouted prettily. "Dan, I'm going to need some
help. Sam wanted me to take the pickup truck and get
about eight hundred pounds in feed. I'm going to need
a strong body to help lift that stuff into the truck. Sam
said Old Man Thomas at the store is in his eighties and
he's too stingy to hire help. The poor old gent can't handle hundred-pound sacks of grain, and I can't, either."
Flexing her arm, she pointed to the almost nonexistent
bulge of her biceps. "I'm a wimp."

He chuckled. The sparkle in her eyes was one of
warmth and welcome. Instantly, Dan felt embraced by
her bubbly enthusiasm and humor. "Okay, Miss Jessica,
let me get my horse unsaddled and cared for. It'll take
about ten minutes."

"Great! I'll drive over to the barn in about ten and
meet you."

Her heart exploded with happiness as she saw him
grin. How little Dan laughed. The more she pried, the
less he allowed her entrance into his unknown life. She
longed for his companionship again. Kate and Sam had
been so busy that Jessica largely left them alone. They
worked from dawn to almost midnight every day and
then fell exhausted into one another's arms, and slept
deeply. The drought was putting a terrible edge on the
struggle for life at the ranch, and they were doing everything in their power to save the lives of their stock.

She knew Dan was working every bit as hard, but she wished she could spend more time with him.

Jessica couldn't still her excitement as Dan drove the beat-up pickup into town. There was no air-conditioning in the truck, so both windows were down as they pulled slowly into uptown Sedona, the area known to the locals as the "tourist trap."

"Can you imagine, six million people a year visit us?" Jessica asked, looking at the line of tourist shops crowded together along the highway.

Dan grimaced. "I stay away from this place as much as possible."

"Why?" She looked at his chiseled profile, her gaze settling on his mouth. His lips were thinned, which meant he was tense. She wondered if this trip was the reason. Rarely did Jessica see Dan leave the ranch premises. It was as if he were hiding out there.

With a shrug, Dan turned the truck into the hay-and-feed-store parking lot. "Crowds bother me, that's all."

"Oh..." She looked at the storefront. It was badly weathered and in dire need of a coat of paint. The wood was graying and splintering from the heat. A rusted old sign hung at an angle and moved slowly back and forth in the inconstant afternoon breeze, creaking in protest. Dan backed the pickup against the wooden loading dock at the barn portion of the building, where the grain and hay were kept.

Jessica caught sight of an old Indian man sitting beneath the cottonwood tree near the entrance. He was probably in his seventies, his white hair down to his shoulders, a bright red wrap around his head as he sat with his back against the tree and weaved from side to side. He was drunk, Jessica realized as she stepped from the truck. The clothes he wore were rags, and very dirty looking. She frowned. Instead of going up the stairs into the store, she moved to the man's side.

Jessica had forgotten most of the Navajo she'd learned as a child. She'd been multilingual, knowing English, Eastern Cherokee, some Navajo and Apache. Now she worked to remember Navajo phrases.

The old man opened his bloodshot eyes and looked at her as Jessica knelt down in front of him. *"Ya at eeh,"* she began tenuously. That was Navajo for "hello." She wasn't sure he *was* Navajo, even though the reservation ended where the city of Flagstaff, an hour north of Sedona, began.

The old man's tobacco brown skin crinkled. He gave her a toothless smile, his gums gleaming. *"Ya at eeh..."* he slurred.

Jessica knew there was a mission in West Sedona that helped the homeless. She was distraught by the man's condition. The odor of alcohol assailed her, and she spotted an empty one-gallon wine bottle lying next to him.

"Jessica, leave him alone."

She looked up to see Dan scowling darkly over her.

"No. He needs help."

"You can't help him. That's Tommy Wolf. He's the local drunk here in Sedona."

She heard the embarrassment in Dan's voice. He was edgy and nervous, looking around as if he were ashamed to be seen with her and Tommy. "I'm not leaving him, Dan. Look at him. He's filthy! He needs a bath and some help. Can you speak Navajo to him and tell him we'll take him to the mission? It's only a few blocks from here."

Pulling his black Stetson lower on his sweaty brow, Dan frowned in irritation. "Jessica, you're throwing your care away. Tommy knows where the mission's at. He'll eventually get over there when he wants a decent meal and a bath. Right now, he's drunker than hell. Just leave him alone."

Her jaw became set. "Dan, just go get the feed and antibiotics, okay? I'll take Tommy over while you do it." She moved forward to lift the old man's arm, placing it around her shoulders. Instead, she felt Dan's strong hands on her arms. He lifted her up and away from Tommy.

"Dan!" She stood there, staring up into his angry features.

"I'll do it," he rasped. "Just get the door of the truck open for me."

Jessica's eyes widened as she heard the grating in his deep voice. She watched as Dan easily hefted the old Navajo to his feet and aimed him in the direction of the pickup. Tommy began a slurred conversation in Navajo with Dan as they walked toward the truck. Jessica hurried ahead of them.

The honk of a horn startled her. She halted as a brand-new pickup truck roared into the hay and feed store next to where they were parked. If she hadn't stopped when she did, she would have been sideswiped by the swift-moving vehicle. Her mouth dropped open in shock as she stood there, the truck passing only a foot away from her. Blinking, she realized she knew the two cowboys in the cab—Chet and Bo Cunningham from the neighboring ranch. Old memories flooded her.

Angrily, Jessica moved around the red pickup and quickly opened the passenger door for Dan, who was slowly easing Tommy along on not too steady feet. The old Navajo had no shoes or socks on, and her heart bled for his condition.

"Well, well, another one of the prodigal daughters has returned to the Donovan Ranch. Whad'ya know...."

Snapping her head to the left, Jessica met the dark eyes of Chet Cunningham. A two-day growth of scraggly beard shadowed his narrow, pale features, and his straw cowboy hat was low over his eyes as he swaggered around the front of his red truck toward her.

"Little Jessica Donovan," he crowed, and then laughed. "Out saving the world again?" He slapped his hand on his jean-covered thigh.

To her consternation, she saw the taller, darker brother, Bo, appear around the front of the truck in turn. "Mind your own business, Chet," she said.

Chet snickered and put his hand over hers where she held the door to the pickup open. "Naw, that's too easy. The Cunninghams run Sedona. You're trespassing, missy."

"Get your hand off her."

Jessica jerked her head toward the dark, lethal-sounding voice. She realized belatedly that it was Dan speaking. He stood there, still holding Tommy in his grip, and glared past her to Chet. She'd never heard Dan speak in such a tone, nor had she ever seen the expression his face held now. There was a dangerous quality radiating around him that made the hair on the back of her neck stand up in reaction. His eyes were colorless, his mouth a hard line, his face emotionless.

Chet snickered again and glanced over at Bo, who came and stood at his shoulder. "Go to hell, you drunken half-breed. You got guts coming into Sedona in the first place," he roared, raising his gloved hand and jabbing it at Dan. "You takin' Tommy over to the mission to dry out again? Together?" And both brothers laughed loudly.

Jessica jerked her hand away from Chet's and held it out to Tommy, who weakly grasped her fingers. "Pay no attention to them," she ordered the older man as Dan helped her maneuver the Navajo into her truck. Before she knew it, she felt Dan's hand on her arm. It was a strong, guiding grip, not hurtful, but meant to remove her from between him and the Cunningham men. She opened her mouth to protest, but it was too late.

"You two sidewinders go about your business," Dan snarled. "And leave off your jawing, too."

"Whooee!" Chet crowed, slapping his brother's shoulder. "Listen to this drunken Indian give orders, Bo. Whad'ya think about that?" Chet's eyes narrowed in fury. "Take your bottle and the old Navajo rug your granny made for you and crawl back into your hole, Black. Better yet, crawl off to Flag, where you were the butt of everyone's jokes."

Dan felt the heat creep into his face. He saw the leering anger in both men's expressions. Worse, Jessica was hearing what they said about him. His heart pounded in fury and dread. Now she would know the truth about him. A serrating pain scored his heart. "Get the hell out of here, Chet. Just leave us in peace and we'll do the same for you."

Chet took in a couple of deep breaths and stuck his chest out. He glanced again at Bo, who barely nodded. Pulling his stained leather gloves a little tighter, Chet grinned. "Gonna be the cock of the walk here, Black? Showing off for Miss Goody Two-shoes, who rescues drunks like you?"

Dan heard Jessica's protest. Before he could answer, he saw Chet draw back his arm, his fist cocked. To hell with it. If he was going to go to jail on assault charges, he might as well make Chet Cunningham pay in full for his actions.

Jessica gasped as she watched Chet's fist barrel forward to strike Dan. Suddenly she saw Dan move with the speed of a striking rattlesnake. Only he didn't use his fists, he used his entire body in a karatelike motion. Blinking, Jessica cried out as Chet went flying backward with a grunt, slamming into the dock and letting out a loud *ooooff* sound.

Bo cursed and leaped toward Dan. Jessica put her hands to her lips and cried out a warning. Dan moved with the grace of a ballet artist and swung around, his booted foot arcing out and catching Bo in the stomach. The older brother was slammed into the side of the red truck. Chet, his nose bloody and crooked, scrambled off the ground and leaped at Dan.

Jessica stood there, stunned by Dan's prowess in fighting. All of a sudden the easygoing, mild-mannered cowboy had turned into a lethal warrior she'd never known existed. She watched as Dan's open hand caught Chet just beneath the nose. Cunningham went down like a felled ox, unconscious this time.

"Stop it!"

A shotgun went off.

Jessica leaped and screamed. She saw Old Man Thomas hobbling out onto the dock, the shotgun aimed at the three cowboys below.

"Now, galdarnit, you three young roosters take yore fights elsewhere. You got that? Or you want yore pants full of buckshot?"

Dan eased out of his karate position. Breathing hard, his hands aching, he looked up at Old Man Thomas, who was red-faced and angry as hell. Holding up his hands, Dan said, "We'll leave, Mr. Thomas."

"Damn right you will! Get outta here! All of ya! Chet, Bo, get a move on. I'm a callin' yore daddy and tellin' him yore up to yore same ol' tricks again. Dagnabit, yore nothing but trouble! Now git! The lot of ya!"

Dan moved swiftly over to Jessica, who stood white-faced and frozen, her hands pressed against her stomach and her eyes large and glazed. Damn! "Come on," he rasped, grabbing her by the arm and leading her around the front of the truck. "Let's get Tommy over to the mission. We can pick up the supplies down at Cottonwood Hay and Feed, instead."

He looked over his shoulder just to make sure the Cunningham men weren't foolish enough to try and attack again. He saw Bo holding a hand up to his bloody nose and mouth.

"You drunken bastard," Bo snarled as he got to his feet, "I'm callin' the sheriff. You're going up on assault charges—"

"No, he ain't!" Old Man Thomas roared, glaring down at them from the dock. He aimed the shotgun directly at Bo. "You two started it. I saw it with my own eyes. You two ain't got the sense of a rock. Get the hell outta here! Any sheriff to be called, I'll be doing that, ya hear? And if you put charges against Black, I'll be slappin' them against you. Understand?"

Bo glared over at Dan, wiping his nose with his gloved hand. "Yeah, I hear you, Mr. Thomas."

Chet stood on wobbly feet, his face a mass of blood coming from his nose and the corner of his badly cut mouth. Bo strode over, jerked his younger brother forward and pushed him back into the pickup. He looked up at them.

"Black, you're on my list now. You'd better watch your back, you drunken son of a bitch." His mouth curved into a hard grin. "Yeah, you'll hit the bottle again and I'll come looking for you. Next time, things will be different," he finished, punching his gloved index finger toward Dan.

"Come on," Dan urged tightly, getting Tommy out of the truck in front of the mission. He didn't dare look at Jessica. Now she knew about his sordid past. Damn! Gently moving the old Navajo up the sidewalk to the two-story wooden house that served as a center for the homeless in Sedona, he avoided Jessica's gaze. But he could feel her eyes on him, his skin scorching hotly at her appraisal. She hadn't said a word as he drove the three blocks to the mission.

The ache in his heart widened. Well, he was stupid to hope that Jessica wouldn't find out about his past—his bout with the bottle after the war. He brought Tommy into the cooler depths of the front lobby, sitting him into a chair near the reception desk.

Jessica moved to the desk and talked to the young woman with glasses behind it, while Dan stood back, his hands shoved into the pockets of his jeans. His knuckles hurt, but it was nothing like the pain he felt in his heart or the shame that burned through him. When Jessica turned, he saw her avoid his gaze and stare down at the floor instead. Humiliation avalanched through him. Grimly, Dan opened the door for her. Tommy was in good hands now and the folks who ran this mission would get him a bath, clean clothes, shoes, some hot, nutritious food and a place for him to sober up.

The heat of the sunlight laced across them as they walked to the pickup parked beneath two huge cotton-woods. He opened the door for Jessica.

"Thank you," she whispered. She got in, pressed her hands into her lap and hung her head. She felt Dan get back in and heard the door slam. Closing her eyes, she took a long, shaky breath.

"Jessica," he began awkwardly, "I'm sorry..."

She slowly opened her eyes and lifted her chin. Dan sat tensely beside her, both his bloodied hands gripping the steering wheel. As she met and held his sad, dark gray eyes, tears stung hers. The incredible sadness around him enveloped her and she just stared at him, at a loss for words. Finally, she saw him scowl and push the cowboy hat off his wrinkled, glistening brow.

"Something came over me," he muttered. "I saw Chet trap your hand against that door and something just snapped inside me. That little rattler is no good. He knew what he was doing."

"Y-yes, I think he did," she managed to answer haltingly. Her gaze shifted to his white-knuckled hands. "At least let me clean up your hands, Dan. They're bleeding pretty badly."

He hadn't even noticed, Dan realized as he watched Jessica lean down and pick up the plastic quart bottle of water she'd brought along for them to drink. From the glove box, she took a clean cloth. Turning in the seat, she eased his right hand off the steering wheel after dampening the cloth. Her touch was incredibly gentle and warm. He felt his heart breaking. It would be the last time she ever touched him this way. The last.

"You don't have to touch me," he muttered, and tried to draw his hand out of hers.

"Stop!" Jessica cried, her voice rising. "I'm upset, Dan. The least you can do is sit still and let me clean you up. Now just relax, will you?"

He heard the strain in her soft voice. Her full mouth was compressed and he knew she was angry—at him. Still, he relished each touch of the cooling cloth against his aching knuckles. He never wanted her to stop. "You make the pain go away," he murmured unsteadily, catching and holding her fleeting blue gaze. "Just your touch…."

Heat swept through Jessica. She closed her other hand over his. Taking a ragged breath, she said brokenly, "Dan, you could've been killed by those two! I've rarely seen evil in this world, but I think Chet and Bo were *born* that way! It's just so upsetting."

Without thinking, Dan tugged his hand from between hers. "Listen to me," he rasped, pulling her into his arms. He felt her trembling like a frightened fawn. Closing his eyes, he buried his face against her soft blond hair. Slowly her trembling ceased and he felt her relax against him. He expected Jessica to fight him, to push away from him in disgust. Instead, he felt her moan softly, her face pressed against his, her arms sliding around his torso.

"It's all right…." he whispered against her ear. She smelled like a meadow full of wildflowers. Her hair was thin and fine, like soft, spun gold against his cheek and nose. All of his barriers dissolved as she sought his protection. "Stop shaking. It's all over, *shi shaa*. You're safe…safe…."

His voice was low and singsong. Jessica felt the strength of Dan's arms around her, holding her protectively. She smelled the odor of hay and horses on his roughened cheek. She felt the powerful thud of his heart against her breasts as he pressed her hard against him. Everywhere she contacted his lean, whipcord strong body, her skin burned with desire.

She heard him speaking low, in the beautiful, rhythmic Navajo language, and she sighed softly and sank more deeply into his arms. She felt his mouth against her hair as he pressed a kiss to her head. How she'd longed for his kiss all these lonely weeks! Summoning all of her courage, all of her driving needs, Jessica turned her face slightly, and this time, as his mouth came down to press another kiss to her hair, his lips met hers instead.

A jolt of heat tore through her as his pliant mouth closed over hers. At first she felt surprise vibrate through Dan, and then, as she moved her lips softly, searchingly against his, she felt the surprise dissolve into a swift, returning pressure against her lips. Suddenly, the world ceased to exist. She was enclosed within his strength, the searching boldness of his mouth. The molten heat of his tongue moved slowly across her lower lip, making her moan with a pleasure she had never before experienced. His roughened hand moved slowly up her bare arm, his touch eliciting fire, yet gentling her at the same time.

This was the Dan Black she had wanted all along, Jessica hazily realized as she sank more deeply into his searching, molding kiss, which stole her breath and bound their aching souls into one. As she ran her hand up across Dan's shoulder, she felt every muscle leap and harden beneath her foray. He felt so good to her! So solid, warm and giving. For an instant, she had thought he would be not only hurt, but killed by the Cunninghams. They were dangerous men. But she'd never realized how dangerous Dan was. To know that the hands that now roved roughly across her arms and shoulders were hands that could hurt as well as protect was shocking to her. He was a man of many surprises. A man wrapped in the darkness of his past.

That realization caused Jessica to pull away unexpectedly. She gazed up into Dan's eyes, which appeared almost silver and black as he studied her. Their breathing was ragged. Their hearts were pounding in unison. Blinking, Jessica realized that Dan was the man Moyra had told her about—the man wrapped in darkness! Her lips tingled wildly from his onslaught. She stared at that mouth, that full lower lip, and then back up into his narrowed eyes. He seemed like a predator right now, and she his willing quarry. Her fingers opened and closed against his broad, powerful shoulders. Her legs felt weak and she didn't want to move. All that existed, all that she'd ever dreamed of having, was here, in Dan Black.

"No...." Jessica whispered faintly.

Chastened, Dan released her. His body was on fire. He ached for her, the pain making him want to bend double. What the hell was he doing? Why had he kissed Jessica? What demon from his darkness had driven him right over the edge to take her? Helping Jessica sit up on her side of the seat, he leaned back, taking off his hat and allowing his head to rest against the rear window. What the hell had he just done? His heart was pounding like a wild horse in his chest. His mouth was warm from her soft, breathless kiss. She tasted like sweet honey and warm sunlight. His skin throbbed wherever she'd touched him with her delicate, hesitant fingertips. Dan cursed himself richly. He could feel shame flooding through him as if a dam had burst. What kind of fool was he? He'd not only overstepped his bounds, he'd probably be getting his walking papers from Sam McGuire tonight when his boss got off the range. Dan had no business kissing the owner of such a huge ranch.

Taking in a deep, ragged breath, he tried to tame his fear and shame. But his desire to make Jessica his, to couple with her not only on the physical level, but to entwine their souls in beautiful lovemaking, overwhelmed him. He ached to take her all the way with him. He wanted to feel her small, firm body against his, to feel their flesh sliding hotly together.

It was all just another broken dream, Dan realized as he opened his eyes and sat up. He risked a look at Jessica. She sat there, hands clasped tightly in her lap, her head tipped back and her eyes closed. Those delicious, pale pink lips were softly parted, and he wondered if he'd hurt her with the power of his kiss. His brows drew downward as he replaced the hat on his head and started the pickup. By tonight, Sam would be asking him to pack his bedroll and leave. By tomorrow morning, the sheriff would probably be out looking for him, to slam him into the county jail on assault charges. Dan couldn't fool himself. Old Man Cunningham ran Coconino and Yavapai Counties, including Sedona.

Dan's hands shook momentarily as he backed the pickup away from the mission. Heaven and hell. He'd just held heaven in his arms and stolen a wild, hot kiss from Jessica. The hell was that he was going to pay for all his indiscretions. Every single last one of them. Worse, he'd never see Jessica again, and he felt his heart crack and begin to break into anguished fragments deep in his chest.

Chapter 7

Dan leaned moodily against the last hundred-pound sack of grain that he'd stored in the barn. The hundred-degree heat was making him sweat profusely. His knuckles ached and he automatically flexed them. Taking his red bandanna from around his neck, he removed his cowboy hat and wiped his perspiring face. Through the large open doors of the red barn, he could see Jessica's house.

Hell and damnation! He might as well pack what few belongings he had into the old carpetbag that he'd inherited from his great-grandmother. It was only a matter of time, Dan concluded, until Sam came to the bunkhouse to give him his walking papers. Especially now that he'd got entangled in a fight—and he'd kissed Jessica.

His lips tingled hotly in memory of her soft, sweet mouth against his hungry, searching one. Frowning, he settled the black Stetson on his head and walked out to the pickup. Climbing in, he drove it around to the front of the main ranch house where it belonged. His gaze caught a rising cloud of dust from the dirt road that led into the ranch from 89A.

Trouble. He could feel it. Getting out of the truck, he looked toward the greenhouse. It was probably the Coconino County sheriff come to slap him in cuffs and take him to jail on assault and battery charges. Rubbing the back of his neck, Dan felt a storm of emotions roll through him. He needed more time. He *had* to talk to Jessica about their unexpected, shocking kiss. He wanted to apologize. Afterward, she'd retreated into a silent shell, and they'd passed the entire trip to the hay and feed store and back to the ranch in stilted, embarrassed silence.

Dan knew she was sorry. The look on her face—the chagrin written across it and the high, red color in her flushed cheeks—told him everything. She didn't like him. He hadn't asked her permission to touch her, much less kiss her. What the hell was the matter with him? He was acting crazy, like that black Arabian stallion when he got around a mare in heat. No brains, just hormones.

Dan decided to wait for the approaching vehicle. As it crested the top of the hill that led down the winding, narrow dirt road to the canyon below, where he stood, he scowled. It wasn't a white car with lights and sirens. No, it was a red car with antennae sticking out of the trunk area. Someone from the fire department. But why? Stymied, Dan folded his arms against his chest and waited, leaning tensely against the back of the pickup. The shade of an overhead cottonwood cooled him slightly and the off-and-on breeze felt good to him. He was sweating plenty, probably out of fear of being jailed again. He never wanted to return to that hateful place.

As the red car drove up and parked near him, Dan saw a man with black hair and blue eyes at the wheel. When the stranger opened the door and unbuckled the seat belt, Dan got a better look at him. Wearing dark blue, serge pants, highly polished black boots and a light blue, short-sleeved shirt, he had a tall, lanky build, reminding Dan of a cougar's lethal grace. He looked vaguely familiar, but Dan couldn't place him. On his shirt he wore a silver badge and his left sleeve bore a red-and-white insignia that said Emergency Medical Technician. Dan tensed as he caught the nameplate affixed to his left pocket: J. Cunningham.

Slowly uncrossing his arms and spreading his feet slightly for balance, Dan studied the man before him. He was the youngest of the three Cunningham brothers, and from town gossip Dan knew that Jim had recently quit his forestry job as a hotshot firefighter and come home to try and mend fences with his cantankerous father and brothers. Rumor had it that Jim had left years ago during a hellacious family fight, swearing never to return. For ten years, he had remained up in Flagstaff. The only time Dan had heard of him coming home was at Christmas. But he always left shortly after to resume his fire fighting duties around the U.S. Now that he was working for Sedona's fire department, everyone wondered if he'd stay for good.

As he quietly closed the car door, Cunningham's blue eyes were dark and disturbed looking, though he held Dan's gauging look. His full mouth was pursed as he moved in Dan's direction.

Dan didn't know what to expect. Had Jim Cunningham come to finish off the fight? His heart began a slow, hard pounding as adrenaline began to pour into his bloodstream.

"You Dan Black?" Cunningham demanded, halting about six feet away, his hands resting tensely on his narrow hips.

"I am."

"You know who I am?"

"Got an idea."

"My brothers just came over to the fire department to get patched up from the fight they just had." Giving Dan a frosty smile, he continued, "I'm an EMT, on the medical staff of the Sedona Fire Department. I came to apologize to you in person for my brothers' actions and to see if you were okay."

Stunned, Dan stared at him in disbelief. Cunninghams weren't known for apologizing for anything they did—they played by their own twisted rules and their reputation in Sedona was nasty. They never had any compassion for folks they chose to take on and destroy. Dan knew many people Old Man Cunningham had torn apart over the years. The father was a merciless bastard just like his two sons. But as Dan heard it, Jim Cunningham had always been different, set apart from the rest of the family, like a black sheep of sorts. Or rather like a *white* sheep.

When Jim thrust out his hand, Dan swallowed hard. "My knuckles are bruised up a little," he muttered, taking the man's offered hand. Cunningham's grip was firm, and Dan found himself respecting the guy for what he was doing. It was absolutely unheard of that a Cunningham apologized for anything.

Jim nodded and released his grip. "And Miss Jessica

Donovan? Is she okay? Chet said she slapped him, but I don't believe my brother. Maybe you can tell me what really happened?"

Dan nodded and told him the entire story. The EMT's oval face and strong chin became tight with anger by the time he'd finished.

"I see," Jim rasped. "Well, both of them have broken noses out of the deal. Just deserts, I'd say." He cocked his head and perused Dan speculatively. "I heard you were in the Corps for four years, or is that just gossip?"

Dan relaxed. He liked Jim Cunningham, even though something about his stance reminded him of a dangerous cougar ready to strike. "Yes, I was."

"What part?"

"Recons."

Cunningham grinned a little. "Thought so."

"Oh?"

"My brothers said they couldn't lay a hand on you. That you'd done all the damage to them. I figured you had some special training to do that."

"I don't like to fight, Mr. Cunningham. It's not in my nature. I'd rather have peace."

He nodded. "I'm with you. Coming back to this family of mine this last month has been hell. I'm going to try and stick it out, but I don't know...." He looked up at the clear blue, cloudless sky for a moment.

"Family troubles are the worst kind," Dan agreed quietly.

Jim looked over at him. "Look, if it's okay with you, I'd like to meet Jessica Donovan and make my apologies directly to her."

"You shouldn't be cleaning up the messes your brothers make."

"No, but if I'm going to break the patterns of abuse that run through my family, somebody is going to have to take responsibility and start changing things, aren't they? My two brothers don't have a clue yet." His eyes flashing, Cunningham muttered grimly, "They sure as hell will when I get off duty tomorrow morning and we have a friendly little chat over breakfast with Dad about it. That's a promise."

Dan didn't envy Jim's position, but he respected the man. He wanted to say that the Cunninghams were a barrel of rotten apples and that if a good apple like Jim were put in among them, they'd infect him, too. Instead, he said, "I admire your mission."

Jim grinned tightly. "Not a job for the faint of heart, is it?"

"No," he murmured, "it isn't." In that moment, Dan realized Jim knew all the sordid tales of his brothers' and father's escapades in Coconino and Yavapai Counties, and that he was well aware of the hatred many people had toward the Cunninghams. Their greed, stinginess and manipulative, underhanded business dealings were famous in these parts. "Come on, I know where Jessica's at. I think she'll feel better hearing that there's one Cunningham who cares about other people's feelings."

Dan was going to leave once he showed Cunningham to the door of the greenhouse, but the EMT persuaded him to come in and make introductions. It was the last thing Dan wanted to do, but he had no choice. Opening the door, he felt an immediate drop in temperature inside the structure and the high humidity enveloped him. He saw Jessica perched up on a stool tending to one of her orchids at the workbench. When she turned to see who was coming in, her eyes widened, first with shock and then surprise mixed with some hidden emotion. Probably disgust for him, for his earlier actions, Dan thought.

Getting a grip on his own feelings, Dan led the EMT over to the workbench and made introductions. Then he stepped back, tipped his hat in Jessica's direction and left. He could see that look in her flawless turquoise eyes. She was so heartbreakingly innocent and beautiful—and he'd abused the privilege of being with her. As he shut the door behind him and crossed the yard, he felt suffocated by his own feelings toward Jessica. How could he have fallen so in love with a woman he'd known only three weeks? How? It had never happened to him before. Not ever.

"I wanted to apologize directly to you for my brothers' actions, Miss Donovan," Jim said to her in an apologetic tone. "I drove over here after they came into the firehouse to get some medical treatment from me and my partner. That's when I found out about it. They told me their side of the story, and I just got the truth as to what really happened from Dan Black. I'm sorry. I want to know if there's anything I can do to patch things up between us."

Stunned, Jessica stared up at the tall, well-muscled EMT. "Y-you're *Jim* Cunningham?"

"Yes, ma'am, I am."

"But," Jessica said, putting the orchid aside, "I thought—"

"I just came home a month ago. Permanently, I hope. My father's ill and—"

"Oh, I'm sorry to hear that." Jessica saw the sadness in his narrowed gaze. She immediately liked Jim Cunningham. "This is such a change from normal Cunningham actions."

"I realize that. I'm trying to break the old habit patterns. They die hard, but someone has got to make Chet and Bo straighten out and become better citizens of Sedona and the county, don't you think?"

His easy smile made him look more handsome, and Jessica warmed to him even more. She wondered if he was married. There was no wedding ring on his left finger. "So, you're home for good now?"

"Yes, I am. For better or worse, I'm afraid."

"Gosh, I admire your tenacity, Jim. You don't mind if I call you by your first name, do you?"

He relaxed slightly, his hand on the edge of her workbench. "No, ma'am, I don't. To tell you the truth, my own lack of formality has gotten me into a lot of trouble with superiors all my life." He looked down at his fire-department uniform. "I'm kinda the wild card around here."

She smiled, enjoying his openness toward her. Jessica was the youngest Donovan girl, and she vaguely remembered Jim in school, but they'd been many grades apart. She knew he'd been a very shy young man, a mere shadow, compared to his two brothers, who were always in fights of one kind or another. Shortly after graduation, he'd been hired by the forest service and had taken a job as a hotshot firefighter. It was the last Jessica had seen of him.

"Sometimes it takes a wild card—or a black sheep— to make the changes, you know?" She saw him relax completely, his broad shoulders drawn back proudly.

"Your reputation around here seems to be true," he murmured.

Jessica raised her eyes and laughed. "Oh, dear, Sedona gossip, I suppose?"

"Well," Jim hedged, "you know there's some truth

to gossip. Not much, usually, but there's a seed in it somewhere."

"And what's the gossip going around about me? I imagine because you're in the fire department you hear a lot of it."

Jim pushed his long, strong fingers through his short black hair. "Just that you were insightful, that you always thought the best of a person and his behavior, that's all. After what my brothers pulled, you didn't have to see me or be this kind to me. I think that speaks volumes about you, personally. At least, it does to me." He scowled. "I want peace between our families. I know the Donovans and Cunninghams have fought for decades, mostly because of our stubborn, wrongheaded fathers." Spreading his hands open in a gesture of peace, he continued, "I want to bury the hatchet, Jessica. I want to come over here some time and tell Kate and Sam the same thing. I've only been back for a month, however, and my hands are full with my new job, plus trying to help run the ranch on my days off."

She felt his commitment, as well as his incredible anguish. Noticing the tiny scars on his brow and right cheek and all over his hands and darkly haired arms, she knew without a doubt that Jim Cunningham carried the scars not only of his own life, but those of his family, too. Her heart went out to him.

"I'll tell Katie and Sam that you dropped by to apologize, Jim. I'm sure they'll be relieved to hear this. We don't want to fight, either. We just want to be able to work with your ranch in the event of some crisis or emergency. We're just as tired of the bad blood between us as you are. Kelly's dead now, so most of the problem is gone. Right now Kate's trying to pick up the pieces, and

Sam's trying to help her save our home." Jessica sighed and looked at his serious, dark features. She saw the Apache blood of his mother in him, in the set of his high cheekbones, his glossy black hair and the reddish tone to his dark golden skin. "I know Katie will be glad to hear you're back and trying to change things."

"I don't know if I can," Jim admitted heavily, frowning down at his hand resting on the workbench. "But I'm going to give it one heck of a try."

"You're a catalyst," Jessica said. "The lightning bolt your family needs. By you coming home, things must change or else."

He grinned a little recklessly and held out his hand to her. "Thanks for the vote of confidence. It's the only one I've gotten around here so far. Maybe I should come over once a week and get a pep talk from you so I can carry on."

Giggling, Jessica shook his proffered hand. "I'll tell you who's a real cheerleader. My sister Rachel. She's coming home in December from London, England. Talk about someone cheering people on to strive to be all they can be—that's Rachel!"

"I remember her. She was two grades behind me in high school," Jim said.

Jessica heard a sudden wistful quality in his voice and saw longing in his blue eyes. It occurred to her that maybe Jim had had a crush on Rachel in school. But Rachel hadn't said anything about it back then, so Jessica shrugged off the intuitive hint. "Hang tight until December. I'm sure Rachel is going to be thrilled to death to hear you're home to change the ways of the Cunningham family. Besides, she's going to be setting up a clinic in

Sedona to practice homeopathy. You're an EMT, I see. You two will have a lot in common—medicine."

"Sounds good to me, ma'am."

"Call me Jessica. Please."

He smiled a little. "Okay... Jessica."

"You already talk to Dan?" she asked, sliding off the stool and walking out of the greenhouse with him.

"Yes, I did. And I apologized to him, too."

Jessica felt the dry heat strike her as they walked around the main ranch house to his dark red car. "I think he was worried the sheriff was going to come out and arrest him or something. I think he worries too much, sometimes."

"Chet and Bo started it. He was only defending himself, you and Tommy." Jim halted at the car and opened the door. "If you wanted, you two could press charges against them and land them in the county jail."

Jessica shook her head. "Why perpetuate bad feelings, Jim? I'm willing to let bygones be bygones."

He climbed into the car and shut the door, rolling down the window. "I hope someday my brothers and father have your kind of understanding heart, Jessica. Thanks." He lifted his hand after starting the vehicle. "If you get a chance, drop over to the main fire department and take a look at our emergency medicine facilities. I hope you don't ever need us out here, but if you do, dial 911 and we'll be here."

Jessica lifted her hand. "I'll do that, Jim. I'm sure Rachel would love to see your medical station, too."

"You've got a deal. Next time I see you, I hope it's for happier reasons."

Jessica watched him drive slowly up the winding road

that led out of the canyon. With a sigh, she turned to find Dan. It was time to talk. More than time.

Jessica found Dan in the barn, moving hay that had been brought in by truck earlier that morning. Her heart beating rapidly, she stood at the doorway, absorbing his lean, hard body and graceful movements as he lifted the hundred-pound bales as if they weighed next to nothing. He had put his cowboy hat aside, and she saw damp black tendrils clinging to his sweaty brow and neck. It was stifling in the barn, and except for the breeze that blew through the open doors, there was little fresh air.

"Dan?" she called, her voice swallowed up by the barn. At first she didn't think he'd heard her, and she was about to call his name again when she saw his head snap in her direction. Instantly, she watched his stormy gray eyes go colorless. She knew that meant he felt he was in danger. Or at least he didn't feel safe—with her. That hurt more than anything, and fear threaded through Jessica as she stepped forward, her fingers twisted together.

"I know you're busy, but could you take a break so we can talk?" Her throat felt dry, and her heart was pounding relentlessly in her breast. Whether Jessica wanted to or not, her gaze settled on Dan's mouth. Oh, that kiss he'd given her had been so incredibly galvanizing! She felt as if he'd breathed life back into her wounded soul, such was the power he'd shared with her in that exquisite moment.

"Yeah, hold on…." he rasped between breaths.

She stood to one side as he grabbed his hat, wiped his face with his bandanna and moved out into the aisle, where there was at least a breeze now and again. She saw his eyes narrow, making his wariness more than evident.

She went over and unscrewed the cap from the jug of water he always kept with him, and taking his beat-up, blue plastic cup she poured him a drink.

"Here," she whispered, "you need this."

In that moment, Dan wished for something a lot stronger to anesthetize the pain he felt in his heart. Alcohol always stopped him from feeling and took the painful knots out of his gut, too. He saw her unsureness; her eyes were shadowed and that soft, delicious mouth was compressed. He knew what was coming. Inside, he cried. Outwardly, he took the glass with his damp, gloved hand.

"Thanks," he said.

Jessica watched as he tipped his head upward, his Adam's apple bobbing with each swallow. Some trickles of water ran down his chin to the strong, gleaming column of his throat. Trying to gird herself emotionally, Jessica sat down beneath his towering form on a bale of hay.

Wiping his mouth with the back of his hand, he placed the blue cup next to the water jug. He saw Jessica hang her head, unable to meet his gaze. She was twisting her fingers nervously in her lap. Crouching down, his hand on the bale behind where she sat, he took a deep breath. "Okay," he rasped in a strained tone, "what do you want to talk about?" He pushed the brim of his hat upward with his thumb.

Jessica tried to smile but couldn't. She risked a very brief glance in his direction. Dan seemed to realize she didn't want him towering over her. Instead, he'd crouched down to be at eye level with her. Her heart mushroomed with strong, powerful feelings toward him. Touching her breast, she managed to say in a strangled voice, "This is so hard for me, Dan. I hope you can forgive me if I bumble through this. I—I just feel so scared and unsure right now. And I feel a lot of other things that I've never felt before."

She gave a helpless little laugh and met and held his gaze. His eyes had gone from colorless to a dove gray and she knew he'd let down some of his guard. Opening her hands artlessly, she said, "Here I am, a woman who was married for eight years. You'd think I'd be a lot less naive than I am. Or I'd know a lot more than most people think I should when it comes to relationships. Or—" her voice shook "—about men and what they want from me..."

Dan shut his eyes tightly for a moment. "Jessica, I never meant to—"

"No," she whispered, twisting toward him. "Please, Dan, let me finish. This is so hard for me to come to terms with, and you more than anyone should know the truth." She watched his eyes open slightly to study her. "Right now, my heart's pounding in my chest. I can taste my fear."

Concerned, Dan reached out and gently grazed her flushed cheek. "Jessica, I swear to God, I *never* meant to make you feel fear...."

Jessica drowned in his darkening, stormy gray eyes, but his gentle touch gave her courage. "Oh, Dan, I was hoping you'd understand, and I believe you do without even realizing it. My heart said you would." She looked away, tears choking her voice. "When you kissed me earlier today, my world just fell apart around my feet. It wasn't your fault. It was my past coming to meet me. I didn't expect it. How could I know?" Jessica opened her hands and gave him a pleading look.

"Your kiss made me feel so clean and good inside, Dan. I would never have thought it was possible to have a man's kiss do that to me instead of…well, making me feel…awful." She avoided his sharpening gaze, hanging her head and staring down at the fingers she'd nervously clasped together. "When I married Carl, I fell in love with the mask he wore, not the man beneath it. I guess if I'd been older, more experienced, or maybe not such an airhead, I'd have realized he was a two-heart underneath that facade. He presented such a wonderful mask to me, Dan. I thought he was the kindest, gentlest, funniest man in the world. I fell for him so hard that I married him three months after meeting him.

"Within a year of being married to him, I realized I'd married an insanely jealous, controlling monster, not a man. He didn't care about me. Over the years, I realized that he just needed someone else to control, to be a slave to his whims and needs, to cook for him and keep house for him. My love, or whatever it was, died over those years. I felt so trapped, like I was in a prison, or a bad nightmare that just got worse and worse with time. It got so I hated his touch. My skin would crawl when he'd touch me…when he'd kiss me. Toward the end, I'd get physically sick to my stomach if he tried to make love to me."

There, the words were out. Jessica took a deep, ragged breath and risked a look at Dan. To her surprise, his face was open and so readable. Gone was his mask; here was the real man beneath. More than anything, she saw anguish in his dark gray eyes, and his lips were parted, as if he wanted to say something to her.

"There's more," Jessica continued in an unsteady whisper. "Only my sisters know about it, and now Sam, because…well, you'll see. I need to tell you all of this, Dan, because it's not fair to you to walk into something without knowing the whole truth. That's why I have to tell you…." She closed her eyes, unable to stand the judgment she knew would be on his face when she was finished.

"Carl would question my every move. If I went to the grocery store, he would accuse me when I returned of seeing another man. He'd accuse me of sleeping with someone else. But he made up everything in his own sick head. I *never* had an affair, Dan. I never could. I'm just not made that way. It got so I had to not only tell Carl where I was going, but what time I expected to be home. If I wasn't home at that time, all hell would break loose. He'd fly into a fury and he'd accuse me again of having an affair. I tried to tell him I would never be with another man…but," Jessica whispered, "he never believed me."

Rubbing her face, she dropped her hands in her lap and stared across the aisle of the barn, her voice losing all trace of emotion. "The last three years of our marriage were pure hell for me. Carl would hit me and knock me down when I denied I was having an affair. At first he'd just shove me around. Then, later, he'd use his fists and hit me in the stomach. He never hit me anywhere a bruise would show. Over time, his attacks escalated. At the end of the third year, he beat me up so badly that I ended up in the emergency room."

Dan whispered, "Jessica—"

"No…please…let me finish this, Dan. You must." Jessica was too ashamed to look at him. She heard the heartbreaking tone of his voice and it drove tears into her eyes. She fought them back and went on, her words coming out stiltedly, in fits and snatches. Caught up in those terrifying times, she could feel the terror eating her up once again.

"That final time, when I was in the emergency room because of what Carl did to me, I lost consciousness. I remember waking up two weeks later in a Vancouver hospital. The nurse told me I'd been in a coma. I was amazed, because when I lost consciousness, I went into the light. I saw my mother, Dan. She held me while I cried. I had needed her so much over those years, but I was afraid to call home, to tell her what I'd done, what I'd gotten myself into. Carl was just like Kelly, only worse. I'd left home and then married someone just like my father. I felt so humiliated, so stupid, that I didn't want my mother to know...but then she died, too, so I was alone. I didn't call Rachel or Kate because of the same reason. I just felt stupid and shamed.

"When I was with my mother in that beautiful white light, I told her everything. I knew she had gone over the rainbow bridge, and I knew I was talking to her spirit. I thought I'd died, too, and now I could be with her forever, which made me very happy. We had so many wonderful talks and I was able to tell her everything.

"Her love was so great that she told me it was all right, that what I had to do when I got 'back' was to leave Carl. This was a test, she said, to break the bondage of the past with my father, and to move forward, free to soar like the eagle I really could become. My mother said someone would be sent to help me leave Carl and my worthless marriage. She said I would always have protection, from the day I decided to divorce Carl.

"When I regained consciousness, I remembered everything my mother had told me. From my bed, I called an attorney, and then I called the police and got protection. I started divorce proceedings that day. I was so scared, but I was more scared of the hospital releasing me, of going back to that house and Carl. I knew he'd kill me eventually." Her voice broke. "I didn't want to die that way.... I knew life had more to offer than this kind of horrible abuse. I didn't feel I deserved it, but Carl kept telling me how worthless I was, that I was no good, that I was a bad seed. After a while, I bought it. I was brainwashed."

Gently, Dan sat down and put his arms around Jessica. Hot tears stung his eyes as he enclosed her in a light embrace. He felt her tremble, and then she leaned back against him, her head against his shoulder as she surrendered to him completely. The precious gift of her trust sent an incredible joy tunneling through him. Closing his eyes, Dan pressed his face against her hair.

"Listen to me," he whispered unsteadily, "you aren't bad, Jessica. You never were. I—I don't know how you stood eight years of something like that. I couldn't have...." He felt her hands fall over his where he'd clasped them against her torso. "You're a survivor. You know that? Just like that black stallion out there who was beaten within an inch of his life by Kelly."

Jessica relaxed in his arms. She could feel the powerful beat of his heart against her back where she lay against him. His arms were strong and caring. His voice was riddled with emotion—for her. "I don't know how you can hold me, Dan. I really don't...."

He smiled softly and squeezed her momentarily. "I know one thing brings an animal that's been abused out of his pain, and that's love and care."

Jessica wanted to tell him she needed his love, but she didn't dare. It was too soon. Her past had taught her that hurrying into a relationship was not smart or healthy. The other thing she'd discovered was that the fact that she had been raised by an abusive father had led her to marry an abusive man. The clarity of that realization was sinking into her now. But Dan was nothing like her father or Carl.

Then she remembered the fight he'd had that day. "When you protected me against Chet, I was so shocked. I don't know why. When he put his hand over mine to trap me at the door of the truck, I panicked inside. It brought back horrible memories of my abusive marriage."

Jessica stirred in his arms, slowly sitting up and turning to him. Dan's face was filled with sadness, and she saw anger burning in his dark gray eyes now, but she knew it wasn't aimed at her. Placing her hands over his, she whispered, "When you fought them, it just shocked me. I never thought of you as a warrior. And the way you fought…"

"I picked up karate when I was a Recon Marine," he told her. "It comes in handy sometimes."

"Yes…it did. You protected Tommy and me." Looking up at the thick rafters of the barn, Jessica said, "I was so shaken up by it all. I'd escaped Vancouver, the violence, to come here and live in peace."

"And your peace was shattered this morning."

Jessica nodded and knew Dan understood better than anyone else what she'd felt. "Yes," she said simply. "I guess it was stupid and idealistic of me to hope that violence wouldn't follow me. But it has…and will…."

Dan gave her a strange look. "The Cunningham boys and I have tangled before, Jessica. They were after me because of my own past, not because of you."

She held Dan's earnest gaze and felt the powerful blanket of his care enveloping her. "There's something else you need to know, Dan, before this goes any further. You need to know the whole truth."

Dan gave her a puzzled look.

"I already told you about my friend Moyra, how she watched out for me while I was living in Vancouver. When I moved down here because Katie needed me to help try and save our home, Moyra warned me that Carl would come after me. Somehow, he'd find out I'd left Canada and would come and hunt me down. She warned me that he would kill me this time if he got a hold of me." Looking at Dan, she said, "But Moyra also said a man 'clothed in darkness' would be sent to me, to protect me and help me. I believe that's you. The day I first met you, I felt something here, in my heart." She touched her breast with her fingertips. "I don't know what it is, but being around you, Dan, makes me feel clean and pure again, like I felt before I met Carl and married him."

Heat thrummed through Dan—a delicious, warming heat that made his heart open wide like a flower in his chest. Jessica was pale as she spoke now, her face etched with strain and so many emotions. He reached out and captured her hand. Normally, her fingers were warm and dry. Now they were cool and clammy.

"And when you kissed me…" She sighed and closed her eyes, relishing the feel of his roughened fingers wrapping around her cooler hand. "I felt things I'd never felt before in my life." She opened her eyes and held his gaze. Tears slipped down her face. "I felt a joy like I'd never knew existed, Dan. All I had known was one man's kisses… Carl's. Your kiss was like life. His were like death. You were so gentle and coaxing when you kissed me. You didn't take, you shared. I was so stunned by your kiss. Nothing had ever felt so right, so good, to me." Quickly, Jessica looked away, unable to stand the pity she saw in Dan's eyes. "That's why I had to tell you everything," she said hurriedly. "I don't know how you really feel toward me, but I know my feelings for you are growing. I don't want to put you in harm's way. Carl could find me. He's so insanely jealous that—that—if he knew you liked me, just a little, he might kill you, too." Pressing her hands against her face, Jessica cried out brokenly, "And I couldn't stand for that to happen, Dan! I just couldn't!"

Chapter 8

Dan slowly released Jessica and turned her around on the bale of hay they sat on, so that she could look directly at him. It was time to be as completely honest with her as she had been with him. Taking off his sweat-stained leather work gloves, he dropped them to the floor of the barn. Her cheeks glistened with spent tears, and her eyes were red rimmed, filled with sadness, betrayal and fear. And yet as she lifted those thick blond lashes, met and held his intense, burning gaze, he felt his heart lift euphorically in his chest, as if for the first time in his life he was flying.

The sensation was new and startling. Beautiful and filled with hope. Hope wasn't something Dan had ever felt much of. Lifting his hands, he brushed away her tears with trembling fingers. Her skin was soft and warm beneath his touch. He ached to lean forward and kiss her mouth, kiss that trembling lower lip as she clung to him.

"Your life path has been hard," he murmured huskily, allowing his fingers to drop from her cheeks and fold around her hands. "I barely knew any of this. Sam only told me that you would need watching out for when you came here. He didn't say more than that."

"It's pretty sordid, don't you think?" Jessica said. How gentle Dan's face had become. She would never have believed he could be so tender if she hadn't seen it for herself. The harshness of the land he'd been raised on made men hard. All she saw now was his dark, stormy eyes burning with a powerful, intense emotion that caught and held her gently in its embrace. His touch was firm and yet gentling. Perhaps it was the same touch he applied to a scared mustang he was breaking for saddle.

He shook his head. "It's a crime what Carl did to you. You're stronger than I believed." One corner of his mouth hitched upward for just a moment. "If you weren't telling me all of this, I'd never believe it secondhand." Gazing at her face, he touched some tendrils of blond hair and smoothed them across the top of her head. "You don't look scarred, Jessica. You're untouched by the darkness life can wrap us in. Like it did me." He saw the puzzled expression in her eyes. "It's funny how we see other people without really knowing them, or what path they had to endure. I see nothing but the beauty in you—in the way you walk, the way you treat others, the way you lead with your heart, not your head."

Dan's mouth curled into a sarcastic line. "I know you heard what Chet and Bo said about me today at the hay and feed store."

Sniffing, Jessica pulled a tissue from the pocket of

her Levi's. "Yes, I did." She blew her nose, apologizing as she tucked the tissue back into her pocket. "Chet and Bo are well known for lying, so I didn't take it seriously."

Dan held her hands firmly. It took every ounce of his escaping courage to hold her gaze and say, "It wasn't lies this time. They were telling the truth about me."

Jessica stared at him, the silence stretching stiltedly between them.

Dan felt his heart begin to beat hard with fear of her rejection. He saw the question, the shock registering in Jessica's easily read expression. Whatever he'd thought he might have with her was rapidly dissolving. Risking it all, he rasped in a low, pain-filled tone, "I never touched alcohol until I entered the Marine Corps. My father was a Recon Marine. He wanted me to be one. That was always his dream for me—to be like him. He was an officer. I went in enlisted because I didn't have the college education that was needed in order to become an officer.

"I wanted him to be proud of me. When I went into the marines, I didn't like it. But I stuck it out and worked hard, and eventually, I was able to go into Recon training. I became a communications specialist for my team of five Recons. Each of us had a skill. Mine was radios, computers and stuff like that.

"I liked the Marine Corps in one way because it was about teamwork. My team was good. One of the best, at Camp Reed out in California. We worked hard together, we played together and—we drank together. It was real easy, after a hard day humping the hills of Reed, to go over to the enlisted men's club and grab a few beers. It never got out of hand.

"When Desert Storm wound up, they sent ten Recon

teams over to Iraq. We worked with army special forces
and black berets, as well. We were part of a contin-
gent no one has ever known about to this day. We were
dropped way behind the lines, to cause havoc among
the elite guard units."

"Oh, dear," Jessica whispered. "It must have been
dangerous...."

Dan tightened his hands around hers, staring down
at their soft, white expanse. "Jessica, what I'm going to
share with you, I've never said to another soul. I—I'm
ashamed of it. I see it almost every night in my dreams.
I wake up drenched in sweat, feeling my heart trying to
beat out of my chest, and I want to die."

Murmuring his name softly, Jessica eased her hand
from his and rested it against the side of his face. She
saw the harshness and judgment in his eyes. "Dan, whatever it is, you can share it with me."

Taking a deep, ragged breath, he rasped, "I ended up
killing five men that night. My team and I parachuted
into an Iraqi stronghold. We'd gotten bad information.
We were surrounded. Once the captain realized what
had happened, we went about our business of causing
havoc. The ammo dump was blown up, and that was the
start of the whole thing. Then we ran out of ammo ourselves. We had no way to get help or support from either
the sky or the land units. It ended up," Dan continued,
scowling heavily, his voice dropping to a bare whisper,
"that the only way we could get out of there alive was
to use our Ka-bar knives as weapons...."

Jessica shut her eyes tightly. "Oh, no...."

Something old and hurting shattered inside of Dan.
He felt it, felt the pain drifting from his chest down to
his knotted gut. "That night I thought I was going to

die. In a way, I wanted to. I had to take five men's lives. Their blood is on my hands to this day. I remember every sound, their cries…. I wonder about their families, their loved ones, and the fact their children no longer have fathers to raise them." He swallowed hard, the lump in his throat making his voice tight. He saw Jessica's eyes widen with such pity that he couldn't handle it.

"Two members of my team were badly wounded. Marines never leave their wounded or dead behind. The other three of us got them out of there, past their lines. Then a rescue team began firing artillery blindly into the night, trying to find us. Well…they did. We were heading down off a sand dune when a shell exploded just behind us. I remember the concussion wave slamming me and the marine I had over my shoulders in a fireman's carry, and that was the last thing I recalled."

Jessica held her breath. "You were hurt, too?"

He shrugged. "The pain I carry inside me every day is much worse than the physical wounds I received."

"How badly were you hurt?"

"I was the only one to survive that blast."

Jessica stared at him, watching his thinned mouth work. He would not look at her, only down at her hand, held so tightly in his own. "Thank the Great Spirit you lived," she breathed softly, leaning over and sliding her fingertips along the hard, unforgiving line of his jaw. She felt the prickles of his beard beneath her flesh.

"I was lucky in one sense. Another returning Recon unit found what was left of us right after dawn. They called in a chopper, which took all of us back to a hospital unit in Kuwait. I didn't wake up until a week later, in some hospital in Germany. I had shrapnel all down my back and both legs. I'd taken a piece of metal into my helmet, which tore it off my head." He grimaced. "I guess the docs thought I was going to die because the shrapnel fractured my skull and caused bleeding underneath. The nurses looked pretty surprised when I woke up. The docs were even more surprised when I didn't seem to suffer any aftereffects of the skull injury. My speech was okay, and so was my memory, unfortunately.

"I got a medical discharge from the Marine Corps after that, and I got transferred to Prescott, Arizona, where they have a Veterans Administration hospital. My wounds were healing up fine on the outside, but inside I was falling apart. I couldn't erase any of what I'd done or seen. As soon as I could, I started drinking hard liquor. It was the only thing that stopped the memories, stopped the sounds careening through my head day and night. By the time I left the VA hospital and headed home to Flagstaff where my parents lived, I was drinking a quart of vodka a day."

Jessica sighed. "Oh, Dan, that's terrible. I can't imagine how much pain you were in, how much you were suffering.…"

He held her tear-filled gaze. "I'm not proud of what I had become, Jessica. You realize that?" It hurt him worse to say those words than any others he'd ever said to anyone in his life. "Chet was right. I was a drunk for a while. My parents tried to help me, and asked me to move in with them."

With a little cry, Jessica whispered, "Your pain was so great. You drank because of the pain, not because you craved alcohol."

"That's right," Dan said with a sigh. "But it doesn't matter. I can't handle alcohol. At all." He couldn't believe she was still sitting there with him. People had disdained him for years because of that painful period of his life. "I dishonored myself, and worse, my parents and their good name. I had hit bottom. I decided that the only way to get out of this cycle was to want to do it. My father looked around for a job for me. He knew if he could get me to stop thinking so much about what I'd done, that I could survive it. There was an opening at a Flag ranch for a horse wrangler. I went over there and got the job. I kept it for five years until they let me go. Then Sam asked me to come down here and be the head horse wrangler for your ranch. He couldn't promise much pay up front, but I needed a change. The people up in Flag remember me as a drunk. The stares, the gossip, the looks they always gave me reminded me of my past, my shame...."

Risking everything, Dan looked up. Jessica's face was filled with suffering. When he realized it was for him, that she was not going to judge him harshly as the people of Flagstaff, and those who had heard gossip about him here in Sedona had, his heart took wing like an eagle that had wanted to fly for a long, long time.

"I know Kelly Donovan was a roaring alcoholic," he admitted hoarsely. "But I'm not like your father, Jessica. I would never hurt you or any other woman. Though I did get into a few brawls, all I wanted to do was go and hide away and—cry. I needed to be alone. The Great Spirit knows, I've hurt and killed enough people already—"

"No!" Jessica said fiercely, grabbing his hands. "You killed to survive, Dan. That's different!"

He shook his head. "It's wrong to take another person's life. I'll never do it again. Not *ever*. I—couldn't. The hell I went through just to get this far away from my past has been the hardest thing I've done in my life. When I finally realized what the alcohol was doing—when I finally got tired of watching my mother grow old because of my choices—I quit." He shook his head. "If I had to kill again, I'd probably go put a bullet in my head afterward because I couldn't handle the pain, the guilt and all the crap that went with it. I'm not that strong. I try and ignore those voices in my head, the faces I see in my nightly dreams."

"Dan, you're an amazing person," Jessica said gently. "You've gone through hell and come out the other side of it. Yes, your spirit was wounded, but you had what it took to pull yourself up by your own bootstraps."

He crooked his mouth a little and looked up at her. "So did you."

"Maybe we don't give ourselves enough credit for our strength and courage," Jessica admitted sadly. "I know I'm horribly ashamed of my past, of my inability to leave Carl before he put me in the hospital."

"Jessica," Dan whispered in a raw tone, "you were like a beaten animal. You came from a family where your father did not respect women. What you have to understand, *shi shaa,* is that when you met Carl, that was the only kind of man you knew. Like draws like. Because you are so intuitive, you, more than most, must realize that. The Navajo have a saying—we attract what we are or we attract what we need. You were young, running away from home, probably homesick, scared and alone in Vancouver. You had no friends, so when Carl saw your beauty, your cleanness, he was like a wolf leaping on an unprotected lamb."

She nodded, amazed by Dan's insight, his under-standing of what had really happened up in Vancouver. "You're right—I was scared and alone. I didn't know what I was going to do. I cried all the time because I

missed Mama, I missed this ranch...but I didn't miss
Kelly. I was so scared of him, Dan. I used to hide under
the bed when he was drunk. I remember crawling under
it and then rolling into the fetal position, my head buried against my knees. Mama did what she could to protect us, but she couldn't be in three places at once. Kelly
usually picked on Kate, not me or Rachel half as much."
She shook her head, tears spilling from her eyes. "It's
all so sad, Dan. So sad.... Kelly destroyed our family
with his drinking binges. And for what?"

"I heard from Sam that Kelly was in the war," Dan
murmured. "That he had post-traumatic stress disor-
der. I'm not making excuses for him, but my gut hunch
was that he drank for the same reasons I did—the horror of what we had to do in a wartime situation, or what
he saw...."

"Probably," she sniffed. "But it didn't give him the
right to abuse us, either."

"No, it didn't," Dan admitted quietly, studying her
flushed, glistening face.

She drowned in his dark gray gaze. "You said something in Navajo just a minute ago. I know you've said it
to me a couple of times. What does it mean?" She took
a clean tissue from her pocket and wiped her face free
of tears.

Avoiding her searching look, Dan tightened his
mouth. "I have no right to call you what I did. I'm
sorry...."

"No!" Jessica slid her hand into his. There were so
many white scars across the darkness of his hand. His
fingers were calloused and rough, and she ached to feel
them once again, moving against her body. What would
it be like to love Dan? The thought was exhilarating,

scary and appealing to Jessica. She was surprised, because she'd thought she was emotionally dead. She thought Carl had destroyed whatever her heart could feel of desire, need and love. "Please," she begged, "share with me what you said."

Heat crept up into his face and he compressed his lips.

The silence hung between them. Did he dare? Dan knew that once she understood what it was, the utter intimacy of it, that it would reveal far too much of how he really felt about her. Jessica knew Navajo ways. She understood that certain sayings, certain words, such as his endearment for her, were never said unless meant from one's heart.

Yes, she had accepted his sordid, drunken history, but so what? She might see him as the spitting image of her father. Maybe Jessica would never get beyond seeing the overlay of Kelly on him, would never accept him for who he was—a man who was falling helplessly in love with her. Dan wanted to say all of this, but he was afraid to. Right now, he felt raw inside from revealing his dark past. He could see the fragility written across Jessica's sweet face, too.

"I had no right to call you what I did," he repeated. "I'm afraid of what you'll do if I share it with you right now, Jessica. We're both hurting...."

She took a deep breath and straightened her shoulders slightly. "I know we're raw, Dan. Maybe we needed to share our pasts with one another for whatever reason. I'm not sorry we did. Are you?"

He shook his head. "No...."

"And your kiss...?"

He snapped a look at her. "That was a mistake...a stupid reaction on my part, Jessica. I had no right, no—"

"Hush," she whispered, placing her fingertips across his strong mouth. "Don't apologize for that, too," she said, a partial smile on her lips. "I liked it, Dan. And since we're telling the truth here, I think I should share with you how much I liked it...."

He took her fingers in his hand, kissed the center of her soft palm and felt a fine tremble go through her. He couldn't believe what he was hearing. Yet as he ruthlessly searched the depths of her glorious eyes, he saw no lies in them. Only a shining warmth that enveloped him like sunshine on a bitterly cold winter day.

"I never thought," Jessica said in a choking voice, "that I would *ever* want a man to kiss me again. Carl, well, he didn't care what I wanted. Ever. He made me hate his kiss. And soon, I hated him. I guess, in the end, I hated all men because of him. Moyra told me that with time, I'd be able to separate Carl from the rest of the men in my life, but I didn't believe her." Jessica slid her hand against Dan's cheek and held his widening gaze.

"When I came here and I met you, something happened, Dan. I still don't know what it is, or pretend to understand it all—yet. I just know that with you, I feel safe—and good. I can feel again. You know, real feelings. Before now, I thought Carl had killed my heart, beaten my spirit. The only time I felt good, felt alive and happy, was when I was working with my orchid girls. My heart would open and I would feel such joy, such pure love from them surrounding me. I would love them back in my own, wounded way, I suppose.

"With you," Jessica continued, giving him a shy look, "I began to experience feelings I'd never felt before in my life. I'd never felt them toward Carl. And all you had to do was be with me. It's kind of wonderful—but kind of scary, too."

Capturing her hand, Dan kissed the back of it gently and said, "You're like that stallion out there in many ways. He's coming around because I'm gentle with him. I use a gentle touch and voice. I would never do anything to hurt him or make him want to distrust me." He smiled a little. "Although he watches me like a hawk, I give him no reason to think I'm like the other men who he's grown to hate and be wary of."

"We're a lot alike, Gan and I," Jessica agreed painfully. "Now you're able to put a saddle on him and ride him. I find that amazing, but in another way, I don't."

"Why?" Dan absorbed the softness of her skin as he moved his thumb across her palm. Touching Jessica was like feeling the sun shining down into his dark, scarred heart. She gave him hope, and so much more....

"It tells me about your quality as a person, what you bring to the situation, Dan. That stallion out there is smarter than most human beings. He's got a wild, innate intelligence, a survival drive. He knows who he can really trust and who he can't." She reached over and pressed her hand, palm down, against the center of Dan's chest and felt the pounding beat of his heart. "No matter how much darkness you've been wrapped in, trapped within, Gan saw your purity, your heart's intentions. He *knows* you won't ever hurt him. You would never lay a finger on someone to hurt them. Even I know that."

"Then why doesn't that stud pick up the fact that I killed five men?"

"He knows the same thing I do," Jessica whispered unsteadily. "That you didn't do it out of enjoyment or pleasure. Gan instinctively knows that you, like him, have the ability to survive some awful storms in life. You're a survivor, as he is. As I am. He trusts you. So do I...."

Closing his eyes, Dan felt her move her hand from the center of his chest upward. His skin tightened deliciously beneath her light, hesitant exploration of his chest and shoulder. As her fingers curved around the back of his neck, an ache built in his lower body. He wanted her. Great Spirit help him, but he wanted all of her, from her bright, shining soul, to her wounded heart and beautiful physical body. And yet, his heart cautioned, Jessica was no different from Gan—badly brutalized and beaten by a man. Dan realized fully that he couldn't just sweep her off her feet, carry her to his bed and love her wildly, fully and with all the hunger he felt. She was still too emotionally wounded from her bad marriage to an abusive man. Dan knew that he had to move slowly, gain her trust and let her tell him when and if she was ready for him to love her.

His heart broke over that realization. Nothing bad should ever have happened to Jessica. She was an innocent victim in all of this. Completely innocent. She'd been a child scared into hiding deep within herself, and then to have a monster like Carl come and complete the damage to her spirit by destroying her femininity was almost too much for him to bear. But as Jessica explored him now with her sweet, almost shy, exquisite touch, he understood what she was doing. For some reason unknown to him, she was giving her trust to him, as that stallion had done. For him to reach out and respond in like manner would scare her away, too.

Opening his eyes, Dan held her luminous blue gaze. "Whatever we have," he rasped, "is good and clean and

pure, Jessica. You never have to be scared of me. You
can keep on trusting me. I won't take your trust and
twist it like Carl did. You're too beautiful…too pure of
heart, to do that to. No human should be disrespected.
No one." He slowly reached up for the hand she had
wrapped around his neck and eased it away. "Right now,
all I want to do is kiss you and return to you in some way
the feelings you're sharing with me, but I won't unless
you tell me you want me to."

A sweet hotness moved through Jessica as he took
her hand between his own. Dan was more than a stallion
tamer; he was taming a wounded, hurting woman—
herself. His gentleness was real. Still, it seemed incredible to her that any man could possess such sensitivity.
And yet, as she clung to Dan's dark gray eyes, she not
only heard his words, she felt them in every dark corner of her scarred spirit. Her lips parted and she shyly
leaned toward him.

"Yes," she whispered unsteadily, "kiss me. Again."
Closing her eyes, she felt his hands fall away from hers.
The seconds seemed so long as she waited to once again
feel his strong mouth upon hers. She no longer knew
what was happening between them or why. She no longer tried to sort it out, nor did she care to.

As Dan's lips covered hers, the warmth of his breath
cascaded down across her cheek. Sighing, she felt his
roughened hands move slowly upward, across her ex-
posed flesh, and a delicious prickle began within her.
The very motion of his hands massaging the tension
away lulled her into a euphoria she'd never felt before.
His mouth moved tenderly across hers, giving, not taking. She felt his power, but she also felt him monitor-
ing how much strength he put against her lips, too. His

beard was rough and sandpapery against her cheek as she turned her head to more fully press her lips to his. His fingers drifted to her shoulders, then traced the outline of her neck until finally, he gently captured her face between his hands. She felt no fear, only a deep ache throbbing between her legs, longing to have him completely, and in all ways.

With each gliding movement, he rocked her lips open a little more, tasted a little more deeply of her. Jessica sighed, realizing with amazement that she wanted to feel and taste him more deeply, too. For the first time, she felt bold, as if she could risk it all and explore this powerful man wrapped in darkness. Carl had always taken from her, hurt her. Now Dan was asking her to take however much of him she wanted. Pressing herself more surely against him until her breasts barely grazed his chest wall, she embraced his strong, corded neck and felt him tremble. But the sensation didn't frighten her, it excited her.

As she moved her lips in a soft, searching motion across his mouth, she felt desire pouring through her. Each time she kissed him, he returned the kiss with equal strength, but he never did anything more than that. Her hands drifted to his head and she removed his hat. She heard it drop to the floor as she lost herself in the sensation of running her fingers through his thick, short black hair. It was so soft and yet strong, like Dan. Moving her fingers downward, she felt his sculpted brow and then the wrinkles at the corners of his eyes. He trembled again and his hands moved to her face. As she slowly absorbed each line in his skin, each part of his face, he felt hers, too.

It was a delicious, pleasurable exploration, Jessica realized. There was safety here in Dan's arms. *And love,* her heart whispered. At first, she didn't catalog her feelings because she was too caught up in the sensation of Dan's breath against her cheek, the movement of his strong mouth against hers and the thudding beat of his heart against her breasts. Finally, she eased her mouth from his. As she did, she barely opened her eyes before she drowned once again in the burning grayness of his. They slowly drew apart, his hands steadying on her shoulders as she created more space between them. Her world spun out of control and she felt heady, almost dizzy, until Dan's hands tightened around her arms to support her.

Her lips felt lush and full and well kissed. She stared up at him and marveled at what she was feeling. "I..." she whispered. "I've never been kissed like that before in my life, Dan. It was so wonderful. You are wonderful...."

Chapter 9

The hot August sunlight was scorching the ranch and sucking out the very lifeblood from the drought-ridden land, Jessica noted with growing dismay. She had just finished filling orders for her flower essences when Kate stepped into the doorway of the greenhouse.

"Anything's better than that heat out there," Kate groused, taking off her cowboy hat and wiping the perspiration from her darkly tanned brow. "How are things going? We haven't seen each other in the past couple of days."

Kate joined Jessica as she sat on her workbench, the cobalt blue bottles labeled and set in groups on the table before her. Jessica looked up and smiled at her older sister as Kate placed a hand on her shoulder and said, "You've been looking awfully happy lately. What's going on?"

"Questions, questions, Katie," she said with a laugh. "You won't even let me answer the first one before you fire off one or two more." Placing the order sheets aside, she brushed back a few crinkly tendrils that had escaped from her ponytail as Kate sat down on the wooden crate next to her workbench.

"First, I'm fine. Secondly, there's lots of orders coming in and yes, I'm happy." She grinned. "Now are *you* happy?"

Kate reached for the plastic bottle of water Jessica always had on her bench and took a swig from it. She recapped it and set it between them. "You look happier than usual. And Dan has sure been changing, too," she hinted.

"How has he changed?"

Kate grinned belatedly. "Like he's walking on cloud nine. You know.... Sam and I have been wondering when things were going to gel between you two."

The serious expression on Kate's face was belied by the dancing sparkle in her eyes. Jessica relaxed. "Pretty obvious, huh?"

"A little...but then, when two people are in love, well, it sort of becomes obvious."

"It's not love," Jessica said quickly. "I like him an awful lot, Katie, but—love? No, I don't think so."

Her sister scrutinized her for a long moment without speaking. "It's Carl, isn't it? You're still scared of him finding you. And that's why you can't openly admit you love Dan?"

"No," Jessica said softly as she folded her hands in the lap of her dark pink skirt decorated with bright yellow marigolds, purple irises and pale pink tulips. "It's—I, well, I'm just wary, I guess, Kate. You know how Carl treated me. My stupid head gets in the way when Dan touches me. It triggers a lot of bad memories."

"Yeah." Kate sighed, reaching out and putting her work-worn hand across Jessica's. "I know that one." She squeezed her sister's clasped fingers. "It takes time, Jessica. You have to give yourself that leeway and don't expect miracles."

"Dan has been so patient with me." Jessica pulled her hands from Kate's and gestured with them. "His kisses are wonderful. I've never been kissed like he kisses me." Sighing, she whispered, "And when he touches me, I feel like I'm on fire and I'm so hungry for him...." She laughed, embarrassed by her admission.

With a crooked smile, Kate nodded. "Sam makes me feel the same way."

"I'm just, well, afraid, Katie, that's all. Dan knows it. He's patient with me. And..." She frowned. "And he's afraid you and Sam won't approve of his feelings toward me."

With a laugh, Kate stood up and stuffed her leather gloves into the belt at her waist. "Why not?"

"He's got this thing in his head that he's not good enough for me, Kate. That because he doesn't own land and have money in the bank, he's in a lower class than me. Isn't that stupid?"

With a shake of her head, Kate muttered, "Well, Dan sure as heck isn't getting rich working here. He's got this class thing hammered into his head from the res. There's a lot of Anglos who think they're better than the Navajo people, but that's pure bull. No, Sam and I consider Dan an equal, like you do. So don't worry about it." Her brow wrinkled as she looked around the lush greenhouse where so many of the orchids were in colorful bloom.

"If only this damn drought would just end. We've lost so many cattle by having to sell them off because we can't feed them. We've lost money." With a sigh, Kate placed her hand on Jessica's sagging shoulder. "Without your financial input, we'd be waiting for the banker to come down the road to foreclose on the ranch. Damn, I just wish this poverty cycle with the ranch would end."

"I pray for rain every day," Jessica said passionately. "I worry about these hot winds we're having. Lightning could strike one of the tinder-dry pastures and we'd have a ranch fire on our hands. So much could be destroyed."

"This is monsoon season," Kate griped, patting her sister's shoulder one more time, "but whoever heard of *dry* monsoons? Usually, we get four inches of rain in three months. Enough to sustain life around here for the following six months." Her mouth moved into a grim line. "All we have now are incredibly beautiful thunderheads that build around ten in the morning. And when the thunder and lightning start around three p.m., that's when Sam and I begin to worry about forest and range fires."

"Speaking of Sam," Jessica said, trying to dissolve the worried look from Kate's eyes, "have you two decided on *when* you're going to get married?"

She shook her head and settled the hat back on her dark hair. "We're working sixteen hours a day. Who has time to discuss the future? Every day we get up, Jessica, there's a hundred things that need to be done and we divide the list between us. By the time we fall into bed at night, we're so exhausted we can't talk." She pulled the gloves from her belt and jerked them back on her hands. "No, until we become more financially stable, I just don't feel we can take the time and energy to finalize wedding plans."

Sadly, Jessica nodded. "I understand. At least you have one another. Sam loves you so much."

"I know," Kate whispered, tears glimmering in her eyes. "I don't know what I did to deserve him, but Lord help me, I love him with every breath I take into this bruised, beaten body of mine."

"If things start turning for the better, maybe a marriage, say, in December? Rachel's coming home at that time," Jessica hinted.

Kate nodded. "Sam mentioned that time frame, too. We can sell some of the Herefords to meet our expenses. I'm all for it." She grinned and ruffled Jessica's bangs. "And you…when are you going to fess up to doing something more than 'liking' Dan? The guy has cow eyes for you every time he sees you."

"Cow eyes," Jessica protested with a giggle. "He does not!"

"That's what we called boys in junior high, remember? If they got a crush on some girl but never had the guts to go over and tell her because they were too scared?" Kate's smile broadened as she considered Jessica's blazing cheeks. "Sam says that since coming here, Dan has really straightened out. I told him it was your influence. He said it probably was, that Dan wanted to put the past behind him and make a more positive statement with his life. He's done that. He works just as hard as we do and he's getting a pittance of what he should be getting. But—" she winked at Jessica "—he's got something else here at the ranch that's giving him reason to work hard—you."

Touching her hot cheeks, Jessica avoided Kate's

laughter-filled eyes. "Oh, Katie, you're reading too much into it. Dan's never said he loved me."

"You said it to him?"

"Well, no… I don't know if I really am in love or not…."

"Silly girl," Kate chided as she walked toward the door, "what's the poor guy to do? If you don't say it, how can he? What's it going to take to get you to see the guy loves you more than life—an act of Congress? I hope your fear goes away soon, or Dan's gonna die of loneliness out there in the bunkhouse."

Squirming inwardly, Jessica watched her big sister open the door to the greenhouse. "Hey, I'm going to leave tomorrow morning and go up near the Rim in the north pasture to try and find some wildflowers to make some new flower essences with."

Kate turned, her gloved hand on the door. "You taking Pete, the packhorse, again? Last time you went out, you made something like ten new essences."

Jessica nodded and slid off the stool. "Yes, Dan's going to get my gelding and the packhorse ready for me tomorrow morning. I hope to scour the Rim itself and see if anything else is up there. I'm taking my wildflower identification books with me and my log and my camera. I'll be up there until about two p.m. I want to be down off the Rim before those lightning bolts start flying."

"Hmm, good idea." Kate patted the redwood frame of the door with her hand. "Okay. But I don't think you're going to find anything alive up on the Rim, especially wildflowers. It's been over a hundred degrees every day and the humidity is so low that the forest service says the pine trees up there are going to start dying off soon because of no rain. I don't know how a wildflower could be alive, much less blooming in those kinds of conditions."

Shrugging, Jessica couldn't disagree. "It's a scouting expedition, is all. I've been wanting to explore that area of the ranch, anyway."

"Probably to get into some cooler air," Kate teased, lifting her hand in a wave. "I'll see you then, tomorrow afternoon sometime? Is Dan going with you? He did last time."

"No, he's at a crucial point in Gan's training."

"Okay, but be careful. There's a lot of rattlers out this time of year."

"I hear you," Jessica said, and watched her sister disappear through the door.

"I wish I were going with you," Dan said as Jessica mounted her small gray Arabian gelding, Jake. Though Jessica wasn't the best of riders, Jake, who was over twenty, was steady and reliable. Dan gazed up into Jessica's face and saw the excitement in her eyes over the daylong adventure ahead of her. She had been working so hard at her business that Dan knew she needed this kind of mini-vacation from the greenhouse activities.

Jessica reached out and touched his gloved hand, which rested on her thigh. "I wish you were coming, too. Are you sure Gan isn't tractable enough to ride so you could?"

He shook his head. "No, Gan's been backing up on me, testing me. I can ride him in pastures and open areas, but when I try to get him into woods, he starts getting real skittish and hard to handle. He's not given his trust to me fully yet. Until he does, he's a danger to ride anywhere but on the flatlands of the ranch."

Jessica leaned down and quickly brushed his mouth

with a kiss, relishing the hot, returning passion of his lips against hers. He gripped her arm, holding her in place to give her a long, thorough goodbye kiss. Her heart pounding, Jessica found herself aching for him again, just as she did every time he kissed her or touched her. "I'll miss you," she said breathlessly, sitting up in the saddle.

"Three p.m. can't come too soon," he rasped, reluctantly releasing her. As he stood there looking up at her, sitting so proudly in the saddle, he wanted to love her so badly he could taste it. He wanted to do more than love Jessica physically. He wanted to speak the words. She wasn't ready for that, he knew, but it didn't help him. Swallowing, he stepped back and smiled up at her. Jessica didn't look like a cowboy, wearing a straw hat with silk flowers affixed to the wide brim. Her white, simple tank top, dark blue jeans and comfortable leather loafers completed the picture. Cowgirl she was not. And he loved her with a fierceness that defied description.

"Hey," Jessica called as she picked up the packhorse's soft cotton lead rope, "do you want to see a movie tonight in Sedona?"

"Sure."

She laughed softly. "Okay, let's make it a date!" Then she clapped her heels and Jake moved off at a steady, slow jog.

Dan watched her form grow small against the towering Rim country that was topped with pine trees thousands of feet above them. The sun was coming up over the canyon wall and he knew it was going to be another blisteringly hot day. He had to get the work done now, while it was still somewhat cool. From one p.m. to seven p.m., he worked indoors because the unrelenting, hundred-degree heat made it nearly impossible to stay outside.

Something bothered him, but he couldn't put a finger on it. Taking off his hat, he rubbed the back of his sunburned neck ruefully before settling the hat back into place. He had an uneasy, gnawing feeling in his gut. The last time he'd had this feeling was when he was dropped behind the lines in Iraq. Why now?

Unable to make heads or tails out of it, Dan moved in long, easy strides back to Gan's pasture to work with the stallion. Right now, he had to concentrate entirely on the stud or he could end up on the ground. That Arabian was smart. Too smart for his own good, Dan thought with a careless grin. But with patience and time, the stallion would reward him with his trust.

Looking over his shoulder one last time, he saw that Jessica had already disappeared behind the ranch buildings. Something niggled at him again. Frowning, he shrugged it off and went to work.

"Dan! Dan!"

Dan was pounding a shoe into place on one of Gan's hooves when he heard Kate's terrified voice. He saw her run into the barn.

"Whoa," he murmured in a low voice to the stallion. "Stand…"

The black Arabian's small ears twitched nervously as Kate came running down the aisle. Dan quickly finished putting the last nails in the shoe and allowed the stallion to stand on all four legs. Automatically, he put a soothing hand on the stud's arched neck. He could feel the sudden tension in him.

"What's wrong, Kate?" he asked as he removed the

thick leather blacksmith's apron from around his waist. He saw that Kate's eyes were wide with terror and his gut shrank as he walked down the aisle to meet her. Gan wasn't too trustful of other human beings yet, and he didn't want the horse starting to rear upward in the cross ties.

"Dan!" she cried, breathless. "Jake's back!"

He frowned as he watched her halt, her breathing harsh. "Jessica's back?" It was three p.m.—time she returned.

"No," Kate rasped, holding up her hand, trying to catch her breath. "Jake just came galloping into the yard. He's covered with sweat! Jessica wasn't on him!"

His eyes narrowed. "Jessica…"

"Yes." Kate leaned over, her hands on her thighs as she took in huge gulps of air. "I'm afraid, Dan. I've had a bad feeling since I woke up this morning. Something's happened to Jessica. Sam's in Flagstaff and I can't reach him. We've got to get out to find Jessica. She said she was going to the north pasture. I'm going to drive out there right now. Maybe Jake just spooked and took off. I don't know, but I'm worried."

So was Dan. Frowning, he hung the leather apron on a nail. "Jake isn't the type of gelding to spook or run off, Kate. He's ground trained." That meant that if anyone dropped the animal's reins, he would halt and not move a muscle until those reins were picked up by the rider once again. Terror began to flood Dan as he stood there, his brain racing with questions and possible answers. "What about Pete, the packhorse?"

"No sign of him."

"Well, even if Jake did startle and take off for some

unknown reason, Jessica could ride Pete back to the ranch."

Kate wiped her brow with trembling hands. "I've already thought of that, Dan. Oh, God, I'm afraid it's Carl."

Dan froze. *Carl.* How could he forget about the insanely jealous ex-husband of Jessica's? A steel hand suddenly gripped his heart, the pain excruciating. "No!" he rasped, his eyes narrowing to slits.

"I don't know for sure," Kate whispered brokenly. "Jessica's enough of a rider. She's not the type to get thrown off. I'm going to drive out there and see if I can locate her or Pete." She gulped, her eyes filled with fear. "Dan, if I can't find them, I *know* Carl has kidnapped her. Just like he threatened he would."

"That means we need to call the police. A search will have to be mounted," he rasped.

"Yes. Look, I'll drive out right now. It shouldn't take more than half an hour by truck at high speed. You stay here. I'll call you on the cell phone and let you know if I find her. In the meantime, if I don't find her, you're going to have to try and track her. You're the best tracker in the county. If Carl has kidnapped her, he's got some heavy forest to get through before he can get to 89A and then drive off with her."

"*If* he drives off with her."

Anguished, Kate looked away. "He said he'd kill her. Oh, Lord…"

Gripping Kate's arm, Dan propelled her down the aisle and out of the barn. "Get out to the north pasture as fast as you can. I'm going to saddle Gan and take a rifle, ammunition, food and a cell phone with me. If Jessica isn't out there, I'll call 911 and get the sheriff out here, then hightail it toward you. I'll tell the police your location and then meet you out there."

Kate nodded. "Gan's the only horse that has the stamina this is going to take. That Rim country is rough and dangerous, Dan. He's got nine lives."

"Yeah," he whispered, opening the door to the white pickup truck for Kate, "and he's going to need every single one of them." He saw the paleness on her face, the fear in her eyes. He felt the same. Giving her a pat on the arm, he said, "Remember, I'll have the other cell phone with me. Call me as soon as you know...."

Kate choked back a sob. "Y-yes. I'm so scared, Dan. I thought this was all over. I hope I'm wrong. Maybe I'm jumping to conclusions."

He was helpless to assuage her pain and worry. "Drive carefully out there," he cautioned. "Keep your eyes open, Kate. If Carl's half as dangerous as Jessica says he is, the man could have a rifle and could train his sights on you, too."

Grimly, Kate nodded. "I'll be in touch very soon...."

Dan had just finished saddling Gan, packing the leather sheath with the 30.06 rifle and his knife scabbard and strapping a heavy set of saddlebags in place with more ammunition, when Kate's call came. Grabbing the cell phone, Dan pressed the On button.

"Kate?" His heart was pounding in his chest. He could barely breathe as he waited to hear Kate's report.

"It's horrible, Dan!"

He gripped the phone hard. "What do you mean?"

"Pete's dead! The gelding's been shot through the head," Kate sobbed, trying to speak coherently. "Jessica's nowhere. All her stuff—her bowls, the water and logbook—

are scattered around the area. I see some signs of scuffling, but I'm not enough of a tracker to know what the hell it means. Oh, Dan, Carl's got her! Call the sheriff!"

Closing his eyes, his mind whirling, Dan whispered, "Get a hold of yourself, Kate. Tell me exactly where you're located."

"I'm at the most northern part of our pasture, at the gate that leads up the path to the Rim."

"Good. I'll call the sheriff. When's Sam due back?"

"Tonight," Kate cried, sniffling. "Everything is such a mess out here. There's paper that's been torn out of Jessica's sketchbook crumpled up all over the place. She'd never do that. She loved her drawings of plants. He'll kill her, Dan! I know he will! He's an insane bastard. Oh, Lord…"

"Kate, come back. Now. You have to be here when the sheriff arrives. I'm going to mount Gan. I'll take a shortcut to the north gate. Just tell the sheriff I'm tracking them from this end. I'll keep the cell phone in my saddlebags. I'll call you if I see anything, all right?"

"O-okay…" She replied with another sob.

Shutting off the cell phone, Dan carefully placed it in the left saddlebag. Gan, sensing his trepidation, pawed the aisle, snorting and moving his head up and down.

Stay calm, stay calm, Dan harshly ordered himself as he mounted the black stallion. But he couldn't. As he turned Gan out of the barn into the intense afternoon sunlight, he felt like crying. Jessica…sweet, innocent Jessica, had been kidnapped by a man who'd sworn to take her life. No! No! He clapped his heels to the flanks of the stallion and instantly Gan responded. The horse was not large, but he was built like a proverbial bull, heavily muscled in the hind quarters with a wide chest and a long slope to his shoulders, indicating larger than normal lung capacity.

As Dan rode the stallion away from the ranch buildings, he felt the powerful surge of the animal beneath him. What would Gan do in the Rim country? The stallion shied at everything. Gan could throw him, or worse, slam him into a tree to get rid of him. Dan's gloved hands tightened on the leather reins as he leaned low, the horse's black mane whipping into his sweaty face as they sped along the hard, dry road toward the north pasture. He was going to need every ounce of Gan's power, his heart and his spirit. He was going to ask everything of this horse, and he prayed that the stallion trusted him enough to give everything in return. Jessica's life was in the balance. He could feel it. He could taste it.

"You little bitch!"

Jessica shrieked as Carl reached out to grab her by the hair, all because she'd tripped and fallen over some black lava rock hidden by dried pine needles on the forest floor. She felt his hand thrust into her hair, his fingers curl and tighten. Her scalp radiated with pain as he hauled her upward. Hands bound behind her, she had no choice as Carl brought her up hard against him. Staggering to catch her balance, Jessica shut her eyes. She expected him to slap her. Instead, Carl shoved her ahead of him again.

"Get moving faster!" he snarled, poking the rifle barrel into her back. "We've got to be at 89A before sundown. And if we aren't—" he grinned "—I'll shoot you anyway."

She gasped for breath. She had been pushed into a jog repeatedly for the last two hours. With her hands bound, she often lost her balance on the slippery, dry pine needles. Her knees were skinned and her joints ached. But that was nothing compared to the unadulterated terror she felt in her heart. Carl had found her. He intended to kill her. It was that simple. That terrifyingly simple.

Chapter 10

By six p.m. Dan was still moving the stallion along at a brisk walk, following the trail barely visible in the pine needles up on the Rim. Three hours had seemed like a lifetime. He'd called in his findings to the sheriff. Overhead, he could hear a helicopter hovering around the general area where he was tracking.

The prints he saw were of two people. A number of times, pine needles were scattered helter-skelter. He was sure Jessica had either fallen or been pushed down on the ground. His mind refused to contemplate why she would be shoved down on the dry, hard forest floor.

Gan was snorting and wringing with sweat, his ebony skin reflecting every muscle movement. Luckily, the stallion had expended a great amount of energy on his heroic climb up the Rim so that by the time they got on top of the three-thousand-foot crest, he didn't have much energy left to be shying at every pine tree they passed.

All of Dan's old military training had come back in startling fashion. He felt as if the forest had eyes—that every dark apparition and shadow was potentially Carl Roman. He didn't know what Jessica's ex-husband looked like. She never spoke of him except when necessary. She was trying to put him and their terrible relationship behind her. Dan couldn't blame her, but right now, he wished he knew what the man looked like. He could tell a lot by looking at a person's face. There was no doubt Carl could kill Jessica—and probably would try. But was the man good at hiding in a forest? Was he a true hunter in that sense? Or only a crazed, insanely jealous man who would make mistakes out here—enough for Dan to continue to track him?

Or maybe Carl knew how to throw a tracker off a trail. Was he that good? Dan was unsure. All he could do was lean over the stallion and follow the wisps of evidence in the disturbed pine needles. The sun's rays were long now. Sunset wasn't until around eight p.m., and then Dan would have just enough light until nine p.m., when it grew totally dark. He had a flashlight and he would use it to follow the trail if necessary. But he also knew he would be a target with that light on. It was a risk he was willing to take.

His mind went back to the dead packhorse. Because of his Recon background, Dan could see that Carl had used a high-powered rifle to shoot the innocent horse in one clean shot. Carl knew how to use the rifle, there was no question. Mouth compressed, Dan halted the stallion, took the canteen from the side of the saddle and drank a little water. Luckily, he knew this country well. He'd chased his fair share of cattle that had broken through the barbed wire fence—sometimes chased them for days at a time. Carl was heading due west, probably trying to intercept 89A. What Carl didn't know was that the sheriff was patrolling that area, too.

The cell phone rang. Dan retrieved it from the saddlebag.

"Dan? It's Sam."

"Yeah, I hear you, but you're breaking up a lot." Dan knew the cell phone wouldn't work well as he rode more deeply into the forest. "What's up?"

"The sheriff found a Ford camper with Canadian license plates parked on the berm along 89A. They broke into it and found the registration for the truck—in Carl Roman's name. It's him. And he's got Jessica."

Mouth flattening, Dan glared ahead at the murky depths of the dry pine forest. "Yes…"

"The helicopter is up and searching. They haven't seen anything yet, but that forest is thick."

"They'll be lucky to spot anything," he growled as he continued to look around. Sweat trickled down his temples.

"Have you found anything?"

"Just two sets of tracks. They're heading due west."

"Toward the highway?"

"Yes."

"Well, that bastard will have a real surprise waiting for him. They've called in the Yavapai SWAT team. They'll be in position in an hour near the camper if Carl manages to evade you and make it that far with Jessica. The sheriff said that if they get a clear shot of Roman, they're taking him down. No questions asked. No negotiations. They got the prison info on this guy and it's not pretty. He murdered a man in cold blood."

A chill ran through Dan. "I understand."

"No, you don't," Sam said harshly. "That means if you find them, Dan, you're to take Carl out if you can. You were a sharpshooter in the Recons. If you find him, take your time, target him and blow him away. He won't let Jessica live. The sheriff thinks, based upon Roman's profile, that he'll more than likely try to rape her first and then kill her. They've got the hospital and police reports from Vancouver. I've seen them. Believe me, this bastard is crazy and he'll kill Jessica."

"Rape?" The word almost strangled him.

"Spousal rape. It's on Roman's rap sheet from the police. Jessica charged him with it after he put her into the hospital and into a coma."

Dan shut his eyes tightly, tasting even more terror. "I—understand."

"I'm going to be riding with the sheriff along 89A. They'll be patrolling it from Flag down to our ranch. I'll be in touch. Just be careful."

"Yeah…"

Taking a ragged breath, Dan put the cell phone back in the saddlebags. Rape. Jessica had been raped repeatedly by the son of a bitch. No wonder she was afraid of *him*. Dan tasted bile in his mouth and he wanted to vomit. Closing his fist over the saddle horn, he tried to get a hold on his unraveling emotions. Jessica had never talked about rape. Oh, she'd skirt around it when pressed, but he'd had no idea. None… Wiping his face with the back of his hand, he grimly swung Gan into a fast walk. Now more than ever he had to find her, before it was too late.

His heart wouldn't stop pounding. His emotions whipsawed. He'd have to kill a man—again. In cold blood.

So much of him rebelled at the idea, and yet another part of him *wanted* to kill Carl Roman for what he'd done to Jessica. Guilt rubbed Dan raw, but his cold rage toward the man pushed him onward. Carl Roman was less than animal. Animals never killed except to eat, to survive. Roman killed because he enjoyed it. He didn't have to kill the packhorse, but he had.

The fact that Carl savored killing scared Dan more than anything. Roman had no feelings. He was a dead man walking. And he had Jessica. How much Dan loved her! Wiping his mouth, he stared hard at the tracks in front of them. Why hadn't he *told* her that? Why? Maybe it would have given her hope, a fighting spirit to try and escape Carl. A serrating loneliness cut through Dan— along with terror for Jessica. He couldn't begin to imagine how she was feeling. Pushing Gan faster, he urged the stallion into a slow jog. The prints on the forest floor were fairly obvious now and he had to try and catch up with their makers.

Up ahead, he knew the Rim began to drop down to the canyon floor three thousand feet below, where Oak Creek wound through the sharp, pinnacled red sandstone, the black lava spires. After passing through there, Carl would have to climb up the other side, another two-thousand-foot incline, to finally reach the highway where his truck was parked. Now was the time to push the stallion. Once they got off the Rim and down among the dangerous, sharp rocks, Dan would have to be very careful or risk his and his horse's life.

"Sit down!" Carl snarled at Jessica.

She collapsed onto the pine needles. Gasping for breath, her mouth dry, she sobbed as Carl strode around her. She winced when his leg brushed against her arm as he passed. She had to *think!* She had to stop panicking. Carl shrugged out of his large backpack and dropped it to the ground, digging in it for a bottle of water.

Jessica lifted her head. Her ex-husband was a large man, densely boned and heavily muscled. He was nearly six foot three and weighed over two hundred pounds. There wasn't an inch of fat on him. He was athletic and powerful. And dangerous. The rifle he'd used to kill Pete stood leaning against the pine tree next to where he was crouched, drinking water to slake his thirst. His red hair was short and plastered wetly against his large skull. Jessica shuddered. If anything, Carl was stronger and more intimidating and dangerous than she'd ever seen him.

How could she escape? He'd tied her wrists tightly with cord behind her back. Looking around, she knew they were heading off the Rim, down to the canyon floor and Oak Creek, though she couldn't see it below. The dusky shadows were deep. Threatening.

And Dan? *Oh, Dan!* Shutting her eyes, Jessica drew up her knees and rested her brow against them. Why hadn't she admitted her love to him? If he knew she was gone, he'd know Carl had her. What was Dan doing? Anguished, Jessica wondered if he was searching for her, though she knew rescue was out of the question. Carl had hunted all his life in the mountains near Calgary where he'd grown up, and was quite resourceful in the woods. Several times he'd gone out of his way to create sets of tracks to throw off anyone who dared to follow them. He kept his rifle—one with a high-powered scope on it for long-range shots—locked and loaded. His green eyes were slits as he glanced up from drinking the water.

Jessica quickly looked away. The icy glitter in his eyes

made her nauseous. She saw what lay in their depths. She knew Carl too well, as if she were still attached psychically with an umbilical cord to his sick, twisted mind. The helicopter overhead told her that someone was looking for them, so that gave her hope. Every time the chopper flew over at treetop level, Carl would haul her against him under a tree until it left. She knew a helicopter had little chance of locating them. Still, it gave her hope, and she desperately needed some to cling to now.

Something told her Dan was following them. Was it her active imagination? Or some gut instinct? Jessica couldn't be sure because she was so scared.

"Get up!" Roman snarled as he jammed the water bottle back into the pack.

Jessica scrambled awkwardly to her feet. "Can't you untie my hands? We're going down into a canyon, Carl. The rocks are sharp. If I slip, I could hurt myself."

He grinned savagely and hoisted the heavy pack back on his thick shoulders. "Pity. No, your hands are staying tied, little girl." He gestured sharply. "Move ahead. Down that way. We'll follow this deer trail into the canyon. They know the easiest ways to get to the water."

Jessica was sorry she was wearing flat loafers with no tread on the bottom. The brown pine needles were like a slippery carpet beneath her feet, which was why she'd fallen so many times earlier. Carl, on the other hand, had leather hiking boots with heavy treads. He wore army camouflage gear and seemed almost to blend into the dusky shadows of the forest.

Trying to concentrate on the thin trail left by deer that traversed this area every day at dawn and dusk to go get water, Jessica tried to steady herself as they began to go down the incline. What was Carl going to do? He hadn't said much. All along, he'd pushed her into a trot or a fast walk, obviously trying to get off the Rim as quickly as possible. He had to have a vehicle stashed along 89A. And then what? Jessica knew he wouldn't try and take her back across the Canadian border. No, he wouldn't even attempt it.

She knew what he'd do: he'd get her to the vehicle, rape her and then shoot her afterward, dumping her body somewhere inaccessible. She remembered what he'd done to the man he'd killed in cold blood—he'd stalked him for weeks, plotted and planned and then, at the right moment, kidnapped him. The police had found forensic evidence in the back of a Ford van where the victim had been tortured and then shot.

They'd found the poor man's body fifty miles away, thrown into a ditch and covered with leaves and branches. Only by luck had another hunter, out during deer season, seen Carl dump the body and cover it up. Otherwise Carl would never have been discovered for the cold-blooded murderer he was.

Dan! As her heart cried out for him, Jessica slipped and skidded, then caught herself. The lava rocks poking up through the brown needles were long, razor sharp and could kill her if she struck her head against one. Breathing hard, her mouth parched, she carefully placed each foot as she descended the long, steep slope. Dusk was coming, the shadows growing deeper and darker. Somewhere in her head, she knew this was her dark night of the soul. Would she live to see the sun rise again? Suddenly, life became even more precious than before.

Jessica desperately wanted to live. She wanted to tell Dan she loved him! She wanted a life where she could marry him, carry the children made out of love they shared, have that family she'd always dreamed of. *Oh, Dan, where are you? Where are you?* she silently cried. Part of her knew it was foolish, but still Jessica prayed that Dan would be on their trail, would find them, would save her. *If only...if only....*

Dan knelt down on a promontory of black lava at dusk, the rifle stock tight against his cheek to steady it. Suddenly, through the rifle's scope, he spotted a big, red-haired man with a huge, awkward backpack working his way down into the canyon. Ahead of him—Dan's heart thudded hard—was Jessica! Yes, he saw her! She was alive! Alive! Worriedly, he gripped the rifle tighter. He could barely see her; he only caught glimpses of her now and then, as she slipped and slid down the steep canyon wall. Her hands were tied behind her, and he could make out a rust-colored patch at each elbow. It had to be blood. She must have fallen a number of times.

Rage tunneled through him as he swung the rifle site back to Carl Roman. It was almost dark. The grayness of the dusk mingled with the dark blue of Roman's pack, and the camouflage clothes he wore made him almost invisible now. It was impossible to get a good, clean shot. Dan couldn't risk it. He knew if he only wounded him, Roman would turn on Jessica and murder her on the spot. Lowering the rifle, the pain in his heart tripling, Dan pulled out the cell phone. Punching in the numbers, he heard nothing but static. Damn! Standing up, he slung the rifle across his shoulder and tried facing several different directions while he dialed again. Nothing. He was too deep in the forest and too low into the canyon for the signal to get out and connect with another phone.

He was alone. Grimly, he put the cell phone away

and mounted Gan. The stallion was restive. He hadn't had water to drink all afternoon and had to be thirsty. Dan's mind spun with plans and possibilities. Turning the stallion away from an outcrop of lava, Dan moved him down a well-used elk path, a shortcut to the creek below. Could he get down before Carl did? Would he have time enough to set up a shot that would kill the murdering bastard and save Jessica's life?

Dan wasn't sure. The stallion grunted, throwing out both front feet and sinking down on his haunches as they started the dangerous descent toward the creek. Halfway down the slope, the grayness began to turn to blackness. Dan held his breath, his legs clamped like steel around the stud's barrel as they slipped and slid, trying desperately to avoid the larger boulders and outcroppings that could rip into flesh and shatter bone.

Finally, they reached the creek. Dan dismounted and allowed the stallion to thrust his muzzle deeply into the icy cold water. The snowmelt off Humphreys Peak, which rose above the city of Flagstaff, helped to fill this creek. In some places it was over a man's head, while in others it was shallow enough to cross. Dan knew they were about half a mile downstream from where Roman would come off the canyon wall with Jessica.

It was completely dark now and he realized only belatedly that his rifle didn't have infrared. There was no way he could pick Carl out in the darkness. No, he'd have to stalk him, jump him and pray to the Great Spirit that he could subdue him before Roman killed him first. Moving to the sated stallion, which stood eagerly eating at the lush grass along the bank, Dan took out a pair of sheepskin-lined hobbles and put them on the horse's front legs. The gurgle of the stream sounded so happy and soothing compared to the violence he would be heading toward in a few minutes.

He tried the cell phone again, but to no avail. In a two-thousand-foot-deep canyon, no signal was going to get in or out. The helicopter that had been flying overhead from time to time was gone now, too, probably heading to Flag. Unless the aircraft had nighttime capability, such as infrared, more than likely it wouldn't return to the area to search until dawn.

Dan took off the stallion's bridle and hung it from the saddle horn. Patting the Arabian affectionately, he knew the horse would remain at the creek eating and drinking. Hopefully, if everything went right, Gan would be their transportation up and out of here later, carrying them to 89A and safety.

The ifs were huge, Dan realized as he got rid of his cowboy boots, trading them for a pair of soft deerskin moccasins instead. There was no doubt Carl Roman was an expert hunter. Dan had been led off the main trail four different times by him. The fact that Roman wore camos and carried a high-powered rifle told Dan he'd hunted and knew what he was doing. Had Roman been in the Canadian military? As Dan stood up and picked up the rifle, he wished he'd asked Sam about that earlier.

Near the banks of Oak Creek, the grass was tender and the earth soft under his silent moccasins. Dan hurried upstream toward where Roman would emerge off the cliff wall. Maybe they had already made the descent. He wasn't sure. What he hoped to do was find a good place to hide, and then jump Roman, surprise him.

How was Jessica? Sweat trickled down Dan's face as he loped along. Did she know they were hunting for her? Trying to save her? She must. She had to. His love for her vied with his building terror. All the old memories of the war—the stealth, the stalking, the terror, the odor of blood and the grunt of men dying—enveloped Dan. He shook his head savagely. Somehow he had to get clear of all of that and concentrate on the here and now.

For a moment, he crouched near the creek, just listening. Picking up the normal night sounds of crickets chirping and frogs croaking, he waited. Suddenly he thought he heard a woman's cry. Jessica? He almost stood, but harshly ordered himself to remain still.

There! He heard it again. It *was* Jessica! She was screaming. He couldn't hear the words. He only knew it was her voice careening off the walls of the canyon in an eerie echo. It was filled with anger—an emotion he'd not heard from Jessica before.

Rising, he hurried along the creek, being careful where he planted his feet. His night vision was good, and with the slice of moon in the sky, he could make out branches and rocks along the bank just well enough to avoid them. Leaping over a fallen log, he gripped the rifle hard. He heard Carl's voice then and froze. It had a deep, threatening tone.

He had to hurry! Dan's heart began to pound, rattling in his chest. He controlled his breathing—it was important not to be heard. Crouching down, he dropped his cowboy hat aside. He knew the color of his skin would help him hide in the shadows, and he wore a dark blue shirt and dark blue jeans. He looked like darkness itself. Roman wouldn't see him coming—until it was too late.

Jessica screamed again. Carl laughed as he lunged for her. She rolled along the bank of the creek, over and over, trying to avoid him. He had shoved her on her back as she'd knelt at the stream, thirstily sucking up badly needed water.

The moonlight was just bright enough for her to see that crazed, wild look in his eyes that meant he intended to rape her—once again. That look filled her with such terror that as he shoved her down on the ground again, Jessica lashed out in self-defense with both her feet. Her shoe caught him along the jaw and, thrown off balance, he roared like a wounded bull.

Gasping for breath, Jessica scrambled to her feet as she watched Carl fall backward. She had to run! Where? No matter where she went, she knew Carl would get her. And he'd tear the clothes off her body, like he had before, and he'd hurt her and make her scream all over again. No! No, she wasn't going to be a victim this time! She'd fight to her death!

Turning, she leaped into the stream. Oak Creek was barely knee-deep at this point, but the rocks were algae covered and slippery. She lunged forward, all the time tugging at her numbed wrists. She had to get free! Her sweat and blood had been loosening the rawhide cords all along. Water splashed around her now as she waded forward. The creek was about a hundred feet wide and the bank was covered with thick brush on the other side. If only…

"You bitch!" Carl roared, scrambling to his feet. "You're dead!"

Crying out, Jessica jerked her head around. She saw Carl leap into the water after her, his face icy with fury. There! She jerked one hand from its bonds. Free! She was free! Leaping from the water, her feet slipping, Jessica crashed up the far bank. Her hands closed over a pine branch the size of her arm. It would do.

She heard Carl's heavy breathing coming up behind her. Thrusting herself onto her feet, Jessica clenched her teeth. She grabbed the limb with both hands and as she whirled to meet her attacker, swung it as hard as she could.

Roman obviously wasn't prepared for her to fight back, and belatedly threw up his arm to protect himself. *Too late!* The wood smashed into the side of his face, catching his hard, square jaw. Her arms vibrated with the impact and her fingers were ripped opened by splinters as the solid connection was made.

With a groan, Carl staggered backward, his hands flying to his bloody, torn face. Jessica blinked uncertainly. Was she seeing things? There was movement, like a dark shadow, back along the creek. Who? What? She froze, unsure, her legs turning to jelly. Carl was roaring and cursing and flailing around in the middle of the creek.

Dan! A cry almost ripped from Jessica's lips as she saw him materialize out of the darkness. Unable to move, she watched in horrified silence as he dropped the rifle he was carrying and pulled out a knife from the scabbard at his side. His face was carved from darkness and light, his eyes narrowed slits of glittering fury as he lunged into the stream after Carl.

Her heart contracted in terror as Dan made two huge leaps. In seconds, he was behind the unsuspecting Carl. She watched in utter fascination and horror as Dan lunged out with one leg and knocked him completely off his feet. Roman grunted hard, falling with a loud splash. Water flew up in sheets all around them. Dan made one, two, three hard jabs with his fist against Carl's face. In moments, her captor was unconscious, his head sinking below the water.

Jessica trembled, watching as Dan hauled Roman to the other side of the creek, quickly tying his hands and then his feet. Was she dreaming this? Was it all her imagination? No!

"Dan!" Her cry echoed through the canyon as she waded jerkily across the creek toward him.

Throwing the knife aside, Dan whirled at the sound of Jessica's cry. He saw her white face, her eyes huge with horror, her arms outstretched as she slogged against the current toward him. Wordlessly, he jumped into the water. In four strides he was at her side, his arms wrapping tightly around her.

"Jessica...." he rasped brokenly, pulling her hard against him, holding her tightly.

Uttering his name, Jessica felt her knees giving way. Her arms numb, she fell against him, feeling the dampness of his shirt against her cheek.

"It's all right, all right," Dan breathed savagely, whispering the words against her tangled, dirty hair. "You're safe, Jessica, safe. I love you... I need you...you almost died...." He squeezed his eyes shut and held her fiercely. He could feel the rapid thud of her heart against his pounding one. Her body felt limp against his and he realized that she'd fainted. Was she wounded? Alarmed, Dan picked her up in his arms. Jessica was like a rag doll, her head lolling against his shoulder, her face pressed to his chest as he hurriedly got her out of the stream and onto dry land.

Raising his head, he whistled sharply, twice. He knew Gan would hear the whistle. He had trained the stallion to come to him. Even though the horse had hobbles on, Dan knew Gan would easily make the trip upstream in about fifteen minutes.

"Jessica? Jessica?" he rasped as he gently laid her down on the green slope of the bank. "*Shi shaa,* can you hear me?" He rapidly scanned her arms, legs and head with his hands. Her flesh felt cold. Shakily, he held his fingers against the carotid artery at the base of her neck. She had a strong, rapid pulse. Besides the blood on both her elbows, he detected a scratch along her brow, but that was all.

Gently, he began to move his hands slowly up and down her arms as he straddled her, calling her name. Shortly, he saw her thick lashes begin to flutter and he breathed a sigh of relief. Taking her into his arms, Dan sat down and cuddled Jessica against him to keep her warm. She was in shock, her flesh cool and damp from being in the water.

Jessica felt the thud of Dan's heart against hers, felt the warm moistness of his breath against her face, the soft kisses he was pressing against her brow and cheek. This was real. She wasn't dead or imagining this. Just the way Dan held her in that gentle, cradling embrace made her sob.

"You're safe, safe," he crooned, running his fingers through her mussed blond hair. "It's okay, Jessica. It's all over. Just lie against me. I'll hold you for as long as you want. We're going home, *shi shaa.* Home. I love you…. I'll always love you…."

Chapter 11

"Don't leave me, Dan...." Jessica whispered. Sam and Kate had just brought her home from the Flagstaff hospital where she'd been taken. Luckily, the Yavapai SWAT team had contacted the Sedona Fire Department, and the medical team had met Dan and Jessica along the highway, when they crested the canyon rim on Gan. Jim Cunningham was the EMT who'd cared for her. With a gentle, quiet voice, he had talked to her soothingly as he treated her many scratches and cuts. He'd allowed Dan to ride in the back of the ambulance with her as she sat on the gurney, still in mild shock. Once at the hospital, a doctor had examined her thoroughly and said she could go home and rest.

She saw Dan hesitate at the door. It was dawn now; a bleak grayness was visible on the western horizon outside her window. Sam and Kate had left her once she was settled in, and had gone back to their ranching duties, despite how tired they were. Absolute exhaustion played on Dan's features as well. "Don't go," she said pleadingly. "I—I don't want to be alone right now. Will you hold me? I think I can sleep if you hold me for just a little while…."

Dan's heart was torn at her tearful plea. "Sure," he said, slowly turning around and coming back into the gloom of her bedroom. The nightmare they'd lived through had chiseled away his normal sense of decorum, of what was right and wrong. Now, all he wanted, needed, was Jessica—to remain in physical contact with her. Though her hair had been washed at the hospital, he saw that the strands needed to be brushed away from her pale features. Picking up the brush lying on the dresser, he came over and sat down, facing her.

"First things first. They should have at least combed your hair up there."

The fleeting touch of his hand against her jaw made Jessica close her eyes. A ragged sigh tore from her lips as Dan gently moved the brush through her tangled, damp hair. Just his touch stopped the pain and fear she was still feeling. With each gentle stroke of the brush, her raw state began to dissolve. Dan was close, and he was caring for her. He loved her. Hadn't she heard him say that? Jessica lifted her lashes and drank in the strong, tired planes of his face.

"You saved my life."

The corner of his mouth twisted. "I think you saved your own. When I saw you pick up that branch and use it like a club against Roman, I was surprised."

An unexpected giggle came from her lips, sounding slightly hysterical. "You were surprised? I was surprised! I'd never done anything to defend myself against him. Ever."

Grimly, Dan brushed her hair until it shone like fine, molten gold. "Then it was about time, Jessica. You empowered yourself in that moment. For a little thing, you can sure heft one hell of a wallop when you want to." A slight, tired smile pulled at his mouth as he dropped his gaze and held her tired, luminous one. Putting the brush on the bed stand, Dan framed her face with his hands. His smile fled as he searched her features. Jessica had many scratches here and there, all from falling so many times.

"Did you hear me out there as I carried you out of the stream?" he said finally.

His hands were so warm, so steadying. Jessica felt like the desert after a turbulent thunderstorm had ravaged it for hours. "I hope I did," she whispered fervently, clinging to his dark gray gaze. "Oh, I hope I did, Dan. I wasn't making it up, was I?"

Leaning over, he met her soft, parting lips with his own. Her breath was moist and warm against his cheek and her hands fell automatically against his upper arms, her fingers digging into his muscles as he caressed her mouth. "I said I loved you," he whispered hoarsely. "I'll always love you even if you never love me, *shi shaa....*" As he pressed his mouth more surely against hers, he tasted the warmth of her salty tears trickling down her cheeks. It was a taste of life, of her, of her strong, courageous heart inside that small body she lived within. A body he wanted to love and hold sacred forever.

Easing away, Dan felt hot tears gathering in his own eyes as he gazed down at her glistening ones. There was such adoring, fierce light in Jessica's eyes, but he didn't trust what he saw there.

"The one thing," she began, sliding her fingers up across his shoulders, "The one thing I regretted after Carl kidnapped me was that I'd never told you how I really felt about you, Dan." Sniffing, she continued, "I was afraid. So afraid. I was like Gan. Me and that stallion are a lot alike, I think...."

Dan smiled tenderly. "You two are like twins in some ways," he agreed. He released her and reached for the box of tissues on the bed stand, pulling a few free and handing them to her. She blew her nose several times and then blotted her eyes. As she sat there in the gloom, his heart opened wide. Here was how he wanted to be with Jessica, sharing the richness of all their feelings with one another. It didn't matter if they were sad, happy, bad or good feelings, it was the simple, beautiful act of sharing them that was important to Dan.

"I recognize myself in Gan. The more you worked with the stallion—the *way* you worked with him, Dan—I found myself wishing you would be like that with me."

He cocked his head and trailed his hand across her smooth, shining hair. "Why didn't you share that with me? I would have." He shook his head and looked at the light spilling through the fragile lace curtains at the window. "I *wanted* to, Jessica. You don't know how many times I wanted to reach out and touch you, kiss you, tell you how beautiful you are to me, how you made a difference in my life, how you made me feel good inside once again...."

"I was scared," she said.

"I realized that after a while." Frowning, he picked up her hand and cradled it between his own. "And after seeing Roman, seeing what he'd done to the horse and what he might do to you, I understood very clearly why you were afraid. That man is a two-heart, like you told me earlier. I've rarely seen a human being like that, but as I looked through the scope of my rifle and I saw his face, I knew why you were afraid of all men." He pressed a soft kiss to the back of her hand. "Even of me."

Sniffing, Jessica took another tissue from the box. She wrapped her fingers more strongly around Dan's hand. "Even knowing the Yavapai SWAT team went down there and got him doesn't make me feel any safer. I know he's up in Flag, in jail under heavy guard, but I'm still scared to death, Dan."

"I know, I know...but listen to me." He gripped her hands and made her focus all her attention on him. "They'll deport him, take him back to Canada. He'll go on trial and this time, he'll be put away for life with no possibility of parole. That's what the captain of the SWAT team told me."

"I'll have to go back to Vancouver to testify," Jessica said with a shudder.

"This time," Dan said grimly, "you won't have to go alone. I'll be there, Jessica. At your side. I'll protect you because I love you."

The words fell softly, soothing her emotional turmoil. "I never told you, did I?" she whispered, reaching up, her fingertips softly brushing his cheek. She felt the prickle of beard beneath her hand. The darkness of his beard made Dan look even more dangerous. "I guess I didn't realize just how much of a warrior you really were until today. I know better than anyone what it took to ride Gan into the Rim country. He could have refused. He could have bucked you off and tried to kill you. To know that you tracked me all that way…to have seen you come out of the darkness like that and jump Carl…" Jessica inhaled raggedly and shifted her gaze to the ceiling for a moment. "You're a man of surprising facets, Dan Black. I think I'm one of the few people who have ever witnessed you in action like that."

Jessica saw him avoid her eyes. He pressed her hands between his and she felt his warmth and care radiating out to her. "The reluctant warrior," she whispered. "I know how you said you'd never kill again—ever. Yet when I saw that knife in your hands and Carl starting to get up out of that stream, I knew that you'd do what you had to do."

Lifting his head, his eyes narrowing, Dan rasped, "Yes, I'd have killed him to save you. There wasn't any question in my heart in that moment. I didn't want to hurt anyone, but I wasn't going to let him hurt you, Jessica. Not *ever* again."

Whispering his name, Jessica leaned forward and wrapped her arms around Dan's shoulders, embracing him. She rested her head against his neck and jaw. "I—I know. As I crouched there, I watched you stalk him. I saw the look in your eyes, the way you moved toward him. There wasn't a doubt in my mind that only one of you would come out of that creek functional. I was so scared for you, Dan." Her voice wobbled dangerously and she tightened her arms around his neck. She felt Dan's hands move gently around her torso and draw her fully against his lean, hard frame.

"I knew all the pain, the horror you'd carried for years from the war, Dan. And to be there and see you set aside your own suffering, and possibly add to your nightmares and more pain to yourself to save me…well, it just blew me away. I couldn't believe you'd do that for me. It was then, as I struggled to get out of the water, that I realized you'd come after me because you loved me. It was the only thing that would make you set aside your own values."

Dan turned his head slightly and pressed a kiss against the warmth of Jessica's cheek. Easing away just enough to meet and hold her tear-filled gaze, he felt a self-deprecating smile tug at his mouth. Moving his hand across the crown of her head, he rasped, "Sometimes when you love someone, you do whatever has to be done, Jessica. This was one of those times. And believe me, I'm not sorry about any decisions I made, or what I did or would have done to keep you safe. In my heart, you are my woman. Even if I never told you so, you are. A man keeps his woman safe. He doesn't step back from that line in the sand when her life is in the balance."

It wasn't until today that Dan had come to realize the violence within him wasn't wrong; in every case, he'd acted out of a protective instinct—to defend himself and his team in the Gulf War. And to protect Jessica now. It would be one thing to enjoy killing, but he didn't. In a way, yesterday's event had helped him realize that not only was he a healer instead of a murderer, he was also a good person who was worthy and deserving of Jessica's love.

Looking deeply into his soft, dove gray eyes, Jessica felt the power of his words, the depth of his love for her in those priceless moments. "I don't know when I fell in love with you, darling, and it doesn't matter. What does matter is that I share how I feel with you now. I prayed out there that the Great Spirit would let me live, let me survive Carl, to tell you that."

"Well," Dan whispered, trailing a finger across the high slope of her flushed cheek, "you survived."

Closing her eyes, Jessica rested her head against his strong, broad shoulder. "And now I'm going to live, Dan. With you at my side."

The words sounded good to him and he embraced her tightly for a moment. "Maybe two wounded human beings with dark pasts can walk into the light together, hand in hand?" he teased her huskily.

Jessica moved her head slightly. "Love creates the light for us," she said, feeling safe, warm and so well loved by Dan. She saw the new sense of confidence in him, saw it in the glimmer of his eyes. Somehow this whole nightmarish event had made him realize what she already saw and knew of him—that he was a wonderful man who had many skills and talents to be proud of. No longer would he walk apologetically. Whatever he'd feared before was gone now. She knew love had a lot to do with it. He'd saved her life and that was the gift he'd given her. Life.

"You're tired, *shi shaa,*" he whispered, gently untangling her from himself. "You need to sleep." And he eased her back on the bed and drew up the blankets to her breasts, covering the pink cotton, lace-trimmed nightgown that she wore. He saw a soft smile play across Jessica's lips as her lashes drooped downward.

"Yes, I'm tired now, Dan. I can sleep because I've told you how I really feel...."

Getting up off the bed, he watched as Jessica quickly sank into the depths of sleep. Exhaustion shadowed her face, but as he stood there, he was aware of that inner strength that had kept her going, that had given her the courage to protect herself in those last few deadly moments.

Jessica's inner bravery had come out and she had, in reality, saved her own life. Dan was proud of her. He loved her fiercely. Lifting his head, he looked toward the dawn, the pinkness of the horizon heralding a new day. A better day. Because of his Navajo upbringing, he said a silent prayer to Father Sun. The east was the direction of new beginnings, of a new day. A new way of life.

As he quietly moved from the room, he left the door ajar. Right now, all he wanted was a hot shower to rid himself of the stink of fear, of sweat and terror. And then he'd come back to Jessica's house and sleep at her side, where she wanted him. Where he wanted to be....

"Isn't this a beautiful place?" Jessica asked as she leaned against Dan. Her arms moved gracefully around his shoulders and she gazed up at him, up at his strong mouth and those burning gray eyes. She felt his arms move firmly around her, capturing her and pressing her fully against him. It was late fall and the autumn leaves on the Rim had turned a multitude of colors. Jessica loved autumn, and here on the Donovan Ranch it was a spectacular time of year. Where they stood near Oak Creek, picnic basket and blanket at their feet, the reds, yellows and oranges of the cottonwoods and sycamores surrounded them like a beautiful chorus of joy.

He grinned and playfully pressed a quick kiss to her full, smiling mouth. "What I'm looking at pleases me the most." In the months since the kidnapping, Dan had reveled in the love that had poured forth from Jessica toward him. They had not made love to one another—yet. In many ways, he was glad to wait because he understood Jessica had to not only heal from her past abuse, but to work at trusting him completely, too. He wasn't Carl, but he was a man. And trust in men hadn't been high on Jessica's list—just as it hadn't been with Gan. In the ensuing months since the kidnapping incident, though, Jessica had worked to change her perceptions. More than anything, Dan knew she needed time. Just as that black stallion had needed time to learn to trust him, too.

The warm, woody smell of decaying leaves surrounded them as Jessica leaned fully against him. He loved her fiercely, ached to have her, but he was content in allowing her to explore him in ways that felt safe to her. Today her hair was shining, molten gold in the sunlight that danced down between the falling leaves.

"Shi shaa," he whispered as he stroked her hair. "My sunshine…."

"You," Jessica whispered, as she stood up on tiptoe and found his mouth, "are my life…." And he was, in every way.

Today was special, Jessica admitted to herself as she pressed her lips more fully against Dan's. Today, she knew, was the first day of her life with him. She'd awakened this morning knowing it, as surely as she breathed air in and out of her lungs.

Since the kidnapping, Dan had been incredibly gentle and understanding with her. Sam and Kate understood clearly that they'd fallen in love, and offered no comment when she asked Dan, a month after the kidnapping, to come and live in her house instead of staying out at the bunkhouse. Little by little, day by day, Jessica had discovered that living with Dan was like living life in the happiest of ways. Sure, they had their differences, but what two people in love didn't? Dan never allowed bad feelings to stay between them for long. He'd sit her down and they'd talk until they'd talked it out. So many times, Jessica discovered, it was misunderstandings, not anything else, upsetting her. How different it was living with Dan than with Carl!

As Jessica relished the rich splendor of Dan's lips against her own now, she surrendered completely to his hands, his mouth and his hard, strong body pressed fully against her. Over the months, he had shown her the positive way to live in a relationship. Because she had had such a bad relationship with Carl, she hadn't known what a good relationship consisted of. That was why, by living with Dan for so many months, Jessica knew she was ready to share the final gift with him. And she knew it would occur naturally, wonderfully, between them.

Dan never pressed her or made her feel she had to make love with him. No, not ever. He made it clear that she had to initiate, that she had to tell him how far he could go with her, and when to stop. Never once did Dan cross that line of discretion with her. She saw him struggle sometimes, and she felt guilty, but when he saw her reaction, he'd sit and talk it out with her to make her understand a hurt animal or human being couldn't be rushed or forced into giving something he or she didn't want to give.

But now his mouth was hot and wet and inviting. Jessica smiled to herself as she ran her fingers through his thick, black hair. Yes, today was the day. A day of loving Dan fully, completely. A day of freedom for them. And where else should they spend it but here beside Oak Creek, where her life had almost ended and then been reborn on that tragic night? It made symbolic sense to

Jessica. And fall was a time for allowing old things to die, to float away, only to be reborn the next spring. Yes, this was the moment....

Dan felt her tugging insistently at the closures on his dark red, long-sleeved shirt. He smiled beneath her lips.

"You in a hurry?"

Giggling, Jessica eased away from his mouth and looked up into his dancing gray eyes. "I guess I am." She proceeded to open his shirt fully, revealing his firm flesh beneath it, and spread her hands against the dark hair of his well-sprung chest. "Mmm, you feel so *good* to me, Dan Black. Today is special, you know."

He drowned in her turquoise gaze, absorbing her searching, exquisite touch. His flesh burned beneath the exploration of her cool, slender fingers and his heart began to pound with need of her. "Oh?"

She stilled her hands against his chest, absorbing the thudding sensation of his heart beneath her palms. "Yes," Jessica whispered more seriously. "I brought you out here for a reason...."

Dan eased his arms around her and held her, rocking her slightly from side to side. The gurgling creek, the soft, intermittent breeze that danced around them, all seemed playful and joyous to him. "Women *always* have reasons," he teased, laughing huskily as he watched her grin. His lower body began to ache, as it always did when Jessica touched him, kissed him and explored him. As badly as he wanted to consummate his relationship with her, he knew it had to be her call, her choice. He wanted her to come willingly, joyfully, to him. He wanted his woman looking forward to his embrace, to his kisses, his adoration of her in all ways. It was the only way.

"What web do you weave today, my spider woman?" he teased, grazing her flushed cheek with a fingertip. Her eyes were so beautiful to him, a haunting mirror of the depths of her priceless soul—a soul he was privileged to see, to share and love fiercely.

Easing the shirt off his shoulders, Jessica stepped back and began to undo the thick leather belt on his jeans. "It's time, darling." Fingers stilling, she lifted her chin and met his flaring gray eyes. "Love me, Dan," she quavered. "Love me fully. In all ways. I'm ready...."

Frowning, he gripped her hands as she tried to push his jeans off his narrow hips. "Are you sure?" Never had he wanted her more than in that moment. The wind played with her hair, which shone like gold and framed her flushed face and sparkling blue eyes. She was a woman of nature, a child to the tree nation and to the flower people. No one was closer to Mother Earth's heartbeat than Jessica, and he loved her for that connection because life flowed so powerfully through her all the time.

Jessica sobered and held his concerned gaze. "I've never been more sure, darling. I love you. I want to share my love with you." She removed his hands and began to slide his jeans downward.

Dan believed her. He saw the change in her eyes, saw a fierce light there, a hunger aimed only at him. Pushing off his boots, then his jeans, he nodded and moved her over to the blanket. Once he'd set the picnic basket aside, he eased her down on the soft, dark blue surface. "Remember," he rasped as she lay down next to him and he began to unbutton her pale green blouse, "you can stop me anytime, Jessica. Just say it or show me...." The blouse opened to reveal her silky camisole. His fingers ached to brush those small breasts beneath it. How would she react to his touch? Suddenly, he was afraid as never before. But he had to push beyond his own fears.

Sighing, Jessica closed her eyes. She took his hand and guided it to the side of her breast. "Touch me, just touch me, Dan. I ache for you. I ache so much...."

Her words fell heatedly over him. Her fingers were so white against his darker hand. He felt the soft, firm roundness of her breast. "You feel so good," he whispered as he leaned down and captured her mouth. "So good...."

The provocative movement of his hand against the swell of her breast, against her camisole and her silken bra, left Jessica wanting more. The sounds of the creek, happy and bubbling, the clatter of the drying leaves moved by the breeze, the far-off call of a blue jay, all blended together in a beautiful song for her. When he tore his mouth from hers, gently removing the soft fabric and settling his lips on the peak of her taut breast, she uttered a cry of absolute pleasure. Her fingers bunched and released on his strong, firm shoulders. A hot, jagged bolt of lightning coursed down through her as he caressed her nipple, suckling it gently. Her body became molten beneath his gentle, exploring touch. A haze of heat throbbed through her, robbing her of any thought processes.

As his lips moved to the other nipple, Jessica arched upward. He slowly removed the rest of her clothing, and when her hip touched his, she realized only belatedly that he was also naked. The movement of his hard, muscular body against her softer one was a mesmerizing experience for her. As his hand grazed her arched spine and he trailed a fiery path of kisses from her throbbing breasts downward, all she could do was gasp raggedly, longing for more of him. The fire between her thighs was hot and burning. She cried out for more of his touch, more of his delicious, dizzying exploration of her. Never had she been touched, kissed, caressed like this.

As she arched more deeply against him, her thighs automatically opened to allow him entrance into her sacred self. Each scorching touch of his lips against her rounded abdomen, moving slowly downward, was a new kind of torture for her. A wild, throbbing ache built and she rolled her head from side to side, frustrated and needing him so badly. As his lips trailed a path of fire to each of her taut thighs and he moved his tongue against her, a moan shattered through her. With each silken movement against her womanhood, she felt the pressure within her build. She reached out, begging him silently to enter her, to consummate their union so that the burning ache within her would be satiated.

Gasping, she felt him move his hand in a languid, caressing motion against that sacred, moist area between her thighs. Consumed in the flames of her need, Jessica lay helplessly in his arms, a prisoner of pleasure to his touches, to kisses that built the fire within her higher and higher, brighter and brighter. Her breath was ragged. Her heart was pounding. How badly she wanted him! She tried to speak, but it was impossible. Just as she sobbed out his name, she felt him move. Within moments, he had opened her thighs even more and she felt the power of his maleness against her, his hard masculine form blanketing her. Jessica barely opened her eyes, her hands coming to rest on his arms. She saw the tender, burning love in his eyes, the way his mouth was twisted in pain as well as pleasure. In that second, she realized he was aching just as much as she was. In the next second, she understood the fierceness of love between a man and a woman.

Without thinking, only responding to the innate knowledge of her body, Jessica lifted her hips upward to allow him entrance into her hot, moist depths. As he surged forward, he bracketed her head with his hands and captured her mouth in a swift, hungry kiss that tore the breath from her. The power of him within her, the rocking motion he established, the cradling of the fire, his hard body pressed surely, provocatively against her— all conspired to dissolve her last coherent senses. In that moment, with that delicious movement tunneling up through her, she understood the mating of moonlight with fierce, hot sunlight that occurs between a woman and a man.

There was such joy, such dizzying elation as he moved within her, taught her the ancient rhythm, that she was amazed by the utter, wild freedom it invoked in her. The pressure, the heat built until she felt as if she would explode internally. And then, as he tore his mouth from hers and suckled her nipple once more, an explosion of such magnitude and power occurred that Jessica arched, cried out and froze in his embrace. It felt as if lightning were dancing across her lower body, sending out forks of light and pleasure through every nerve ending within her.

She felt Dan move his hand beneath her hips and lift her slightly. The sensation, the volcanic molten feeling of pleasure, heightened and continued. He moved within her, danced with her rhythmically, sang in unison with her body, with her heart and soul as he thrust again and again to prolong the incredible feeling for her. Moments later, as the golden light burning within her began to ebb, she felt him stiffen and groan. He buried his head against her breast and held her hard against him and she knew it was her turn to love him, to cherish him as much as he'd cherished her. With a knowledge as old as woman, she moved her hips in a rolling, rhythmic motion and captured him tightly against her with her legs to prolong his release deep within her.

She saw his face tighten almost as if in pain, but with exquisite pleasure, too. With a groan, he suddenly collapsed against her, his hands tangled in her hair, his breathing harsh and shallow against her breasts. An incredible feeling of satiation, of completion, moved through her like soft moonlight caressing the earth. With a sigh of surrender, Jessica understood as never before about real love. What it was really all about. Her abdomen tingled beneath his weight as she slowly opened her eyes, moving her hands weakly through his dark, shining hair, and absorbed his gleaming profile as he lay against her. How fiercely she loved Dan!

In that moment, Jessica felt a breathtaking sensation move through her. Her heart was wide-open, receiving and giving. As she moved her hand languidly across his back and felt the strength of his spine, she smiled softly. To bear his children would be the ultimate gift. Yes, a child created out of love, born not of darkness, but of light, would be welcomed fully. Completely.

As she lay there, the sounds of the forest registering around her once again, Jessica realized that she and Dan would create a child from this first coming together. She didn't know how she knew it, but she did. Lying there in the cooling breeze, she gazed overhead as colorful leaves twirled and spiraled down around them, as if

Mother Earth were celebrating their consummation of love with them. Smiling tenderly, Jessica slid her hands around Dan's face. She saw the dove gray of his eyes, the love shining in them for her alone. He eased up off her and leaned forward just enough to capture her smiling mouth. The kiss was tender. Filled with love. Her heart swelled even more and Jessica wondered if it was possible to die from happiness.

"You are my *shi shaa,*" he rasped, sliding his hand against her full lower lip, "the sunshine in my life. You're all I'll ever need or want, my woman of the earth."

His words were filled with passion and love for her. Dan eased out of her, pulling her into his arms so that she could rest her head against his shoulder. Savoring the way he brought her against him, she closed her eyes, content as never before.

"You are the lightning of Father Sky," she whispered. "You love me so fully, so beautifully. I thought I was going to die if you didn't complete me, darling."

He rose up on one elbow and kept her near as he looked down at her flushed face, her glistening blue eyes and well-kissed mouth. Smiling tenderly, Dan traced her cheek with his fingertip. "And you are the daughter of Mother Earth." His dark hand fell against her rounded abdomen and he caressed her gently. "Our children will be welcome here, between us."

"Oh, yes." Jessica sighed as she moved her hand over his own. She could feel the strength, the roughness of it against her feminine softness. "Children created out of our love for one another, Dan…."

"Marry me, Jessica?"

She opened her eyes and met his very serious ones.

"I'm poor," Dan rasped. "And I don't have a college

education. I'll probably work myself into a grave someday, but it's good, honest work. I want you by my side
every night, every day. We've come so far together.
Let's go the rest of the way." He saw Jessica's expression change to one of tear-filled happiness. The luminous
look in her eyes, Dan knew, was her way of saying yes.
His heart soared in response like an unfettered eagle.
Stilling his hand against her abdomen, he murmured, "I
want you to be the mother of my children. They'll be so
lucky to have you. I want to grow old seeing our children and grandchildren around us. I think they'll have
a good life. Good growing-up years, not like what you
had, but what we can give them with our love."

Tears choked her and she nodded once. "Y-yes, darling. Yes to all our dreams. And I don't care if you're a
horse wrangler and you won't make that much money."

"I don't own any land. I'm poor," he said.

"In one way, maybe," Jessica whispered, "but in so
many other ways, you're a treasure to me, Dan. You
bring me love, respect and care. What's that worth compared to money?" She touched his cheek and watched
his gray eyes narrow with hunger for her. It was a delicious feeling.

"When you put it that way, you're right," he admitted.
A slight smile played at the corners of his mouth. "I'm
going to love you forever and a day, Jessica. *Shi shaa,*
my sunshine. My life and heart...."

Epilogue

"I can hardly wait until Rachel gets home," Jessica eagerly confided to Kate as they sat out on the porch swing in the warmth of late November. Everywhere else in the nation people were experiencing harsh temperatures and even snow, but not here in Arizona. No, on Thanksgiving Day, it was in the sixties and they were enjoying the pale blue sky and sunshine.

Jessica wore a pink angora sweater with a cowl neck, and a soft cream skirt that fell to her ankles. Her hair was caught back behind her head, a beautiful pink-and-white orchid in it. The fuchsia color of the orchid brought out the flushed quality of her cheeks. Dan had given her a gold heart locket shortly after he'd helped rescue her and it hung just above her collarbone as it always did. Inside the locket was a photo of him and her. Together.

Like it should always be. He'd also given her a small pair of gold, heart-shaped earrings, which she adored.

Smoothing her fingers over the red velvet skirt she wore with a crisp white blouse, Kate said, "I can't wait to see Rachel, either. I just wish she could have made it home for Thanksgiving, that's all."

"She has to finish up her commitments," Jessica murmured. "Her teaching contract ends in early December. Just think, she'll be home soon." She smiled over at her older sister. Inside, Dan and Sam were finishing up the last of the dishes and cleaning up after the wonderful midday meal. Jessica was so happy to have been able to restart the tradition her mother had begun so many years before—of feeding the homeless of Sedona. A bus from the Sedona mission had just taken twenty homeless people back to town. Yes, Thanksgiving had been very special this year. In so many wonderful, joyous ways.

"December fifteenth, if everything goes according to plan." Kate sighed. "Rachel said she'd rent a car down in Phoenix and drive north to the ranch. I just hope we don't get any of those sudden, unexpected snowstorms."

Jessica nodded. Weather in November, particularly in Oak Creek Canyon, could be unpredictable. "She's probably used to driving in rain at least, having lived so long over in England."

"Probably," Kate agreed. She smiled a little. "I guess I'm just being big sister worrywart, is all."

Warmth touched Jessica's heart as she met and held Kate's gaze. "You love us, that's why." She watched as Kate wrestled with her obvious affection. Little by little, her sister had let down her guard, and over the months, Jessica had watched her begin to bloom in a way she'd never seen before. Kate was more vulnerable, more open emotionally, and Jessica relished those wonderful, unexpected gifts from her older sister.

Kate pointed to Jessica's left finger. "I think it was romantic of Dan to give you his grandmother's engagement ring this holiday morning. He's such a great guy."

Sighing, Jessica rocked in the swing with her sister. "Isn't he though? Sometimes," she murmured, closing her eyes and fingering the gold-and-diamond ring, "I think I'm in this neverending dream. Sometimes I worry I'll wake up and Dan will be gone." Jessica opened her eyes and stole a look at Kate. "Do you know what I mean?"

Kate laughed. "I sure do." She looked back across her shoulder toward the screen door, through which she could hear the two men working noisily in the kitchen. "I feel the same about Sam. He loves me so much. I sometimes wake up at night in his arms and wonder what he saw in me in the first place. And then I go back to sleep and worry that I'm dreaming it all, and that I'm back in prison again." She frowned. "Boy, are we a jumpy lot or what?"

Giggling, Jessica shook her head, reaching out and gripping Kate's hand. "We have a right to be scared. Dan told me one time that we had such a rough childhood he's surprised any of us turned out so well. He's seen members of his own family who were abused. Some of those kids have scattered to the four winds, and most of them are in trouble in one way or another, lost forever."

Kate became serious. "We were all lost in our own way, Jessica. We all ran the minute we turned eighteen. You went to Canada. Rachel found sanctuary in England. My life went awry and I got involved with fanatical activists and ended up in prison."

"At least," Jessica replied softly, "with the love of two good men who helped us find our way home, we have a chance to change things for the better. Not only for ourselves, but for our children."

"*If* we can keep this ranch afloat for any children that might happen after marriage," Kate warned her grimly. She gestured toward the dried, yellow grass in the front yard. "No rain. Not an inch of it all autumn. I'm really worried about fire, Jessica. And if we don't get rain this winter, I don't know how we can survive. We're going to have to sell off the rest of the herd, the pregnant cows… If that happens, we're done for. Sam and I are counting on that spring crop of calves for—"

"Katie, let it go. Sometimes we just have to have blind faith about these things. Dan says it's the darkness before the dawn for all of us as a family. He sees it in symbolic terms. It's a test. He said all three sisters must come home and pour our lifeblood back into this ranch to get its heart beating again. And once we do that with our care, our love and commitment, he said the rain would come to nourish that seed we've all nurtured here by coming home again."

"Beautiful symbol. But everything still sucks."

Jessica laughed. She shook her head. "Oh, Katie, you're such a pessimist!"

"I have a right to be," Kate growled, though a grin crawled across her mouth. "I'm the one riding the range every day and checking on our cattle and horses, on the drought conditions, the loss of our alfalfa crop."

"Okay," Jessica said, matching her grin, "I'll hold the faith. Rachel was always big on hope. We'll let you be the grouch of the three. I guess every family has to have a pessimist, right?"

Tousling Jessica's hair, Kate laughed. "Right, I've *always* been the grouch in this family. Not much has changed, has it?"

"A lot has changed," Jessica said, more serious now. "On Christmas Eve, we're having a double marriage. You're going to marry Sam and I'm going to marry Dan. Rachel will be our joint maid of honor. *That,* my older, grouchy sister, is *change.*"

Kate enjoyed her younger sister's prim look. "Confident little thing, aren't you?" And she laughed.

"Life is *good,* Katie. Okay, so the ranch is still hanging by a thread, and the bank is salivating over our shoulders, eager to snatch it away the moment we fail to make a monthly payment. On the other side of the ledger, the personal and emotional side, you and I have struck it rich. We've got gold in our hands."

Chuckling, Kate said, "How I wish some of that gold could be alchemically changed into money!"

"Quit!" Jessica playfully hit her sister on the shoulder. "You don't mean that and I know it."

"I guess I don't," Kate said, a little wearily. She lowered her voice so only Jessica could hear her. "What if we can't save the ranch? What will Sam and Dan do? None of us can afford to buy another spread. All we're good for is the open range, being part of this land as cowboys. They might as well shoot us in the head and put us out of our misery if this ranch goes under. I don't want to do anything else in my life except what I'm doing now. I'd like to die in the saddle."

"Ugh. How about in Sam's arms? That's a lot more preferable. I know you love horses, Katie, but geez…."

"You know what I'm trying to say," Kate muttered fiercely.

"I hear you, Katie. Maybe, with Rachel coming home to establish a wellness clinic in Sedona, it will help us with the bills and stave off the inevitable from this terrible drought."

"Rachel isn't exactly rich, you know. She gave us her whole life savings to pay off the bulk of what was owed to the bank so they wouldn't foreclose before. Sure, she's got talent, ideas and plenty of hope, but that's not going to convert into money right away." Kate shook her head worriedly. "No, we've got some long, hard months ahead of us. I just pray for a miracle. Any miracle to help us through, that's all."

"See," Jessica chided, "you're not so pessimistic after all. You believe in miracles."

Chuckling, Kate rose from the porch swing and smoothed out her skirt. "It's all we've got left between us with the bank ready to foreclose on us, you twit."

Giggling, Jessica followed her sister back into the house. The living room had been set up to feed the homeless earlier and the scent of roasting turkey still permeated the air. As Jessica sauntered into the small kitchen, she watched in amusement as Dan and Sam kept bumping unceremoniously into one another as one washed and the other dried dishes. Dan wore a deep cranberry red cowboy shirt, a bolo tie made from silver and a turquoise nugget, dark blue jeans and newly polished black cowboy boots. His sleeves were rolled up to his elbows.

"I should have a picture of this," Kate teased, laughing. She went to the pecan-colored cupboards, opened them and started to put away the plates that Sam had dried.

"I think," Sam grumbled, "we should get silver stars for action above and beyond the duty of males."

Dan grinned and winked at Jessica, who rested her elbows on the white tile counter near the stove. She colored fiercely and smiled that soft smile that was so much a part of her.

"Where I come from on the res," Dan said, up to his elbows in soapsuds, "men did their fair share of housework. About the only thing we didn't do was learn how to weave."

"I'll take dishwashing over that," Sam said, drying the plates furiously with a white towel.

"Thought you might," Dan murmured, grabbing a handful of silverware to wash.

While Kate and the men chatted amiably, Jessica busied herself cutting the last pumpkin pie into four large slabs. Placing the slices on the small oak table covered with a lacy, white linen tablecloth, she added big dollops of whipped cream. Dan had found some pyracantha bushes with bright orange berries against dark green leaves, and had put some cuttings in a small, cut glass vase in the center of the table. It looked Christmassy to Jessica.

Her heart expanded with joy as she saw Dan steal a look across his shoulder to check where she was. Her hands stilled on the last plate as she caught and held his smoldering gray gaze. Automatically, her body responded fully to his unspoken invitation. Surely today was a day of thanksgiving as no other she'd ever had. Her finger burned warmly where his grandmother's engagement ring rested on her hand. Dan had bestowed the gift on her in front of everyone. Jessica had been so humbled and surprised that she'd cried shamelessly. She'd seen tears in Dan's eyes, too. And everyone else's.

There was nothing she wanted more than to have

Dan as her husband, her partner for life. Each morning she woke up with him at her side, and it was a miracle to her. A wonderful, unfolding miracle. Jessica realized she had never known love until Dan, the man wrapped in darkness, had walked quietly into her life.

"Is that for us?" Dan queried, raising his brows and eyeing the pumpkin pie.

Grinning, Jessica traded a look with Kate. "Well, we took pity on you cowboys and thought you deserved some kind of treat for doing all this kitchen duty. Right, Katie?"

"Oh, sure, right." Kate looked at them with mock sternness. "We cooked all day, so you boys can clean up the mess."

Dan crowed and shared a laugh with Sam. "Do we get whipped cream on our reward?"

Jessica colored fiercely at the innuendo. "On the pie, yes."

The foursome broke into ribald laughter. The kitchen rang with the sounds of love and joy. How much had changed since she was a child! Jessica realized. With Kelly around, they had always walked as if stepping on eggs, afraid they would break at any moment. Now there was teasing, good-natured competition between Dan and Sam, and obvious love for her and Katie. Enough to go around and then some.

There was a knock at the front door.

"I'll get it!" Jessica said, quickly putting the tub of whipped cream aside and fleeing through the kitchen.

"Who's comin'?" Sam asked, trading looks with Dan and Kate.

"I don't know," Kate said. "We're not expecting anyone else."

Dan chuckled. "By now I think you would have caught on. With Jessica around, surprises are the order of the day."

Jessica appeared at the doorway to the kitchen, breathless and flushed. "Look who's coming for a late dinner!"

All three of them turned in unison.

Jessica smiled and stepped aside. "I found out last week that Jim Cunningham and his crew had Thanksgiving duty at the fire department. None of them could go home and have turkey with their families, so…" She skipped to the refrigerator as Jim entered the kitchen, "I packed up ten meals, for all of his crew at the fire station."

Jim nodded shyly to everyone. "Hi," he said, a bit awkwardly.

Dan shook his head and laughed. "Come on in, Jim."

Sam stepped forward and extended his hand. "Glad you could drop by."

Kate nodded. "Yes," she said, her voice a bit strained.

Jessica knew that the old war between the Cunninghams and Donovans had gone on for a long, bitter time. But Jim Cunningham had reached out to her, Sam and Kate to try and make up for the many wrongs done to them by his cantankerous father. Dressed in his dark blue, serge trousers and light blue, long-sleeved shirt, the silver badge on his chest glinting in the lamplight, Jim gave her a look of thanks for the dinners.

"Can you at least have a cup of coffee with us?" Jessica pleaded as she brought out the foil-wrapped meals and set them on the table. Kate went to find paper bags to place them in.

"Uh, no.… With the permission of my captain, I

faked a call to come up here to get the meals, so I'm living on borrowed time as it is," Jim said with a slight, hesitant smile. His dark blue gaze pinned Kate as she returned with the paper bags, her expression grim. "The crew down at the fire station is beholden. Donovan generosity is well known in these parts. I hear you served thirty needy families as well as the homeless at the mission earlier today."

Kate compressed her lips and put the meals into the paper bags. "I'm sorry you have to work today."

Jim shrugged. "Well, with the way things were going at home this last week, I'm kinda glad I have the duty, to tell you the truth."

Jessica gave him a compassionate look. She *liked* Jim Cunningham. He was quiet, clean-cut, terribly handsome in a rough kind of way and respectful toward everyone. "Maybe a meal made with lots and lots of love will help then," she whispered, bringing over both bags for him to carry. "There's pumpkin pie and whipped cream in there for dessert."

Jim brightened as he put the two bags beneath his arms and Sam moved by him to open the front door. "Thanks—all of you." He caught and held Kate's dark stare. "I mean it...."

Kate barely nodded and wrapped her arms defensively against her breasts.

Jessica placed her hand on Jim's upper arm and led him out of the kitchen, with Dan following. She could feel Jim's firm muscles beneath his shirt and noted how fit he was. "I just hope you don't have any calls. I hope you have a nice, quiet night."

"Thanks, Jessica," Jim murmured, smiling down at her.

Out on the front porch, they saw that the sun had set

behind the thousand-foot lava wall that protected the ranch property. The sky was a light blue and gold as Jessica, Dan and Sam walked with Jim to the red-and-white ambulance with the Sedona crest on the front door. Dan opened the rear doors of the ambulance and helped Jim place the food where it wouldn't fall over during transit.

Jim hesitated as he opened the driver's door, then turned and extended his hand to Dan. "Congratulations. I hear you're going to marry this flower child at Christmas."

Jessica laughed and felt heat flow into her cheeks as Jim's eyes danced with gentle teasing. "Flower child! Oh, come on, Jim. Is that what the gossip going around in Sedona is calling me?"

Dan released Jim's hand and put his arm around Jessica. "Be happy they're calling you something nice, *shi shaa,*" he said with a grin. "Instead of a blooming idiot or something like that."

Jim laughed, got into the ambulance and shut the door. "No kidding. You don't want to know what they call me. I can guarantee you it ain't nice." He raised his hand in a mock salute to the three of them. "Thanks. All of you. I know everyone at the station will want you to know how much your care means to them."

Her hands clasped to her breast, Jessica leaned warmly against Dan. "Just take care, Jim. I'll see you in town next week. I'll drop by and pick up the dishes and silverware, okay?"

"Okay, Jessica." He started the ambulance and slowly turned around on the gravel driveway.

Back on the porch, Sam rested his hands on his hips as the ambulance disappeared up the winding road out of the canyon. He turned his gaze on Jessica. "That was a good move, politically," he said in congratulations.

She looked at him in surprise. "What do you mean?"

"Hadn't you heard?" he rumbled. "Old Man Cunningham is fixin' to slap our ranch with a lawsuit later this month. Over water rights."

Groaning, Jessica raised her hands to her open mouth. "No! How can he? We've always shared that well between our properties—for nearly a hundred years."

Sam ran his fingers through his hair and looked grimly over at Dan. "Explain it to her, Dan?"

Dan rubbed his hand against Jessica's tense arm. "Yes… I will…."

Sam grunted before slowly walking back inside the house.

Jessica turned in Dan's arms, feeling secure as his hands moved gently down her back to capture her against him. "Dan, what's going on? Is there something you three know that I don't? Is Katie hiding things from me again?"

"Come on," he urged, leaning down and kissing her lips tenderly, "let's go for a walk and let this dinner settle."

Petulantly, Jessica surrendered and fell into step with him as they walked toward the horse corrals near the red barn. "What's Sam talking about, Dan? What lawsuit?"

Dan settled his black Stetson on his head and drew her more surely against him. He wished he could protect Jessica from some of the harshness of life. He saw the consternation in her expression and the worry in her eyes. Everyone hid the truth from Jessica because they knew how easily she could become upset, and how much it distressed her. He tightened his fingers on her shoulder as they walked.

"About two weeks ago, Jim's father called Sam over there," Dan confided in a low tone. "The day before that, Jim had come to the ranch here and talked with Sam, to warn him that the call was coming in. Jim tried to talk his father out of it, but the old man refused to listen to him. The drought has dried up all the wells on Cunningham property and he told Sam he was going to court to get full rights to the well that both ranches have shared for the last hundred years."

"That's why Kate looked so unsettled, then," Jessica said. "She wasn't very happy to see Jim here. Now I know why."

"Kate doesn't trust Jim or his motivations. She thinks that he's in cahoots with his father and he's just bluffing us."

Jessica rolled her eyes. "That's silly! Jim Cunningham is the only good apple from that rotten barrel, and she knows it!"

"That's probably true," Dan conceded, "but Cunningham could destroy us if he goes to court. We don't have the money to fight that kind of a lawsuit. He's got money. And money talks."

"But we need that well, too!" Jessica protested, her voice high with indignation. "All our pasture wells have dried up with the exception of that one! What are we to do? Let our stock die of thirst?"

"Take it easy," Dan soothed, placing both hands on her tense shoulders as she faced him. He saw the anguish in her eyes. "It could be a bluff. Old Man Cunningham, from what Sam has said, often uses threat of a lawsuit to scare off someone who gets in his way."

Bitterly, Jessica gripped his upper arms. "But if he takes that well, our livestock will die, Dan."

"I know that...." Helplessly, he caressed her strained mouth with his fingertips. "We can always pump water from Oak Creek if it comes down to that, so stop worrying. At least the creek runs through our property and not Cunningham's. If their well goes dry, we have a second water source. They don't. I was hoping that today would be happy for you in all ways, Jessica."

She gazed down at the ring on her finger. The small diamond twinkled in the early evening light. "I'm sorry. I was happy, Dan. So very, very happy." She struggled to smile for his sake as she placed her arms around his neck.

"I wish," Dan said in a frustrated tone, "that I could make these problems at the ranch go away. This family doesn't deserve any more hard luck than it already has."

Anger, worry and concern warred within Jessica. "Jim isn't a two-heart like Kate thinks," she said fiercely. "I have a feeling he'll fight for us. He won't let his father get away with this. Jim is fair-minded."

Dan nodded. He didn't tell Jessica that Old Man Cunningham owned the ranch until he died, and that the property rights were not to be divided among the three sons. The ranch was going to Bo and Chet. Jim had absolutely no leverage at all, even if he wanted to try and help the Donovans in the lawsuit over water rights.

Gently, Dan stroked her warm, flushed cheek. Instantly, Jessica responded to his touch and he smiled inwardly. Little by little, as he caressed her cheek, her brow and soft, silky hair, she quieted. Much of the worry was replaced with that serene look in her eyes again. The effect she had on him was similar.

"I'm putting Gan out with his band of mares today," he told her as he led her toward the stallion's pen. "Sam agreed. The stallion is tame now and he isn't going to be attacking a man on foot or horseback, so it's safe to let him be with his ladies."

Jessica sighed and wrapped her arm around Dan's waist as they walked. Her heart was heavy with worry, but she knew he had worked hard to get the stallion trained to the point where such a gift could be bestowed upon the animal. It would be one more job they wouldn't have to do. Natural breeding could take place instead. "Yes, let's watch him race out of his pen for the pasture."

Gan was waiting at the corral gate, his head extended, his fine ears pricked forward. He nickered as Dan drew near. Jessica stood back and smiled softly. The stallion, over time, had grown to love Dan. It was obvious in the way the animal nudged his shoulder as he opened the gate. As Gan moved, the shining ripple of his muscles was something to behold. She watched the stallion lift his tail like a flag once Dan had opened the gate, and give a deep, bugling cry that echoed throughout the canyon.

Looking over at the south pasture, where all the broodmares were kept, Jessica saw a number of them lift their heads from grazing on the dry, withered grass, and whinny in return.

Gan dug his rear hooves into the dirt, the dust flying as he lunged out of his corral. His long black mane and tail flowed as he galloped full speed toward his mares, a little over a mile away. Jessica heard Dan chuckle as he closed the gate. She liked the smile on his handsome face, the warm look in his gray eyes as he watched the stallion fly across the hard clay floor of the pasture. Gan's joyous bugling sounded again and again.

Jessica felt her spirits lift unaccountably. With the coming lawsuit she should feel sad and afraid. Miraculously, she didn't, and she knew why. It was because of the man wrapped in darkness who was walking toward her. His eyes were banked with coals of hunger—for her. Reaching out, she touched his fingers.

"He's free," she whispered. "You helped free Gan— and me...."

Sliding his arms around Jessica, Dan nuzzled her cheek. The past few weeks had convinced him that he was worthy of Jessica in every way. Dan was going to let his past go—completely. His bout with alcohol wouldn't be forgotten, but now, thanks to Jessica, he had put it into perspective. She had helped him retrieve his dignity and reembrace who and what he was. He was a man with an incredible gift with horses, a gift that he would use here at the ranch. Over time, the money he'd save from his work would build toward their bright future— together. He no longer worried about his place in Jessica's life. Everything he was had helped to save Jessica. The power of that knowledge had given him back his shredded self-esteem.

Pressing his mouth against her soft cheek, he whispered, "We're free to love one another, like that stallion will love his mares." Gently framing Jessica's face, Dan whispered, "And I'm going to love you forever...."

* * * * *

A career Air Force officer, **Merline Lovelace** served
at bases all over the world. When she hung up her
uniform for the last time, she decided to try her hand
at storytelling. Since then, more than twelve million
copies of her books have been published in over thirty
countries. Check her website at merlinelovelace.com or
friend Merline on Facebook for news and information
about her latest releases.

Books by Merline Lovelace

Harlequin Special Edition

Three Coins in the Fountain

"I Do"…Take Two!
Third Time's the Bride
Callie's Christmas Wish

Harlequin Romantic Suspense

Course of Action (with Lindsay McKenna)

Course of Action
Crossfire
The Rescue

Harlequin Desire

The Paternity Proposition
The Paternity Promise

Duchess Diaries

Her Unforgettable Royal Lover
The Texan's Royal M.D.
The Diplomat's Pregnant Bride
A Business Engagement

Visit the Author Profile page
at Harlequin.com for more titles.

RETURN TO SENDER

Merline Lovelace

This one's for Sherrill and Elisha and Peggy and all the folks at the S. Penn Post Office—thanks for your friendly smiles when I show up all drawn and haggard to put a finished manuscript in the mail. Thanks, too, for your cheerful professionalism. You're outstanding representatives of the finest postal system in the world!

Chapter 1

Rio de Janeiro.

Mount Sugarloaf rising majestically above the city.

Streets crowded with revelers in costumes of bright greens and yellows and reds.

The glossy postcard leaped out at Sheryl Hancock from the thick sheaf of mail. Her hand stilled its task of sorting and stuffing post office boxes. The familiar early-morning sounds of co-workers grumbling and letters whooshing into metal boxes faded. For the briefest moment, she caught a faint calypso beat in the rattle of a passing mail cart and heard the laughter of Carnival.

"Is that another postcard from Paul-boy?"

With a small jolt, Sheryl left the South America festival and returned to the Albuquerque post office where she'd worked for the past twelve years. Smiling at the woman standing a few feet away, she nodded.

"Yes. This one's from Rio."

"Rio? The guy sure gets around, doesn't he?"

Elise Hart eased her bulk around a bank of opened postal boxes to peer at the postcard in Sheryl's hand. From the expression in Elise's brown eyes, it was obvious that she, too, was feeling the momentary magic of faraway places.

"What does this one say?"

Sheryl flipped the card over. "'Hi to my favorite aunt. I've been dancing in the streets for the past four days. Wish you were here.'"

Sighing, Elise gazed at the slick card. "What I wouldn't give to dump my two boys with my mother and fly down to Rio for Carnival."

"Oh, sure. I can just see you dancing through the streets, eight months pregnant yet."

"Eight months, one week, two days and counting," the redhead replied with a grimace. "I'd put on my dancing shoes for a hunk like Mrs. Gunderson's nephew, though."

"You'd better not put on dancing shoes! I'm your birthing partner, remember? I don't want you going into premature labor on me. Besides," Sheryl tacked on, "we only have Mrs. Gunderson's word for it that her nephew qualifies as a hunk."

"According to his doting aunt, Paul-boy sports a thick mustache, specializes in tight jeans and rates about 112 on the gorgeous scale." Elise waggled her dark-red brows in an exaggerated leer. "That's qualification enough in my book."

"Paul-boy, as you insist on calling him, is also pushing forty."

"So?"

So Sheryl didn't have a whole lot of respect for jet-setting playboys who refused to grow up or grow into their responsibilities. Her father had been a pharmaceutical salesman by profession and a wanderer by nature. He'd drifted in and out of her life for short periods during her youth, until her mother's loneliness and bitter nagging had made him disappear altogether. Sheryl didn't blame him, exactly. More often than not, she herself had to grit her teeth when her mother called in one of her complaining moods. But neither did she like to talk about her absent parent.

Instead, she teased Elise about her fascination with the man they both heard about every time the frail, white-haired woman who'd moved to Albuquerque some four months ago came in to collect her mail.

"Don't you think Mrs. Gunderson might be just a bit prejudiced about this nephew of hers?"

"Maybe. He still sounds yummy." Sighing, Elise rested a hand on her high, rounded stomach. "You'd think I would have learned my lesson once and for all. My ex broke the gorgeous scale, too."

Sheryl had bitten down hard on her lip too many times in the past to keep from criticizing her friend's husband. Since their divorce seven months ago, she felt no such restraints.

"Rick also weighed in as a total loser."

"True," Elise agreed. "He was, is and always will be a jerk." She traced a few absent circles on her tummy. "We can't all find men like Brian, Sher."

At the mention of her almost-fiancé, Sheryl banished any lingering thoughts of Elise's ex, Latin American carnivals and the globe-trotting Paul Gunderson. In their place came the easy slide of contentment that always accompanied any thought of Brian Mitchell.

"No, we can't," she confirmed.

"So have you two set a date yet?"

"We're talking about an engagement at the end of the year."

"You're engaged to get engaged." Her friend's brown eyes twinkled. "That's so…so Brian."

"I know."

Actually, the measured pace of Sheryl's relationship with the Albuquerque real estate agent satisfied her almost as much as it did him. After dating for nearly a year, they'd just started talking about the next step. They'd announce an engagement when the time was right, quite possibly at Christmas, and set a firm date for the wedding when they'd saved up enough to purchase a house. Brian was sure interest rates would drop another few points in the next year or so. Before they took the plunge into matrimony, he wanted to be in a position to buy down their monthly house payments so they could live comfortably on her salary and his commissions.

"I think that's what I like most about him," Sheryl confided. "His dependability and careful planning and—"

"Not to mention his cute buns."

"Well…"

"Ha! Don't give me that Little Miss Innocent look. I know you, girl. Under that sunshine-and-summer exterior, you crave excitement and passion as much as the next woman. Even fat, prego ones."

"What I crave," Sheryl replied, laughing, "is for you to get back to work. We've only got ten minutes until opening, and I don't want to face the hordes lined up in the lobby by myself."

Elise made a face and dipped into the cardboard tray

in front of her for another stack of letters. She and Sheryl had come in early to help throw the postal box mail, since the clerk who regularly handled it was on vacation. They'd have to scramble to finish the last wall of boxes and get their cash drawers out of the vault in time to man the front counter.

Swiftly, Sheryl shuffled through the stack in her hand for the rest of Mrs. Gunderson's mail. Today's batch was mostly junk, she saw. Coupon booklets. Advertising fliers. A preprinted solicitation from the state insurance commissioner facing a special runoff election next week. And the postcard from Paul-boy, as Elise had dubbed him. With a last, fleeting glance at the colorful street scene, Sheryl bent down to stuff the mail into Mrs. Gunderson's slot.

It wouldn't stuff.

Frowning, she dropped down on her sneakered heels to examine the three-by-five-inch box. It contained at least one, maybe two days' worth of mail.

Strange. Mrs. Gunderson usually came into the post office every day to pick up her mail. More often than not, she'd pop in to chat with the employees on the counter, her yappy black-and-white shih tzu tucked under her arm. Regulations prohibited live animals in the post office except for those being shipped, but no one had the heart to tell Inga Gunderson that she couldn't bring her baby inside with her. Particularly when she also brought in homemade cookies and melt-in-your-mouth Danish spice cakes.

A niggle of worry worked into Sheryl's mind as she shoved Mrs. Gunderson's mail into her box. She hoped the woman wasn't sick or incapacitated. She'd keep an eye out for her today, just to relieve her mind that she was okay. Pushing off her heels, she finished the wall of boxes with brisk efficiency and headed for the vault. She had less than five minutes to count out her cash drawer and restock her supplies.

She managed it in four. She was at the front counter, her ready smile in place, when the branch manager unlocked the glass doors to the lobby and the first of the day's customers streamed in.

Sheryl didn't catch a glimpse of Mrs. Gunderson all morning, nor did any of her co-workers. As the day wore on, the unclaimed mail nagged at Sheryl. During her lunch break, she checked the postal box registry for the elderly renter's address and phone number.

The section of town where Inga Gunderson lived was served by another postal station much closer to her house, Sheryl noted. Wondering why the woman would choose to rent a box at a post office so far from her home, she dialed the number. The phone rang twice, then clicked to an answering machine. Since leaving a message wouldn't do anything to assure her of the woman's well-being, Sheryl hung up in the middle of the standard I-can't-come-to-the-phone-right-now recording.

Having come in at six-thirty to help "wall" the letters for the postal boxes, she got off at three. A quick check of Mrs. Gunderson's box showed it was still stuffed with unclaimed mail. Frowning, Sheryl wove her way slowly through the maze of route carriers' work areas and headed for the women's locker room at the rear of the station. After peeling off her pin-striped uniform shirt, she replaced it with a yellow tank top that brightened up the navy shorts worn by most of the postal employees in summer. A glance at the clock on the wall had her grabbing for her purse. She'd promised to meet Brian at three-thirty to look at a property he was thinking of listing.

After extracting a promise from Elise to go right home and get off her feet, Sheryl stepped outside. Hot, dry heat hit her like a slap in the face. With the sun beating down on her head and shoulders, she crossed the asphalt parking lot toward her trusty, ice-blue Camry. She opened the door and waited a moment to let the captured heat pour out. As she stood there in the hot, blazing sun, her nagging worry over Mrs. Gunderson crystallized into real concern. She'd swing by the woman's house, she decided. Just to check on her. It was a little out of her way, but Sheryl couldn't shake the fear that something had happened to the frail, white-haired customer.

With the Toyota's air conditioner doing valiant battle against the heat, she pulled out of the parking lot behind the post office and headed west on Haines, then north on Juan Tabo. Two more turns and three miles took her to the shady, residential neighborhood and Inga Gunderson's neat, two-story adobe house. She didn't see a car in the driveway, although several were parked along the street. Maybe Mrs. Gunderson's car was in the detached rear garage. Or maybe she'd gone out of town. Or maybe…

Maybe she was ill, or had fallen down the stairs and broken a leg or a hip. The woman lived alone, with only her precious Button for company. She could be lying in the house now, helpless and in pain.

More worried than ever, Sheryl pulled into the driveway and climbed out of the car. Once more the heat enveloped her. She could almost feel her hair sizzling. The thick, naturally curly mane tended to turn unmanageable at the best of times. In this soul-sucking heat, it took on a life of its own. Tucking a few wildly corkscrewing strands into the loose French braid that hung halfway down her back, Sheryl followed a pebbled walk to the front porch. A feathery Russian olive tree crowded the railed porch and provided welcome shade. Sighing in relief, she pressed the doorbell.

When the distant sound of a buzzer produced a series of high, plaintive yips and no Mrs. Gunderson, Sheryl's concern vaulted into genuine alarm. Inga Gunderson wouldn't leave town without her Button. The two were practically joined at the hip. They even looked alike, Elise had once joked, both possessing slightly pug noses, round, inquisitive eyes and hair more white than black.

Sheryl leaned on the doorbell again, and heard a chorus of even more frantic yaps. She pulled open the screen and pounded on the door.

"Mrs. Gunderson! Are you in there?"

A long, piteous yowl answered her call. She hammered on the door in earnest, setting the frosted-glass panes to rattling.

"Mrs. Gunderson! Are you okay?"

Button howled once more, and Sheryl reached for the old-fashioned iron latch. She had just closed her hand around it when the door snapped open, jerking her inside with it.

Gasping, she found herself nose to nose with a wrinkled linen sport coat and a blue cotton shirt that stretched across a broad chest. A *very* broad chest. She took a quick step back, at which point several things happened at once, none of them good from her perspective.

Her foot caught on the door mat, throwing her off balance.

A hard hand shot out and grabbed her arm, either to save her from falling or to prevent her escape.

A tiny black-and-white fury erupted from inside the house. Gums lifted, needle-sharp teeth bared, it flew through the air and fastened its jaws on the jean-clad calf of her rescuer-captor.

"Ow!"

The man danced across the porch on one booted foot, taking Sheryl with him. Cursing, he lifted his leg and shook it. The little shih tzu snarled ferociously and hung on with all the determination of the rat catcher he was originally bred to be. Snarling a little herself, Sheryl tried to shake free of the bruising hold on her arm. When the stranger didn't loosen his grip, she dug her nails into the back of his tanned hand.

"Dammit, let go!"

She didn't know if the command shouted just above her ear was directed at her or the dog, and didn't particularly care. Pure, undiluted adrenaline pumped through her veins. She had no idea who this man was or what had happened to Mrs. Gunderson, but obviously *something* had. Something Button didn't like. Sheryl's only thought was to get away, find a phone, call the police.

Her attacker gave his upraised leg another shake, and Sheryl gouged her nails deeper into his skin. When that earned her a smothered curse and a painful jerk on her arm, she took a cue from the shih tzu and bent to bite the hand that held her.

"Hey!"

Still half-bent, Sheryl felt herself spun sideways. Her captor released his grip, but before she could bolt, his arm whipped around her waist. A half second later, she thudded back into the solid wall of blue oxford.

Her breath slammed out of her lungs. The band around her middle cut off any possibility of pulling in a replacement supply. As frantic now as the dog, she kicked back. One sneakered heel connected with the man's shin.

"Oh, for…!" Lifting her off her feet, her attacker grunted in her ear. "Calm down! I won't hurt you."

"Prove…it," she panted. "Let…me…go!"

"I will, I will. Just calm down."

Sheryl calmed, for the simple reason that she couldn't do anything else. Her ribs felt as though they'd threaded right through one another and squeezed out everything in between. Red spots danced before her eyes.

Thankfully, the excruciating pressure on her waist eased. She drew great gulps of air into her starved lungs. The sounds of another snarl and another curse battered at her ears. They were followed by a wheezy whine. When the spots in front of her eyes cleared, she turned to face a belligerent male, holding an equally belligerent shih tzu by the scruff of its neck.

For the first time, she saw the man's face. It was as hard as the rest of his long, lean body, Sheryl decided shakily. The sun had weathered his skin to dark oak. White lines fanned the corners of his eyes. They showed whiskey gold behind lashes the same dark brown as his short, straight hair and luxuriant mustache.

His mustache!

Sheryl whipped her gaze down his rangy form. Beneath the blue cotton shirt and tan jacket, his jeans molded trim hips and tight, corded thighs. She made the connection with a rush of relief.

The hunky nephew!

She'd have to tell Elise that Mrs. Gunderson wasn't all

that far-off in her description. Although Sheryl wouldn't quite rate this rugged, whipcord-lean man as 112 on the gorgeous scale, he definitely scored at least an 88 or 90. Well, maybe a 99.

Wedging the yapping shih tzu under his arm like a hairy football, he gave Sheryl a narrow-eyed once-over. "Sorry about the little dance we just did. Are you all right?"

"More or less."

"Be quiet!"

She jumped at the sharp command, but realized immediately that it was aimed at Button. Thankfully, the shih tzu recognized the voice of authority. His annoying, high-pitched yelps subsided to muttered growls.

Swinging his attention back to Sheryl, Button's handler studied her with an intentness that raised little goose bumps on her arms. She couldn't remember the last time a man had looked at her like this, as though he wanted not just to see her, but into her. In fact, she couldn't remember the last time any man had *ever* looked at her like this. Brian certainly didn't. He was too considerate, too polite to make someone feel all prickly by such scrutiny.

"What can I do for you, Miss…?"

"Hancock. Sheryl Hancock. I know your aunt," she offered by way of explanation. "I just came by to check on her."

Those golden brown eyes lasered into her. "You know my aunt?"

"Yes. You're Paul Gunderson, aren't you?"

He was silent for a moment, then countered with a question of his own. "What makes you think so?"

"The mustache," she said with a tentative smile. And

the thigh-hugging jeans, she added silently. "Your aunt talks about you all the time."

"Does she?"

"Yes. She's really proud of how well you're doing in the import-export business." Belatedly, Sheryl recalled the purpose of her visit. "Is she okay? I was worried when I didn't see her for a day or two."

"Inga's fine," he replied after a small pause. "She's upstairs. Resting."

Sheryl didn't see how anyone could rest through Button's shrill yapping, but then, Mrs. Gunderson was used to it.

"Oh, good." She started for the porch steps. "Would you tell her I came by, and that I'll talk to her tomorrow or whenever?"

Paul moved to one side. It was only a half step, a casual movement, but Sheryl couldn't edge past him without crowding against the wrought-iron rail.

"Why don't you come inside for a few minutes?" he suggested. "You can give me the real lowdown on what my aunt has to say about me, and we can both get out of the heat for a few minutes."

"I wish I could, but I'm running late for an appointment."

"There's some iced tea in the fridge. And a platter of freshly baked cookies on the kitchen table."

"Well…"

The cookies decided it. And Button's pitiable little whine. Obviously unhappy at being wedged into Paul's armpit, the dog snuffled noisily through its pug nose. The rhinestone-studded, bow-shaped barrette that kept his facial fur out of his eyes had slipped to one side. His bulging black orbs beseeched Sheryl to end his indignity.

She felt sorry for him but didn't make the mistake of reaching for the little stinker. The one time she'd tried to pet him at the post office, he'd nipped her fingers. As he now tried to nip Paul's. His sharp little teeth just missed the hand that brushed a tad too close to him. With a muttered oath, Paul jerked his hand away.

"How anyone could keep a noisy, bad-tempered fur ball like this as a pet is beyond me."

Somehow, the fact that Inga Gunderson's nephew disliked his aunt's obnoxious little Button made Sheryl feel as though they were allies of sorts. Smiling, she accepted his invitation and preceded him into the house.

Cool air wrapped around her like a sponge. The rooftop swamp cooler, so necessary to combat Albuquerque's dry, high-desert air, was obviously working overtime. As Sheryl's eyes made the adjustment from blazing outside light to the shadowed interior, she looked about in some surprise. The house certainly didn't fit Mrs. Gunderson's personality. No pictures decorated the walls. No knickknacks crowded the tables. The furniture was a sort of pseudo-Southwest, a mix of bleached wood and brown Naugahyde, and not particularly comfortable looking.

Turning, she caught a glint of sunlight on Paul's dark hair as he bent down to deposit Button on the floor. To her consternation, she also caught a glimpse of what looked very much like a shoulder holster under the tan sport coat. She must have made some startled sound, because Paul glanced up and saw the direction of her wide-eyed stare. He released the dog and straightened, rolling his shoulders so that his jacket fell in place. The leather harness disappeared from view.

Sheryl had seen it, though.

And he knew she had.

His face went tight and altogether too hard for her peace of mind. Then Button gave a shrill, piercing bark and raced across the room. With another earsplitting yip, he disappeared up the stairs. He left behind a tense silence, broken only by the whoosh of chilled air being forced through the vents by the swamp cooler.

Sheryl swallowed a sudden lump in her throat. "Is that a gun under your jacket?"

"It is."

"I, uh, didn't know the import-export business was so risky."

"It can be."

She took a discreet step toward the door. Guns made her nervous. Very nervous. Even when carried by handsome strangers. Especially when carried by handsome strangers.

"I think I'll pass on the cookies. It's been a long day, and I'm late for an appointment. Tell your aunt that I'll see her tomorrow. Or whenever."

"I'd really like you to stay a few minutes, Miss Hancock. I'm anxious to hear what Inga has to say about her nephew."

"Some other time, maybe."

He stepped sideways, blocking her retreat as effectively as he had on the porch. But this time the movement wasn't the least casual.

"I'm afraid I'll have to insist."

Chapter 2

She knew about Inga Gunderson's nephew!

As he stared down into the blonde's wide, distinctly nervous green eyes, Deputy U.S. Marshal Harry Mac-Millan's pulse kicked up to twice its normal speed. He forgot about the ache in his gut, legacy of a roundhouse punch delivered by the seemingly frail, white-haired woman upstairs. He ignored the stinging little dents in his calf, courtesy of her sharp-toothed dust mop. His blood hammering, he gave the new entry onto the scene a thoroughly professional once-over.

Five-six or -seven, he guessed. A local, from her speech pattern and deep tan. As Harry had discovered in the week he'd been in Albuquerque, the sun carried twice the firepower at these mile-high elevations than it did at lower levels. It had certainly added a glow to this woman's skin. With her long, curly, corn-silk hair, tip-tilted nose and nicely proportioned set of curves, she looked more like the girl next door than the accomplice of an escaped fugitive. But Harry had been a U.S. marshal long enough to know that even the most angelic face could disguise the soul of a killer.

His jaw clenched at the memory of his friend's agonizing death. For a second or two, Harry debated whether to identify himself or milk more information from the woman first. He wasn't about to jeopardize this case, which had become a personal quest, by letting a suspect incriminate herself without Mirandizing her, but this woman wasn't a suspect. Yet.

"Tell me how you know Inga Gunderson."

Her eyes slid past him to the door. "I, uh, see her almost every day."

"Where?"

"At the branch office where I work."

"What branch office?"

She started to answer, then forced a deep, steadying breath into her lungs. "What's this all about? Is Mrs. Gunderson really all right?"

She had guts. Harry would give her that. She was obviously frightened. He could detect a faint tremor in the hands clenched at the seams of her navy shorts. Yet instead of replying to Harry's abrupt demands for information, she was throwing out a few questions of her own.

"Are you her nephew or not?"

He couldn't withhold his identity in the face of a direct question. Lifting his free hand, he reached into his coat pocket. The woman uttered a yelp every bit as piercing as the damned dog's, and jumped back.

"Relax, I'm just getting my ID."

He pulled out the worn brown-leather case containing his credentials. Flipping it open one-handed, he displayed the five-pointed gold star and a picture ID.

"Harry MacMillan, deputy U.S. marshal."

Her gaze swung from him to the badge to him and back again. Her nervousness gave way to a flash of indignation.

"Why didn't you say so?!"

"I just did." Coolly, he returned the case to his pocket. "May I see your identification, please."

"Mine? Why? I've told you my name."

Her response came out clipped and more than a little angry. That was fine with Harry. Until he discovered her exact relationship to the fugitive he'd been tracking for almost a year, he didn't mind keeping her rattled and off balance.

"I know who you said you were, Miss Hancock. I'd just like to see some confirmation."

"I left my purse in the car."

"Oh, that's smart."

The caustic comment made her stiffen, but before she could reply Harry cut back to the matter that had consumed his days and nights for so many months.

"Tell me again how you know Inga Gunderson."

Sheryl had always thought of herself as a dedicated federal employee. She enjoyed her job, and considered the service that she provided important to her community. Nor did she hesitate to volunteer her time and energies for special projects, such as selling T-shirts to aid victims of the devastating floods last year or coordinating the Christmas Wish program that responded to some of the desperate letters to Santa Claus that came into the post office during the holidays. She'd never come close to any kind of dangerous activity or bomb threats, but she certainly would have cooperated with other federal agencies in any ongoing investigation...if asked.

What nicked the edges of her normally placid temper was that this man didn't ask. He demanded. Still, he was a federal agent. And he wanted an answer.

"Mrs. Gunderson stops in almost every day at the station where I work," she repeated.

"What station?"

"The Monzano Street post office."

"The Monzano post office." He shoved a hand through his short, cinnamon-brown hair. "Well, hell!"

Sheryl bristled at the unbridled disgust in his voice. Although her friendly personality and ready smile acted as a preventive against the verbal abuse many postal employees experienced, she'd endured her share of sneers and jokes about the post office. The slurs, even said in fun, always hurt. She took pride in her work, as did most of her co-workers. What's more, she'd chosen a demanding occupation. She'd like to see anyone, this lean, tough deputy marshal included, sling the amount of mail she did each day and still come up smiling.

"Do you have a problem with the post office?" she asked with a touch of belligerence.

"What?" The question seemed to jerk him from his private and not very pleasant thoughts. "No. Have a seat, Miss Hancock. I'll call my contacts and verify your identity."

"Why?" she asked again.

His hawk's eyes sliced into her. "You've just walked into the middle of an ongoing investigation. You're not walking out until I ascertain that you're who you say you are...and until I understand your exact relationship with the woman who calls herself 'Mrs. Gunderson.'"

"*Calls* herself 'Inga Gunderson'?"

"Among other aliases. Sit down."

Feeling a little like Alice sliding down through the rabbit hole, Sheryl perched on the edge of the uncomfortable, sand-colored sofa. Good grief! What in the world had she stumbled into?

She found out a few moments later. Deputy U.S. Marshal MacMillan dropped the phone onto its cradle and ran a quick, assessing eye over her yellow tank top and navy shorts.

"Well, you check out. The FBI's computers have your weight at 121, but the rest of the details from your background information file substantiate your identity."

Sheryl wasn't sure which flustered her more, the fact that this man had instant access to her background file or that he'd accurately noted the few extra pounds she'd put on recently. Okay, more than a few pounds.

MacMillan's gaze swept over her once more, then settled on her face. "According to the file, you're clean. Not even a speeding ticket in the past ten years."

From his dry tone, he didn't consider a spotless driving record a particularly meritorious achievement.

"Thank you. I think. Now will you tell me what's going on here? Is Mrs. Gunderson…or whoever she is… really all right? Why in the world is a deputy U.S. marshal checking up on that sweet, fragile lady?"

"Because we suspect that sweet, fragile lady of being involved in the illegal importation of depleted uranium."

"Mrs. *Gunderson?*"

The marshal, Sheryl decided, had been sniffing something a lot more potent than the glue on the back of stamps!

"Let me get this straight. You think Inga Gunderson is smuggling uranium?"

"Depleted uranium," he corrected, as though she should know the difference.

She didn't.

"It's the same heavy metal that's used in the manufacture of armor-piercing artillery shells," he explained in answer to her blank look. Almost imperceptibly, his voice roughened. "Recently, it's also been used to produce new cop-killer bullets."

Sheryl stared at him, stunned. For the life of her, she couldn't connect the tiny, chirpy woman who brought her and her co-workers mouthwatering spice cakes with a smuggling ring. A uranium smuggling ring, for heaven's sake! Of all the thoughts whirling around in her confused, chaotic mind, only one surfaced.

"I thought the Customs Service tracked down smugglers."

"They do." The planes of MacMillan's face became merciless. "We're working with Customs on this, as well as with the Nuclear Regulatory Commission, the FBI, the CIA and a whole alphabet of other agencies on this case. But the U.S. Marshals Service has a special interest in the outcome of this case. One of our deputies took a uranium-tipped bullet in the chest when he was escorting Inga Gunderson's supposed nephew to prison."

"Paul?" Sheryl gasped.

The hazy image she'd formed of a handsome, mustached jet-setter lazing on the beach at Ipanema among the bikinied Brazilians surfaced for a moment, then shattered forever.

She shook her head in dismay. She should have known better than to let herself become intrigued, even slightly, by a globe-trotting wanderer! Her father hadn't stayed in one place long enough for anyone, her mother included, to get to know him or his many varied business concerns. For all Sheryl knew, he could have been a smuggler, too. But not, she prayed, a murderer.

At the memory of her father's roving ways, she gave silent, heartfelt thanks for her steady, reliable, soon-to-be fiancé. Sure, Brian occasionally fell asleep on the couch beside her. And once or twice he'd displayed more excitement over the prospect of closing a real estate deal than he did over their plans for the future. But Sheryl knew he would always be there for her.

As he was probably there for her right now, she realized with a start. No doubt he was waiting in the heat at the house he wanted to show her, flicking impatient little glances at his watch. She'd promised to be there by three-thirty. She snuck a quick look at her watch. It was well past that now, she saw.

"What do you know about Paul Gunderson?"

The curt question snapped her attention back to Deputy Marshal MacMillan.

"Only what Inga told me. That he's a sales rep for an international firm and that he travels a lot. From his postcards, it looks like his company sends him to some pretty exotic locales."

MacMillan dropped his hands from his hips. His well-muscled body seemed to torque to an even higher degree of tension.

"Postcards?" he asked softly.

"He sends her bright, cheery cards from the various places he travels to. They come to her box at the Monzano branch. We—my friends at the post office and I—

thought it was sweet the way he stayed in touch with his aunt like that."

"Yeah, real sweet." His face tight with disgust, Mac-Millan shook his head. "We ordered a mail cover the same day we tracked Inga Gunderson to Albuquerque. The folks at the central post office assured us they had the screen in place. Dammit, they should have caught the fact that she had another postal box."

Sheryl's defensive hackles went up on behalf of her fellow employees. "Hey, they're only human. They do their best."

The marshal didn't dignify that with a reply. He thought for a moment, his forehead furrowed.

"We didn't find any postcards here at the house. Obviously, Inga Gunderson destroyed them as soon as she retrieved them from her box. Did you happen to see the messages on the cards?"

Sheryl squirmed a bit. Technically, postal employees weren't supposed to read their patrons' mail. It was hard to abide by that rule, though. More than one of the male clerks slipped raunchy magazines out of their brown wrappers for a peek when the supervisors weren't around. *Cosmo*s and *Good Housekeeping* had been known to take a detour to the ladies' room. The glossy postcards that came from all over the world weren't wrapped, though, and even the most conscientious employee, which Sheryl considered herself, couldn't resist a peek.

"Well, I may have glanced at one or two. Like the one that arrived this morning, for instance. It—"

The marshal started. "One came in this morning?"

"Yes. From Rio."

"Damn! Wait here. I'm going to get my partner." He

spun on one booted heel. His long legs ate up the distance to the hallway. "Ev! Bring the woman down!"

Sheryl heard a terse reply, followed by a series of shrill yaps. A few moments later, she recognized Mrs. Gunderson's distinctive Scandinavian accent above the dog's clamor. When she made out the specific words, Sheryl's jaw sagged. She wouldn't have imagined that her smiling, white-haired patron could know such obscenities, much less spew them out like that!

She watched, wide-eyed, as a short, stocky man hauled a handcuffed Inga Gunderson into the living room.

"Get your hands off me, you fat little turd!"

The elderly lady accompanied her strident demand with a swing of her foot. A sturdy black oxford connected with her escort's left shin. Button connected with his right.

Luckily, the newcomer was wearing slacks. As Mac-Millan had earlier, he took several dancing hops, shaking his leg furiously to dislodge the little dog. Button hung on like a snarling, bug-eyed demon.

The law enforcement officer sent MacMillan a look of profound disgust. "Shoot the damned thing, will you?"

"No!"

Both women uttered the protest simultaneously. As much as Sheryl disliked the spoiled, noisy shih tzu, she didn't want to see it hurt.

"Button!" she commanded. "Down, boy!"

The dog ignored Sheryl's order, but its black eyes rolled to one side at the sound of its mistress's frantic pleas.

"Let go, precious. Let go, and come to Mommy."

The warbly, pleading voice was so different from the

one that had been spitting vile oaths just moments ago that both men blinked. Sheryl, who'd heard Inga Gunderson carry on lengthy, cooing conversations with her pet many times before, wasn't as surprised by the abrupt transition from vitriol to syrupy sweetness.

"Let go, sweetie-kins. Come to Mommy."

The shih tzu released its death grip on the agent's pants.

"There's a pretty Butty-boo."

With his black eyes still hostile under the lopsided rhinestone hair clip, the little dog settled on its haunches beside its mistress. In another disconcerting shift in both tone and temperament, Inga Gunderson directed her attention to Sheryl.

"What are you doing here? Don't tell me you're working with these pigs, too?"

"No. That is, I just stopped by to make sure you were all right and I—"

"She's been telling us about some postcards," MacMillan interrupted ruthlessly.

Inga's seamed face contorted. Fury blazed in her black eyes. "You just waltzed in here and started spilling your guts to these jerks? Is that the thanks I get for baking all those damn cookies for you and the other idiots at the post office, so you wouldn't lose my mail like you do everyone else's?"

Shocked, Sheryl had no reply. Even Button seemed taken aback by his mistress's venom. He gave an uncertain whine, as if unsure whom he should attack this time. Before he could decide, MacMillan reached down and once again scooped the dog into the tight, restraining pocket of his arm.

"Get her out of here," he ordered his partner curtly.

"Call for backup and wait in the car until it arrives. I'll meet you at the detention facility when I finish with Miss Hancock."

The older woman spit out another oath as she was tugged toward the front door. "Hancock can't tell you anything. She doesn't know a thing. *I* don't know a thing! If you think you can pin a smuggling rap on me, you're pumping some of that coke you feds like to snitch whenever you seize a load."

Yipping furiously, Button tried to squirm free of the marshal's hold and go after his mistress. MacMillan waited until the slam of the front door cut off most of Mrs. Gunderson's angry protests before releasing the dog. Nails clicking on the wood floor, the animal dashed for the hallway. His grating, high-pitched barks rose to a crescendo as his claws scratched frantically at the door.

Sheryl shut out the dog's desperate cries and focused, instead, on the man who faced her, his eyes watchful behind their screen of gold-tipped lashes.

"She's right. I don't know anything. Nothing that pertains to uranium smuggling, anyway."

"Why don't you let me decide what is and isn't pertinent? Tell me again about these postcards."

"There's nothing to tell, really. They come in spurts, every few weeks, from different places around the world. The messages are brief—from the little I've noticed of them," Sheryl tacked on hastily.

"Can you remember dates to go with the locations?"

"Maybe. If I think about it."

"Good! I want to take a look at the card that arrived this morning. If you don't mind, we can take your car back to the branch office."

"Now?"

"Now."

"But I have an appointment."

"Cancel it."

"You don't understand. I'm supposed to meet my fiancé."

The marshal's keen gaze took in her ringless left hand, then lifted to her face.

"We're, uh, unofficially engaged," Sheryl explained for the second time that day.

"This shouldn't take long," MacMillan assured her, taking her elbow to guide her toward the door. "You can use my cell phone to call your friend."

His touch felt warm on her skin and decidedly firm. They made it to the hall before a half whine, half growl stopped them both in their tracks. The shih tzu blocked the front door, his black eyes uncertain under his silky black-and-white fur.

"We can't just leave Button," Sheryl protested.

"I'll have someone contact the animal shelter. They can pick him up."

"The shelter?" Her brows drew together. "They only keep animals for a week or so. What happens if Mrs. Gunderson isn't free to claim him within the allotted time?"

"We'll make sure they keep the mutt as long as necessary."

A touch of impatience colored MacMillan's deep voice. He reached for the door, and the dog gave another uncertain whine. Sheryl dragged her feet, worrying her lower lip with her teeth.

"He doesn't understand what's happening."

"Yeah, well, he'll figure things out soon enough if he tries to take a chunk out of the animal control people."

"I take it you're not a dog lover, Mr....Sheriff... Marshal MacMillan."

"Call me 'Harry.' And, yes, I like dogs. Real dogs. Not hairy little rats wearing rhinestones. Now, if you don't mind, Miss Hancock, I'd like to get to the post office and take a look at that postcard."

"We can't just let him be carted off to the pound."

The marshal's jaw squared. "I don't think you understand the seriousness of this investigation. A law enforcement officer died, possibly because of Inga Gunderson's complicity in illegal activity."

"I'm sorry," she said quietly. "But that's not Button's fault."

"I didn't say it was."

"We can't just leave him."

"Yes, we can."

With her sunny disposition and easygoing nature, Sheryl didn't find it necessary to dig in her heels very often. But when she did, they stayed dug.

"I won't leave him."

Some moments later, Sheryl stepped out of the adobe house into the suffocating heat. A disgruntled deputy U.S. marshal trailed behind her, carrying an equally disgruntled shih tzu under his arm.

She slid into her car and winced as the oven-hot vinyl seat covers singed the backs of her thighs. Trying to keep the smallest possible portion of her anatomy in direct contact with the seat, she keyed the ignition and shoved the air-conditioning to max.

With the two males eyeing each other warily in the passenger seat, Sheryl retraced the route to the Monzano station. She was pulling into the parking lot behind the building when she realized that she'd forgotten all about Brian. She started to ask Harry MacMillan if she could use his phone, but he had already climbed out.

He came around the car in a few man-sized strides. Opening her door, he reached down a hand to help Sheryl out. The courteous gesture from the sharp-edged marshal surprised her. Tentatively, her fingers folded around MacMillan's hand. It was harder than Brian's, she thought with a little tingle of awareness that took her by surprise. Rougher. Like the man himself.

Swinging out of the car, she tugged her hand free with a small smile of thanks. "We can go in the back door. I have the combination."

Button went with them, of course. They couldn't leave him in the car. Even this late in the afternoon, heat shimmered like clear, wavery smoke above the asphalt. Stuffed once more under MacMillan's arm and distinctly unhappy about it, the little dog snuffled indignantly through his pug nose.

Sweat trickled down between Sheryl's breasts by the time she punched the combination into the cipher lock and led the way into the dim, cavernous interior. Familiar gray walls and a huge expanse of black tile outlined with bright-yellow tape to mark the work areas welcomed her. As anxious now as MacMillan to retrieve the postcard from Mrs. Gunderson's box, she wove her way among hampers stacked high with outgoing mail toward her supervisor's desk, situated strategically in the center of the work area.

"You do have a search warrant, don't you?" she asked Harry over one shoulder.

He nodded confidently. "We have authority to screen

all mail sent to the address of Inga Gunderson, alias Betty Hoffman, alias Eva Jorgens."

"Her home address or her post office box?"

"Does it make a difference?"

At MacMillan's frown, Sheryl stopped. "You need specific authority to search a post office box."

"I'm sure the warrant includes that authority."

"We'll have to verify that fact."

Impatience flickered in his eyes. "Let's talk to your supervisor about it."

"We will. I'd have to get her approval before I could allow you into the box in any case."

Sheryl introduced Harry to Pat Martinez, a tall, willowy Albuquerque native with jet-black hair dramatically winged in silver. The customer service supervisor obligingly called the main post office and requested a copy of the warrant. It whirred up on the fax a few moments later.

After ripping it off the machine, Pat skimmed through it. "I'm sorry, this isn't specific enough. It only grants you authority to search mail addressed to Mrs. Gunderson's home address. It'll have to be amended to allow access to a postal box."

Sheryl politely kept any trace of "I told you so" off her face. Harry wasn't as restrained. He scowled at her boss with distinct displeasure.

"Are you sure?"

"Yes, Marshal, I'm sure," Pat drawled. With twenty-two years of service under her belt, she would be. "But you're welcome to call the postal inspector at the central office for confirmation."

He conceded defeat with a distinct lack of graciousness. "I'll take your word for it." Still scowling, he shoved Button at Sheryl. "Here, hold your friend."

He pulled a small black address book out of his pocket, then punched a number into the phone. His face tight, he asked the person who answered at the other end about the availability of a federal judge named, appropriately, Warren. He listened intently for a moment, then requested that the speaker dispatch a car and driver to the Monzano Street post office immediately.

Sheryl watched him hang up with a mixture of relief and regret. Her part in the unfolding Mrs. Gunderson drama was over. She certainly didn't want to get any more involved with smugglers and kindly old ladies who spewed obscenities, but the trip to Inga's house had certainly livened up her day. So had the broad-shouldered law enforcement officer. Sheryl couldn't wait to tell Brian and Elise about her brush with the U.S. Marshals Service.

MacMillan soon disabused her of the notion that her role in what she privately termed the post office caper had ended, however.

"I'll be back in forty-five minutes," he told her curtly. "An hour at most. I'm sorry, but I'll have to ask you to wait for me here."

"Me? Why?"

"I want you to take a look at the message on this postcard and tell me how it compares with the others."

"But I'm already late for my appointment."

He cocked his head, studying her with a glint in his eyes that Sheryl couldn't quite interpret.

"Just out of curiosity, do you always make appointments, not dates, with this guy you're sort of engaged to?"

Since the question was entirely too personal and none

of his business, she ignored it. "I'm late," she repeated firmly. "I have to go."

"You're a material witness in a federal investigation, Miss Hancock. If I have to, I'll get a subpoena from Judge Warren while I'm downtown and bring you in for questioning."

She hitched Button up on her hip, eyeing MacMillan with a good deal less than friendliness.

"You know, Marshal, your bedside manner could use a little work."

"I'm a law enforcement officer, not a doctor," he reminded her. Unnecessarily, she thought. Then, to her astonishment, his mustache lifted in a quick, slashing grin.

"But this is the first time I've had any complaints about my bedside manner. Just wait for me here, okay? And don't talk about the case to anyone else until I get back."

Sheryl was still feeling the impact of that toe-curling grin when Harry MacMillan strode out of the post office a few moments later.

Chapter 3

With only a little encouragement, the Albuquerque police officer detailed to Harry's special fugitive task force got him to the Dennis Chavez Federal Building in seventeen minutes flat. Luckily, they pushed against the rush-hour traffic streaming out of downtown Albuquerque and the huge air force base just south of I-40. The car had barely rolled to a stop at the rear entrance to the federal building before Harry had the door open.

"Thanks."

"Any time, Marshal. Always happy to help out a Wyatt Earp who's lost his horse."

Grinning at the reference to the most legendary figure of the U.S. Marshals Service, Harry tipped him a two-fingered salute. A moment later, he flashed his credentials at the courthouse security checkpoint. The guard obligingly turned off the sensors of the metal detector to accommodate his weapon and waved him through.

Harry took the stairs to the judge's private chambers two at a time. Despite his impatience over this detour downtown for another warrant, excitement whipped through him. He was close. So damned close. With a sixth sense honed by his fifteen years as a U.S. marshal, Harry could almost see the fugitive he'd been tracking for the past eleven months. Hear him panting in fear. Smell his stink.

Paul Gunderson. Aka Harvey Millard and Jacques Garone and Rafael Pasquale and a half-dozen other aliases. Harry knew him in every one of his assumed personas. The bastard had started life as Richard Johnson. Had gone all through high school and college and a good part of a government career with that identity. His performance record as an auditor for the Defense Department described him as well above average in intelligence but occasionally stubborn and difficult to supervise. So difficult, apparently, that a long string of bosses had failed to question the necessity for his frequent trips abroad.

While conducting often unnecessary audits of overseas units, Johnson had also used his string of aliases to establish a very lucrative side business as a broker for the sale and shipment of depleted uranium, a by-product of the nuclear process. As Harry had discovered, most of the uranium Johnson illegally diverted went to arms manufacturers who used it to produce armor-piercing artillery and mortar shells for sale to third-world countries. But recently a new type of handgun ammunition had made an appearance on the black market, and the

U.S. government had mounted a special task force to find its source.

When he was arrested a little over two years ago, Johnson had claimed that he didn't know the product he brokered was being used to manufacture bullets that shredded police officers' protective armor like confetti. The man who gunned down the marshals escorting Johnson to trial certainly knew, though. He left one officer writhing in agony. In the ensuing melee, Johnson finished off the other.

Harry had lost a friend that day. His best friend.

He'd been tracking Johnson ever since. After months of frustrating dead ends, chance information from a snitch had established a tenuous link between Johnson and the Gunderson woman. She'd slipped through their fingers several times before Harry finally traced her to Albuquerque. Through the damned dog yet! Harry didn't even want to think about all the calls they'd made to veterinarians and grooming parlors before they got a lead on an elderly woman with a Scandinavian accent and a black-and-white shih tzu!

They'd no sooner found her than she'd almost slipped away again. Harry had barely set up electronic surveillance of her home when the same dog groomer who IDed her alerted him that Inga Gunderson had canceled her pet's regularly scheduled appointment. She was, according to the groomer, going out of town. Harry had been forced to move in…and had gotten nothing out of the woman.

Then Sheryl Hancock had stumbled on the scene.

With her tumble of blond hair and sunshine-filled green eyes, she would have made Harry's pulse jump in the most ordinary of circumstances. The fact that she provided a definitive link to Paul Gunderson sent it shooting right off the Richter scale. He shook his head, still not quite believing that the Gundersons had been using the U.S. mail to coordinate their activities all this time.

The mail, for God's sake!

In retrospect, he supposed it made sense. Phones were too easily tapped these days. Radio and satellite communications too frequently intercepted by scanners set to random searches of the airwaves. For all the heat the postal system sometimes took, it usually delivered… which was more than could be said for a good many other institutions, private or public. The card sitting in Inga Gunderson's box right now could very well hold vital information. Every nerve in Harry's body tightened at the thought of studying its message.

He cornered the judge and did some fast talking to obtain an amended warrant. A quick call to his partner to check on Inga Gunderson's status confirmed what Harry already suspected. The woman refused to talk until her lawyer arrived. Since the man was currently cruising the interstate somewhere on the other side of Amarillo, it would be some hours yet before he arrived and they could confront the suspect.

"Everything we've got on her is circumstantial," Ev warned. "I don't know if it's enough to hold her unless we establish a hard connection between her and Richard Johnson or Paul Gunderson or whatever he's calling himself now."

"I'm working on it. Just sit on the woman as hard as you can. Maybe she'll crack. And give me a call when her lawyer shows."

"Will do."

Harry hung up, more determined than ever to get his hands on that postcard.

* * *

"Box 89212?"

Buck Aguilar glanced from Sheryl and Pat Martinez to the man facing him across a sorting rack. Oblivious to the tension radiating from the marshal, the postal worker handed Pat back the amended warrant.

"Closed that box this afternoon."

He picked up the stack of mail he'd been working before the interruption. Letters flew in a white blur into the sorting bins.

His face a study in disbelief, Harry leaned forward. "What do you mean, you closed it?"

At the fierce demand, Buck lifted his head once again. Slowly, his gaze drifted from the marshal's face to his boots and back up again. From the expression on the mail carrier's broad, sculpted face, Sheryl could tell that he didn't take kindly to being grilled.

"Got a notice terminating the box," Buck replied in his taciturn way. "Closed it."

The clatter of wheels on concrete as another employee pushed a cart across the room drowned Harry's short, explicit reply. Sheryl caught the gist of it, though. The marshal was *not* happy. She waited for the fireworks. They weren't long in coming.

"What did you do with the contents of the box? Or more specifically—" Harry sent a dagger glance at Sheryl and her supervisor "—what did you do with the postcard that was in there?"

"Returned to sender. Had to. BCNO."

"What the hell does that mean?"

Buck glanced at the marshal again, his eyes flat. Spots of red rose in his cheeks, darkening the skin he'd inherited from his Jacarillo Apache ancestors. Sheryl and the other employees at the Monzano branch office knew that look. Too well. It settled on her co-worker's face whenever he was about to butt heads with another employee or an obnoxious customer. Since Buck stood six-four and carried close to 250 pounds on his muscled frame, that didn't occur often. But when it did, the results weren't pretty.

Pat Martinez replied for him. "*BCNO* means 'Box closed, no order.' Without a forwarding order, we have no choice but to return the mail to sender."

"Dammit!"

"You got a problem with that, Sheriff?"

Buck's soft query lifted the hairs on Sheryl's neck.

"Yeah, I've got a problem with that. And it's 'Marshal.'"

The two men faced each other across the bin like characters in some B-grade Western movie. *The Lawman and the Apache.* At any minute, Sheryl expected them to whip out their guns and knives. Even Button sensed the sudden tension. Poking his nose through the straps of Sheryl's purse, he issued a low, throaty growl.

Hastily, she stepped into the breech. "Maybe it's not too late to retrieve the card. What time did you close the box, Buck?"

His gaze shifted once again. Infinitesimally, his expression softened. "'Bout three-thirty, Sher."

"Oh, dear."

Although it seemed impossible, the marshal bristled even more. "What does 'oh, dear' mean?"

She turned to him, apology spilling from her green eyes. "I'm afraid it means that the contents of Mrs. Gunderson's box went back to the Processing and Distribution Center on the four o'clock run."

"You mean that postcard left here even before I went chasing downtown after the blasted amended warrant?"

"Well...yes."

Harry stared at her, aggravation apparent in every line of his body. For a moment, she wasn't quite sure how he'd handle this new setback. Finally, he blew out a long, ragged breath.

"So where is this distribution center?"

"The P&DC is on Broadway, but..."

"But what?"

Sheryl shared a look with her supervisor and co-worker. They were more than willing to let her handle the thoroughly disgruntled marshal. Bracing herself, she gave him the bad news.

"But the center uses state-of-the-art, high-speed sorters. It also makes runs to the airport every half hour. Since we rent cargo space on all the commercial carriers, your postcard would have gone out—" she glanced at the clock on the wall "—an hour ago, at least. Depending on how it was routed, it's halfway to Dallas or Atlanta or New York right now."

A muscle twitched on the side of MacMillan's jaw. "I suppose there's no way to trace the routing?"

"Not unless it was certified, registered or sent via Global Express, which it wasn't."

"Great!"

A heavy silence descended, broken when Pat Martinez handed Harry his useless warrant.

"I'm sorry about sending you downtown on a wild-goose chase, Marshal, but I won't apologize for the fact that my employees followed regulations. If you don't need me for anything else, I'll get back to work."

"No. Thanks."

Buck moved off, too, rolling his empty hamper away to collect a full one from the row at the back of the box area. Sheryl and Button waited while Harry rubbed a hand across the back of his neck, flattening his cotton shirt against his stomach and ribs.

At the sight of those lean hollows and broad surfaces, a sudden and completely unexpected tingle of awareness darted through Sheryl. Content with Brian, she hadn't looked at other men in the year or so they'd been dating. She'd certainly never let her gaze linger on a set of washboard ribs or a flat, trim belly. Or noticed the tight fit of a pair of jeans across muscled thighs and...

"Are you hungry?"

Sheryl jerked her gaze upward. "Excuse me?"

"Are you hungry? I skipped breakfast, and Ev and I were too busy taking physical and verbal abuse from the Gunderson woman to grab lunch. Why don't we have dinner while we talk about these postcards?"

"Tonight?"

The tightness left his face. A corner of his thick, luxuriant mustache tipped up in a reluctant smile. "That was the general idea. I know I made you miss your... appointment...with this guy you're sort of engaged to. Let me make it up to you by feeding you while I squeeze your brain."

"Squeeze my brain, huh? Interesting approach. Does it get you a lot of dinner dates?"

"It never fails." His smile feathered closer to a grin. "Another example of my charming bedside manner, Miss Hancock. So, are you hungry?"

She was starved, Sheryl realized. She was also obligated to provide what information she could to the authorities, represented in this instance by Deputy U.S. Marshal Harry MacMillan.

Still, she hesitated. When she'd called Brian a while ago to apologize for standing him up, he'd sounded more than a little piqued. Sheryl couldn't blame him. In an attempt to soothe his ruffled feathers, she'd promised to cook his favorite chicken dish tonight. They'd fallen into the routine of eating at her apartment on Tuesdays and his on Fridays. This was supposed to have been her night. Oh, well, she'd just have to make it up to him next week.

"I need to make a phone call," she said, hitching her purse and its furry passenger up on her shoulder.

Graciously, MacMillan handed her his mobile phone. With both dog and man listening in, Sheryl conducted a short, uncomfortable conversation with Brian.

"I'm sorry I've kept you waiting all this time, but something's come up. I'm going to be tied up awhile longer. Yes, I know it's Tuesday night. No, I can't put this off until tomorrow."

She caught MacMillan's speculative gaze, and turned a shoulder. "Yes. Maybe. I'll phone you when I get home."

Sheryl ended the call on a small sigh. Brian's structured approach to life usually gave her such a comfortable feeling. Sometimes, though, it made things just a bit difficult.

"Trouble in almost-paradise?" Harry inquired politely, slipping his phone back into his pocket.

"Not really. Where would you like to eat?"

"You pick it. I don't know Albuquerque all that well."

She thought for a minute. "How about El Pinto? They have the best Mexican food in the city and we can get a table outside, where we can talk privately."

"Sounds good to me."

Sheryl led the way to the rear exit, absorbing the fact that he was apparently a stranger to the city.

"Where's home? Or can you say?"

As soon as she articulated the casual question, she wondered if he would…or should…answer. She had no idea what kind of security U.S. marshals operated under. He'd told her not to talk about the case. Maybe he wasn't supposed to talk about himself, either.

Evidently, that wasn't a problem.

"I'm assigned to the fugitive apprehension unit of the Oklahoma City district office," he replied, "but I don't spend a whole lot of time there. My job keeps me on the road most of the time."

Another wanderer! They seemed to constitute half the world's population. Sheryl's minor annoyance with Brian's inflexibility vanished instantly. He, at least, wouldn't take off without warning for parts unknown. She led the way outside, blinking at the abrupt transition from dim interior to dazzling sunlight.

"I'd better meet you at the restaurant. I'll have to go by my apartment first to drop off Button. Unless you want to take him back to your place?" she finished hopefully.

"I can't," he replied without the slightest hint of regret. "I'm staying in a motel."

She sighed, resigning herself to an unplanned houseguest. "Do you know how to get to El Pinto?"

"Haven't got a clue. Just give me the address. I'll find it."

She chewed her lip, thinking perhaps she should suggest a more accessible place. "It's kind of hard to locate if you're not familiar with Albuquerque."

He sent her a look of patented amusement. "U.S. mar-shals have been tracking down bad guys since George Washington pinned gold stars on the original thirteen deputies. I'm pretty sure I can find this restaurant."

"I stand corrected," Sheryl said gravely.

She drove out of the parking lot a few moments later, with Button occupying the seat beside her. Harry trailed in a tan government sedan. Following her directions, he turned south at the corner of Haines and Juan Tabo, and she headed north.

By this late hour, Albuquerque's rush-hour traffic had thinned to a steady but fast-moving stream. The trip to her apartment complex took less than fifteen minutes. As always, the cream-colored adobe architecture and profusion of flowers decorating the fountain in the center of the tree-shaded complex gave her a quiet joy. Sheryl had moved into her one-bedroom apartment soon after her last promotion and loved its cool Southwestern col-ors and high-ceilinged rooms. It was perfect for her, but the pale-mauve carpet hadn't been pet-proofed. After unlocking the front door, she set the shih tzu down in the tiled foyer.

"We have to establish a few ground rules, fella. No yapping, or you'll get me thrown out of here. No taking bites out of me or my furniture. No accidents on the rug."

Busy sniffing out the place, Button ignored her.

"I'm serious," she warned.

Once she'd plopped her purse down on the counter separating the kitchen from the small dining area, she pulled a plastic bowl from the cupboard and filled it with water.

"It's either me or the pound, so you'd better… Hey!"

With regal indifference to her startled protest, the

shih tzu lifted his raised leg another inch and sprayed the dining table.

Obviously, Button didn't believe in rules!

Sheryl went to work with paper towels, then scooped up the unrepentant dog. A moment later, she set him and the water dish down on the other side of the sliding-glass patio doors. Hands on hips, she surveyed the small, closed-in area. The leafy Chinese elm growing on the other side of the adobe wall provided plenty of shade. The few square yards of grass edging the patio tiles provided Button's other necessary commodity.

"This is your temporary residence, dog. Make yourself comfortable."

After sliding the patio door closed behind her, she heeled off her sneakers and padded into the bathroom to splash cold water on her face. Then she shucked her shorts and tank top and pulled on a gauzy sundress in a cool mint green. She had her hair unbraided and was pulling a brush through its stubborn curls when a series of high-pitched yips told her Button wanted in.

Too bad. He'd better get used to outdoor living.

She soon learned that what Button wanted, Button had his own way of getting. Within moments, the yips rose to a grating, insistent crescendo.

The brush hit the counter with a thud. Muttering, Sheryl retraced her steps and cut the dog's protests off with a stern admonition.

"I guess I didn't make myself clear. You've lost your house privileges. You're going to camp out here on the patio, Buttsy-boo, or take a trip to the pound."

Ten minutes later, Sheryl slammed the front door behind her and left a smug Button in undisputed possession of her air-conditioned apartment. It was either cave in to his hair-raising howls or risk eviction. In desperation, she'd spread a layer of newspapers over the bathroom floor. She could only hope that the dog would condescend to use them. The next few days, she thought grimly, could prove a severe strain on her benevolence toward animals in general and squish-faced lapdogs in particular.

As she shoved the car key into the ignition, a sudden thought struck her. If even half of what Harry had told her about Mrs. Gunderson's activities was true, Sheryl could be stuck with her unwanted houseguest for a lot longer than a few days.

Groaning, she backed out of the carport. No way was she keeping that mutt for more than a day or two. Harry had to have stumbled across some relative or acquaintance of Mrs. Gunderson during his investigation, someone who could take over custody of her pet. She put the issue on the table as soon as they were seated in El Pinto's shaded, colorful outdoor dining area. Harry stretched his long legs out under the tiled table and graciously refrained from pointing out that it was her insistence on taking the dog with them that had caused her dilemma in the first place.

"There's nothing I'd like better than to identify a few of Inga Gunderson's friends and acquaintances."

Sheryl had to scoot her chair closer to catch his reply over the noise of the busy restaurant. A fountain bubbled and splashed just behind them, providing a cheerful accompaniment to the mariachi trio strumming and thumping their guitars as they strolled through the patio area. Harry had chosen the table deliberately so they could talk without raising the interest of other diners.

Even so, Sheryl hadn't counted on practically sitting in his lap to carry on a conversation.

"As far as we know," he continued, "Inga doesn't have any acquaintances here. She made a few calls to local businesses, but no one's phoned her or visited her." His gold-flecked eyes settled on his dinner partner. "Except you, Miss Hancock."

"'Sheryl,'" she amended absently. "So what will happen to her?"

"We have sufficient circumstantial evidence to book her on suspicion of smuggling. The charge might or might not stick, but she's not the one I really want. It's her supposed nephew I'm after."

Despite Harry's relaxed pose, Sheryl couldn't miss the utter implacability in his face. He slipped a pen and small black-leather notebook out of his jacket pocket, all business now.

"Tell me about the postcards."

She waited to reply until the waitress had placed a brimming basket of tortilla chips on the table and taken their drink orders.

"They usually come in batches," she told Harry. "Two or three will arrive within a week of each other, then a month might go by before another set comes in."

"I figured as much," the marshal said, almost to himself. "He'd have to send backups in case the first didn't arrive. Have any others come in with this one from Rio?"

"Two. The first was from Prague. The second from Pamplona."

"Pamplona?" His brow creased. "Isn't that where they run bulls through the streets? With the locals running right ahead of them?"

"That's what the scene on the card showed." Sheryl

hunched forward, recalling the vivid street scene with a shake of her head. "Can you imagine racing down a narrow, cobbled street a few steps ahead of thundering, black bulls?"

"I can imagine it, but it's not real high on my list of fun things to do," Harry admitted dryly. He loaded a chip with salsa. "How about you?"

"Me? No way! I have enough trouble staying ahead of my bills, let alone a herd of bulls. Uh, you'd better go easy on that stuff. I heard the green chili crop came in especially hot this year."

"Not to fear, I've got a lead-lined stom— Arrggh!"

He shot up straight in his chair, grabbed his water glass and downed the entire contents in three noisy gulps. Blinking rapidly, he stared at the little dish of salsa in disbelief.

"Good Lord! Do you New Mexicans really eat this stuff?"

"Some of us do," Sheryl answered, laughing. "But we work up to it over a period of years."

The waitress arrived at that moment. Harry shot her a look of profound gratitude and all but snatched the Don Miguel light he'd ordered out of her hand. The ice-cold beer, like the water, went down in a few long, gulping swallows.

The waitress turned an amused smile on Sheryl. "Didn't you warn him?"

"I tried to."

Winking, she picked up her tray. "Another gringo bites the dust."

Sheryl eyed the marshal, not quite sure she'd agree with the waitress's assessment. His golden brown eyes watered, to be sure. A pepper-induced flush darkened his cheeks above the line of his mustache. He drained his mug with the desperation of a man who'd just crawled across a hundred miles of burning desert.

She would categorize him as down, but certainly not out. He showed too much strength in those broad shoulders. Carried himself with too much authority. Even in his boots and jeans and casual open-necked shirt, he gave the impression of a man who knew what he wanted and went after it.

For an unguarded moment, Sheryl wondered if he would pursue a woman he desired with the same single-minded determination he pursued the fugitives he hunted. He would, she decided. He'd pursue her, and when he caught her, he'd somehow manage to convince her she'd been the hunter all along. The thought sent a ripple of excitement singing through her veins. She shook her head at her own foolishness.

Still, the tingle stayed with her while Harry dragged the heel of his hand across his eyes.

"Remind me to listen to your warnings next time."

The offhand remark made Sheryl smile, until she realized that there probably wouldn't be a next time. As soon as she filled Marshal MacMillan in on the details from the postcards, he'd ride off into the sunset in pursuit of his quarry.

How stupid of her to romanticize his profession. She'd better remember that he lived the same life-style her father had. Here today, gone tomorrow, with never a backward glance for those he left behind.

Recovering from his bout with the green chilies, Harry got back to business.

"Prague, Pamplona and Rio," he recited with just a

hint of hoarseness. "We've suspected all along that our man is triangulating his shipments."

"Triangulating them?"

"Sending them through second and third countries, where they're rebundled with other products like coffee or bat guano, then smuggled into the States."

"Why in the world would someone bundle uranium with bat guano and...? Oh! To disguise the scent of the metal containers and get them past the Customs dogs, right?"

"You got it in one." He leaned forward, all business now. "Can you remember any of the words on the cards?"

"On two of them. I didn't see the one from Prague. My friend Elise described it to me, though."

"Okay, start with Rio. Give me what you can remember."

"I can give it to you exactly." She wrinkled her brow. "'Hi to my favorite aunt. I've been dancing in the streets for the past four days. Wish you were here.'"

Harry stared at her in blank astonishment. "You can recall it word for word?"

"Sure."

"How?" he shot back. "With the thousands of pieces of mail you handle every day, how in the hell can you remember one postcard?"

"Because I handle thousands of pieces of mail every day," she explained patiently. "The white envelopes and brown flats—the paper-wrapped magazines and manila envelopes—all blur together. Not that many postcards come through, though, and when they do, they catch our attention immediately."

She decided not to add that the really interesting postcards got passed from employee to employee. The male workers particularly enjoyed the topless beach scenes that American tourists loved to send back to their relatives. Some cards went well beyond topless and tipped into outright obscenity. Those they were required to turn into the postal inspectors. Sheryl had long ago ceased being surprised at what people stuck stamps on and dropped in a mailbox.

Harry had her repeat the message. He copied the few sentences in his pad, then studied their content.

"I don't think this is Carnival season. I'm sure that happens right before Lent in Rio, just as it does in New Orleans."

He made another note to himself to check the dates of Rio's famous festival. Sheryl was sitting so close she could make out every stroke. His handwriting mirrored his personality, she decided. Bold. Aggressive. Impatient.

"Maybe the four days has some significance," she suggested.

"It probably does." He frowned down at his notes. "I don't know what yet, though."

"Do you want to know about the picture on the front side?" she asked after a moment.

"Later. Let's finish the back first. What else do you remember about it?"

"What do you want to start with? The handwriting? The color of ink? The stamp? The cancellation mark?"

He sat back, his eyes gleaming. He looked like a man who'd just hit a superjackpot.

"Start wherever you want."

They worked their way right through sour cream enchiladas, smoked charro beans, rice and sopapillas dripping with honey. The mariachi band came to their table and left again, richer by the generous tip Harry passed them. The tables around them emptied, refilled. They were still working the Rio postcard when Harry's phone beeped.

"MacMillan." He listened for a moment, his brow creasing. "Right. I'm on my way."

Snapping the phone shut, he rose to pull out Sheryl's chair. "I'm sorry. Inga Gunderson's lawyer just showed up and wants to see his client. We'll have to go over the rest of the cards tomorrow. I'll call you to set up a time."

A small, unexpected dart of pleasure rippled through Sheryl at the thought of continuing this discussion with Marshal MacMillan. Shrugging, she chalked it up to the fact that she still had something worthwhile to contribute to his investigation.

She drove out of the parking lot a few moments later, thinking that she'd better reschedule the last-minute layette shopping spree she and Elise had planned for tomorrow night. As determined as Harry was to extract every last bit of information from her, they might have to work late.

She couldn't know that he would walk into the post office just after nine the next morning and reschedule her entire life.

Chapter 4

"I'm sorry, sir," Sheryl repeated for the third time. "I can't hand out a DHS check over the counter. Even if I could, I wouldn't give you a check addressed to someone else."

The runny-eyed scarecrow on the other side of the counter lifted an arm and swiped it across his nose. His hand shook so badly that the tattoos decorating the inside of his wrist were a blur of red and blue.

"That's my old lady's welfare check," he whined. "I gotta have it. I want it."

Yeah, right, Sheryl thought. What he wanted was another fix, courtesy of the Department of Human Services. She wondered how many other women this creep had bullied or beaten out of their food and rent money over the years to feed his drug habit.

"I can't give it to you," she repeated.

"My old lady's moved, I'm tellin' ya, and she didn't get her check this month. She sent me in to pick it up."

"I'm sure someone explained to her that the post office can't forward a DHS check. We're required by regulations to deliver it to the address where she physically resides or send it back."

"Send it back? Why, dammit?"

The angry explosion turned the heads of the other customers who'd come in with the first rush of the morning. In the booth next to Sheryl's, Elise glanced up sharply from the stamps she was dealing out.

Holding on to her patience with both hands, Sheryl tried again. "We have to send the checks back to DHS because a few people abused the system by moving constantly and collecting checks from several different counties at once. Now everyone has to pay the price for their fraud."

The lank-haired junkie fixed her with a malevolent glare. "Yeah, well, I don't give a rat's ass about them other people. I just want my old lady's money. You'd better give it to me, bitch, or I'm gonna—"

"You're going to what?"

At the dangerous drawl, both Sheryl and her unpleasant customer jerked around.

The sight of Harry MacMillan's broad-shouldered form sent relief pinging through her. Relief and something else, something far too close to excitement for Sheryl's peace of mind. Swallowing, she ascribed the sudden flutter in her stomach to the fact that the marshal looked particularly intimidating this morning.

As he had yesterday, he wore jeans and a well-tailored sport coat, this one a soft, lightweight, blue broadcloth. As it had yesterday, his jacket strained at the seams of his wide shoulders. Adding to his overall physical presence, his jaw had a hard edge that sent off its own silent warning. The gold in his eyes glinted hard and cold.

Sheryl could handle nasty characters like the one standing in front of her at this moment. She'd done it many times. But that didn't stop her from enjoying the pasty look that came over the druggie's face when he took in Harry's size and stance.

"Nah, no problem," he replied to Harry, but his mouth pinched when he turned back to Sheryl. "Me 'n' my old lady need that money."

"Tell her to contact DHS," She instructed once again. "They'll issue an emergency payment if necessary."

His thin, ravaged face contorted with fury and a need she could only begin to guess at. "I wouldn't be here if it wasn't necessary, you stupid—"

He broke off, slinging a sideways look at Harry.

The marshal jerked his head toward the lobby doors. "You'd better leave, pal. Now."

The watery eyes flared with reckless bravado. "You gonna make me, *pal?*"

"If I have to."

Like waves eddying around a rock, the other customers in the post office backed away from the two men. A tight, taut silence gripped the area. Sheryl's knee inched toward the silent alarm button just under her counter.

The thin, pinch-faced junkie broke the shimmering tension just before she exerted enough pressure to set off the alarm. With another spiteful glance at Sheryl, he pushed past Harry and shouldered open the glass door. A collective murmur of relief rose from the other customers as the door thumped shut behind him.

Harry didn't relax his vigilance until the departing

figure had stalked to a battered motorcycle, threw a leg over the seat, jumped on the starter and roared out of the parking lot.

"Nice guy," one of the women in line murmured.

"Wonder what his problem was?" another groused.

"Do you get many customers like that?" Harry inquired, moving to Sheryl's station.

No one objected to the fact that he cut ahead of them in line, she noticed.

"Not many. What are you doing here? I thought you were going to call and set up a time for us to meet?"

"I decided to come in person, instead. Can you get someone to cover for you here? I need to talk to you privately."

"Yes, of course. Wait for me in the lobby and I'll let you in through that door to the back area."

With a nod to the other customers, Harry turned away. Elise demanded an explanation the moment the glass doors swung shut behind him.

"Who *is* that?"

"He's—"

Sheryl caught herself just in time. Harry had told her not to discuss the case with anyone other than her supervisor. She hadn't, although the restriction had resulted in another uncomfortable phone conversation with Brian after she'd driven home from El Pinto.

"He's an acquaintance," she finished lamely, if truthfully.

"Since when?"

"Since last night."

Elise's dark-red brows pulled together in a troubled frown. "Does Brian know about this new acquaintance of yours?"

"There's nothing to know." With an apologetic smile at the lined-up customers, Sheryl plopped a Closed sign in front of her station. "I'll send Peggy up to cover the counter with you."

She found the petite brunette on the outside loading dock, pulling in long, contented drags of cigarette smoke mixed with diesel fumes from the mail truck parked next to the ramp.

"I know you're on break, but something's come up. Can you cover for me out front for a few minutes?"

"Sure." Peggy took another pull, then stubbed out her cigarette in the tub of sand the irreverent carriers always referred to as the butt box. Carefully, she tucked the half-smoked cigarette into the pocket of her uniform shirt.

"I have to conserve every puff. I promised myself I'd only smoke a half a pack today."

"I thought you decided to quit completely."

"I did! I will! After this pack. Maybe." Smiling ruefully at Sheryl's grin, she strolled back into the station. "How long do you think you'll be? I'm supposed to help Pat with the vault inventory this morning."

"Not long," Sheryl assured her. "I just need to set up an appointment."

Contrary to her expectations, she soon discovered that Harry hadn't driven to the Monzano station to make an appointment.

She stared at him, dumbfounded, while he calmly informed her and her supervisor that Albuquerque's postmaster had agreed to assign Miss Hancock to the special fugitive apprehension task force that Harry headed.

"Me?"

Sheryl's startled squeak echoed off the walls of the stationmaster's little-used private office.

"You," he confirmed, pulling a folded document out of his coat pocket. "This authorizes an indefinite detail, effective immediately."

"May I see that?" her supervisor asked.

"Of course."

Pat Martinez stuck her pencil into her upswept jet-black hair and skimmed the brief communiqué he handed her.

"Well, it looks like you're on temporary duty, Sheryl."

"Hey, hang on here," she protested. "I'm not sure I want to be assigned to a fugitive apprehension task force, indefinitely or otherwise. Before I agree to anything like this, I want to know what's required of me."

"Basically, I want your exclusive time and attention for as long it takes to extract every bit of information I can about those postcards."

"Exclusive time and attention? You mean, like all day?"

"And all night, if necessary."

Sheryl gaped at him. "You're kidding, right?"

He didn't crack so much as a hint of a smile. "No, Miss Hancock, I'm not. My team's been at it pretty much around the clock since we tracked Inga Gunderson to Albuquerque. I won't ask that you put in twenty-four hours at a stretch, of course, but I will ask that you work with me as long as necessary and as hard as possible."

"Look, I don't mind working with you, but we're shorthanded here. The box clerk is on vacation and Elise could go out on maternity leave at any moment."

"So the postmaster indicated." Calmly, Harry nodded to the document held by Sheryl's supervisor. "We took that into consideration."

"The postmaster is sending a temp to cover your absence," Pat explained. "If Elise goes out, he'll cover that, too." Her eyes lifted to Harry. "You're thorough, Mac-Millan."

"I learned my lesson after the fiasco with the warrant," he admitted. "This time, I made sure we dotted every i and crossed every t."

Sheryl wasn't sure she liked being lumped in with the i's and t's, but she let it pass. Now that she'd recovered from her initial surprise, she didn't object to the detail. She just didn't care for Harry's high-handed way of arranging it.

As if realizing that he needed to mend some bridges with his new detailee, the marshal gave her a smile that tried for apologetic but fell a few degrees short. Sheryl suspected that MacMillan rarely apologized for anything.

"I didn't have time to coordinate this with you and Ms. Martinez beforehand. My partner and I were up most of the night running air routes that service Prague, Pamplona and Rio through the computers. We're convinced our man is bringing in a shipment soon, and we're not going to let it or him slip through our fingers. We've got to break the code that was on those postcards, and to do that we need your help, Sheryl."

Put like that, how could she refuse?

"Well, if you're sure someone's coming out here to cover for me…"

"The postmaster assured me that wasn't a problem."

Sheryl looked to Pat, who nodded. "We'll manage until the temp gets here. Go close down your station."

Still a little bemused by her sudden transition from postal clerk to task force augmentee, Sheryl headed for the front. Naturally, her curious co-workers peppered her with questions.

"What's going on, Sher?" Elise wanted to know. "Why are you closing out?"

Peggy grinned wickedly over the divider separating the stations. "And who's the long, tall stud with the mustache? Tell us all, girl."

"I can't right now. I'll tell you about it later."

When she could, Sheryl amended silently, hitting a sequence of keystrokes to tally her counter transactions. The printer stuttered out a report for her abridged workday. Another quick sequence shut down the computer.

Her hand resting on her mounded tummy, Elise waited for the next customer. "Where are you going now?"

That much at least Sheryl could reveal. "Downtown. The postmaster has assigned me to a special detail."

"With the stud? No kidding?" Peggy waggled her brows. "How do I go about getting assigned to this detail?"

"By stopping by to check on little old ladies on your way home from work."

"Huh?"

"I'll tell you about it later," Sheryl repeated.

With swift efficiency, she ejected her disk from her terminal and removed her cash drawer. After stacking her stock of stamps on top of the drawer, she carried the lot to the vault. A quick inventory tallied her cash receipts with the money orders, stamps and supplies she'd sold so far this morning. She scribbled her name across the report, then left it for the T-6 clerk who had the unenviable task of reconciling all the counter clerks' reports with the master printout produced at the end of each day. That done, she hurried back to her counter to retrieve her purse and extract a promise from Elise.

"Brian's supposed to pick me up at eleven-thirty. He wanted to show me a house during lunch that he's going to list. He needs a woman's opinion about the renovations that might be necessary to the kitchen. Would you go with him? Please? You know how he always raves about what you did with your kitchen."

Brian wasn't the only one who raved about the miracles Elise had performed with the small fixer-upper he'd found for her after her divorce. With two kids to house and a third about to make an appearance, she'd taken wallpapering and sheet curtains to a higher plane of art. She'd also turned a dilapidated kitchen into a marvel of bleached cabinets, hand-decorated tiles and artfully disguised pipes.

"I'll be happy to go with him, but..."

"Thanks! Tell him I'll call him tonight."

Sheryl left Elise with a frown still creasing her forehead and hurried toward the back. Now that she'd gotten used to the idea, she had to admit the prospect of taking part in a criminal investigation sent a little thrill of excitement through her. The Wanted posters tacked to the bulletin board in the outer lobby and the occasional creeps who came into the post office, like the one this morning, were the closest she'd come to the dark, seamy side of life. Besides, she was only doing her civic duty by helping Harry piece together the puzzle of the postcards.

Which didn't explain the way her pulse seemed to stutter with that strange, inexplicable excitement when she saw the marshal. Hands shoved into his pockets, ankles

crossed, he lounged against one of the carriers' sorting
desks as though he had nothing else in the world more
important to do than wait for her. The pose didn't fit his
character, she now knew. Harry MacMillan was anything but patient. She'd just met him yesterday—fallen
into his arms, more correctly—and now he'd pulled her
off her job to work on his team.

At the sound of her footsteps, he glanced up, and
Sheryl's excitement took on a deeper, keener edge. His
toffee-colored eyes swept her with the same intent scrutiny that had raised goose bumps on her skin yesterday. Suddenly self-conscious, she glanced down at her
pin-striped shirt with its neat little cross tab tie and her
navy shorts.

"Should I change out of my uniform?"

His gaze skimmed from her nose to her knees and
back again. "You're fine."

She was a whole lot better than fine, Harry thought
as he followed her to the exit. He'd never paid much attention to postal uniforms, but Sheryl Hancock filled
hers out nicely. Very nicely.

Her pin-striped shirt with its little red tab was innocu-
ous enough, but the long, curving stretch of leg displayed
by those navy shorts pushed his simple observation into
swift, gut-level male appreciation. It also put a knot in
his belly that didn't belong there right now.

Frowning, Harry gave himself a mental shake. He'd
better keep his mind focused on the information Sheryl
could supply, not on her tanned legs or the seductive
swing of her hips. And he'd darn well better remember
why he'd yanked her from her workplace and put her on
his team. She held the key to those damned postcards.
He felt it with every instinct he possessed. He wasn't

going to rest until he'd pulled every scrap of information out of this woman.

Despite his stern reminder that his business with Sheryl was just that, business, his pulse tripped at the thought of the hours ahead. On the advice of her lawyer, Inga Gunderson flatly refused to talk to the investigators. Harry and Ev had spent several frustrating hours with the woman last night. Finally, they'd left her stewing in her own venom. The clerk of the court had assured them that she wouldn't get a bail hearing until late tomorrow, if then, given the overloaded court docket.

Earlier this morning, Ev had left to drive up to the labs at Los Alamos to talk to one of the government's foremost experts on the use and physical properties of depleted uranium. The New Mexico state trooper assigned to the task force was now out at the local FAA office, compiling a list of secondary airstrips within a hundred-mile radius. The Customs agent working with them on an as-needed basis had returned to his office to cull through foreign flight schedules. For the next few hours at least, Harry would have the task force headquarters—and Sheryl—to himself.

He intended to make good use of that time.

"Why don't I drive, since my vehicle is cleared for the secure parking at the Chavez Federal Building? We can come back for your car later."

"Okay. Just let me open my windows a bit to keep from baking the seats."

A moment later, Sheryl buckled herself into the blast furnace heat of the tan sedan. "So you're operating out of the downtown courthouse?"

"We've set up task force headquarters in the U.S. Marshals' offices."

Task force headquarters!

A vague image formed in her mind of a busy, high-tech command post, complete with wall-sized screen satellite maps displaying all kinds of vital information, humming computer terminals, beeping phones and a team of dedicated, intense professionals. The idea of becoming a part, however briefly, of the effort kindled a sense of adventure.

Reality came crashing down on her the moment she stepped inside the third-floor conference room in the multistory federal building in the heart of the city. Hand-scribbled paper charts decorated the nondescript tan walls. Foam coffee cups and cardboard boxes of records littered the long conference table. Wires from the phones clustered in the center of the table snaked around the cups and over the boxes like gray streamers. A faint, stale odor drifted from the crushed pizza cartons that had been stuffed into metal wastebaskets in a corner. Sheryl looked around, gulping.

"This is it? Your headquarters?"

"This is it." Harry shrugged off the clutter with the same ease he shrugged out of his jacket. "Make yourself comfortable."

She might have been able to do just that if her gaze hadn't snagged on the blue steel gun butt nestled against his left side. Even holstered, the weapon looked ugly and far too dangerous for her peace of mind.

Harry tossed his jacket over a chair back and turned, catching her wary expression. "Don't worry. I know how to use it."

Somehow, that didn't reassure her.

"I don't like guns," she admitted, dropping her shoulder bag into a chair. "They make me nervous. Very nervous."

Calmly, he rolled up the cuffs of his white cotton shirt. "They make me nervous, too. Especially when they're loaded with uranium-tipped bullets. Ready to get to work?"

After that unsubtle reminder of the reason she was here, Sheryl could hardly say no. Pulling out one of the chairs, she rolled up to the table.

"I'm ready."

"We pretty well took apart the postcard from Rio last night. Let's start with the one from Pamplona today. We'll reverse the process and work the front side first. Can you describe the scene?"

She shot him an amused glance.

"Of course you can," he answered himself. "You talk, I'll listen."

Summoning up a mental image of the card, Sheryl painted a vivid word picture that included a narrow, cobbled street lined with two-story stone houses. Geranium-filled window boxes. White-shirted young men racing between the buildings, looking over their shoulders at the herd of black bulls just visible at a bend in the street.

Harry copied down every word, so intent on searching for similarities with the card from Rio that it was some time before he noticed the subtle difference in Sheryl's voice. It sounded softer, he realized in surprise, almost dreamy. He glanced up to find her staring at the wall, her mouth curving slightly. She'd gotten lost somewhere on a high, sunny plain in Spain's Basque province.

Harry got a little lost himself just looking at her. The faint trace of freckles across the bridge of her nose fascinated him, as did the mass of tawny hair tumbling down her back. She'd pulled the hair at her temples back and caught it in one of those plastic clips with long, danger-ous-looking teeth. His hand itched to spring the clip free, to let those curls take on a life of their own.

"There was a cathedral in the background," she mur-mured, drawing his attention away from the curve of her cheek. "An old Gothic cathedral complete with fly-ing buttresses and a huge rose-colored window in the south transept. One of man's finest monuments to God."

Sighing, she shifted in her seat and caught Harry star-ing at her. "I've read a little bit about medieval Gothic cathedrals," she confessed with an embarrassed shrug. "Some people consider them the architectural wonders of the modern world."

"Have you ever been inside one?"

"No. Have you?"

He nodded. "Notre Dame."

"In Paris?"

Her breathless awe made Harry bite back a grin. He'd visited the majestic structure on a wet, dreary spring day. All he could recall were impenetrable shadows, cold dampness and thousands of votive candles flicker-ing in the darkness. Of course, he was a marine gunny sergeant on leave at the time, and far more interested in the *filles de joie* working the broad embankments along the Seine than in the gray stone cathedral

"Maybe your sort-of fiancé will spring for a trip to Paris for a honeymoon," he commented casually.

He saw at once that he'd said the wrong thing. The soft, faraway look disappeared from her green eyes. She sat up, a tiny frown creasing her brow.

"Brian isn't interested in traveling, any more than I am. We prefer to save our money for something more practical, like a house or a new car or the kids' college education."

Without warning, a thought rifled through Harry's mind. If he wanted to stake his claim to a woman like this one, he'd whisk her off to a deserted island, peel off her clothes and make love to her a dozen times a day before either of them started thinking about a house and a new car and the kids' college education.

His belly clenched at the image of Sheryl sprawled in the surf, her tanned body offered up to the sun like a pagan sacrifice. Her arms reached for him. Her eyes...

Dammit!

A quick shake of his head banished the crashing surf. He had to remember why he was here. And that Sheryl was spoken for...almost. Pushing aside her vague relationship with the jerk who made appointments instead of dates, he brought them both back to the matter at hand.

"Let's talk about the message on the back."

She blinked at his brusque instruction, but complied willingly enough.

"As best I recall, it was short and sweet. 'Hi, Auntie. I've spent two great...'" She paused, chewing on her lower lip. "No, it was three. 'I've spent three great days keeping a half step ahead of the bulls. See you soon, Paul.'"

"Run it through your mind again," Harry ordered. "Close your eyes. See the words. Picture the—"

One of the phones on the table shrilled. He grabbed the receiver, listened for a few minutes and hung up with a promise to call back later.

"Close your eyes, Sheryl."

Obediently, she blanked out the chart-strewn walls.

"Visualize the words. Follow every curl of every letter. Describe them to me."

Like a dutiful disciple of a master mesmerizer, she let Harry's deep, slow voice lull her into a state of near somnolence. Slowly, lines of dark swirls began to take shape.

She didn't even notice when morning faded into afternoon, or when the uninspiring conference room began to take on an aura of a real live operations center. She did note that the phones rang constantly, and that a seemingly steady stream of people popped in to talk to Harry or pass information.

Sometime around the middle of the afternoon, the short, stocky Everett Sloan returned from Los Alamos Laboratories. Sheryl soon discovered that, unlike Harry, he was assigned to the Albuquerque office of the U.S. Marshals and had been tapped as the local coordinator for the task force. Shedding his wrinkled suit jacket, Ev informed his temporary partner that he'd collected more information than he'd ever wanted to know about the properties and characteristics of the heavy metal known as U-235.

A short time later, a slender, striking brunette in the brown shirt, gray pants and Smoky the Bear hat of a New Mexico state trooper joined the group. After brief introductions, Fay Chandler tossed her hat on the table and unrolled a huge aerial map showing every airstrip, paved or otherwise, within a hundred-mile radius. The three-letter designation code for each strip had been highlighted in yellow. If their suspect intended to bring his contraband in someplace other than Albuquerque International, Fay would coordinate the local response team.

In the midst of all this activity, Harry somehow remained focused on Sheryl and the postcards. After hours of work, he reduced the sheets of information he'd pulled from her to a few key words and phrases. He repeated them now in an almost singsong mantra.

"Rio… Carnival… April…four."

Sheryl picked up the chorus. "Pamplona…bulls… July…three."

"Prague… Wenceslas Square… September…two."

MacMillan stared at the words, as though the sheer intensity of his scrutiny would solve the riddle they represented. "I know there's a pattern in there somewhere. A reverse order of numbers or letters or something!"

"Maybe the computers will find it." Ev Sloan slid his thumbs under his flashy red-and-yellow Bugs Bunny suspenders to hitch up his pants. "I'll go down to the data center and plug the key words in. The airstrip designation codes, too. Be back in a flash with the trash."

Harry caught Sheryl's smile and put a more practical spin on Ev's blithe remark. "You'll think it's trash, too, when you see the endless combinations the computers will kick out. It'll take us the rest of the evening, if not the night, to go over them."

Sheryl's smile fizzled. Good grief! He hadn't been kidding about working day and night. She snuck a peek at the clock on the wall. It was after five. They'd worked right through lunch. The Diet Pepsis and bags of Krispy Korn Kurls Harry had procured from the vending machines down the hall had long since disappeared. Practical considerations such as real food and a cool shower and retrieving her car from the post office parking lot crept into Sheryl's mind.

As if to echo her thoughts, a loud, rolling growl issued from her tummy.

"I'm a creature of habit," she offered apologetically

when Harry glanced her way. "I tend to crave food… real food…a couple of times a day."

He speared a look at the clock, then reached for the jacket he'd tossed over a chair back hours ago. "Sorry. I didn't intend to starve you. There's a decent Italian sub shop across the street. Ev, Fay, you two up for another round of green peppers and sausage?"

Ev shook his head. "I want to get the computers rolling. Bring me back a garlic sausage special."

"I'll pass, too," Fay put in. "My youngest has a T-ball game at six-thirty and I swore on his stack of Goosebumps that I'd make this one. I'll come back here after the game's over, Harry."

MacMillan shrugged into his jacket. "You've been at this hard for the past three days and nights. Relax and enjoy the game."

Laughing, Fay rerolled her aeronautical maps. "Your single status is showing, Marshal. Anyone with kids would know better than to advise a parent to relax at a T-ball game."

"I stand corrected."

So he was single. Without knowing why she did so, Sheryl tucked that bit of information away for future reference. She'd noticed that he didn't wear a wedding ring. A lot of men didn't, of course, but the confirmation that the marshal was neither married nor a parent added a new dimension to the man…and triggered a whole new set of questions in her mind. Was he divorced? Currently involved with someone? Seeing someone who didn't mind the fact that he spent almost all his time away from home, chasing fugitives?

Sheryl shook off her intense curiosity about the marshal with something of an effort. His personal life had nothing to do with her, she reminded herself, or with her part in his investigation. She shifted her attention to Fay, who winked and settled her hat on her sleek, dark hair.

"Some people think that high-speed chases in pursuit of fleeing suspects and cement-footed drunks are tough, but I'm here to tell you that keeping up with my four rug-rats takes a whole lot more stamina."

"I don't have any rug-rats at home, but I can imag—" Sheryl stopped abruptly, her eyes widening. "Oh, no! I do!"

"If you're referring to the obnoxious rodent you insisted on taking home with you," Harry drawled, "I can't think of a more perfect description."

She grabbed her purse, trying not to think of the damage the shih tzu might have done to her dining-room chairs and pale-mauve carpet during his long incarceration.

"I have to swing by the post office to get my car, then go home to let Button out," she said worriedly.

"Good enough. We can grab some dinner on the way."

The thought of sharing another meal with Harry sent a tingle of anticipation down Sheryl's spine...followed by an instant rush of guilt. Belatedly, she realized that she hadn't even thought of Brian since early morning. The marshal's forceful personality and fierce determination to bring Richard Johnson-Paul Gunderson to justice had swept her right into the stream of the investigation, to the exclusion of all else.

"I'd better pass on dinner, too," she said. "I'll grab a sandwich at home."

And call Brian.

The task force leader conceded the point with a small shrug. "Whatever works."

Just as well, Harry thought as he waited beside Sheryl for the elevator to the underground parking. This man-hunt had consumed him for almost a year, yet today he'd had to fight to stay focused on the information his new-est team member was providing. Harry knew damn well that Sheryl didn't have any idea of the way his muscles had clenched every time she'd leaned over to check his notes. Or the havoc she'd caused to his concentration whenever she'd stretched out those long, tanned legs. After almost eight hours of breathing her scent and reg-istering every nuance in her voice and body language, Harry figured he'd better put some distance between them. He needed to regain his sharp-edged sense of pur-pose, which was proving more difficult than he would have imagined around Sheryl.

They turned into the Monzano station well after six. To the east, the jagged Sandia Mountains were begin-ning to take on the watermelon-pink hue that the Span-iards had named them for. To the west, the sun blazed a fiery gold above the five volcanoes that rose from the lava fields like stubby sentinels.

The station's front parking lot had long since emp-tied, and a high, sliding gate blocked the entrance to the fenced-in rear lot. Rows of white Jeeps with the postal service's distinctive red-and-blue markings filled the back parking area. Sheryl spied her ice-blue Camry at the far end of the lot.

"You can let me out here," she told Harry. "I have a key card to activate the gate. I'll see you back at the courthouse in an hour or so."

"I'll wait here until you drive out."

She didn't argue. Although the station was located

in a quiet, residential neighborhood, it took in large amounts of cash every day. They'd never had a robbery at the Manzano station, but postal bulletins regularly warned employees to stay alert when coming in early or leaving late. After keying the gate, Sheryl waited while the metal wheels rattled and bumped across the concrete. Her footsteps made little sucking noises as she crossed asphalt still soft from the scorching afternoon sun.

She was almost to her car when she heard a clink behind her. It sounded as though someone or something had bumped into a parked Jeep. Sheryl glanced over her shoulder. Nothing moved except the elongated shadow that floated at an angle behind her. Frowning, she dug in her purse for her keys and wound through the last row of vehicles at a brisk pace. Relief rippled through her as she approached her trusty little Camry. When she got her first full look at the car, relief melted into instant dismay. The vehicle sat low to the ground. Too low. Keys in hand, Sheryl stood staring at its board-flat tires.

Slowly, she moved closer and bent to examine the front tire. It hadn't just gone flat, she saw with a sudden, hollow sensation. It had been slashed. She was still poking at the gaping wounds in the rubber with her finger when another sound cut through the stillness like a knife.

Her heart leaping into her throat, Sheryl spun around. The slanting rays of the sun hit her full in the face… and blurred the dark silhouette of the figure looming over her.

Chapter 5

"What the hell...?"

Sheryl recognized Harry's broad-shouldered form at almost the same moment his voice penetrated her sudden, paralyzing fear.

Without stopping to think, without taking a breath, she flowed toward him. She didn't expect him to curl an arm around her and draw her hard against his body, but she certainly didn't protest when he did. She closed her eyes, taking shameless comfort in his presence. It was a moment before she managed to murmur a shaky explanation.

"Someone slashed my tires."

"So I see," he rasped, his voice low and tight above her head. "I got antsy about letting you walk back here alone. Looks like I had reason to."

His muscles twisting like steel under her cheek, he

turned to survey the parking lot and the wire fence surrounding it.

"Not a security camera in sight," he muttered in disgust.

Slowly, Sheryl disengaged from his hold. She was still shaken enough to miss the security of his arms, but not so much that she didn't realize the feel of his body pressed against hers wasn't helping her regain her equilibrium. Swallowing, she tried to steady her nerves while he completed a scowling survey of the area.

The vista on the other side of the fence didn't afford him any more satisfaction than the lack of outside cameras in the parking lot. A tumbleweed-strewn field cut by a jagged arroyo separated the station from the residential area. The landscape shimmered with a silvery beauty that only someone used to New Mexico's serene, natural emptiness could appreciate. At this moment, all Sheryl could think of was how easily someone could have crossed the emptiness and scaled the wire link fence.

Echoing her thoughts, Harry scanned the residences in the distance and shook his head. "Those houses are too far away for anyone to spot a fence climber. The post office should have better security."

"That's assuming whoever cut my tires climbed the fence. He could've just walked into the lot. With all the carriers coming and going, we don't keep the gates locked during the day."

"I know."

Belatedly, she remembered that Harry had driven in and out of those open gates with her several times. She wasn't thinking clearly, she realized.

He went down on one knee to examine the tires. "We're also assuming that an outsider caused this damage."

A new series of shocks eddied through Sheryl. "You can't think anyone at the post office would cut my tires like that."

He rose, dusting his hands. "Why not?"

"They're my friends as well as my co-workers!"

"All of them?"

"Well…"

She could name one carrier whose coarse, barroom style of humor had resulted in a couple of private and very heated discussions about what was considered acceptable language in the workplace. Then there was that temporary Christmas clerk who'd pestered her for dates long after she and Brian started seeing each other. Neither of those men had ever shown any animosity toward her, however. Certainly not the kind of animosity that would lead to something like this.

"Yes," she finished. "All of them."

Harry lifted a skeptical brow but didn't argue. "Well, I suspect you can't say the same about all of your customers."

"No." She shuddered, thinking of the thin, hostile doper who'd confronted her across the counter this morning. "I can't."

"That's why I followed you into the parking lot. I got to thinking about the crackhead who'd threatened you." He hesitated, then continued slowly. "I also got to thinking about the fact that right now you're my only link to Inga Gunderson's nephew."

Sheryl stared up at him in confusion. "What could that have to do with my slashed tires?"

"Maybe nothing," he answered, his face tight. "Maybe everything."

Before she could make any sense of that, he pulled

out his phone. "Let's get the police out here to check the area before I call Ev."

Her mind whirling, Sheryl listened while he contacted the Albuquerque police and asked them to send a patrol car to the Monzano station right away. A moment later, he made a short, succinct call to his partner.

"Find out if the Gunderson woman contacted anyone other than her lawyer, or if she sent out any messages, written or otherwise. I want every second of her time accounted for since we brought her in yesterday afternoon."

Yesterday afternoon? Sheryl shook her head in disbelief. Was it only yesterday afternoon that she'd driven to Inga Gunderson's house, worried about the woman's well-being? Just a little more than twenty-four hours since she'd practically fallen into Harry MacMillan's arms? It seemed longer. A whole lot longer!

No wonder, considering all that had happened in those hours. She'd stood Brian up not once but twice. She'd gained a thoroughly obnoxious houseguest. She'd transitioned from postal clerk to task force augmentee without so much as five minutes' notice. And she'd just lost four tires that she'd planned to squeeze another thousand miles out of, despite the fact that the tread had pretty well disappeared. She was wondering if her insurance would cover the cost of replacements when she caught the tail end of Harry's conversation.

"Finish up at Miss Hancock's apartment. I'll call you when I get through." He snapped the phone shut.

"Finish up what at my apartment?"

"I'm going to follow you home after we get done here. I want to check your locks."

"Check my locks? Why?"

"Just in case the person who did this also knows where you live."

"Oh."

Harry's eyes narrowed at the sudden catch in her voice. Sliding the phone into his pocket, he nodded toward the loading dock.

"Let's wait over there, out of the heat."

Sheryl trailed beside him, but she didn't need the shade offered by the overhanging roof to cut the effects of the sun. The idea that the person responsible for the damage to her car might also know her home address had cooled her considerably. Harry's carefully neutral expression only added to that chill.

"I'm not trying to scare you," he said evenly, "but this wasn't a random act. The perpetrator didn't vandalize any of the other vehicles. Only yours."

"I noticed that."

"He could have done it out of spite." He slanted her a careful look. "Or he might have been trying to disable your car so you couldn't drive off when you came back to the post office…although there are certainly less obvious ways of doing that."

"For someone who isn't trying to scare me, you're doing a darn good job of it!"

"Sorry."

Blowing out a long breath, he tried to recover the ground he'd just lost.

"Look, all cops are suspicious by nature, and most of us are downright paranoid. I'm reaching here, really reaching, to even imagine a connection between this incident and the fact that Inga Gunderson knows you're providing us information about her postcards."

"I hope so!"

The near panic in her voice brought his brows down in a quick frown. Cursing under his breath, he backpedaled even more.

"I'll wait to see if the police can lift any prints from the car before I speculate any further. In the meantime, try to think of anyone who might hold a grudge against you or want to get even over something."

"Other than the creep this morning, I can't think of anyone. I lead a pretty quiet life aside from my work."

"That doesn't say a lot for your fiancé," MacMillan offered as an aside. "Correction, sort-of fiancé."

A tinge of heat took some of the chill from Sheryl's cheeks. "Brian and I are very comfortable together."

His brow went up. "That says even less."

"Yes, well, not everyone wants to go chasing all over the world after bad guys, Marshal. Some of us prefer a more settled kind of life, not to mention unslashed tires."

"We'll get the tires fixed and put a—"

He broke off, his head lifting at the sound of a siren in the distance. It drew closer, the wail undulating through the evening stillness. Sheryl gave a little breath of relief.

"They got here fast."

Harry pushed away from the dock. "That's one of the benefits of having a representative from the Albuquerque Police Department on the task force. Come on, let's go direct them to the crime scene."

Hearing her trusty little Camry described as a "crime scene" didn't exactly soothe the victim's ragged nerves. She trailed after MacMillan, sincerely wishing Mrs. Inga Gunderson had never brought her melt-in-your-mouth cookies and yappy little dog into the Monzano Street station.

The reminder that the yappy little dog had no doubt spent the day demolishing Sheryl's apartment didn't particularly help matters, either.

By the time the police finished their investigation of the scene and a twenty-four-hour roadside service had replaced the Camry's tires, the spectacular light show that constituted a New Mexico sunset had begun. The entire western horizon blazed with color. Streaks of pink and turquoise layered into vibrant reds and velvet purples. The sun hovered like a shimmering gold fireball just above the Rio Grande. As Sheryl drove up the sloping rise toward her east-side apartment with Harry following close behind, the city lights twinkled like earthbound stars in her rearview mirror.

The serenity and beauty of the descending night helped loosen the tight knot of tension at the back of her neck. The police hadn't found anything that would identify the slasher. No prints, no footprints, no personal item conveniently dropped at the scene as so often occurred in movies and detective novels. The police had promised to canvas the houses that backed onto the fields around the station, but didn't hold out any more hope than Harry had that someone might have witnessed the vandalism. Tomorrow, they would interview Sheryl's co-workers. Rumors would speed like runaway roadrunners around the post office with this incident coming on top of her sudden detail. Elise must be wondering what in the world her friend had gotten herself into.

She'd call her tonight, Sheryl decided. And Brian.

Despite the marshal's orders, she had to tell them something. They were her best friends.

When she caught her train of thought, Sheryl's hands tightened on the steering wheel. When had she started thinking of Brian as a friend, not a lover, for goodness' sake? And why did Harry's little editorial comments about their relationship raise her hackles?

Frowning, she waited for the easy slide of comfort that always accompanied any reminder of Brian and their future together. It came, but it brought along with it another traitorous thought. Was comfort really what she wanted in a marriage?

Oh, great! As if escaped fugitives, smuggled uranium and slashed tires weren't enough, Sheryl had to pick now of all times to question a relationship that she'd happily taken for granted until this minute.

The events of the past two days had rattled her, she decided. Both her home and her work schedule had been thrown off-kilter, as had the comfortable routine she and Brian had fallen into. As soon as she finished this detail and Harry MacMillan went chasing after his fugitive, her life would return to its normal, regular pace.

Sheryl pulled into her assigned parking slot, wondering why in the world the prospect didn't cheer her as much as it should have. A car door slammed in the area reserved for visitor parking, then Harry appeared beside the Camry. As he had before, he opened Sheryl's door and reached down a hand to help her out.

Oddly reluctant, she put her hand in his. The small electrical jolt that raced from her palm to her wrist to her elbow did *not* help resolve the confusion that welled in her mind. With a distinct lack of graciousness for the small courtesy, Sheryl yanked her hand free and led the way through the two-story adobe buildings.

While she fumbled through the keys for the one to her front door, Harry swept an appreciative eye around the tiled courtyard shared by the eight apartments in her cluster. Soft light from strategically placed luminaria bathed the little bubbling fountain and wooden benches carved with New Mexico's zia symbol. Clay pots spilled a profusion of flowers that hadn't yet folded their petals for the night. Their fragrance hung on the descending dusk like a gauzy cloud.

"This is nice," he commented. "Very nice. A place like this might tempt even me into coming home once in a while."

Once in a while.

The phrase echoed in Sheryl's head as she shoved the key into the lock. If she'd needed anything more to banish the doubts that had plagued her a few moments ago, that would have done it. She had no use for men who returned home every few weeks or months and stayed only long enough to get their laundry done.

"It's comfortable," she replied with deliberate casualness. "And I like the view. From the back patio, you can see—Oh, no!"

She halted in the entryway, aghast. Dirty laundry trailed in a colorful array from the foyer to the living room. Bras, panties, socks, tank tops and uniform shirts decorated the tiles, along with what looked like every shoe she owned.

"Button?" Harry inquired from behind her.

"No," Sheryl said in a huff. Slamming the door, she tossed her purse and her keys on the kitchen counter and bent to scoop up an armful of underwear. "This is the latest decorating scheme for working women who have to dress on the run."

"It works for me."

At his amused comment, she shot a glance over her shoulder. Her face heated when she spied the filmy, chocolate-and-ecru lace bra dangling from his hand. She'd splurged on the bra and matching panties just last week. As any woman who'd ever had to wear a uniform to work could attest, a touch of sinfully decadent silk under the standard, company-issued outer items did wonders for one's inner femininity.

"I'll take that." She snatched the bra out of his hand. "Why don't you wade through this stuff and go into the living room. Since we haven't heard a peep out of Butty-boo, he's obviously—"

"Butty-boo?"

"That's what Inga called him, among other, similarly nauseating names. He must be hiding." She started down the hall. "You check the living room. I'll check the bedroom."

She found the shih tzu stretched out in regal abandon on her bed. He'd made a nest of the handwoven Zuni blanket she used as a spread. His black-and-white fur blended in with the striking pattern on the blanket, and she might have missed him completely if he hadn't lifted his head at her entrance and given a lazy, half-hearted bark.

"That's it?" Sheryl demanded indignantly. "Two people walk into the house who could be burglars for all you know, and that's the best you can do? One little yip?"

In answer, Button yawned and plopped his head back down.

"Had a hard day, did you?"

Disgusted, she used one foot to right the overturned straw basket she used as a clothes hamper.

"Well, so did I, and I'm telling you here and now that I'd better not come home to any more messes like this one."

With that totally useless warning, Sheryl dumped her laundry in the basket and steeled herself to check the bathroom. To her surprise and considerable relief, Button had used the newspapers she'd spread across the tiles. She hoped that meant he hadn't also used the living-room carpet.

She took a few moments to swipe a little powder on her shiny nose and tuck some stray tendrils of hair back behind her ear, then headed for the living room. Button's black eyes followed her across the room. With another yawn and an elaborate stretch, he climbed out of his nest, leaped down from the bed and padded after her.

Sheryl had taken only a step or two into the living room when the dog gave a shrill bark that seemed to pierce right through her eardrums. Like a small, furry cannonball, Button launched himself across the mauve carpet at the figure jimmying the locks on the sliding-glass patio doors.

This time, Harry met the attack head-on. Jerking around, he growled at the oncoming canine.

"Take another bite out of my leg and you're history, pal!"

The shih tzu halted a few paces away, every hair bristling.

His target bristled a bit himself. "If it were up to me, you'd be chowing down at the pound right now, so back off. Back off, I said!"

Button didn't take kindly to ultimatums. His black

lips drew back even farther. Bug eyes showed red with suppressed fury. The growls that came from deep in his throat grew even more menacing. Guessing that the standoff might break at any second, Sheryl hurried forward and scooped the dog into her arms.

"This is Harry, remember? He's one of the good guys. Well, not a good guy to you, since he sent your mistress off in handcuffs, but he's okay. Really."

Murmuring reassurances, she stroked the small, quivering bundle of fur.

"Helluva watchdog," the marshal muttered in disgust. "What was he doing back there, anyway? Trying on the rest of your underwear?"

Despite the fact that she herself didn't feel particularly benevolent toward the animal, Sheryl didn't have the heart to expose him to more criticism. Harry didn't need to know that Button had sprawled in indolent indifference while persons unknown had entered her apartment. Besides, the dog had leaped to the attack quickly enough once roused. Deciding to treat the marshal's question as rhetorical, she didn't bother to answer.

"How are the locks?"

"The dead bolt on the front door is sturdy enough. These patio doors are another story. If you don't mind, I'd like to get some security people up here to install a drop bar and kick lock, as well as a rudimentary alarm system. I'll have them wire your car while they're at it. They can be here in an hour or so."

"Tonight?"

"Tonight."

Sheryl's fingers curled into the dog's silky topknot. The fear that had gripped her for a few paralyzing mo-

ments in the parking lot reached out long tentacles once
more. She shivered.

Harry's keen glance caught the small movement. He
gave a smothered oath. "My paranoia's working overtime. The alarm probably isn't necessary, but I'd feel
better with it in."

"Probably?" she repeated hollowly.

Harry cursed again and closed the short distance between them. Button issued a warning growl, which the
marshal ignored. Lifting a hand, he smoothed an errant
curl back from her cheek.

"I'm sorry, Sher. I didn't mean to scare you again."

The touch of his palm against her cheek startled
Sheryl so much that she barely noticed his use of her
nickname. She did, however, notice the tiny bits of gold
warming his brown eyes. And the way his mustache
thickened slightly at the corners, as if to disguise the
small, curving laugh lines that appeared whenever his
mouth kicked into one of his half-rogue, all-male grins.

The way it did now.

Except this grin was more rueful than roguish. It
matched the look in his eyes, Sheryl thought, as his hand
slid slowly from her cheek to curl at the back of her neck.

She shivered once more, but this time it wasn't from
fear. This time, she realized with something close to dismay, it was from delight. Caught on a confusing cross
of sensations, she could only stand and watch the way
Harry's grin tipped from rueful into a smile that trapped
her breath in the back of her throat.

He shouldn't do this! Harry's mind shouted the warning, even as his fingers got lost in the silky softness of
her hair. He knew better than to mix business with per-

sonal desire. But suddenly, without the least warning, desire had grabbed hold of him and wouldn't let go.

She felt so soft. Smelled so intoxicating, a mixture of hot sun and powdery talcum, with a little shih tzu thrown in for leavening. She was also scared, Harry reminded himself savagely. Off balance from all that had happened in the past few days. Almost engaged.

Another man might have drawn back at that sobering thought. Someone else might have respected the territory this Brian character had tentatively staked out. Instead of deterring Harry, the very nebulousness of the other man's claim angered him. Any jerk who kept a woman like Sheryl dangling in some twilight never-never land didn't deserve her.

So when she didn't draw back, when her lips opened on a sigh instead of a protest, Harry bent his head and brushed them with his own. She tasted so fresh, so irresistible, that he brought his mouth back for another sample.

The kiss started out slow and soft and friendly. Within seconds, it powered up to fast and hard and well beyond friendship. A dozen different sensations exploded in Harry's chest and belly. The urge to pull Sheryl into his arms, to feel every inch of her against his length, clawed at him. He started to do just that when another, sharper sensation bit into his lower right arm.

"Dammit!"

He jumped back, almost yanking the stubby little monster locked onto his jacket sleeve out of Sheryl's arms. She caught the dog just in time and held on to it by its rear legs. It hung there between them, a growling, snarling mop with one end firmly attached to Harry's sleeve and the other to the woman who held him.

"You misbegotten, mangy little…"

"He was just trying to protect me," Sheryl got out on a gasp. "I think."

Harry thought differently, but he was too busy working his fingers onto either side of the dog's muzzle to say so at that moment. Exerting just enough pressure to spring those tiny, steel jaws open, he pulled his coat sleeve free. He then reached over and extracted the animal from Sheryl's unresisting arms.

Two long strides took him back to the sliding doors. A moment later, the glass panel slammed shut. Buggy black eyes glared at him from the outside. Ignoring the glare and the bad-tempered yips that accompanied it, Harry turned back to Sheryl.

His fierce, driving need to sweep her into his arms once more took a direct hit when he caught her expression. It held a combination of regret and guilt…and not the least hint of any invitation to continue.

Chapter 6

"I'm sorry."

The apology came out with a gruffer edge than Harry had intended, for the simple reason that he couldn't think of anything he felt less sorry about than taking Sheryl into his arms. Yet that kiss ranked right up there among the dumbest things he'd ever done.

That said something, considering that he'd pulled some real boners in his life. Two in particular he'd always regret. The first was succumbing to a bad case of lust and marrying too young, much too young to figure out how to get his struggling marriage through the stress of his job. The second occurred years later, when he decided to take a few long-overdue days off to go fishing in Canada. That fateful weekend his best buddy was gunned down. By the time Harry had returned and taken charge of the operation to track down Dean's killers, the trail had gone stone cold.

Now it had finally heated up, and he couldn't allow himself to get sidetracked by a moss-eyed blonde who raised his blood pressure a half-dozen points every time she glanced his way. Nor, he reminded himself with deliberate ruthlessness, could he afford to confuse her by coming on to her like this. He needed her calm and rational and able to concentrate on the task she'd been detailed to do. She still had information Harry wanted to pull out of her.

"That was out of line," he admitted, less gruffly, more firmly. "It won't happen again."

"N-no. It won't."

The guilt in her voice rubbed him raw. Cursing the predatory instincts that had driven him to poach so recklessly on another man's territory, he tried to recapture her trust.

"I guess this damned investigation has sanded away the few civilized edges I possessed."

It had sanded away a few of Sheryl's edges, too. She couldn't remember the last time a kiss had seared her like that. Dazed, she struggled to subdue the runaway fire racing through her veins. A massive dose of guilt helped speed the process considerably.

She was almost engaged, for heaven's sake! How could she have just stood there and let Harry kiss her like that? How could she have been so shallow, so disloyal to Brian? She'd never even looked at another man in all the time they'd been seeing each other. What's more, she'd certainly never dreamed that a near stranger could generate this combination of singing excitement and stinging regret with just the touch of his mouth on hers. She stared at Harry, seeing her own consternation in his frown.

"We've got a good number of hours of work ahead of us yet," he got out curtly. "You can't concentrate if you're worried that I might pounce at any minute. I won't, I promise."

A small sense of pique piled on top of Sheryl's rapidly mounting guilt. She knew darn well she was as much to blame for what had just happened as Harry. Her instinctive, uninhibited response to his touch shook her to her core, and she didn't need him to tell her it wouldn't happen again. She wouldn't do that to Brian or to herself. Still, it rankled just a bit that the marshal regretted their kiss as much as she did, if for entirely different reasons.

Feeling flustered and thoroughly off balance, Sheryl had a need to put some distance between her and Harry. She moved into the kitchen, where she snatched up Button's plastic water dish and shoved it under the faucet to rinse it out.

"Why don't you head back downtown," she suggested with what she hoped was a credible semblance of calm. "I'll follow after I feed Button, and we can put in a few more hours' work."

Harry looked as though there was nothing he'd like better than to get back to business, but he shook his head. "I'd like to stay here until the security folks arrive and do their thing, if you don't mind."

Sheryl stared at him while water ran over the sides of the dish. In the aftermath of his shattering kiss, she'd totally forgotten what had led up to it.

"No, of course I don't mind."

"I'll call them and get them on the way."

With brisk efficiency, he mobilized the necessary

specialists. Another quick call alerted Ev to the fact that he'd have to scrounge his own dinner.

"I guess I could make us some sandwiches," Sheryl said slowly when he snapped the phone shut. "Or I could cook lemon chicken. I have all the fixings. We can eat and work while we wait."

The idea of preparing Brian's favorite meal for Harry disconcerted Sheryl all over again. Honestly, she had to get a grip here. Harry had certainly recovered his poise fast enough. He'd faced the awkwardness head-on and moved beyond it. She could do the same. Briskly, she swiped a paper towel around the bowl and filled it with the dried dog food she'd picked up yesterday.

"I'll feed Button and get something started."

"I have a better idea." Harry shrugged out of his coat, then rolled up his sleeves. "You feed the rodent while I pour you a glass of wine or whatever relaxes you. Then I'll cook the chicken."

"There's some wine in the fridge," Sheryl said doubt-fully, "but you don't have to fix dinner."

"I don't have to, but I'd like to."

He flashed her a grin that strung her tummy into tight knots. Good grief, what in the world was the mat-ter with her?

"Being on the road so much, I don't get to practice my culinary skills very often. But my ex-wife trained me well. She never opened a can or flipped on a burner when I was home."

"Well…"

He traded places with Sheryl, taking over the kitchen with an easy competence that put the last of her doubts to rest. A quick investigation of her cupboards and fridge produced skillet, chicken, flour, lemons, onions, cracked pepper, butter and a half-full bottle of chilled Chablis.

While Harry assembled the necessary ingredients, Sheryl fed Button. Naturally, the dog displayed his displeasure over his banishment to the patio by turning up his pug nose at the dry food. She left him and his dinner outside, then occupied one of the tall rawhide-and-rattan counter stools. Sipping slowly on the wine Harry had poured for her, she tried to understand the welter of confused emotions this man stirred in her.

She gave up after the second or third sip and contented herself with just watching. He hadn't been kidding about his culinary skills. Within moments, he had the floured chicken fillets sizzling in the skillet. While they browned, he made short work of dicing the onion. Seconds later, the onion, more butter and a generous dollop of Chablis went into the pan. Sheryl sniffed the delicious combination of scents, conscious once more of the inadequacy of the Korn Kurls she'd eaten for lunch.

"My compliments to your ex-wife," she murmured. "You really do know your way around a kitchen."

"Unfortunately, cooking is my one and only domestic skill...or so I've been told."

"How long were you married?" she asked curiously.

He squeezed a wedge of lemon over the chicken. The drops spurted and spit in the hot pan, adding their tangy scent to the aroma of butter and onions rising from the cooktop.

"Eight years by calendar reckoning. Three, maybe four, if you count the time my wife and I spent at home together. She's an account executive for a Dallas PR firm now, but when we met she was just starting in the

business. Her job took her on the road as much as mine
did, and…"

"And constant absences don't necessarily make the
heart grow fonder," she finished slowly.

He shrugged, but Sheryl had been in this man's company enough by now to catch the tight note in his voice.
Harry MacMillan didn't give up on anything easily, she
now knew, whether it was a marriage or the relentless
pursuit of a fugitive.

"Something like that," he concurred, sending her a
keen glance through the spiraling steam. "You sound as
though you've been there, too."

"In a way."

She traced a circle on the counter with her glass. She
rarely spoke about the father whose absence had left such
a void in her heart, but Harry's blunt honesty about his
divorce invited reciprocation. Reluctantly, she shared a
little of her own background.

"My father traveled a lot in his job, too. My mother
stewed and fretted every minute he was gone, which
didn't make for happy homecomings."

"I imagine not. Is he still on the road?"

"As far as I know. He and Mom divorced when I was
six. He showed up for a Christmas or two, and we wrote
each other until I was about ten. The letters got fewer
and farther between after he took an overseas position.
Last I heard, he was in Oman."

"Want me to track him down for you? It would only
take a few calls."

He was serious, Sheryl saw with a little gulp.

"No, thanks," she said hastily. "I don't need him wan-
dering in and out of my life anymore."

"Well, the offer stands if you change your mind," he

replied, flipping the slotted wooden spoon into the air like a baton. He caught it with a smooth ripple of white shirt and lean muscle. "Do you have any rice in the cupboard? I'm even better at rice Marconi than lemon chicken."

"And so modest, too."

He grinned. "Modesty isn't one of the skills they emphasize in the academy. Relax, enjoy your wine and watch a master at work."

Maybe it was the Chablis. Or the sight of this tall, rangy man moving so matter-of-factly about her little kitchen. In any case, Sheryl relaxed, enjoyed her wine and managed to ignore the fact that the master chef sported a leather shoulder holster instead of a tall, white hat. Her prickly sense of guilt stayed with her, though, and kept her from completely enjoying the meal Harry served up with a flourish.

It also kept her on the other side of the dining-room table after they finished eating and got down to work. Button, released from his banishment, perched on the back of the sofa and watched the marshal with unblinking, unwavering hostility. With the wine and food to soothe the nerves made ragged by Harry's kiss, Sheryl was able to recall the details on several batches of postcards.

"Venice, the Antibes, Barbados." Harry tapped his pen on the tabletop. "You're sure the cards that arrived before the Rio set came from those three locations?"

"I'm sure. It's hard to mistake gondolas and canals. I remember Antibes because of the little gold emblem in the corner of the card that advertised the Côte d'Azur. And Barbados…"

Sheryl gazed at the wall, seeing in its wavy plaster

a sea so polished it glittered like clear, blue topaz, and white beaches lined with banyan trees whose roots hung downward like long, scraggly beards.

"If the picture on the card came anywhere close to reality," she murmured, "Barbados must have the most beautiful beaches in the world."

Harry's pen stilled. Against his will, against his better judgment, he let his glance linger on Sheryl's face. Damn, didn't the woman have any idea what that soft, dreamy expression did to a man's concentration? Or how much of herself she revealed in these unguarded moments? Despite her assertions to the contrary, Harry suspected that the daughter had inherited more than a touch of her father's wanderlust. She tried hard to suppress it, but it slipped out in moments like this, when she mentally transported herself to a white sweep of beach.

Despite *his* intentions to the contrary, Harry mentally transported himself there with her.

The sound of a low, rumbling growl wrenched him back to Albuquerque. A quick look revealed that Button had shifted his attention from Harry to the front door. The dog's entire body quivered as he pushed up on all four paws and stared at the entryway. His gums pulled back. Another low growl rattled in his throat.

Carefully, Harry laid down his pen. "Are you expecting anyone?"

Sheryl's eyes widened at his soft query. Gulping, she shifted her gaze to the door. "No," she whispered.

"Stay here!"

Harry moved toward the door, his mind spinning with possibilities. The dog might have alerted on a neighbor arriving home. Maybe the security team was outside. Whoever it was, Harry had been a cop too long to take a chance on mights and maybes. He waited in the entryway, his every sense straining.

He heard no murmur of voices, no passing footsteps, no doorbell. Only Button's quivering growls...and a small, almost inaudible scrape.

Pulse pounding, back to the wall, Harry edged toward the door. With no side windows to peer out, he had to resort to the peephole. He made out a bent head, a pale blur of a shirt, a glint of moonlight on steel.

With a kick to his gut, he saw the dead bolt slowly twist.

His hand whipped across his chest. The Smith & Wesson came out of its leather nest with a smooth, familiar slide. He reached for the doorknob and waited until the dead bolt clicked open.

The knob moved under his palm. He exploded into action at the exact instant Button flew off the sofa, snarling, and Sheryl shouted at him.

"Harry! Wait!"

Her cry was still echoing in his ears when he yanked the door open with his free hand. A second later, the stranger standing on the other side of the door slammed up against the hallway wall. The Smith & Wesson dug into his ribs.

His cheek squashed into the plaster, the tall, slender man couldn't do much more than gape over his shoulder at his attacker.

"Wh—What's going on here?" he stuttered. "Who are you?"

In response, Harry torqued the stranger's arm up his spine another few inches. His adrenaline pumped like high-octane jet fuel. Button's high-pitched yaps scratched on his strung-tight nerves like fingernails on a chalkboard.

"You first," he countered roughly. "Who the hell are you?"

Before he got an answer, Sheryl locked both hands on his arm. "It's Brian," she shouted, yanking at his bruising hold. "Let go, Harry. It's Brian. Brian Mitchell."

Slowly, he released his grip and stepped back. Button didn't give up as readily. It took Sheryl's direct intervention before the still-snarling dog retired from the field. A good-sized strip of gray twill pants dangled from his locked jaws.

The two men faced each other, blood still up and faces flushed. Sheryl dumped the dog on the sofa and hurried back to calm the roiled waters.

"Brian, I'm so sorry! I didn't expect you, and it's been such a crazy day. Are you okay? Button didn't break the skin on your leg, did he?"

"No." Jaw clamped, the younger man watched his attacker holster his gun. "Who's this?"

"This is, er…" She turned, her face a study in frustration. "I can tell him, can't I?"

Harry took his time replying. Now that he knew the man didn't pose an immediate threat, his sharp-edged tension should have eased. Instead, Sheryl's fluttering and fussing raised his hackles all over again. It didn't take any great deductive skills to identify the man as Brian, her almost-fiancé.

Eyes glinting, he assessed the newcomer. An inch or two shorter than Harry's own six-one, he carried a good deal less weight on his trim frame. He also, the marshal noted, didn't take kindly to having his face shoved up against the wall.

"Elise said someone came into the station this morning and pulled you for a special detail. I take it this is the guy."

"Yes."

His gaze sliced from Sheryl to Harry. "Working kind of late, aren't you?"

She answered for them, a tinge of pink in her cheeks. "Yes, we are. Why don't you come in? I want to check your leg to make sure Button didn't do any serious damage."

Unmoving, Brian looked the marshal up and down. His lip curled. "I wouldn't have picked you for a shih tzu owner."

"You got that much right, anyway," Harry replied with a careless shrug. "I would have dumped the mutt in the pound. Sher insisted on bringing it home."

He used the nickname deliberately, not exactly sure why he wanted to get a rise out of the younger man. Whatever the reason, Brian's scowl sent a spear of satisfaction through his belly.

Sheryl listened to their terse exchange with increasing consternation flavored with a pinch of irritation. They sounded like two boys baiting each other. She could understand why Brian might feel antagonistic, given Harry's rough handling and his presence in her apartment so late at night, but she could do without the marshal's deliberate provocation.

"Let's go into the living room," she said firmly. "Harry will explain what we're doing while I check your leg."

The remains of the meal still sitting on the table didn't help matters, of course. Nor did the empty wine bottle on the kitchen counter. Frowning, Brian took in the littered table, the half-empty wineglasses and the dog once more stretched along the back of the sofa, his duty done. Slowly, he turned to face Sheryl.

"My leg's fine," he said quietly, all trace of antagonism gone now. "But I can certainly use a little explaining."

Before she could reply, Harry stepped forward. The gold star gleamed from the leather credentials case lying in his palm.

"I'm Deputy U.S. Marshal Harry MacMillan. Since Sheryl vouches for you, I'll tell you that I'm tracking a fugitive who escaped while being transported for trial a year ago. His trail led to Albuquerque and, obliquely, to the Monzano branch of the post office."

Brian's face registered blank astonishment, followed by swift concern. "Is this fugitive dangerous?"

"He's suspected of killing the marshal escorting him to trial."

"And you pulled Sheryl into a hunt for a cop killer?"

"I requested that she be assigned to my team, yes."

"Well, you can just unrequest her," Brian declared. "I don't want her taking part in any manhunt for a cop killer."

Sheryl gave a little huff of exasperation. "Excuse me. I'm getting a little tired of this two-sided conversation. In case you've forgotten, this is my apartment and my living room, and it's my decision whether or not I'm going to work on this detail."

Brian conceded her point stiffly. "Of course it's your decision, but I don't like it. Aside from the possible danger, this detail of yours has already disrupted our schedule. I waited almost an hour for you yesterday afternoon, and we missed our Tuesday night together."

As she looked up into his gray eyes, Sheryl's momentary irritation disappeared, swept away by a fresh wave of guilt. She loved Brian. She'd loved him for almost a year now. Yet she'd gotten so caught up in Harry's investigation that she hadn't spared much thought to this kind, considerate man—until the marshal kissed her.

She felt a sudden, urgent need to fold herself into Brian's arms and feel his mouth on hers. She turned, offering Harry a forced smile. "Would you keep Button entertained for a few minutes? I'm going to walk Brian to his car."

"You stay here and talk," he countered. "Much as I hate to be seen in public with this sorry excuse for a dog, he can keep me company while I reconnoiter the outside layout for the security folks."

Sheryl grabbed the leash she'd purchased when she bought the dog food and shoved it in his hand gratefully. Frowning, Brian watched the oversized marshal depart with the undersized mop of fur at the end of a bright-red lead.

"Security folks?" he echoed as the door closed. "What security folks?"

Sighing, Sheryl abandoned her need to be held in favor of Brian's need to know. Taking a seat beside him on the sofa, she tucked a foot under her and recapped the events of the past few days. When she got to the part about the slashed tires, Brian voiced his growing consternation.

"At the risk of repeating myself, I have to say I don't like this. I wish you'd take yourself off this detail."

"We don't know that my slashed tires had anything to do with my participation on the task force. Anyone could have done it, but Harry insists it's better not to take chances. He's got a team coming out to install new locks and an alarm system."

"I still don't like it," Brian repeated stubbornly.

Sheryl bit back the retort that she'd didn't particularly like that part, either. She probably should feel flattered by Brian's protective streak. Instead, she resented it just a little bit. No, more than a little bit.

Suddenly, Sheryl remembered that she'd curled into Harry's side for protection only this afternoon, without feeling the least hint of resentment.

Guilt, confusion and a desperate need to reestablish her usual sense of comfortable ease with Brian brought her forward. Sliding her arms around his neck, she smiled up at him.

"I'm sorry you don't like it, and I appreciate your concern. I want to be part of this team, though. If I have any knowledge that could lead to the capture of a murderer, I have to share it. After this detail, we'll get back to our regular routine. I promise."

Conceding with his usual good-natured grace, he bent his head and met her halfway. Their mouths fit together with practiced sureness...and none of the explosive excitement that Sheryl had experienced only a half hour ago.

Dismayed, she rose up on her knees. Her body melted against Brian's. Her fingers tunneled through his hair. Brian was more than willing to deepen the embrace. His arms went around her waist, drawing her closer.

Afterward, she could never sort out whether he pulled back first or she did. Nor would she ever forget the look in his eyes. Puzzled. Surprised. Not hurt, but close. Too close.

"I guess I'd better leave," he said slowly. "So you and—what's his name?—Harry can get back to work."

When his arms dropped away, her ache spread into a slow, lancing pain. Deep within her, she knew that she would never find her usual comfortable satisfaction in his embrace again. She'd changed. Somehow, she'd become a different person.

She loved Brian. She would always love him. But she knew now that she'd mistaken the nature of that love. Comfort didn't form the basis for a marriage. Security couldn't ensure happiness. For either of them.

If nothing else, Harry's searing kiss had demonstrated that. Sheryl didn't fool herself that she'd fallen in love with Harry MacMillan, or even in lust. She'd barely known the man for thirty-six hours. Yet in that brief period, he'd knocked the foundations right out from under Sheryl's nice, placid existence.

Aching, she wet her lips and tried to articulate some of her confused thoughts.

"Brian…"

He shook his head. "I need to do some thinking. I guess you do, too. We'll talk about it when you finish this detail, Sher."

He pushed himself off the sofa. Miserable, Sheryl followed him to the door. He paused, one hand on the knob, as reluctant to walk out as she was to let him.

"Elise said you rescheduled your shopping expedition for a bassinet for tomorrow night. You need to call her if you're going to be working late again."

"I will." She grabbed at the excuse to delay his departure for another few moments. "Or maybe you could take her?"

He nodded. "Sure, if you can't make it. And don't forget to call your mother. You know she expects to hear from you every Thursday."

"I won't."

He opened the door, and a small silence fell between them. Sheryl felt her heart splinter into tiny shards of pain when he curled a hand under her chin.

"Bye, Sher," he said softly.

"Goodbye, Brian."

He tilted her head up for a final kiss.

Harry watched from the shadows across the court-yard. He needed to see this, he thought, his jaw tight. He needed the physical evidence of Brian's claim. Of Sheryl's affection.

It made Harry's own relationship with her easier, clearer, sharper. She was part of his team.

Nothing more.

Nothing less.

Which didn't explain why he had to battle the irrational temptation to unclip Button's leash and turn the man-eating fur ball loose on Brian Mitchell again.

Chapter 7

Sheryl walked into the task force operations center twenty minutes late on Thursday morning. A taut, unsmiling Harry greeted her.

"Where the hell have you been? I was about to send a squad car up to your place to check on you."

"Button set the darn alarm off twice before I figured out how to bypass the motion detectors."

The marshal bit back what Sheryl suspected was another biting comment about hairy little rodents. Instead, he raked her with a glance that left small scorch marks everywhere it touched her skin.

"Call in the next time you have a problem."

The curt order raised her brows and her hackles. "Yes, sir!"

Harry narrowed his eyes but didn't respond.

Tossing her purse onto a chair, Sheryl headed for

the coffeepot in the corner of the conference room. She didn't know what had gotten into Harry this morning, but his uncertain mood more than matched her own. She felt grouchy and irritable and unaccountably off-kilter in the marshal's presence.

Much of her edginess she could ascribe to the fact that she hadn't gotten much sleep last night. She'd spent countless hours tossing and turning and thinking about Brian. She'd spent almost as many hours trying *not* to think about Harry's shattering kiss. She couldn't, wouldn't, allow herself to dwell on the sensations the marshal had roused in her, not when she owed Brian her loyalty.

To make matters even worse, Button had added his bit to her restless night. The mutt insisted on burrowing under the covers and curling up in the bend of her knees. Every time Sheryl had tried to straighten her legs, she'd disturbed his slumber...a move that Button didn't particularly appreciate. He'd voiced his displeasure in no uncertain terms. Between the dog's growls and her own troubled thoughts, Sheryl was sure she'd barely closed her eyes for an hour or so before the alarm went off.

Grumbling, she'd dragged out of bed, pulled on a pair of white slacks and a cool, sleeveless silk blouse in a bright ruby red, then grabbed a glass of juice and a slice of toast. She still might have made it down to the federal building by eight if she'd hadn't had to struggle with the unfamiliar alarm system. Twenty minutes and three calls to the alarm company later, she'd slammed the door behind her and headed for her car.

Her day hadn't gotten off to a good start, even before Harry's curt greeting. As she greeted the assembled team members, she guessed that it wouldn't get much better.

Crisp and professional in her New Mexico state trooper's uniform, Fay Chandler shook her head in response to Sheryl's query about her son's T-ball game.

"They got creamed," she said glumly. "I had to take the whole team for pizza to cheer them up. They perked up at the first whiff of pepperoni, but my husband was still moping when I left the house this morning. He's worse than my seven-year-old."

Folding her hands around the hot, steaming coffee, Sheryl took cautious injections of the liquid caffeine. She carried the cup with her to the conference table and greeted Everett Sloan. The poor man was almost buried behind a stack of computer printouts.

"Hi, Ev. Looks like you're hard at it already."

The short, barrel-chested deputy marshal waved a half-eaten chocolate donut. "'Hard' is the operative word. The computers crunched the numbers and words you gave us from the first set of postcards. Take a look at what they kicked out."

Sheryl's eyes widened at the row of cardboard boxes stacked along one wall, each filled with neatly folded printouts.

"Good grief! Do you have to go through all those?"

"Every one of them."

"What in the world are they?"

"We bounced the numbers and letters of the words you gave us against the known codes maintained by the FBI and Defense Intelligence Agency to see if there's a pattern. So far, no luck." Grimacing, he surveyed the boxes still awaiting his attention. "It'll take until Christmas to find a needle in that haystack...if there is one."

"We don't have until Christmas," Harry put in from the other end of the table. "We've got to break that code fast. We caught Inga Gunderson with her bags packed, remember? We have to assume the drop is scheduled for sometime soon…if it hasn't already gone down," he added grimly.

Fay hitched a hip on the edge of the conference table. "My bet is that Inga sent a message through her lawyer. She probably alerted either the sender or the receivers to the fact she's been tagged. If they didn't call off the shipment, they've no doubt diverted it to an alternate location."

Ev shook his head. "I know her lawyer. Several of us in the Albuquerque Marshals' office had to provide extra courtroom security when he defended one of his skinhead clients against a charge of communicating a threat against a federal law enforcement official. The scuzzball swore his buddies would blow up the Federal building if he was found guilty."

Since the Oklahoma City bombing, Sheryl knew, those threats were taken very, very seriously. She remembered the tension that had gripped the city during that trial.

"Don Ortega gave the guy one helluva defense," Ev continued, "but he told me afterward he fully expected to go up in smoke with his client. He's tough but straight. He wouldn't knowingly aid an escaped prisoner or contribute to the commission of a crime."

"But he might do it unknowingly," Fay argued. "Maybe Inga and company used some kind of a coded message. They're certainly handy enough at that sort of thing."

Ev shook his head emphatically. "Not Don. He's too smart to act as a courier for a suspected felon. Besides, the supervisor of the women's detention center swears

Inga hasn't made any calls to anyone other than her attorney. So the odds are that the drop is still on...for a time we've yet to determine at a place we haven't identified."

"We'll identify both," Harry swore, his face as tight and determined as his voice. "Keep working those computer reports. If you don't find anything that makes sense, run them again with the day-month combinations for the next five days."

His partner groaned. "I'm going to need more energy for this."

Polishing off his donut, Ev dug another out of the box in the center of the table. While he munched his way through the report in front of him, Harry turned to the state trooper.

"I want you to drive out to all the airports we've IDed as possible landing sites. Talk to the Customs people and airport managers personally. Ask them to info us on any flight plans with South America as originating departure point or cargo manifests showing transport from or through Rio. Also, tell them to notify us immediately of any unscheduled requests for transit servicing on aircraft large enough to carry this kind of a cargo load."

Fay reached for her Smoky the Bear hat. "Will do, Chief."

Topping off his coffee, Harry walked back to his seat. "All right, Sheryl, let's get to work."

She shot him a quick glance as she settled in the chair next to his. He'd shed his jacket, but otherwise wore his standard uniform of boots, jeans and button-down cotton shirt, this one a soft, faded yellow. His clean-shaven jaw and neatly trimmed mustache looked crisply professional, but the lines at the corners of his eyes and mouth suggested that he'd hadn't slept much more than she had.

No doubt his investigation had kept him awake. It certainly seemed to consume him this morning. He gave no sign that he even remembered brushing a hand across her cheek last night or sending her into a shivering, shuddering nosedive with the touch of his mouth on hers. Not that Sheryl wanted him to remember, of course, any more than she wanted him to kiss her again.

Not until she'd sorted out her feelings for Brian, anyway.

"Where do you want to start?" she asked briskly.

"Let's go over the wording from the Venice-Antibes-Barbados cards again. Start with Barbados."

"Fine."

They worked for several hours before Harry was satisfied that he'd extracted all the information he could on that set of postcards. After sending the key words down to the computer center for analysis, they moved on to other cards that had arrived during Inga Gunderson's four months in Albuquerque. The further back Sheryl reached into her memory, the hazier the dates and stamps and messages got. The scenes on the front side of the cards remained vivid, however.

"Give me what you can on this one from Heidelberg," Harry instructed.

"It came in early April, a week or so before the fifteenth. I remember that much, because it provided such a colorful counterpoint to all the dreary income tax returns we had to sort and process."

Harry scribbled a note. "Go on."

"It was one of my favorites. It had four different scenes on the front. One showed a fairy tale castle perched above the Neckar River. Another depicted the old bridge that spans the river. Then there was a group of university students lifting their beer steins and singing, just like Mario Lanza and his friends did in the *Student Prince.*"

At the other end of the table, Ev groaned. "Mario Lanza and the *Student Prince.* I can just imagine what the computers will do with that one!"

Harry ignored him. "What about the fourth scene?"

"That was the best." Sheryl assembled her thoughts. "It showed a monstrous wine cask in the basement of the castle. According to Paul's note, the cask holds something like fifty thousand gallons. Supposedly, the king's dwarf once drained the whole thing."

Harry stared at her. A slow, almost reluctant approval dawned in his eyes, warming them to honey brown. "Fifty thousand gallons, huh? That gives us an interesting number to work with. Good going, Sher."

For the first time that morning, Sheryl relaxed. A sense of partnership, of shared purpose, replaced her earlier irritation with Harry's brusque manner. When he wasn't glowering at her or barking out orders, the marshal had his own brand of rough-edged charm.

As she'd discovered last night.

From the other end of the table, Ev whistled softly. "How the heck can you remember that kind of detail?"

"A good memory is one of the primary qualifications for a postal worker," she replied, smiling. "Especially those of us who are scheme qualified."

"Okay, I'll bite. What's 'scheme qualified'?"

"Although I primarily work the front counter, I'm also authorized to come in early and help throw mail for the carrier runs. Everything arrives in bulk from the central distribution center, you see, then we have to sort it by zip."

"I thought you had machines to do that."

"I wish!" Sheryl laughed. "No, most of the mail is hand-thrown at the branch level. I worked at two different Albuquerque stations before I moved to the Monzano branch. I can pretty well tell you the zip for any street you pick out of the phone book," she finished smugly.

"No kidding?"

Ev looked as though he wanted to put her to the test, but Harry intervened.

"Unless they're pertinent to this investigation, I'm not interested in any zips but the ones on these postcards. Let's get back to work."

"Yes, sir!" Ev and Sheryl chorused.

Harry grilled her relentlessly, extracting every detail she could remember about Mrs. Gunderson's correspondence and then some. They worked steadily, despite constant interruptions.

The phones in the task force operations center rang frequently. In one call, the DEA advised that the informant who'd tipped them to Paul and Inga Gunderson had just come up with another name. They were working to ID the man now. Just before noon, the CIA came back with an unconfirmed field report that six canisters of depleted uranium had indeed passed through Prague four days ago. Their contact was still working Pamplona and Rio to see if he could pick up the trail. His face alive with fierce satisfaction, Harry reported the news to his small team.

"Hot damn!" Ev exclaimed. "Prague! Good going, Sheryl."

A thrill shot through her. She couldn't believe the

information she'd provided only yesterday had already borne fruit. Her eyes met Harry's above his latest ream of notes.

"I owe you," he said quietly. "Big time."

Her skin tingled everywhere his gaze touched it. She smiled, and answered just as softly.

"All in the line of duty, Marshal."

The call that came in from their contact in the APD a little later took some of the edge off Sheryl's sense of satisfaction. The police hadn't turned up any leads regarding her slashed tires, nor had they located the man who'd hassled her yesterday morning over his girlfriend's welfare check. The woman had moved, and none of the neighbors knew her or her boyfriend's current address.

"They're going to keep working it," Harry advised.

"I hope so."

In addition to the many incoming calls, the task force also had a number of visitors, including the deputy U.S. district attorney working the charges against Inga Gunderson. Harry and Ev conferred with the man in private for some time. Just before noon, the three of them went downstairs for Inga Gunderson's custody hearing. The marshals returned an hour later, elated and more determined than ever. The government's lawyer had convinced the judge to hold Inga pending a grand-jury review of the charges against her, they reported. The good guys had won another two, possibly three days while the woman remained in custody.

"That's great for you," Sheryl said with a sigh, "but it looks like I've got Button for at least two, possibly three, more days."

"There's always the pound," Harry reminded her.

When she declined to reply, Ev picked up on the conversation.

"Inga's attorney asked about the dog. Said his client was worried about her precious Butty-Boo. We assured him the mutt was in good hands." His pudgy face took on a thoughtful air. "Maybe we should check the mutt out again."

Harry's head jerked up sharply. "You said you went over him while we were at Inga's house."

"I took his collar apart and searched what I could of his fur without losing all ten of my fingers. I might have missed something."

"Great."

"Or he could be carrying something internally," Ev finished with a grimace. He eyed the other marshal across the table. "I'll let you handle this one, MacMillan. You lugged the mutt around under your arm for most of yesterday. He knows you."

"I've done a lot of things in the pursuit of justice," Harry drawled, "but I draw the line at a body cavity search of a fuzz ball with teeth. If you don't mind giving me your house keys and the alarm code, Sheryl, I'll send a squad car out to pick him up and take him to the vet who works the drug dogs. He's got full X-ray capability."

Sheryl dug her keys out of her purse, then passed them across the table. Poor Button. She suspected he wouldn't enjoy the next hour or so. Neither would the vet.

Harry dispatched the squad car, resumed his seat next to hers and reviewed his notes. "Okay, we've got details on eight postcards now. Can you remember any more?"

Sheryl sorted through her memory. "I think there were two, perhaps three, more."

* * *

They worked steadily for another hour. A uniformed police officer returned Sheryl's keys and a report that the dog was clean. Fay Chandler called in from Farmington, where she was waiting for the manager of the local airport to make an appearance. Ev went downstairs to confer with his buddies in the computer center.

Finally, Harry leaned back in his chair and tapped his stub of a pencil on his notes. "Well, I guess that's it. We've covered the same ground three times now, with nothing new to add to our list of key words or numbers."

"I wish I could remember more."

"You've given us and the computer wizards downstairs enough to keep us busy the rest of the night. If we don't break whatever code these cards carried, it won't be from lack of trying."

Feeling oddly deflated now that she'd finished her task, Sheryl swept the empty conference room with a glance. After only two days, the litter of phones and maps and computerized printouts seemed as familiar to her as her own living room.

"Do you need me for anything else?"

Harry's gaze drifted over her face for a moment. "If… when…we make sense of what you've told us, I'll give you a call. We might need you to verify some detail. In the meantime, I want you to stay alert…and let me know if any more postcards show up, of course."

"Of course."

"Preferably *before* you return them to sender."

"We'll try to be less efficient," she said gravely.

A small silence gripped them, as though neither wanted to make the next move. Then Harry pushed back his chair.

"I know I've put you through the wringer for the past couple of days. I appreciate the information you've provided, Sheryl. I'll make sure the postmaster knows how much."

He held out his hand. Hers slipped into it with a warm shock that disturbed her almost as much as the realization that she might not see him again after today.

"You'll let me know when…if… Inga gets out of custody, so I can send Button back to her?"

"I will, although if I have my way, that won't occur for seven to ten years, minimum."

"Well…" She tugged her hand free of his.

"I'll walk you down to your car."

Their footsteps echoed in the tiled corridor. Side by side, they waited for the elevator.

Why couldn't he just let her go? Harry wondered. Just let her walk away? There wasn't any need to prolong the contact. He'd gotten what he wanted out of her.

No, his mind mocked, not quite all he wanted.

With every breath he drew in he caught her scent and knew he wanted more from this woman. A lot more. He'd spent most of last night thinking about the feel of her mouth under his, tasting again her wine-flavored kiss. And most of today trying not to notice how her tawny hair curled at her temples, or the way her red silk blouse showed off her golden skin.

If Harry hadn't witnessed the scene in her doorway last night, he might have come back to Albuquerque after he cornered his quarry and given this Brian character a run for his money. But the aching tenderness in Sheryl's face when she'd bid her almost-fiancé good-night had killed that half-formed idea before it really took root. His predatory instincts might allow him to challenge another male for a woman's interest, but he wouldn't loose those instincts on one so obviously in love with another man…as much as he burned to.

The elevator swooshed open, then carried them downward in a smooth, silent descent. With a smile and a nod to the guard manning the security post, Harry escorted Sheryl to the underground parking garage.

Her little Camry sat waiting in the numbered slot Harry had arranged for her. She deactivated the newly installed alarm with the remote device, unlocked the door and tossed her purse inside. Then she unclipped her temporary badge and handed it to him.

"I guess I won't need this anymore."

His hand fisted over the plastic badge. "Thanks again, Sheryl. You've given me more to work with than I've had in almost a year."

"You're welcome."

Let her go! Dammit, he had to let her go! Deliberately, he stepped back.

"I'll keep you posted on what happens," he said again, more briskly this time. "And what to do with Button."

She took the hint and slid into the car. "Thanks."

Harry closed the door for her and stood in a faint haze of exhaust while Sheryl backed out of the slot and drove up the exit ramp. Turning on one heel, he returned to the conference room.

He made a quick call to the task force's contact in the APD to confirm that they'd keep an eye on the Monzano Street station and Miss Hancock's apartment for the next few days. Then he got back to the glamorous, adventurous work of a U.S. marshal.

"All right, Ev, let me have some of those computer printouts."

* * *

They worked until well after midnight. Wire tight from the combination of long hours and a mounting frustration over his inability to break the damned code of the postcards, Harry drove to his motel just off of I-40.

The door slammed shut behind him. The chain latch rattled into place. The puny little chain and flimsy door lock wouldn't keep out a determined ten-year-old, but the .357 Magnum Harry slid out of its holster and laid on the nightstand beside his bed provided adequate backup security.

Enough light streamed in through curtains the maid had left open to show him the switches on the wall. He flicked them on, flooding the overdone Southwestern decor with light. The garish orange-and-red bedspread leaped out at him. Decorated with bleached cattle skulls, tall saguaro cacti and stick figures that some New York designer probably intended as Kachinas, it was almost as bad as the cheap prints on the wall. The room was clean, however, which was all Harry required.

He closed the curtains and headed for the shower, stripping as he went. Naked, he leaned back against the smooth, slick tiles and let the tepid water sluice over him.

They were close. So damned close. He and Ev had winnowed the thousands of possible combinations of letters and numbers on the postcards down to a hundred or so that made sense. Tomorrow, they'd go over those again, looking for some tie to the local area, some key to a date, a time, a set of coordinates.

They'd worked hard today. Tomorrow, they'd work even harder. The drop had to happen soon. If Paul Gunderson had passed the stuff through Prague four days ago and was triangulating the shipment through

Spain and Rio, he had to bring it into the States any day now. Any hour.

Frustration coiled like a living thing in Harry's gut. Prague. Pamploma. Rio. At last he had a track on the bastard. He wouldn't let him slip through his fingers this time.

He lifted his face to the water, willing himself to relax. He needed to clear his mind, so he could start fresh in a few hours. He needed sleep.

Not that there was much chance of that, he acknowledged, twisting the water off. If last night was any indication, he'd spend half of tonight trying not to think of Sheryl Hancock naked and heavy eyed with pleasure from his kisses, the other half thoroughly enjoying the image.

He slung a towel around his neck and padded into the bedroom. Just as well she had such an amazing memory, he thought grimly. Two days in her company had done enough damage to his concentration. Tomorrow, at least, he wouldn't have to battle the distraction of her smile and her long, endless legs.

Harry almost succeeded in putting both out of his mind. After a short night and a quick breakfast of coffee and *huevos rancheros* in the motel's restaurant, he entered the conference room just after six. Ev arrived at six-thirty, Fay a little later. They slogged through the remaining reports for a couple of hours and had just been joined by an FBI agent with a reputation as an expert in codes and signals when one of the phones rang.

Impatiently, Harry snatched it up. "MacMillan."

"This is Officer Lawrence with the APD. I have a

note here to keep you advised of any unusual activity at the Monzano Street post office."

He went still. "Yes?"

"A call came into 911 a few minutes ago, requesting an ambulance at that location."

Ev's desultory conversation with the FBI agent faded into the background. Harry gripped the phone, his eyes fixed on an aeronautical map tacked to the far wall.

"For what reason?"

"I didn't get the whole story. Only that they needed an ambulance to transport a white female to the hospital immediately."

"Did you get a name?"

"No, but I understand it's one of the employees."

His pulse stopped, restarted with a sharp, agonizing kick. "What hospital?"

"University Hospital at UNM."

In one fluid motion, Harry slammed the phone down, shoved back his chair and grabbed his jacket. Throwing a terse explanation over his shoulder to the others, he raced out of the conference room.

Chapter 8

Sheryl called in to work early the next morning to let her supervisor know that Harry had released her from the special task force. Things were quiet for a Friday, Pat Martinez informed her. The temp had her counter station covered, but they could use her help throwing mail on the second shift.

Feeling an unaccountable lack of enthusiasm for a return to her everyday routine, Sheryl decided to run a few errands on her way in. She indulged Button with a supply of doggie treats and herself with a new novel by her favorite romance author before pulling into the parking lot of the Monzano Street station.

The moment she walked through the rear door and headed for the time clock, Sheryl got the immediate impression that things were anything but quiet. Tension hung over the back room, as thick and as heavy as a cloud. The mail carriers who hadn't already started their daily runs crowded around the station supervisor's desk. In the center of the throng, Pat paced back and forth with a phone glued to her ear, her face grave as she spoke to the person on the other end. Peggy, who should have been on the front counter with Elise, was hunched on a corner of Pat's desk. Even Buck Aguilar stood with arms folded and worried lines carved into his usually impassive face.

Sheryl punched in and wove her way through the work stations toward the group clustered around Pat. The station manager's worried voice carried clearly in the silence that gripped her audience.

"Yes, yes, I know. I'll try to reach her again. Just keep us posted, okay?"

The receiver clattered into its cradle.

"They don't know anything yet," she announced to the assembled crowd. "Brian's going to call us as soon as he gets word."

"Brian?" Sheryl nudged her way to the front. "What's Brian going to call about?"

"Sheryl!" Pat sprang up, relief and worry battling on her face. "I've been trying to reach you since right after you called to tell me you were coming in this morning."

"Why? What's going on?"

"Elise fell and went into labor."

"Oh, no!" A tight fist squeezed Sheryl's heart. "Is she okay? And the baby?"

"We don't know. They took her to the hospital by ambulance an hour ago. She was frantic that we get hold of you, since you're her labor coach. I tried your house, then Brian's office, thinking he might know where you were. He didn't, but he went to University Hospital to stay with Elise until we found you."

"Get hold of Brian at the hospital," Sheryl called, already on the run. "Tell him I'll be there in fifteen minutes."

It took her a frustrating, anxious half hour.

She sped down Juan Tabo and swung onto Lomas quickly enough, only to find both westbound lanes blocked by orange barrels. A long line of earthmovers rumbled by, digging up big chunks of concrete. Dust flew everywhere, and Sheryl's anxiety mounted by the second as she waited for the last of them to pass. Even with one lane open each way, traffic crawled at a stop-and-go, five-mile-an-hour pace.

Cursing under her breath, she turned off at the next side street and cut through a sprawl of residential neighborhoods. The Camry's new tires squealed as she slowed to a rolling stop at the stop signs dotting every block, then tore across the intersections. By the time the distinctive dun-colored adobe architecture of the University of New Mexico came into view, she trembled with barely controlled panic.

Elise wasn't due for another two weeks…if then. The baby's sonogram had showed it slightly undersized, and the obstetrician had revised the due date twice already. With the stress of her divorce coming right on top of the discovery that she was pregnant, Elise hadn't been vague about the possible date of the baby's conception. She and Rick had split up and reconciled twice before finally calling it quits. She could have gotten pregnant during either one of those brief, tempestuous reconciliations.

And Pat had said that Elise had fallen! Every time

Sheryl thought of the hard, uncarpeted tile floors at the post office, the giant fist wrapped a little tighter around her heart. Offering up a steady litany of prayers for Elise and her baby, she squealed into the University Hospital parking lot, slammed out of the Camry, and ran for the multistory brown-stucco building.

Since she and Elise had toured the facility as part of their prenatal orientation, she didn't need to consult the directory or ask directions to the birthing rooms. The moment the elevator hummed to a stop on the third floor, she bolted out and ran for the nurses' station in the labor and delivery wing.

"Which room is Mrs. Hart in? Is she all right? I'm her birthing partner—I need to be with her."

A stubby woman in flowered scrubs held up a hand. "Whoa. Slow down and catch your breath. Mrs. Hart's had a rough time, but the hemorrhaging stopped before she went into hard labor."

"Hemorrhaging! Oh, my God!"

"She's okay, really. Last time I checked, she was about to deliver."

"Which room is she in?"

The nurse hesitated. "You'll have to scrub before you can go in, but I'm not sure it's necessary at this point. Her husband's with her. From what I saw a little while ago, he's filling in pretty well as coach."

Sheryl's brows shot up. "Rick's here?"

"I thought he said his name was Brian."

Belatedly, Sheryl remembered the hospital rule restricting attendance in the birthing room during delivery to family members and/or designated coaches.

"We, er, call him 'Rick' for short. Look, I won't burst

in, I promise, but I need to be with Elise. Where can I scrub?"

"I'll show you."

A few moments later, a gowned-and-masked Sheryl entered the birthing sanctuary. Doors on either side of the long corridor revealed rooms made homelike by reclining chairs, plants, pictures and low tables littered with magazines. Most of the doors stood open. Two were shut, including Elise's. Mindful of the nurse's injunction, she approached it quietly.

An anguished moan from inside the room raised the hairs on the back of her neck. She nudged the door open an inch or two, and stopped in her tracks.

A trio of medical specialists stood at the foot of the bed, poised to receive the baby. Brian leaned over a groaning, grunting Elise. At least, she thought it was Brian. He was gowned and masked and wearing a surgical cap to keep his auburn hair out of his eyes, and she barely recognized him. She recognized his voice, though, as hoarse and ragged as it was.

"You're doing great. One more push, Elise. One more push."

Sweat glistened on his forehead. His right hand clenched the laboring woman's. With his left, he smoothed her damp hair back from her forehead.

"Breathe with me, then push!"

"I...can't."

"Yes, you can."

"The baby's crowning," the doctor said from the bottom of the bed. "We need a good push here, Mom."

"Breathe, Elise." The command came out in a desperate squeak. Brian swallowed and tried again. "Breathe, then push. Puff. Puff. Puff."

"Puff. Puf…arrrgh!" Elise lifted half off the mattress, then came down with a grunt. Limp and panting, she snarled out a fervent litany.

"Damn Rick! Damn all men! Damn every male who ever learned how to work a zipper!"

Startled, Brian drew back. Elise grabbed the front of his gown and dragged him down to her level.

"Not you! Oh, God, not you! Don't… Don't leave me, Brian. Please, don't leave me."

"I won't, I promise. Now push."

Sheryl peered through the crack in the door, her heart in her throat. After sharing the ups and downs of her friend's divorce and training with her for just this moment, she longed to rush into the room, shove Brian aside and take Elise's hand to help her through the next stage of her ordeal. But her friend's urgent plea and Brian's reply kept her rooted in place. The two of them had bonded. The drama of the baby's imminent birth had forged a link between them that Sheryl couldn't bring herself to break or even intrude on.

"The head's clear," the doctor announced calmly. "Relax a moment, Mom, then we'll work the shoulders. You're doing great. Ready? Okay, here we go."

Sheryl felt her own stomach contract painfully as Elise grunted, then gave a long, rolling moan.

"We've got him."

One of the nurses smiled at the two anxious watchers. "He's a handsome little thing! The spitting image of his dad."

Brian started, then grinned behind his mask. With a whoop of sheer exhilaration, he bent and planted a kiss on Elise's forehead.

She used her death grip on the front of his hospital

gown to drag him down even farther. Awkwardly, Brian took her into his arms. She clung to him, sobbing with relief and joy. A second later, the baby gave a lusty wail.

"Don't relax yet," the doctor instructed when Elise collapsed back on the bed, wiped out from her ordeal. "We've still got some work to do here."

Elated, relieved and hugely disappointed that she hadn't participated in the intense drama except as an observer, Sheryl watched Brian smooth back Elise's hair once more. A fierce tenderness came over the part of his face that showed above the mask. The sheer intensity of his expression took Sheryl by surprise. Swiftly, she thought back through the months she and Brian had been dating. She couldn't ever remember seeing him display such raw, naked emotion.

The realization stunned her and added another layer to the wrenching turmoil that had plagued her for two nights now. If she'd had any doubts about the decision she'd made in the dark hours just before dawn this morning, she only needed to look at his face to know it was the right one.

She loved Brian, but she wasn't *in* love with him. Nor, apparently, was he in love with her. Never once had she roused that kind of intense emotion in him. Never had she caused such a display of fierce protectiveness.

Slowly, Sheryl let the door whisper shut and backed away...or tried to. A solid wall of unyielding flesh blocked her way. Turning, she found herself chest to chest with Marshal MacMillan.

"Harry!" She tugged off her face mask. "What are you doing here?"

"I got word that EMS was transporting a female employee from the Monzano Street post office to the hospital. I thought…"

A small muscle worked on one side of his jaw. He paused, then finished in a voice that sounded like glass grinding.

"I thought it might be you."

"Oh, no! Did you think the slasher had come back?"

"Among other things," he admitted, taking Sheryl's elbow to move her to one side as an orderly trundled by with a cart. "By the time EMS verified the patient's identity, I was already in the parking lot, so I came up to see what the problem was."

"Did they tell you? My friend Elise fell and went into labor."

He nodded. "They also told me you were on the way down here, so I waited. How's she doing?"

Sheryl relaxed against the hallway wall, strangely comforted by Harry's presence. "Okay, I think. She and the baby both."

"Good! The nurse said her husband was in with her. From the glimpse I had over your shoulder a moment ago, he's certainly a proud papa."

"Well, there's a little mix-up about that. Elise is divorced. I was supposed to act as her coach, but I didn't get here in time, so Brian filled in for me."

"Brian?" A puzzled frown flitted across his face. "That was your Brian in there?"

So Harry had seen it, too. The raw emotion. The special bond Brian had forged with Elise.

Sheryl fumbled for an answer other than the one her aching heart supplied. No, he wasn't her Brian. Not any more. Maybe he never had been. But until she talked to him, she wouldn't discuss the matter with anyone else.

Thankfully, one of the nurses walked out of Elise's room at that moment and spared her the necessity of a reply. Sheryl sprang away from the wall and hurried toward her.

"Is everything okay? How are Elise and the baby?"

"Mother and son are both fine," she answered with a smile. "And Dad's so proud, he's about to pop. Give them another few minutes to finish cleaning up, then you can go in."

Their voices must have carried to the occupants of the birthing room, because Brian came charging out a second later. His dark-red hair stuck straight up in spikes. The hospital gown had twisted around his waist. Huge, wet patches darkened his underarms and arrowed down his chest. Sheryl had never seen him looking so ruffled...or so excited.

"Sher! You missed it!" He tore off his mask. "It was so fantastic! Elise is wonderful. And the baby, he's... he's wonderful!"

"Yes, I..."

"Look, can you call the school? Elise is worried about the boys. Tell them I'll pick them up this afternoon and bring them down to see their new brother."

"Sure, I—"

"Thanks! I have to go back in. The doc says it'll be a few minutes yet before you can come in. You, too..."

He blinked owlishly, as if recognizing for the first time the man who stood silently behind Sheryl. If Brian wondered why Harry had turned up at the hospital, he was too distracted to ask about it now.

"You, too, MacMillan."

He turned away to reenter the birthing room, then spun back. "You're never going to believe it, Sher! He's got my hair. Elise's is sort of sorrel, but this little guy has a cap of dark red fuzz." He grinned idiotically. "Just like mine."

"Brian!" Sheryl caught him just before he disappeared. "Do you want me to call your office? If you're going to pick the boys up from school, should I tell your secretary to reschedule your afternoon appointments?"

He flapped a hand. "Whatever."

The door whirred shut behind him.

"Well, well," Harry murmured in the small, ensuing silence. "Is that the same man who had to schedule everything, even his meetings with his almost-fiancée?"

"No," Sheryl answered with a sigh. "It isn't."

Turning, she caught a speculative gleam in the marshal's warm brown eyes. Unwilling to discuss her relationship with Brian until she'd had time to talk to him, she deliberately changed the subject.

"If you want to go in and see Elise and the baby, I'll show you where to find a gown and mask."

"I'd better pass. They don't need a stranger hovering over them right now."

"No, I guess not."

She hesitated, torn between the need to join Elise and a sudden, surging reluctance to say goodbye to Harry for the second time in as many days.

"Thanks for coming down to check on me, even if it wasn't me who needed checking."

"You're welcome."

It took some effort, but she summoned a smile. "Maybe I'll see you around."

The gleam she'd caught in his eyes a moment ago returned, deeper, more intense, like the glint of new-struck gold.

"Maybe you will."

* * *

Sheryl spent the rest of the morning and most of the afternoon at the hospital. Brian left after lunch, promising to be back within an hour with Elise's other two boys. His jubilation had subsided in the aftermath of the birth, but his eyes still lit with wonder whenever he caught a glimpse of the baby.

Lazy and at peace in the stillness of the afternoon, Elise cradled her son in her arms and smiled at the woman perched on the edge of her bed. The friendship that had stretched across years of shared work and a variety of family crises, big and small, cocooned them.

"I'm sorry you missed your tour of duty as birthing partner, Sher. I could have used your moral support. The others were easy, but I was a little scared with this one after my fall."

"We were all scared."

Elise brushed a finger over the baby's dark-russet down. "I was going to call him Terence, after my grandfather, but I think I'll name him Brian, instead. Brian Hart. How does that sound to you, little one?"

It must have sounded pretty good, as the baby pursed its tiny lips a few times, scrunched its wrinkled face, then settled once more into sleep.

"I don't know what I would have done without Brian," Elise murmured. "He's...wonderful."

Sheryl found a smile. "He says the same thing about you and little Red here."

Her friend's gaze lifted. "I know I've told you this before, but you're so lucky to have him. There aren't many like him around."

"No, there aren't."

Sheryl's smile felt distinctly ragged about the edges.

She had to talk to Brian. Soon. This burden of confusion and guilt and regret was getting too heavy to lug around much longer.

As it turned out, she didn't have to talk to Brian.

He talked to her.

They met at the hospital later that evening. Elise's room overflowed with flowers and friends from the post office. Murmurs of laughter filled the small room as Peggy and Pat and even Buck Aguilar cooed and showered the new arrival with rattles and blankets and an infant-sized postal service uniform.

Deciding to give the others time and space to admire Baby Brian, Sheryl slipped out and went in search of a vending machine. A cool diet soda fizzed in her hand as she paused by a window, staring out at the golden haze of the sunset.

"Sher?"

She turned and smiled a welcome at Brian. He looked very different from the man who'd rushed out of Elise's room this morning, his face drenched with sweat and his eyes alive with exultation. Tonight, he wore what Sheryl always teasingly called his real-estate-agent's uniform— a lightweight blue seersucker jacket, white shirt, navy slacks. His conservative red tie was neatly knotted.

Leaning against the window alcove, Sheryl offered him a sip of her drink. He declined. His gaze, like hers, drifted to the glorious sunset.

"Have you been in to see Elise and the baby yet?" she asked after a moment.

He nodded. "For a few minutes. I could barely squeeze in the room."

"Did she tell you what she'd decided to name him?"

"Yes."

The single word carried such quiet, glowing pride that Sheryl's heart contracted. God, she hated to hurt this man! They'd shared so many hours, so many dreams. Caught up in her own swamping guilt and regret, she almost missed his next comment.

"I need to talk to you, Sher. I don't know if this is the right time… I don't know if there is a right time." He raked a hand through his hair. "But this morning, when I saw what Elise went through, when I was there with her, I realized what marriage is really about."

Sheryl wanted to weep. She set her drink on the window ledge and took his hands in hers.

"Oh, Brian, I…"

He gripped her fingers. "Let me say this."

"But…"

"Please!"

Miserable beyond words, she nodded.

He took a deep breath and plunged ahead. "Marriage means…should mean…sharing everything. Giving everything. Joining together and, if it's in the picture, holding on to each other at moments like the one that happened this morning."

"I know."

He swallowed, gripping her hands so tightly Sheryl thought her bones would crack. "It shouldn't be something comfortable, something easy and familiar or something we just drift into because it's the next step."

"What?"

His words were so unexpected she was sure she hadn't heard him right.

"Oh, God, Sher, I'm sorry. This hurts so much."

"What does?"

"When I was with Elise this morning, I realized that…that I love you. I'll always love you. But…"

That small "but" rang like a gong in her ears. In growing incredulity, Sheryl stared up at him.

"But what?"

"But maybe… Maybe I don't love you enough," he finished, his eyes anguished. "Maybe not the way a man who might someday stand beside you and hold your hand while you give birth to his children should. I think… I think maybe we shouldn't see each other for a while. Until I sort through this awful confusion, anyway."

Sheryl wouldn't have been human if she'd hadn't experienced a spurt of genuine hurt before her rush of relief. After all, the man she'd spent the better part of the past year with had just dumped her. But she cared for him too much to let him shoulder the entire burden of guilt.

"I love you, too, Brian. I always will. But…"

He went still. "But?"

She gave him a weak, watery smile. "But not in the way a woman who might someday cling to your hand while she gave birth to your children should."

Chapter 9

Sheryl arrived home well after nine that night. Wrung out from the long, traumatic day and her painful discussion with Brian, she dropped her uniform in the basket of dirty clothes that Button, thankfully, had left unmolested.

She thought about crawling into bed. A good cry might shake the awful, empty feeling that had dogged her since she woke up this morning. Arriving at the hospital too late to share the miracle of birth with Elise after all those months of anticipation had only added to her hollowness. The subsequent breakup with Brian had taken that lost feeling to a new low.

As if those disturbing events weren't enough, another lowering realization had hit her as she'd driven home through the dark night. Just twenty-four hours off the task force, and she missed Harry MacMillan as much as she missed her ex-almost.

If not more.

Sighing, Sheryl pulled on a pair of cutoffs and a well-worn pink T-shirt adorned with a covey of roadrunners. Try as she might, she couldn't seem to get her mind off the marshal. As soon as he bagged Paul Gunderson, which she sincerely hoped he would soon do, he'd be off after the next fugitive. That was his job. His life. Chances were that she'd never see him again. Utterly depressed by the thought, she scooped Button out of the nest he'd made in the middle of her bed.

"Come on, fella. You're going to keep me company while I sob my way through a schmaltzy movie or two." She knuckled his head around the topknot she'd tied with a red ribbon. "Since I don't have to work tomorrow, we might just make it an all-nighter."

They were halfway through *Ghost,* her all-time favorite tearjerker, when the doorbell rang. Treating Sheryl to an ear-shattering demonstration of newly awakened watchdog instincts, Button dug his claws into her bare thighs and sprang off her lap. Yapping furiously, he raced for the foyer.

Sheryl swiped at her tear-streaked cheeks with the bottom of her T-shirt and followed. To her surprise and instant, bubbling pleasure, she identified Harry MacMillan's unmistakable form through the peephole. Reaching for the door chain, she shouted a command at the dog.

"Quiet!"

Naturally, Button didn't pay the least attention to her. His ear-shattering barks bounced off the walls.

"Will you hush! It's Harry."

She jerked the chain off, flicked the alarm switch and threw open the door. If anything, Button's shrill yips went up a few decibels when he recognized his nemesis, but the marshal had come armed this time. Flashing a grin at Sheryl, he knelt down and wafted a cardboard carton under the dog's nose.

"Like pizza, pug-face? I got double pepperoni for you, pineapple and Canadian bacon for us."

The nerve-shredding barking ceased as if cut off with a knife. To Sheryl's astonishment, Button plopped down on the tiles, rolled all the way over, then scrambled back onto his paws. Jumping up on his hind legs, he danced backward, inviting Harry and the pizza in.

The marshal rose, smirking. "Even hairy little rodents can be bribed. It was just a matter of finding the right price."

Sheryl stood aside, her heart thumping at the crooked grin. "Did you come all the way over here just to bribe your way into Button's good graces?"

"That, and to cheer you up."

Palming the pizza high in the air, he followed her into the apartment. He placed the carton on the whitewashed oak dining table and shrugged out of his jacket. The leather holster followed his sport coat onto the back of a chair. Sheryl turned away from the gun and drank in the sight of Harry's broad shoulders and rugged, tanned face. The smile in his warm brown eyes acted like a balm to her spirits, pulling her out of her depression like a fast-climbing roller coaster.

"What made you think I needed cheering up?" she asked curiously.

"Let's just say my cop's instincts were working overtime again. I also want to go over the info you gave us on the Rio card one more time. Even the FBI's so-called expert can't crack the damned code."

Ahhh. Now the real reason for his visit was out. She didn't mind. Working a few hours with Harry would do her more good than sobbing while Patrick Swayze tried to cross time and space to be with Demi Moore. Or lying in bed, thinking about Brian.

"Have a seat," the marshal instructed, heading for the kitchen. "I think I remember where everything is."

Button trailed at his heels, having abandoned all pride in anticipation of a late-night treat. Sheryl settled into one of the rattan-backed dining-room chairs as instructed and hooked her bare feet on the bottom rung. With a little advance notice of this visit, she might have traded her cutoffs and T-shirt for something more presentable. She might even have pulled a brush through her unruly hair. As it was, Harry would just have to put up with a face scrubbed clean of all makeup and a tumble of loose curls spilling over her shoulders.

He didn't seem to mind her casual attire when he emerged a moment later with plates, napkins and a wineglass filled with the last of the leftover Chablis. In fact, his eyes gleamed appreciatively as his gaze drifted over her.

"I like the roadrunners."

A hint of a flush rose in Sheryl's cheeks. She definitely should have changed…or at least put on a bra under the thin T-shirt.

"We have a lot of them out here," she said primly, then tried to divert his attention from the covey of birds darting across her chest. "Why do you want to go over the Rio card again?"

The glint left his eyes, and his jaw took on a hard angle that Sheryl was coming to recognize.

"I'm missing something. It's probably so simple it's staring me right in the face, but I'll be damned if I can see it."

"Maybe we'll see it tonight."

"I hope so. My gut tells me we're running out of time."

He passed her the wine and plates, then dug in his jacket pocket for a dew-streaked can of beer. The momentary tightness around his mouth eased as he popped the top and hefted the can in the air.

"Shall we toast the baby?"

"Sounds good to me."

Smiling, Sheryl chinked her wineglass against the can. She sipped slowly, her eyes on the strong column of Harry's throat as he satisfied his thirst. For the first time that day, she felt herself relax. Really relax. As much as she could in Harry's presence.

Sure enough, she enjoyed her sense of ease for ten, perhaps twenty, seconds. Then he set his beer on the table, brushed a finger across his mustache and dropped a casual bomb.

"So did you give Brian his walking papers?"

Sheryl choked. Her wineglass hit the whitewashed oak tabletop with more force than she'd intended. While she fought to clear her throat, Harry calmly served up the pizza.

"Well?"

"No, I didn't give Brian his walking papers! Not that it's any of your business."

"Why not?"

She glared at him across the pizza carton. Getting

dumped by Brian was one thing. Telling Harry about it was something else again.

"What makes you think I would even want to?"

He leaned back in his chair, his expression gentle. As gentle as someone with his rugged features could manage, anyway.

"I was there, Sheryl. I saw him with Elise. I also saw your face when he went dashing back into her room."

"Oh."

A small silence spun out between them, broken only by the noisy, snuffling slurps coming from the kitchen. Button, at least, was enjoying his pizza.

Sheryl chipped at the crust with a short, polished nail. She wanted…needed…to talk to someone. Normally, she would have shared her troubled thoughts with Elise. She couldn't burden her friend with this particular problem right now, though, any more than she could call her own mother in Las Cruces to talk about it. Joan Hancock adored Brian, and had told her daughter several thousand times that she'd better latch onto him. Men that reliable, that steady, didn't grow in potato patches.

Maybe… Maybe Harry was just the confidant Sheryl needed. He knew her situation well enough to murmur sympathetically between slices of pineapple and Canadian bacon, but not so well that he'd burden her with unsolicited advice, as her mother assuredly would.

She stole a glance at him from beneath her lashes. Legs stretched, ankles crossed, he lounged in his chair. He looked so friendly, so relaxed that she couldn't quite believe this was the same man she'd almost taken a bite out of on Inga Gunderson's front porch. His air of easy companionship invited her confidence.

"Brian and I had a long talk tonight in the hospital

waiting room," she said slowly. "I didn't give him his walking papers, as you put it. I, uh, didn't get the chance. He gave me mine."

A slice of pizza halted halfway to Harry's mouth. "What?"

"He said that his time with Elise this morning changed every thought, every misconception, he'd ever formed about marriage." She nudged a chunk of pineapple with the tip of her nail. "And about love. It shouldn't be easy, or comfortable, or something we just sort of drift into."

Snorting in derision, the marshal dropped his pizza onto his plate. "No kidding! He's just coming to that brilliant conclusion?"

Sheryl couldn't help smiling at the utter disgust in his voice. Harry MacMillan wouldn't drift into anything. He'd charge in, guns blazing...figuratively, she hoped!

"Don't come down on Brian so hard," she said ruefully. "It took me a while to figure it out, too."

Across the table, golden brown eyes narrowed suddenly. "Are you saying that's all this guy was to you? Someone easy and comfortable?"

"Well..."

The single, hesitant syllable curled Harry's hands into fists. At that moment he would have taken great pleasure in shoving the absent real-estate-agent's face not just into the hallway wall but through it. Hell! It didn't take a Sherlock Holmes, much less a U.S. marshal, to figure out that the jerk hadn't fully committed to Sheryl. If he'd wanted her, really wanted her, he wouldn't have moved so slowly or made any damned appointments! He would've staked his claim with a ring, or at least with a more definitive arrangement than their sort-of engagement.

But after seeing them in each other's arms the other night, Harry had assumed…had thought…

What?

That Sheryl loved the guy? That she wanted Brian Mitchell more than he showed signs of wanting her?

The idea that she might be hurting was what had brought Harry to her apartment tonight. That and the sudden lost look in her eyes when the idiot had rushed back into her friend's hospital room and left her standing there. That look had stayed with Harry all afternoon, until he'd startled Ev and Fay and the FBI expert still struggling with the key words from the postcards by calling it a night. Driven by an urge he hadn't let himself think about, he'd stopped at a pizzeria just a few blocks from Sheryl's apartment and come to comfort her.

He now recognized that urge for what it was. Two parts sympathy for someone struggling with an unraveling relationship: anyone who'd gone through a divorce could relate to that hurt. One part concern for the woman he'd worked with for two days now and had come to like and respect. And one part…

One part pure, unadulterated male lust.

Harry could admit it now. When she'd opened the door to him in those short shorts and figure-hugging T-shirt, a hot spot had ignited in his gut. He knew damned well that the slow burning had nothing to do with any desire to comfort a friend or to grill a team member yet again about the postcards.

It had taken everything he had to return her greeting and nonchalantly set about feeding her and the mutt. He couldn't come anywhere close to nonchalant now, though. Any more than he could keep his gaze from dipping to the thrust of her breasts under the thin layer of pink as she rose and shoved her hands into her back pockets.

"I don't know why I didn't see it sooner, Harry." She paced the open space between the dining and living rooms. "I loved Brian. I still do. But I wasn't *in* love with him. I guess I let myself be seduced by the comfortable routine he represented."

Thoroughly distracted by the sight of those long, tanned legs and bare toes tipped with pink nail polish, Harry forgot his self-assigned role of friend and listener.

"Comfortable routine?" He snorted again. "The man has a helluva seduction technique."

"Hey, it worked for me."

The way she kept springing to Brian's defense was starting to really irritate Harry. Almost as much as her admission that she still loved the jerk.

"Right," he drawled. "That's why you're pacing the floor and ole Bry's off on his own somewhere, pondering the meaning of life and love."

She turned, surprise and indignation sending twin flags of color into her cheeks. "Whose side are you on, anyway?"

"Yours, sweetheart."

He rose, barely noticing the way the endearment slipped out. Three strides took him to where she stood, all stiff and bristly.

"You deserve better than routine, Sheryl. You deserve a dizzy, breathless, thoroughly exhausting seduction that shakes you right out of predictable and puts you down somewhere on the other side of passion."

"Is… Is that right?"

"That's right." He stroked a knuckle down her

smooth, golden cheek. "You deserve kisses that wind you up so tight it takes all night to unwind."

Harry could have fallen into the wide green eyes that stared up at him and never found his way out. Her lips opened, closed, opened again. A slow flush stole into her cheeks.

"Yes," she whispered at last. "I do."

Her breasts rose and fell under their pink covering. A pulse pounded at the base of her throat. Slowly, so slowly, her arms lifted and slid around his neck.

"Kiss me, Harry."

He kissed her.

He didn't think twice about it. Didn't listen to any of the alarms that started pinging the instant her arms looped around his neck. Didn't even hear them.

He'd hold her for a moment only, he swore fiercely. Kiss her just once more. Show her that there was life after Brian. That life *with* Brian hadn't come close to living at all. Then his mouth came down on hers, and Sheryl showed him a few things, instead.

That her taste had lingered in his mind for two days. But not this sweet. Or this wild. Or this hot.

That her lips were softer, firmer, more seductive than he remembered.

That her body matched his perfectly. Tall enough that he didn't have to bend double to reach her. Small enough to fit into the cradle of his thighs.

At the contact, he went instantly, achingly, hard. He jerked his head up, knowing that one more breath, one more press of her breasts against his chest, would drive him to something she couldn't be ready for. Not this soon after Brian.

Or maybe she could.

Her eyes opened at his abrupt movement. Harry saw himself in the dark pupils. Saw something else, as well. The passion he'd taunted her about. It shimmered in the green irises. Showed in her heavy eyelids. Sounded in the short, choppy rush of her breath.

This time, she didn't have to ask for his kiss. This time, he gave it, and took everything she offered in return.

By the time she dragged her mouth away, gasping, every muscle in Harry's body strained with the need to press her down on the nearest horizontal surface. With an effort that popped beads of sweat out on his forehead, he loosened his arms enough for her to draw back.

"Harry, I…"

She stopped, swiped her tongue along her lower lip. The burning need in Harry's gut needled into white, hot fingers of fire.

"You what, sweetheart?"

"I want to wind up tight," she whispered, her eyes holding his. "And take all night to unwind."

Few saints would fail to respond to that invitation, and Harry had no illusions that anyone would ever nominate him for canonization. Still, he forced himself to move slowly, giving her time to pull back at any move, any touch.

He lifted a hand to her throat and stroked the smooth skin under her chin. "I think we can manage a little winding and a lot of unwinding. If you're sure?"

A wobbly smile tugged at lips still rosy from his kiss. "Who's being cautious and careful now? What happened to breathless and dizzy and thoroughly exhausting?"

Grinning, he slid his arm under the backs of the thighs that had been driving him insane for the past half hour. Sweeping her into a tight hold, he headed for the hall.

"Breathless and dizzy coming right up, ma'am. Thoroughly exhausting to follow."

Sheryl barely heard Button's startled yip as Harry swept past with her in his arms. She didn't think about the idiocy of what she'd just asked this man to do. Tomorrow, she'd regret it. Maybe later tonight, when Harry left, as he inevitably would.

At this moment, she wanted only to end the swirling confusion he'd thrown her into the first moment he'd appeared in her life. To get past the pain of her break with Brian. To do something insane, something unplanned and unscheduled and definitely unroutine.

She buried her face in the warm skin of his neck. When he crossed the threshold to her bedroom, he twisted at the waist. With one booted heel, he kicked the door shut behind him. Sharp, annoyed yips rose from the other side.

"I might not hesitate at a little bribery," he told her, his voice a rumble in her ear, "but I draw the line at voyeurism."

"He'll bark all night," Sheryl warned, lifting her head. "Or however long it takes to unwind."

"Let him." His mustache lifted in a wicked grin. "And in case there's any doubt, it's going to take a long time. A very long time."

The husky promise sent ripples of excitement over every inch of her skin. The way he lowered her, sliding her body down his, turned those ripples into a near tidal wave. Her T-shirt snagged on his buttons. It lifted, baring her midriff. Cooled air raised goose bumps above her belly button. Harry's hard, driving kiss raised goose bumps below.

Her shirt hit the floor sometime later. His jeans and boots followed. In a tangle of arms and legs, they tumbled onto the downy black-and-white blanket that covered her bed. Gasping, Sheryl let Harry work the same magic on her breasts that he'd worked on her mouth. His soft, silky mustache teased. His fingers stroked. His tongue tasted. His teeth took her from breathless to moaning to only a kiss or two away from spinning out of control.

Sheryl wasn't exactly a passive participant in her unplanned, unroutine seduction. Her hands roamed as eagerly as his. Her tongue explored. Her body slicked and twisted and pressed everywhere it met his. She was as wet and hot and eager as he was when he finally groaned and dragged her arms down.

"Wait, sweetheart. Wait! Let me get something to protect you."

He rolled off her. Wearing only low-slung briefs and the shirt she'd tugged halfway down his back, he padded across the room to his jeans.

Sheryl flung an arm up over her head, almost as dizzy and befuddled as he'd predicted. Harry's posterior view didn't exactly unfuddle her. Lord, he was magnificent! All long, lean lines. Bronzed muscles. Tight, trim buttocks.

When he scooped up his jeans and turned, she had to admit that his front view wasn't too shabby, either. Her heart hammered as he dug out his wallet and rifled through it with an impatience that fanned the small fires he'd lit under her skin. A moment later, several packages of condoms fell onto the blanket.

Sheryl eyed the abundant supply with a raised brow. Harry caught her look and his mustache tipped into another wicked grin.

"U.S. marshals always come prepared for extended field operations."

"So I see."

Still grinning, he sheathed himself and rejoined her on the bed. He settled between her legs smoothly, as if she were made to receive him. His weight pressed her into the blanket. With both hands, he smoothed her hair back and planted little kisses on her neck.

"I don't want to give you the wrong impression," he murmured against her throat. "Dedicated law enforcement types have all kinds of uses for those little packages."

Torn between curiosity and a wild, blazing need to arch her hips into his, Sheryl could only huff a question into his ear.

"Like…what?"

"Later," he growled, nipping the cords of her neck. "I'll tell you later."

Would they have a later? The brief thought cut through her searing, sensual haze. Then his hand found her core and there was only now. Only Harry. Only the incredible pleasure he gave her.

The pleasure spiraled, spinning tighter and tighter with each kiss, each stroke of his hand and his body. When Sheryl was sure she couldn't stand the whirling sensations a moment longer without shattering, she wrapped her legs around his and arched her hips to receive him. It might have been mere moments or a lifetime later that she exploded in a blaze of white light.

Another forever followed, then Harry thrust into her

a final time. Rigid, straining, joined with her at mouth
and chest and hip, he filled her body. Only later did she
realize that he'd filled the newly empty place in her
heart, as well.

The realization came to her as she hovered between
boneless satiation and an exhausted doze. Her head cradled on Harry's shoulder, she remembered sleepily that
they hadn't gotten around to the postcards. They'd get
to them tomorrow, she thought, breathing in the musky
scent of their lovemaking.

Tomorrow came crashing down on them far sooner
than Sheryl had anticipated. She was sunk in a deep
doze, her head still cradled on a warm shoulder, when
the sound of a thump and a startled, pain-filled yelp
pierced her somnolent semiconsciousness.

Instantly, Harry spun off the bed. Sheryl's head hit
the mattress with a thump

"Wh...?"

"Stay here!"

With a pantherlike speed, he dragged on his jeans
and yanked at the zipper. They rode low on his hips as
he headed for the door. Gasping, Sheryl pushed herself
up on one elbow. Still groggy and only half-awake, she
blinked owlishly.

"What is it?"

"I don't know, and until I do, stay here, okay? No he-
roics and no noise."

Before his low instructions had even sunk in, he'd
slipped through the door and disappeared into the shadowed hallway. Sheryl gaped at the panel for a second
or two, still in a fog. Then she threw back the sheet and

leaped out of bed. She had her panties on and her T-shirt half over her head when the door swung open again.

She froze, her heart in her throat.

To her infinite relief, Harry stalked in. Disgust etched in every line of his taut body, he carried a tomato-and-grease-smeared Button under his arm.

"The greedy little beggar climbed up onto the table. He and our half of the pizza just took a dive."

Chapter 10

Although the little heart-shaped crystal clock on her nightstand showed just a few minutes before eleven, by the time Sheryl finished dressing she was experiencing all the awkwardness of a morning-after.

Button's noisy accident had shaken her right out of her sleepy, sensual haze. Like a splash of cold water in her face, reality now set in with a vengeance. She couldn't quite believe she'd begged Harry to kiss her like that. To seduce her, for pity's sake!

She walked down the hall to the living room, cringing inside as she realized how pathetic she must have sounded. First, by admitting that Brian had dumped her. Then, by practically demanding that the marshal take her to bed as a balm to her wounded ego. She couldn't remember when she'd ever done anything so rash. So stupid. So embarrassing to admit to after the fact.

Heat blazed in both cheeks when she found Harry in the dining room. Hunkered down on one knee, he was scrubbing at the grease stains in her carpet with a sponge and muttering imprecations at the dog that sat a few feet away, watching him with a show of blasé interest.

"You don't have to do that," Sheryl protested, her discomfiture mounting at the sight of Harry's naked chest. Had she really wrapped her arms and legs and everything else she could around his lean, powerful torso?

She had, she admitted with a new flush of heat. She could still feel the ache in her thighs, and taste him on her lips. How in the world had she lost herself like that? She hardly knew much more about this man than his name, his occupation, his marital status and the fact that he logged more travel miles in a month than most people did in two years. That alone should have stopped her from throwing herself at him the way she had! Hadn't she learned her lesson from her parents?

Obviously not. Even now, she ached to wrap her arms around him once again. Smart, Sheryl! Real smart. Dropping to her knees, she reached for the sponge.

"I'll do that while you get dressed."

He looped an arm across his bent knee and regarded her with a lazy smile.

"Unwound already, Sher? And here I promised that it would take all night."

His teasing raised the heat in her cheeks to a raging inferno. She attacked the pizza stain, unable to meet his eyes.

"Yes, well, I know you came here to work, not to, uh, help me get past this bad patch with Brian, and you don't have all night for that."

His hand closed over her wrist, stilling her agitated

movements. When she looked up, his air of lazy amusement had completely disappeared.

"Is that what you think just happened here? That I played some kind of sexual Good Samaritan by taking you to bed?"

She wouldn't have put it in quite those words, but she couldn't deny the fact that he'd done exactly that.

"Don't think that I'm not..." She swallowed. "That I'm not grateful. I needed a...a distraction tonight and you—"

With a swiftness that made her gasp, he rose, bringing her up with him. Sudden, fierce anger blazed in his brown eyes.

"A distraction?" he echoed in a tone that raised the fine hairs on the back of her neck. "You needed a distraction?"

Sheryl knew she was digging herself in deeper with every word, but she didn't have the faintest idea how to get out of this hole. She'd only wanted to let Harry know that she didn't expect him to continue the admittedly spectacular lovemaking she'd forced on him. Instead, she'd unintentionally ruffled his male ego. More embarrassed than ever, she tugged her wrist free.

"That didn't come out the way I meant it. You were more than a distraction. You were..." Her face flaming, she admitted the unvarnished truth. "You were wonderful. Thank you."

Harry stared at her, at a total loss for words for one of the few times in his life. Anger still pounded through him. Incredulity now added its own sideswiping kick. He couldn't believe that Sheryl had just *thanked* him, for God's sake! If this whole conversation didn't make him so damned furious, he might have laughed at the irony of it. He couldn't remember the last time he'd lost himself so completely, so passionately, in a woman's arms. Or the last time he'd drifted into sleep with a head nestled on his shoulder and a soft, breathy sigh warming his neck.

Harry hadn't exactly sworn off female companionship in the years since his divorce, but neither had he ignored the lessons he'd learned from that sobering experience. As long as he made his living chasing renegades, he couldn't expect any woman to put up with his here-today, gone-tonight lifestyle. Deliberately, he'd kept his friendships with women light and casual. Even more deliberately, he dated women whose own careers or interests coincided with the transitory nature of his. In any case, he sure as hell had never jeopardized an ongoing investigation by seducing one of the key players involved.

He'd broken every one of his self-imposed rules tonight. Deep in his gut, Harry knew damned well that he'd break them again if Sheryl turned her face up to his at this moment and asked him in that sweet, seductive way of hers to kiss her. Hell, he didn't need asking. Wide-awake now and still tight from the crash that had brought him springing out of bed, he had to battle the urge to sweep Sheryl into his arms and take her back to bed to show her just how much of a *distraction* he could provide. Just the thought of burying himself in her slick, satiny heat once again sent a spear of razor-sharp need through him.

With something of a shock, Harry realized that he wanted this woman even more fiercely now than he had before she'd given herself to him. And here she was, brushing him off with a polite thank-you.

Despite her red cheeks, she met his gaze with a dignity that tugged at something inside him. Something sharper than need. Deeper than desire.

"I'm sorry," she said quietly. "I didn't mean to insult you or cheapen what happened between us. It *was* wonderful, Harry. I just didn't want you to think that I want…or expect…anything more. I know why you're in Albuquerque, and that you'll be gone as soon as something breaks on your fugitive."

She had just put his own thoughts into words. Harry didn't particularly like hearing them.

"Sheryl…"

Her eyes gentled. Her hand came up to stroke his cheek. "It's all right, Marshal. Some men are wanderers by nature as much as by profession. My father was one. So, I think, are you. I understand."

Harry wasn't sure he did. He heard what she was saying. He agreed with it completely. So why did he want to—

The muted shrill of his cellular phone interrupted his chaotic thoughts. Frowning, he extracted the instrument from the jacket he'd left hanging on the back of a dining-room chair.

"MacMillan."

"Harry!" Ev's voice leaped out at him. "Where the hell are you?"

"At Sheryl's apartment." He didn't give his partner a chance to comment on that one. "Where are you?"

"Outside your motel room. I was on my way home when I got the news. I swung by your place to give you the word personally."

"What word?"

"The Santa Fe airport manager just called. He's got a

small, twin-engine jet about two hours out, requesting permission to land."

Harry's gut knotted. "And?"

"And the pilot also requested that Customs be notified. He wants to off-load a cargo of Peruvian sheepskin hides destined for a factory just outside Taos that manufactures those Marlboro-man sheepskin coats. From what I'm told, the hides stink. Like you wouldn't believe. Customs isn't too happy about processing the cargo tonight."

"This could be it," his listener said softly.

"I think it is. The FAA ran a quick check on the aircraft's tail number and flight plan. This leg of the flight originated in Peru, but the aircraft is registered in Brazil, Harry. Brazil!"

"Get a helo warmed up and ready for us."

"Already done. It's on the pad at State Police headquarters. Fay's on her way there now."

"I'll meet you both in ten minutes."

Harry snapped the phone shut and jammed it into his jacket. Every sense, every instinct, pushed at him to race into the bedroom and grab his clothes. To slam out of the apartment, jump into his car and hit the street, siren wailing.

For the first time that he could remember, his cop's instincts took second place to a stronger, even more urgent demand. In answer to the question in Sheryl's wide eyes, he paused long enough to give her a swift recap.

"We've got a break, Sher. A plane registered in Brazil is coming into the Santa Fe airport in a couple of hours."

"No kidding!"

She was still standing where he'd left her when he came running back, shoving his shirttail into his jeans.

He grabbed his holster and slipped into it with a roll of his shoulders. Then he snatched up his jacket and strode to where she stood. His big hands framed her face.

"I've got to go."

"I know. Be careful."

He gave himself another second to sear her eyes and her nose and the tangled silk of her hair into his memory. Then he kissed her, hard, and headed for the door.

"Harry!"

"What?"

"Come back when you can. I, uh, want to know what happens."

"I will."

The nondescript government sedan squealed out of the apartment complex. With one eye on the late-night traffic, Harry fumbled the detachable Kojak light into its mounting and flipped its switch. The rotating light slashed through the night like a sword. A half second later, he activated the siren and shoved the accelerator to the floor. The unmarked, unremarkable vehicle roared to life.

Ten minutes later, the car squealed through the gates leading to the headquarters of Troop R of the New Mexico Highway Patrol. Grabbing the duffel bag containing his field gear from the trunk, Harry raced for the helo pad. Ev and Fay met him halfway, both jubilant, both lugging their own field gear.

"Give me a rundown on who we've got playing so far," Harry shouted over the piercing whine of the helicopter's engine.

"Our Santa Fe highway patrol detachment is pulling in every trooper they've got to cordon off the airport,"

Fay yelled. "The Santa Fe city police have alerted their SWAT team. They'll be in place when we get there."

They ducked under the whirring rotor blades and climbed aboard through the side hatch. The copilot greeted them with a grin and directed them to the web rack that stretched behind the operators' seats.

Panting, Ev buckled himself in. "Customs has a Cessna Citation in the air tracking our boy as we speak. They've also got two Blackhawks en route from El Paso, with a four-man bust team aboard each."

Fierce satisfaction shot through Harry at the news. The huge Sikorsky UH-60 Blackhawk helicopters came equipped with an arsenal of lethal weapons and enough candlepower to light up half of New Mexico.

"Good. We might just give them a chance to show their stuff."

While the copilot buckled himself in, the pilot stretched around to show the passengers where to plug in their head-sets.

"What's the flying time to Santa Fe?" Harry asked, his words tinny over the static of the radio.

"Twenty minutes, sir."

"Right. Let's do it."

The aviator gave him a thumbs-up and turned her attention to the controls. Seconds later, the chopper lifted off. It banked steeply, then zoomed north.

Harry used the short flight to coordinate the operation with the key players involved. The copilot patched him through to the Customs National Aviation Center in Oklahoma City, which was now tracking the suspect aircraft, the New Mexico state police ops center and the Santa Fe airport manager.

"Our boy is still over an hour out," he summarized

for Ev and Fay. "That gives us plenty of time to familiarize ourselves with the layout of the field and get our people into position. No one moves until I give the signal. No one. Understood?"

Harry didn't want any mistakes. No John Waynes charging in ahead of the cavalry. No hotshot Rambos trying to show their stuff. If the man he'd been tracking for almost a year was flying in aboard this aircraft, the bastard wasn't going to get away. Not this time.

The short flight passed in a blur of dark mountains to their right and the sparse lights of the homes scattered along the Rio Grande valley below. The helo set down at the Santa Fe airport just long enough for Harry and the two others to jump out. Bent double, they dashed through the cloud of dust thrown up by the rotor wash. As soon as they were clear, Harry shed his coat and pulled his body armor out of his gear bag. A dark, lightweight windbreaker with "U.S. Marshal" emblazoned on the back covered the armor and identified him to the other players involved. After shoving spare ammo clips into his pockets, he checked his weapon, then went to meet the nervous airport manager waiting for him inside the distinctive New Mexico-style airport facility.

In a deliberate attempt to retain Santa Fe's unique character and limit its growth, the city planners had also limited the size of the airport that serviced it. To make access even more difficult, high mountain peaks ringed its relatively short runway. Consequently, no large-bodied jetliners landed in the city. The millions of tourists a year who poured into Santa Fe from all over the world usually flew into Albuquerque and drove the fifty-five-mile scenic route north. Even the legislators who routinely trav-

eled to the capital to conduct their business did so by car
or by small aircraft.

The inconvenient access might have constituted an
annoyance for some travelers, but it added up to a major
plus for Harry and the team members who gathered
within minutes of his arrival. With only one north-south
runway and the parallel taxiway to cover, he quickly
orchestrated the disposition of his forces. They melted
into the night like dark shadows, radios muted and lights
doused.

After a final visual and radar check of their handheld
secure radios, Ev headed for the tower to coordinate the
final approach and takedown. Harry and Fay climbed
into the airport service vehicle that would serve as their
mobile command post. When the truck pulled into its
customary slot beside the central hangar, Harry stared
into the night.

A million stars dotted the sky above the solid blackness
of the mountains. Richard Johnson, aka Paul Gunderson,
was out there somewhere. With any luck, that somewhere
would soon narrow down to a stretch of runway in the
high New Mexico desert.

A shiver rippled along Harry's spine, part primal anticipation, part plain old-fashioned chill. Even in mid-
June, Sante Fe's seven-thousand-foot elevation put a nip
in the night air. He zipped his jacket, folded his arms.
His eyes on the splatter of stars to the south, the hunter
settled down to await his prey.

The minutes crawled by.

The secure radio cackled as Ev gave periodic updates
on the aircraft's approach. Forty minutes out. Thirty.
Twenty.

The Blackhawks swept over the airport, rotors thumping in the night, and touched down behind the hangars. One would move into position to block any possible take-off attempt should anything spook the quarry once it was on the ground. The second would come in from the rear.

Quiet settled over the waiting, watching team. Even Ev's status reports were hushed.

Fifteen minutes.

Ten.

This was for Dean, Harry promised the dark, silent night. For the man who'd razzed him as a rookie, and stood beside him at the altar, and asked him to act as god-father to his son. And for Jenny, who'd cried in Harry's arms until she had no more tears left to shed. For every marshal who'd ever died in the line of duty, and every son or mother or husband or wife left behind.

Without warning, an image of Sheryl formed in Harry's mind. Her hair tumbling around her shoulders. Her eyes wide with excitement and the first, faint hint of worry on his behalf. It struck him that he'd left Sheryl, as Dean had left Jenny, to chase after Paul Gunderson.

Dean had never returned.

Harry might not, either. Dammit, he shouldn't have made that rash promise to Sheryl. Even without the haz-ards inherent in his job, success bred its own demands. If Gunderson stepped off an airplane in Santa Fe in the next few minutes, as Harry sincerely prayed he would, he'd climb right back on a plane, this time in handcuffs and leg irons. Harry would go with him. He wouldn't be driving back to Sheryl's place to give her a play-by-play of the night's events…or to redeem the promise of the hard, swift kiss he'd left her with.

He had no business making her any kind of promises at all, he thought soberly.

Even if he wanted to, he couldn't offer her much more than a choice between short bursts of pleasure and long stretches of loneliness. And a husband whose job might or might not leave her weeping in someone's arms, as Dean's had left Jenny.

Suddenly, the radio cackled. "He's on final approach. Check out that spot of light at one o'clock, 'bout two thousand feet up."

Harry blanked his mind of Sheryl, of Jenny, even of Dean. His eyes narrowed on the tiny speck of light slowly dropping out of the sky.

The takedown was a textbook operation.

Following the tower's directions, the twin-engine King Air rolled to a stop on the parking apron, fifty yards from where Harry waited in the service vehicle. As soon as the engines whined down and the hatch opened, the Blackhawks rose from behind the adjacent hangar like huge specters. They dropped down, their thirty-million-candlepower spotlights pinning the two figures who emerged from the King Air in a blinding haze of white light. The helo crews poured out.

Harry clicked the mike on the vehicle's loudspeaker and shouted a warning. "This is the U.S. Marshals Service. Hit the ground. Now!" He was out of the vehicle, his weapon drawn, before the echoes had stopped bouncing off the hangar walls.

The two figures took one look at the dark-suited figures converging on them from all directions and dropped like stones.

Harry reached them as they hit the pavement. Disappointment rose like bile in his throat. Even from the back, he could see that neither of the individuals spread-eagled on the concrete fit Paul Gunderson's physical description.

Ev Sloan reached the same conclusion when he panted up beside Harry a moment later.

"He's not with 'em. Damn!"

"My sentiments exactly," Harry got out through clenched jaws. Raising his voice, he issued a curt order. "All right. On your feet. We need to inspect your cargo."

A two-man Customs team went through the King Air's cargo with dogs, handheld scanners and an array of sophisticated chemical testing compounds. A second team searched the plane itself, which had been towed into a hangar for privacy.

By the time the first streaks of a golden dawn pierced the darkness of the mountain peaks outside, unbaled sheepskin hides lay strewn along one half of the hangar. Barely cured and still wearing a coat of gray, greasy wool, they gave off a stench that had emptied the contents of several team members' stomachs and put the drug dogs completely out of action.

The plane's guts lay on the other side of the hangar floor…along with a neat row of plastic bags. Even without the dogs, the stash in the concealed compartment in the plane's belly had been hard to miss.

The senior Customs agent approached Harry, grinning. Sweat streaked his face, and he carried the stink of hides with him.

"Five hundred kilos and a nice, new King Air for the Treasury Department to auction off. Not a bad haul, Marshal. Not bad at all."

"No. Just not the one we wanted."

The agent thrust out his hand. "Sorry you didn't get your man this time. Maybe next time."

"Yeah. Next time."

Leaving the other agency operatives to their prizes, Harry walked out into the slowly gathering dawn. Ev leaned against the hood of a black-and-white state police car, sipping coffee from a leaking paper cup. Then he tossed out the dregs of his coffee and crumpled the cup.

"Well, I guess it's back to the damned computer print-outs and postcards. You get anything more from Sheryl when you were up at her place last night?"

"No."

And yes.

Harry had gotten far more from her than he'd planned or hoped for. The need to return to her apartment, to finish this damnable night in her arms, tore through his layers of weariness.

He thought of a thousand reasons why he shouldn't go back…and one consuming reason why he should.

Chapter 11

Sheryl curled in a loose ball on top of the black-and-white blanket. Button lay sprawled beside her. She stroked his silky fur with a slow, light touch, taking care not to wake him while he snuffled and twitched in the throes of some doggie dream. Her gaze drifted to the small crystal clock on the table beside her bed.

Five past six.

Seven hours since Harry had left. Seven hours of waiting and worrying. Of wondering when…if…he'd come back. He'd been gone for only seven hours, yet it seemed as though days had passed since he'd rolled out of this bed and raced into the kitchen in response to Button's attack on the pizza.

Until tonight, Sheryl had never really appreciated the loneliness that had turned her mother into such a bitter, unhappy woman. She'd seen it happening, of course.

Even as a child, she'd recognized that her father's extended absences had leached the youth from her mother's face and carved those small, tight lines on either side of her face. Mentally, she'd braced herself every time her father walked out the door. She'd shared her mother's hurt and dissatisfaction, but she'd never *felt* the emptiness deep inside her, as she had these past hours. Never experienced this sense of being so alone.

Despite the hollow feeling in her chest, Sheryl could summon no trace of bitterness. Instead of hurt, a lingering wonder spread through her veins every time she thought of the hours together with Harry. Her breasts still tingled from his stinging kisses. One shoulder still carried a little red mark from his prickly mustache. She'd never experienced anything even remotely resembling the explosions of heat and light and skyrocketing sensation the marshal had detonated under her skin. Not once but twice.

Recalling her fumbling attempt to thank him for services rendered, Sheryl almost groaned aloud. Talk about putting her foot in it! Harry had bristled all over with male indignation. For a moment, he'd looked remarkably like Button with his fur up.

Smiling, she combed her fingers through the soft, feathery ruff decorating the paw closest to her. The shih tzu snuffled and jerked his leg away. One black eye opened and glared at her though the light of the gathering dawn.

"Sorry."

He gave a long-suffering look and rolled onto his back, all four paws sticking straight up in the air. Sheryl speared another glance at the clock. Six-fifteen.

Too restless to even pretend sleep any longer, she

tickled the dog's pink belly. "Want to get up? You can finish off the pizza for breakfast."

Black gums pulled back. A warning growl rumbled up from the furry chest. Hastily, Sheryl pulled her fingers out of reach.

"Okay, okay! You don't mind if I get up, do you?"

Silly question. Before she'd was halfway across the bedroom, Button was already sunk back into sleep.

A quick shower washed away the grittiness of her sleepless night. Since it was Saturday, Sheryl didn't even glance at the uniforms hanging neatly in her closet. Instead, she pulled out her favorite denim sundress. With its thin straps, scooped neck and loose fit, it was perfect for Albuquerque's June heat. Tiny wooden buttons marched down the front and stopped above the knee, baring a long length of leg when she walked. The stone-washed blue complemented her tan and her streaky blond hair, she knew. Now all she had to do was erase the signs of her sleepless night. Making a face at her reflection in the mirror, she applied a little blush and a swipe of lipstick. A few determined strokes with the brush subdued her hair into a semblance of order. Clipping it back with a wooden barrette that matched the buttons on the dress, she padded barefoot into the kitchen.

The first thing she saw was the pizza carton on the counter. Instantly, she started worrying and wondering again.

Where was Harry? What had happened after he'd left her last night?

Leaning a hip against the counter, she filled the automatic coffeemaker and waited while it brewed. Slowly, a rich aroma spread through the kitchen. Even more slowly, the soft, golden dawn lightened to day.

The sound of Button's nails clicking on the tiles alerted her to the fact that he'd decided to join the living. He wandered into the kitchen and gave her a disgruntled look, obviously as annoyed with her early rising as he'd been with her tossing and turning.

"Do you need to go out? Hold on a sec. I'll get the paper and pour a cup of coffee and join you on the back patio."

Sheryl flicked off the alarm and went outside to hunt down her newspaper. As usual, the deliveryman had tossed it halfway across the courtyard. She didn't realize Button had slipped out the front door with her until his piercing yip cut through the early morning quiet.

Startled, Sheryl spun around. From the corner of one eye, she saw Button charge across the courtyard toward the silver-haired Persian that had been sunning itself at the base of the small fountain. The cat went straight up in the air, hissing, and came down with claws extended.

"Oh, no!"

Oblivious to her dismayed exclamation, Button leaped to attack. His quarry decided that discretion was the better part of valor. Streaking across the tiled courtyard, it disappeared through the arched entryway that led to the parking lot. The shih tzu followed in noisy pursuit.

The darned dog was going to wake every person in the apartment complex with that shrill bark. Dropping the paper, Sheryl joined in the chase.

"Button! Here, boy! Here!"

She rounded the entryway corner just in time to see both cat and dog dart across the parking lot. Another cluster of apartments swallowed them up. Sheryl started across the rough asphalt. Suddenly, her bare heel came down on a pebble. Pain shot all the way up to the back of her knee.

"Dammit!"

Wincing, she took a few limping steps, then ran awkwardly on the ball of her injured foot. To her consternation, the noisy barking grew fainter and fainter. A moment later, it disappeared completely, swallowed up by the twisting walkways, picturesque courtyards and multistory buildings of the sprawling complex.

Seriously concerned now, Sheryl ran through archway after archway. Button would never find his way back through this maze. Stepping up the pace as much as the pain in her heel would allow, she searched the apartment grounds. Her dress skirt flapped around her knees. The wooden barrette holding her hair back snapped open and clattered to the walkway behind her. Sweat popped out on her forehead and upper lip.

"Button!" she called in gathering desperation. "Here, boy! Come to Sheryl!"

Her breath cut through her lungs like razor blades when she caught the sound of a crash, followed by a yelp. She tore down another path and through an archway, then came to a skidding, one-heeled halt. If she'd had any breath left, Sheryl would have gasped at the scene that greeted her. As it was, she could only pant helplessly.

An oversized clay pot had been knocked on its side. It now spilled dirt and pink geraniums onto the tiles. Beside the overturned pot lay a tipped-over sundial. Colorful fliers and sections of a newspaper littered the courtyard. In the midst of the havoc, not one but two silver Persians now stood shoulder to shoulder. Fur up, backs arched, they hissed for all they were worth. Their indignant owner stood behind them, flapping her arms furiously at the intruder. Button was belly to the ground, but hadn't given up the fight.

By the time Sheryl had scooped up the snarling shih tzu, apologized profusely to the cats' owner, offered to pay for the damages and listened to an irate discourse on dog owners who ignore leash laws, the sun had tipped over the apartment walls and heated the morning. Limping and hot and not exactly happy with her unrepentant houseguest, she lectured him sternly as she retraced her steps to her apartment. She took a wrong turn twice, which didn't improve her mood or Button's standing. Unconcerned over the fact that he was in disgrace, the dog surveyed the areas they passed through, ears up and eyes alert for his next quarry.

Sheryl was still lecturing when she rounded the corner of her building. The sight of two squad cars pulled up close to the arch leading to her courtyard stopped her in midscold. Curious and now a little worried, she hurried through the curving entrance. Worry turned to gulping alarm when she saw a uniformed officer standing just outside her open apartment door.

Oh, God! Something must have gone wrong last night! Maybe Harry was hurt!

Her heart squeezed tight. So did her arms, eliciting an indignant squawk from Button.

"Sorry!"

Easing the pressure on the little dog, she ran across the courtyard. "What's going on? What's happened?"

"Miss Hancock?"

"Yes. Is Harry all right?"

"Harry?"

"Harry MacMillan. Marshal MacMillan."

"Oh, yeah. He's inside. He's the one who called us when he found your front door open."

Sheryl fought down an instant rush of guilt. She'd forgotten all about the security systems in her worry over Button.

"Are you all right, Miss Hancock?"

"Yes, I'm fine."

"Then where the hell have you been?"

The snarl spun Sheryl around. Harry filled her doorway, his body taut with tension and his eyes furious. Another uniformed police officer hovered at his shoulder.

She took one look at his face and decided this wasn't the time to tell him about the wild chase Button had led her through the apartment complex. In the mood he was obviously in, he'd probably skin the dog whole.

"I, uh, went out to get the newspaper."

His blistering look raked her from her sweat-streaked face to her bare toes, then moved to the rolled newspaper lying a few yards away...right where Sheryl had dropped it.

"You want to run that by me one more time?"

She didn't care for his tone. Nor did she appreciate being dressed down like a recruit in front of the two police officers.

"Not particularly."

Although she wouldn't have thought it possible, his jaw tightened another notch. Turning to the police officer, he held out a hand.

"Looks like I called you out on a false alarm. Sorry."

"No problem, Marshal."

"Thanks for responding so quickly."

"Anytime."

With a nod to Sheryl and Button, the two policemen

departed the scene. Harry turned to face her, his temper still obviously simmering. In no mood for a public fracas, Sheryl brushed past him and headed for the cool sanctuary of her apartment.

Harry trailed after her, scowling. "Why are you limping?"

"I stepped on a stone."

For some reason, that seemed to incense him even further. He followed her inside, lecturing her with a lot less restraint than she'd lectured Button just a few moments ago.

"That could have been glass you stepped on."

"Well, it wasn't."

"Running around barefoot is about as smart as leaving your front door wide-open! Speaking of which…"

The oak door slammed behind her, rattling the colorful Piña prints on the entryway wall.

"You want to tell me what good a security system is if you don't even bother to close the damned door?"

Enough was enough. Sheryl had run a good mile or more after the blasted mutt. She was hot and sweaty. Her hair hung in limp tendrils around her face. Her heel still hurt like hell. And she'd spent most of the night worrying about a U.S. marshal who, judging from his foul temper, obviously hadn't apprehended the fugitive he wanted.

Bending, she released the dog. Button promptly scampered off, leaving her to face the irate Harry on her own. She turned to find him standing close. Too close. She could see the stubble darkening his cheeks and chin… and the anger still simmering in his whiskey-gold eyes.

Drawing in a deep breath, she decided to go right to the source of that anger. "I take it Paul Gunderson wasn't aboard the plane you intercepted."

"No, he wasn't."

"I'm sorry."

"Yeah," he rasped. "Me, too. And it didn't exactly help matters when I arrived to find your apartment wide-open and you gone."

"Okay, that was careless."

"Careless? How about idiotic? Irresponsible?"

"How about we don't get carried away here?" she snapped back.

Her spurt of defiance seemed to fuel his anger. He stepped even closer. Sheryl refused to back away, not that she could have if she'd wanted to. Her shoulder blades almost pressed against the wall as it was.

"Do you have any idea what I went through when I found the door open and you missing?"

The savagery in his voice jolted through her like an electrical shock. In another man, the suppressed violence might have frightened her. In Harry, it thrilled the tiny, adventurous corner of her soul she'd never known she possessed until he'd burst into her life.

How could she have fooled herself into believing she wanted safe and secure and comfortable? The truth hit her with devastating certainty.

She wanted the fierce emotion she saw blazing in this man's eyes.

She wanted the fire and excitement and the passion that only he had stirred in her.

She wanted Harry…however she could have him.

"No," she whispered. "I don't know what you went through. Tell me."

He buried his hands in her hair and pulled her head back. "I'll show you."

This kiss didn't even come close to resembling the

ones they'd shared last night. Those were wild and tender and passionate. This one was raw. Elemental. Primitive. So powerful that Sheryl's head went back and her entire body arched into his.

Nor did Harry display any of the teasing finesse he'd used on her before. His mouth claimed hers. Rough and urgent, his hands found her hips and lifted her into him. Sweat-slick and breathless and instantly aroused, Sheryl felt him harden against her.

He dragged his head up. Nostrils flaring, he stared down at her. Raw male need stretched the skin over his cheekbones tight and turned the golden lights in his eyes to small, blazing fires.

Sheryl wasn't stupid. She knew that this barely controlled savagery sprang as much from his frustration over his failure to nab Paul Gunderson last night as from the worry and anger she'd inadvertently sparked in him this morning. She didn't care. Wherever it sprang from, it consumed her.

Wanting him every bit as fiercely as he wanted her, she slid an arm around his neck and dragged his head back down. She knew the instant his mouth covered hers that a kiss wasn't enough. She fumbled for his belt buckle. He stiffened, then attacked the wooden buttons on her denim sundress. The little fasteners went flying. They landed on the tiles with a series of sharp pops. The dress hit the floor somewhere between the entryway and the bedroom. His jeans and shirt followed.

On fire with a need that slicked her inside and out, Sheryl pushed Harry to the bed and straddled him. He was ready for her. More than ready. But when he reached for her hips to lift her onto his rigid shaft, she wiggled backward.

"Oh, no! Not this time. This time, I want to give you what you gave me last night."

"Sheryl…"

"I'm going to wind you up tight," she promised. "And leave you breathless and dizzy and wanting more."

Much more. So much more.

Her fingers combed the hair on his belly. Moved lower. At her touch, his stomach hollowed. Hot, velvety steel filled her hand. Sheryl's throat went dry. She ran her tongue over her lips.

His shaft leaped in her hand. With a wicked smile that surprised her almost as much as it did Harry, she bent and proceeded to leave him breathless and groaning and wanting more.

Much more.

She was still smiling when she and Harry both dropped into an exhausted stupor.

A bounce of the bedsprings woke her with a jerk some time later. Harry shot straight up, his face a study in sleep-hazed confusion.

"Oh, God!" she moaned. "What now?"

"Did you just—"

He broke off, his entire body stiffening. An expression of profound disgust replaced his confusion. Yanking back the rumpled black-and-white Zuni blanket, he glared at the animal wedged comfortably between their knees.

Button lifted his head and snarled, obviously as displeased at having his rest disturbed as Harry was. The two males wore such identical expressions of dislike that Sheryl fell back on the bed, giggling helplessly.

"You should see your face," she gasped.

Harry didn't share her amusement. "Yeah, well, you should try waking up to a set of claws raking down your thigh."

"I have," she told him, still giggling. "Believe me, I have."

For a moment, he looked as though he intended to take Button on for undisputed possession of the bed. Bit by bit, the light of battle went out of his eyes. Rasping a hand across his chin, he let out a long breath.

"I've got to go."

Sheryl's giggles died, but she managed to keep her smile going. "I know."

"Even though we didn't get Gunderson, we've still got some matters to clear up from last night. Ev will be waiting for me."

She nodded.

"Mind if I use your shower?"

"Be my guest," she said with deliberate nonchalance. "I've even got a razor in there. It's contoured for a woman's legs, but I think it'll scrape off everything but your mustache."

While the water pelted against the shower door, Sheryl slipped out of bed and retrieved her sundress. She wouldn't regret his leaving, she repeated over and over, as if it were a mantra. She wouldn't try to hold him.

She couldn't, even if she wanted to.

She could only keep her smile fixed firmly in place when he walked out of the shower, his chest bare above his jeans and his dark hair glistening.

He gathered his clothes. By the time he buckled on his holster, a frown creased his brow. He crossed to where she sat on the edge of the bed.

"I'll call you."

"Ha! That's what they all say."

Her feeble attempt at humor fell flat. If anything, the line in his forehead grooved even deeper.

"I'll call you. That's all I can promise."

Sheryl sympathized with the wrenching conflict she saw in his eyes. He wanted to leave. Needed to leave. Yet something he couldn't quite articulate tugged at him. That something gave her the courage to rise slowly and lift her palms to his cheeks.

Like Harry, she'd gone through a bit of wrenching herself in the past few days. Without wanting to, without trying to, she'd slipped out of her nice, easy routine and discovered that she wanted more of life than comfort and security.

Harry had shown her what life could...should...be. He'd given her a taste of excitement, of adventure. Of something that she was beginning to recognize as love. She wasn't sure when she'd fallen for this rough-edged marshal, but she had. She suspected it had happened last night, when she'd opened the door and found him standing there with his pineapple-and-Canadian-bacon pizza. She'd known it this morning, when he pinned her against the wall and everything inside her had leaped at his touch.

She was willing to take a chance that what she felt could withstand the test of time. The trial of separation and the tears of loneliness. She wanted to believe that what she could share with Harry was special, different... unlike what her parents had shared.

He hadn't reached that point yet. She saw the hesitation in his eyes. Heard it in his voice. Maybe he'd never reach it. Maybe he'd walk out the door, get caught up in his investigation and forget her.

And maybe he wouldn't.

Sheryl would risk it.

"I didn't ask for any promises, Marshal," she said softly. "I don't need them."

Her smile gentling, she rose on tiptoe and brushed his mouth with a kiss.

"Call me when you can."

For the next few hours, she jumped every time the phone rang…which didn't make for a restful morning, considering that it rang constantly.

Elise called first. After a glowing recount of the baby's first night, she mentioned that the doctor had cleared them both to go home tomorrow.

"So soon?"

"It'll be forty-eight hours, Sher. That's long enough for either of us."

"I'll drive you."

"Thanks, but Brian said he would take us home. Do you suppose you could swing by my house to pick up some clean clothes, though? Mine got a little messed up when I fell."

"Sure." Wedging the phone between her ear and her shoulder, Sheryl reached for a pad and pen. "Tell me what you need."

She scribbled down the short list and hung up, promising to see Elise and the baby later this morning. Just seconds after that, the phone rang again. Her heart jumping, she snatched up the receiver.

It took some doing, but she finally managed to convince the telemarketer at the other end that she did *not* want to switch her long distance carrier.

The third call came shortly after that. Her mother wanted to hear about Elise's delivery.

Sheryl sank onto the sofa. This conversation would take a lot longer than the one she'd just had with the telemarketer, she knew. Scratching Button's ears absently, she told her mother what had happened at the hospital... and afterward. The news that Sheryl had failed to perform her coaching duties surprised Joan Hancock. The news of her breakup with Brian left her stuttering.

"But...but...you two were almost engaged!"

"'Almost' is the operative word, Mom."

"I don't understand. What happened?"

Sighing, Sheryl crossed her ankles on the sturdy bleached-oak plank that served as her coffee table. She'd abandoned her now almost buttonless denim dress for a cool, gauzy turquoise top and matching flowered leggings. With Button snuggled against her thighs, she tried to explain to her mother the feelings she'd only recently discovered herself.

"We decided that we wanted more than what we had together."

"You don't even know *what* you had! You'd better think twice, Sheryl Ann Hancock, before you let a man like Brian slip through your fingers."

Joan's voice took on the brittle edge her daughter recognized all too well. Mentally, Sheryl braced herself.

"He's so nice," her mother argued. "So reliable. He'd never leave you to lie awake at night wondering where he was, or make you worry about whether he had a decent meal or remembered to take his blood pressure medicine."

Recalling the near-sleepless night she'd just spent

wondering and worrying about Harry, Sheryl could only agree.

"No, he wouldn't."

"Call him," Joan urged. "Brian loves you. I know he does. Tell him you made a mistake. Tell him you want to patch things up. And I suggest you do it before that so-called friend of yours sinks her claws in him."

Sheryl blinked at the acid comment. "What are you talking about?"

"Oh, come on! I may get up to Albuquerque only a few times a month, but that's more than enough for me to see that Elise knows very well what a prize Brian is, if you don't. She's been mooning after him ever since her divorce."

Struck, Sheryl thought back over the past few months. Elise hadn't exactly mooned over Brian, but she, like Joan, was forever singing his praises. Then there was that kiss at the hospital to consider, when Elise had dragged the man down by his tie. And the substitute father's wide-eyed wonder in the baby.

A huge grin tracked across Sheryl's face. Harry had all but wiped away the ache in her heart caused by her breakup with Brian. She and the marshal might or might not ever reach the "almost" point she'd reached with Brian. Right now, though, she couldn't think of anything that would please her more than for her two best friends to find the same passion, the same wild need, that she'd discovered in Harry's arms.

She sprang up, dislodging the sleeping dog in the process. He gave her a disgusted look and plopped down again.

"I've gotta go, Mom. I have to swing by Elise's house

to pick up some clothes for her. Then I'm heading for the hospital. She and I need to talk."

"Yes," her mother sniffed. "You do."

Still grinning, Sheryl hung up and headed for the bedroom. She was halfway across the room when the phone rang again. She spun around, ignoring the protest of her bruised heel, and grabbed the phone.

It had to be Harry this time!

"Miss Hancock?"

She swallowed her swift disappointment. "Yes?"

"My name is Don Ortega. I'm an attorney representing a woman you know as Mrs. Inga Gunderson."

"Oh! Yes, I think I heard your name mentioned."

"I understand from Marshal Everett Sloan that you're keeping my client's dog."

She eyed the animal sprawled in blissful abandon on her sofa.

"Well, I'm not sure who's keeping whom, but he's here. Why? Does Mrs. Gunderson want me to take him to someone else?"

She frowned, wondering why the thought of losing her uninvited houseguest didn't fill her with instant elation. The mutt had chewed up her underwear, sprayed her dining-room chair and led her on a not-so-merry chase through the apartment complex this morning. Even worse, his sharp claws had brought Harry jerking straight up this morning, as they had her more than once the past few nights. She ought to be dancing with joy at the prospect of dumping him on some other unsuspecting victim.

Instead, she breathed an inexplicable sigh of relief when the lawyer responded to her question with a negative.

"No, my client doesn't have any close friends or acquaintances in Albuquerque. She's just worried about her, er, Butty-boo. She asked me to check with you and find out if you'd given him his heartworm pill," he finished on a dry note.

"I didn't know he needed one."

"According to my client, he has to have one today. She was quite insistent about it. Evidently, her dog almost died last year when the worms got into his bloodstream and wrapped around his heart."

The gruesome description made Sheryl gulp.

"She says that he could pick up another infestation if he misses even one dose of the medication," Ortega advised her.

"So where can I get this medication?"

"If you wouldn't mind going to the pet store on Menaul, where Mrs. Gunderson does business, you can pick up the pills and charge them to her account. My client has instructed me to call ahead and authorize the expenditure."

"Well…"

She hesitated, wondering if she should contact Harry or Ev Sloan before she acceded to the attorney's request. But Ev had vouched for the lawyer himself, she recalled, swearing that he was tough but straight. Evidently, he also cared enough about his clients to relay their concern for their pets.

"I don't mind," she told Ortega. "Give me the address of this store."

She jotted it down just below the list of items Elise had asked her to bring to the hospital.

"I was just leaving to visit a friend at University Hospital. I'll stop at the pet store on my way."

"Thank you, Miss Hancock. I'm sure my client will be most grateful."

* * *

His client, Sheryl discovered when she walked out of the pet store a little over an hour later, was more than grateful. She was lying in wait for her...in the form of two men with slicked-back hair, unsmiling eyes, shiny gray suits and black turtlenecks that must have made them miserable in Albuquerque's sweltering heat.

One of the men appeared at Sheryl's side just as she unlocked her car door. The other materialized from behind a parked car. Before she had done more than glance at them, before she could grasp their intent, before she could scream or even try to twist away, the shorter of the men slapped a folded handkerchief over her mouth.

She fought for two or three seconds. Two or three breaths. Then the street and the car and the gray suits tilted crazily. Another breath, and they disappeared in a haze of blackness.

Chapter 12

"Dammit, where is she?"

Harry paced the task force operations center like a caged, hungry and very irritated panther. He'd been trying to reach Sheryl since just after ten, and it was now almost three.

Ev Sloan leaned back in his chair and watched his partner's restless prowling. Like Harry's, his face showed the effects of his previous long night in the tired lines and gray shadows under his eyes.

"Want me to call central dispatch and have them put out an APB?"

Harry shoved his hands in his pockets and jiggled his loose change. His gut urged him to agree to the all-points bulletin, but this morning's fiasco held him back. He didn't want to use up any more chits with the Albuquerque police than he already had. Sheryl was probably be surprised if one of the guards hasn't skinned him by now and nailed his hide over the front door."

They soon discovered that Button was still in one piece, although the same couldn't be said for the security guards. One sported a long tear in his uniform sleeve. The other pointed out the neat pattern of teeth marks in his leather brogans.

Sheryl apologized profusely and retrieved the indignant animal from the lidded trash can where the guards had stashed him. Button huffed and snuffled and ruffled up his fur, but let himself be carried from the federal building with only a few parting snarls at the guards. After a few greeting snarls at Ev, he settled down on Sheryl's chest.

She buried her nose in his soft, silky fur. The lights of Old Town, only a few blocks from the federal building, sped by unnoticed. The bright wash of stars overhead didn't draw her eyes. Even Ev's excited recounting of the night's tumultuous events barely penetrated. In her mind, she followed the flight of a small silver jet over the Sandias and across New Mexico's wide, flat plains.

He'd be back. He'd promised.

But when?

"Looks like it's going to be next week before Gunderson's arraignment."

Turning her back on the noise of the lively group who'd just arrived at her apartment to celebrate young Master Brian Hart's christening, Sheryl strained to hear Harry's recorded message.

"You have my office number. They can reach me anytime, night or day, if you have an emergency. I'll talk to you soon."

The recorder clicked off.

Frustrated, she hit the repeat button. Except for one short call soon after Harry had arrived in D.C., he and Sheryl had been playing telephone tag for almost three days now. From what she'd gleaned through his brief messages, the man she now thought of as Richard Johnson had held out longer than anyone had expected before finally breaking his stubborn silence. Once the dam gave, the assistant DA working the case had kept Harry busy helping with the briefs for the grand jury. Now, it appeared, he'd have to stay in D.C. until next week's arraignment.

"Sheryl, where are the pretzels? I can't—Oh, I'm sorry, honey. I didn't know you were on the phone."

Replacing the receiver, Sheryl pasted on a smile and turned to face her mother. "I'm not. I was just checking my messages."

"Well? Did he call?"

"Yes, he called."

"Where is he?"

"Still in Washington."

"I want to meet this man. When is he coming back to Albuquerque?"

"He doesn't know."

Her mother's thin, still-attractive face took on the pinched look that Sheryl had seen all too often in her youth. Joan Hancock wanted to say more. That much was obvious from the way she bit down on her lower lip.

Thankfully, she refrained.

She had driven up to Albuquerque from Las Cruces three days ago, after Elise's frantic call informing her that her daughter was missing. She'd stayed through the rest of the weekend, demanding to know every detail about Sheryl's involvement in a search for a dangerous fugitive.

Needless to say, the cautious bits her daughter let drop about the deputy marshal who'd swept in and out of her life hadn't pleased Joan any more than observing Brian Mitchell's growing attachment to his namesake...and his namesake's mother.

The christening ceremony tonight had only added to her disgruntlement. Sheryl and Brian had stood as godparents to the baby. Seeing them together at the altar had rekindled Joan Hancock's grievances against Elise. She was still convinced that the new mother had schemed to steal Sheryl's boyfriend right out from under her nose.

"Just look at her," she griped, pressing the pretzel bowl against the front of the pale-gray silk dress she'd worn to the church. "The way she's making those goo-goo eyes at Brian, you'd think he'd fathered her child instead of her shiftless ex-husband."

Sheryl's gaze settled on the scene in the living room. Elise had anchored the baby's carrier in a corner of the sofa, where it couldn't be jostled by her two lively boys. They were showing off their baby brother to the assembled crowd with patented propriety. Brian leaned against the arm of the sofa, one finger unconsciously stroking the baby's feathery red curls while he chatted with Elise. Even Button had gotten into the act. Perched on the back of the sofa, he waved his silky tail back and forth and guarded the baby with the regal hauteur that had made the shih tzu so prized by the emperors of China.

It was a picture-perfect family tableau. With all her heart, Sheryl wished everyone in the picture happiness.

She'd told Elise so when the two friends had snatched a half hour alone yesterday. Even now, she had to smile at the emotions that had chased across Elise's face, one after another, like tumbleweeds blown by a high wind. Pain for Sheryl over her break with Brian. Guilty relief that he was free. Disbelief that her friend had fallen for Harry so hard, so fast. Worry that she was in for some hurting times ahead.

Like Joan, Elise couldn't quite believe that her friend had opted to settle for a life of loneliness, broken by days or weeks or even months of companionship. Sheryl couldn't quite believe it, either, but sometime in the past few days, she had.

Joan gave a long, wistful sigh. "Are you sure you and Brian can't patch things up?"

"I'm sure."

Her gaze left the group on the sofa and settled on her daughter's face. "Oh, Sherrie, I hoped you'd do better than I did."

Sheryl's smile softened. "You did fine, Mom."

A haze of tears silvered Joan's green eyes, so like her daughter's. "I wanted you to find someone steady and reliable. Someone who'd be there when you needed him to kiss away your hurts and share your laughter and fix the leaky faucets."

"You taught me to be pretty handy with a wrench," Sheryl replied gently. "And Harry was there when I needed him."

He'd been there, and he'd done more than kiss away her hurts, she acknowledged silently. After her breakup with Brian, he'd driven the hurt right out of her mind. At the airport, he'd wiped away a good measure of her terror and trauma by the simple act of acknowledging her as part of his team.

Along the way, Sheryl thought with an inner smile,

he'd also taken her to dizzying heights of pleasure that she'd never dreamed of, let alone experienced. She craved the feel of his hands on her breasts, ached for the brush of his prickly mustache against her skin. She longed to curl up with him on the couch and share a pepperoni-and-pineapple pizza, and watch his face when he bit into one of New Mexico's man-sized peppers.

In short, she wanted whatever moments they could snatch and memories they could make together. Everyone else might count their time together in hours, but Sheryl measured it by the clinging, stubborn love that had taken root in her heart and refused to let go.

Her mother sighed again. "You're going to wait for this man, aren't you? Night after night, week after week?"

"Yes, I am."

Joan lifted a hand and rested a palm against her daughter's cheek. "You're stronger than I was, Sherrie. You'll…you'll make it work."

She hoped so. She sincerely hoped so.

"Come on, Mom. Let's get back to the party."

Despite her conviction that Harry was worth waiting for, Sheryl found the wait more difficult than she'd let on to her mother. The hours seemed to stretch endlessly. Thankfully, she had her job to keep her busy during the day and Button to share her nights.

According to Ev Sloan, she could expect to have the mutt's company for some time to come. He called with the news the evening after little Brian's christening. Just home from work and about to step into the shower, Sheryl ran out of the bathroom and snatched the phone up on the second ring. With some effort, she kept the fierce disappointment from her voice.

"Hi, Ev."

Clutching the towel she'd thrown around her with one hand, she listened to his gleeful news. Patrice Jörgenson/ Johnson, aka Inga Gunderson, cut a deal with the federal authorities. In exchange for information about her nephew's activities, she would plead guilty to a lesser battery of charges that would give her the possibility of parole in a few years.

"We're transporting her to D.C. Got a plane standing by. She wants to say goodbye to the mutt first."

"You mean, like, now? Over the phone?"

"Yeah."

The note of disgust in Ev's voice told Sheryl he hadn't quite recovered from his initial bout with Button, when the dog had locked onto his leg.

"I'll, er, put him on."

Perching on the side of the bed, she prodded the sleeping dog awake. At the sound of his mistress's voice, he yipped into the phone once or twice before curling back into a ball and leaving Sheryl to finish the conversation. Somehow, she found herself promising to write faithfully and keep the older woman apprised of Button's health and welfare.

Sniffing, Inga provided a list of absolute essentials. "He takes B-12 and vitamin E twice a week. His vet can supply you with the coated tablets. They're easier for him to swallow. And don't forget his heartworm pills."

"How could I forget those?" Sheryl countered with a grimace.

"Make sure you keep his hair out of his eyes to prevent irritation of the lids."

"I will."

"Don't use rubber bands, though! They pull his hair."

"I won't."

"Oh, I canceled his standing appointment at the stud. You'll have to call them back and reinstate him."

"Excuse me?"

"Button's descended from a line of champions," Inga explained in a teary, quavering voice so different from the one that had shouted obscenities at Harry and Ev that her listener found it hard to believe she was the same woman. "We could charge outrageous stud fees if we wanted to, you know, but we just go there so my precious can, well, enjoy himself."

Sheryl blinked. She hadn't realized her responsibilities would include pimping for Button. She was still dealing with that mind-boggling revelation when Inga sniffed.

"He's very virile. They always offer me pick of the litter." She paused. "You may keep one of his pups in exchange for taking care of him. Or perhaps two, since you work and a pet shouldn't be left alone all day."

"Th-thank you."

Underwhelmed by the magnanimous offer, Sheryl glanced at the tight black-and-white ball on her bed. She could just imagine Harry's reaction if two or three Buttons crawled under the covers with him in the middle of the night.

Assuming Harry ever got back to Albuquerque to get under the covers.

Sighing, she copied down the last of Inga's instructions, held the phone to the dog's ear a final time and hung up. She stood beside the bed for a moment, staring down into her companion's buggy black eyes.

"What do you say, fella? Wanna share a pizza after I get out of the shower?"

Chapter 15

The glossy postcard leaped out at Sheryl from the sheaf of mail in her hand.

Tahiti.

A pristine stretch of sandy beach. A fringe of deep-green banyan trees. An aquamarine sea laced with white, lapping at the shore.

Resolutely, she fought down the urge to turn the postcard over and peek at the message on the back. She'd had enough vicarious adventures as a result of reading other people's mail to last her a while.

She won the brief struggle, but still couldn't bring herself to shove the card in the waiting post office box. For just a moment, she indulged a private fantasy and imagined herself on that empty stretch of beach with Harry. She saw him splashing toward her in the surf. The sun bronzed his lean, hard body. The breeze off the sea ruffled his dark hair. His gold-flecked eyes gleamed with—

"You okay, Sher?"

"What?" Startled out of the South Pacific, she glanced up guiltily to meet Elise's look. "Yes, I'm fine."

"You're thinking about the marshal again, aren't you? You've got that…that lost look on your face."

Sheryl flashed the postcard at her friend. "I was thinking about Tahiti."

Elise pursed her lips.

"All right, all right. I was thinking about Tahiti and Harry."

Nudging aside a stack of mail, the new mom cleared a space on the table between the banks of postal boxes and hitched a hip on the corner. She'd insisted on coming back to work, declaring that her ex-mother-in-law, her parents, her two boys and her regular baby-sitter were more than enough to care for the newest addition to the Hart family. She still hadn't fully regained the endurance required for postal work, though. Sheryl scooped up her bundle and added it to the stack in her hand.

"How long has it been now since Harry left?" Elise demanded as her friend fired the mail into the appropriate boxes. "A week? Eight days?"

"Nine, but who's counting?"

"You are! I am! Everyone in the post office is."

"Well, you can stop counting. He promised he'd come back. He will."

"Oh, Sher, he said he'd come back after the arraignment last week. Then he had to fly to Miami. I hate for you to…"

Buck Aguilar rumbled by with a full cart, drowning

out the rest of her comment. Sheryl didn't need to hear it. The worry in her eyes spoke its own language.

"He'll be back, Elise. He promised."

"I believe you," the other woman grumbled. "I just don't like seeing you jump every time the phone rings, or spending your evenings walking that obnoxious little hair ball."

"Give Button time," Sheryl replied, laughing. "He grows on you."

"Ha! That'll be the day. He almost took off my hand at the wrist when I made the mistake of reaching for the baby before Butty-boo was finished checking him out. Here, give me the last stack. I'll finish it."

"I've got it. You just sit and gather your strength for the hordes waiting in the lobby. We have to open in a few minutes."

Elise swung her sneakered foot, a small frown etched on her brow. Sheryl smiled to herself. Her friend still couldn't quite believe that she would prefer the marshal—or anyone else!—over Brian Mitchell. Despite the long talk the two women had shared, Elise had yet to work through her own feelings of guilt and secret longing.

She would. After watching her and Brian together, Sheryl didn't doubt that they'd soon reach the point she herself had come to this past week. They were meant for each other. Just as she and Harry were.

She'd wait for him. However long it took. Wherever his job sent him. She wasn't her mother, and Harry certainly wasn't her father. They'd wring every particle of happiness out of their time together and look forward to their next reunion with the same delicious anticipation that curled in Sheryl's tummy now.

After zinging the last of the box mail into its slot, she

slammed the metal door. "Come on, kiddo. We'd better get our cash drawers from the safe. We've only got…"

She glanced at the clock in the central work space and felt her heart sommersault. Striding through the maze of filled mail carts was a tall, unmistakable figure in tight jeans, a blue cotton shirt and a rumpled linen gray sport coat.

"Harry!"

Sheryl flew toward him, scattering letters and advertising fliers and postcards as she went. He caught her up in his arms and whirled her around. The room had barely stopped spinning before he bent his head and covered her mouth with his. Instantly, the whole room tilted crazily again.

Flinging her arms around his neck, she drank in his kiss. It was better than she remembered. Wild. Hot. Hungry. When he lifted his head, she dragged in great, gulping breaths and let the questions tumble out.

"When did you get in? Why didn't you call? What happened in Miami?"

Grinning, he kissed her again, much to the interest of the various personnel who stopped their work to watch.

"Twenty minutes ago. I didn't want to take the time. And we nailed the arms manufacturer Gunderson was supplying."

"Good!"

Laughing at her fierce exclamation, he hefted her higher in his arms and started for the back door.

"Wait a minute!" Sheryl was more than willing to let him carry her right out of the post office, but she needed to cover her station. "I've got to get someone to take the front counter for me."

"It's all arranged," he told her, his eyes gleaming.

"What is?"

"The postmaster general got a call from the attorney general early this morning, Miss Hancock. You're being recommended for a citation for your part in apprehending an escaped fugitive and suspected killer." The gleam deepened to a wicked glint. "You've also been granted the leave you requested. There's a temp on the way down to fill in for you."

"I seem to be having some trouble recalling the fact that I asked for leave."

"I wouldn't be surprised, with all you've gone through lately." Harry wove his way through the carriers' stations. "You asked for two weeks for your honeymoon."

Sheryl opened her mouth, shut it, opened it again. A thousand questions whirled around in her head. Only one squeaked out.

"Two weeks, huh?"

"Two weeks," he confirmed. "Unless you don't have a current passport, in which case we'll have to tack on a few extra days so we can stop over in Washington to pull some strings."

He slowed, his grin softening to a smile so full of tenderness that Sheryl's throat closed.

"I want to take you to Heidelburg, sweetheart, and stand beside you on the castle ramparts when the Neckar River turns gold in the sunset. I want to watch your face the first time you see the spires of Notre Dame rising out of the morning mists. I want to make love to you in France and Italy and Germany and wherever else we happen to stop for an hour or a day or a night."

"Oh, Harry."

He eased his arm from under her knees. Sheryl's feet slid to the floor, but she didn't feel the black tiles under her sneakers. Not with Harry's hands locked loosely around her waist and his heart thumping steadily against hers.

"I know you said it was too soon for commitments and promises, but I've had a lot of time to think this past week."

"Me, too," she breathed.

"I don't want almost, Sheryl. I want you now and forever."

He brushed back her hair with one hand. All trace of amusement left his eyes.

"The regional director's position here in the Albuquerque office comes open next month. The folks in D.C. tell me the job's mine if I want it."

Her pounding pulse stilled. She wanted Harry, as much as he wanted her. But she wouldn't try to hold him with either tears or a love that strangled.

"Do you want it, Harry?"

"Yes, sweetheart, I do. It'll mean less time on the road, although I can't guarantee I'll have anything resembling regular office hours or we'll enjoy a routine home life."

Sheryl could have told him that she'd learned her lesson with Brian. On her list of top-ten priorities, a comfortable routine now ranked about number twenty-five. All that mattered, all she cared about, was the way his touch made her blood sing, and the crinkly lines at the corners of his eyes, and his soft, silky mustache and...

"I'm a deputy marshal," he said quietly. "The service is in my blood."

"I know."

"So are you. I carried your smile and your sun-streaked hair and your little moans of delight with me day and night for the past week. I love you, Sheryl. I want to live the rest of my life with you, if you'll have me, and take you to all the places you dreamed about."

A sigh drifted on the air behind her. She didn't even glance around. She didn't care how many of her co-workers had gathered to hear Harry's soft declaration. One corner of his mustache tipped up.

"I thought about buying a ring and getting down on one knee and doing the whole romantic bit," he told her ruefully, "but I don't want to waste our time with almost-anythings. I want to go right for the real thing. Right here. Right now."

He would, she thought with a smile.

"There's a judge waiting for us at the federal building," he said gruffly. "He'll do the deed as soon as we get the license."

An indignant sputter sounded just behind Sheryl. Elise protested vehemently. "You have to call your mother, Sher! At least give her time to drive up from Las Cruces!"

"The judge will do the deed as soon as your mother gets here," Harry amended gravely, holding her gaze with his own.

Someone else spoke up. Pat Martinez, Sheryl thought.

"Hey, we want to be there, too! Wait until the shift change this afternoon. We'll shred up all that mail languishing in the dead-letter bin and come down to the courthouse armed with champagne and confetti."

"Champagne and confetti sounds good to me." Harry smiled down at her. "Well?"

"I love you, too," she told him mistily. "I'll have you, Marshal, right here, right now and for the rest of our lives."

Stretching up on her tiptoes, she slid her arms around his neck. He bent his head, and his mouth was only a breath away from hers when she murmured, "There's only one problem. We'll have to take Button with us on this honeymoon. Unless you know someone who will take care of him while we're gone?" she asked hopefully.

"You're kidding, right?"

When she shook her head, he closed his eyes. Sheryl closed her ears to his muttered imprecations. When he opened them again, she saw a look of wry resignation in their golden brown depths.

"All right. We'll pick up a doggie-rat carrier on our way to the airport."

At that moment, she knew she'd never settle for almost-anything again.

* * * * *

The silence on the car ride to the public hearing at the Chicago
Board of Education building on Madison Street was jaw-dropping.
Mingus maneuvered his car through traffic, his expression smug
as he stole occasional glances in her direction. Joanna stared out
the passenger-side window, still lost in the heat of Mingus's touch.
That kiss had left her shaking, her knees quivering and her heart
racing. She couldn't not think about it if she wanted to.

His kiss had been everything she'd imagined and more. It
was summer rain in a blue sky, fudge cake with scoops of praline
ice cream, balloons floating against a backdrop of clouds, small
puppies, bubbles in a spa bath and fireworks over Lake Michigan.
It had left her completely satiated and famished for more. Closing
her eyes and kissing him back had been as natural as breathing.
And there was no denying that she had kissed him back. She hadn't
been able to speak since, no words coming that would explain the
wealth of emotion flowing like a tidal wave through her spirit.

They paused at a red light. Mingus checked his mirrors and
the flow of traffic as he waited for his turn to proceed through

the intersection. Joanna suddenly reached out her hand for his, entwining his fingers between her own.

"I'm still mad at you," Joanna said.

"I know. I'm still mad at myself. I just felt like I was failing you. You need results and I'm not coming up with anything concrete. I want to fix this and suddenly I didn't know if I could. I felt like I was being outwitted. Like someone's playing this game better than I am, but it's not a game. They're playing with your life, and I don't plan to let them beat either one of us."

"From day one you believed me. Most didn't and, to be honest, I don't know that anyone else does. But not once have you looked at me like I'm lying or I'm crazy. This afternoon, you yelling at me felt like doubt, and I couldn't handle you doubting me. It broke my heart."

Mingus squeezed her fingers, still stalled at the light, a line of cars beginning to pull in behind him. "I don't doubt you, baby. But we need to figure this out and, frankly, we're running out of time."

The honking of a car horn yanked his attention back to the road. He pulled into the intersection and turned left. Minutes later he slid into a parking spot and shut down the car engine. Joanna was still staring out the window.

"Are you okay?" he asked.

Joanna nodded and gave him her sweetest smile. "Yeah. I was just thinking that I really like it when you call me 'baby.'"

Don't miss
Tempted by the Badge *by Deborah Fletcher Mello,*
available March 2019 wherever
Harlequin® Romantic Suspense books
and ebooks are sold.

www.Harlequin.com

He knew she was shaken, but he wasn't ready to let her out of his
sight. "Melissa, you could have been hurt tonight." Killed, but
he couldn't allow himself to voice that awful thought aloud. "I'll
see that you get home safely, so don't argue."

Melissa rubbed a hand over her eyes. She was obviously so
exhausted she simply nodded and slipped from his SUV. Just as
he thought, the beat-up minivan belonged to her.

She jammed her key in the ignition, the engine taking three
tries to sputter to life.

Anger that she sacrificed so much for others mingled with
worry that she might have died doing just that.

She deserved so much better. To have diamonds and pearls.
At least a car that didn't look as if it had been rolled twice.

He glanced back at the shelter before he pulled from the
parking lot. Melissa was no doubt worried about the men she'd
had to move tonight. But worry for her raged through him.

He knew good and damn well that many of the men who
ended up in shelters had simply fallen on hard times and needed a
hand. But others…the drug addicts, mentally ill and criminals…

He didn't like the fact that Melissa put herself in danger by
trying to help them. Tonight's incident proved the facility wasn't
secure.

The thought of losing her bothered him more than he wanted
to admit as he followed her through the streets of Austin. His gut
tightened when she veered into an area consisting of transitional
homes. A couple had been remodeled, but most looked as if they

were teardowns. The street was not in the best part of town, either, and was known for shady activities, including drug rings and gangs.

Her house was a tiny bungalow with a sagging little porch and paint-chipped shutters, and sat next to a rotting shanty, where two guys in hoodies hovered by the side porch, heads bent in hushed conversation as if they might be in the middle of a drug deal.

He gritted his teeth as he parked and walked up the graveled path to the front porch. She paused, her key in hand. A handcrafted wreath said Welcome Home, which for some reason twisted his gut even more.

Melissa had never had a real home, while he'd grown up on the ranch with family and brothers and open land.

She offered him a small smile. "Thanks for following me, Dex."

"I'll go in and check the house," he said, itching to make sure that at least her windows and doors were secure. From his vantage point now, it looked as if a stiff wind would blow the house down.

She shook her head. "That's not necessary, but I appreciate it." She ran a shaky hand through her hair. "I'm exhausted. I'm going to bed."

She opened the door and ducked inside without another word and without looking back. An image of her crawling into bed in that lonely old house taunted him.

He wanted to join her. Hold her. Make sure she was all right tonight.

But that would be risky for him.

Still, he couldn't shake the feeling that she was in danger as he walked back to his SUV.

Don't miss
Hostage at Hawk's Landing *by Rita Herron,*
available March 2019 wherever
Harlequin® Intrigue books and ebooks are sold.

www.Harlequin.com

Love Harlequin romance?

DISCOVER.

Be the first to find out about promotions,
news and exclusive content!

Facebook.com/HarlequinBooks

Twitter.com/HarlequinBooks

Instagram.com/HarlequinBooks

Pinterest.com/HarlequinBooks

ReaderService.com

EXPLORE.

Sign up for the Harlequin e-newsletter and
download a free book from any series at
TryHarlequin.com.

CONNECT.

Join our Harlequin community to share
your thoughts and connect with other
romance readers!
Facebook.com/groups/HarlequinConnection

**ROMANCE WHEN
YOU NEED IT**

HSOCIAL2018

Reward the book lover in you!

Earn points on your purchase of new Harlequin books from participating retailers.

Turn your points into **FREE BOOKS** of your choice!

Join for FREE today at
www.HarlequinMyRewards.com.

Harlequin My Rewards is a free program (no fees) without any commitments or obligations.